SERGEANT NELSON OF THE GUARDS

Sergeant Nelson of the Guards

GERALD KERSH

faber and faber

This edition first published in 2013
by Faber and Faber Ltd
Bloomsbury House, 74–77 Great Russell Street
London WC1B 3DA

Printed and bound by CPI Group (UK) Ltd, Croydon, CR0 4YY

A CIP record for this book is available from the British Library

ISBN 978–0–571–30454–7

My Dear Morrow,

The last time we met we talked about this book. You hoped to see it published in the States, and I told you that it might be regarded as too English, and therefore limited in its appeal. I was quoting readers' opinions. You said: "Boloney." With this sentiment I heartily agreed: we had a drink on it in the pub around the corner, and I said to you: "If ever *Bill Nelson* comes out in America, I'll dedicate it to you."

"Swell," you said. And then you went away, took the wings of the morning, and died in the region of Iceland; and I was deeply sorry because, in the few weeks between our first meeting and our last, we had become friends. I liked you: you were a man I could work with. I shall always think of you with affection and with a sense of loss.

You wanted to see this edition: you felt as I felt—that Bill Nelson, as a type, belongs to your country as well as mine. Our Bill Nelsons shorten our wars and lengthen our periods of peace; they are our hard and gentle warriors, our rationed men, our austerity soldiers; our de-hydrated fighters that travel light, shorn of superfluities, living cheaply, surviving economically, and only dying dearly. They are brave souls that will not accept defeat: they are the lights that burn in the windows of History.

Between good, clean-cut men there should never be any misunderstanding. They must accept one another's accents and backgrounds, look one another between the eyes, and join forces against the menace of the outer darkness . . . We discussed all this, deploring the fact that

v

all too often, a language-in-common emphasises points of difference between peoples instead of eliminating them. And we agreed that nothing
could be more ridiculous. You and I, for instance, had our little differ-
ences about the pronunciation of words, and our misunderstandings concerning their interpretation. Yet we were friends, and we wanted our
peoples also to be friends.

Well, whatever may happen, you won't be here to celebrate it. However . . . here is the American edition of *Bill Nelson*. Your Nelsons and
ours are brothers—they have the same things to say: only their accents
are different. I am following your advice and putting in a glossary of
British soldiers' slang as used in this book.

Rest in peace!

Yours ever,

GERALD KERSH

CONTENTS

PART ONE

They Die With Their Boots Clean

PART TWO

The Nine Lives of Bill Nelson

PART ONE

They Die With Their Boots Clean

PROLOGUE

"A MAN gets knifed. A throat gets slit. A bomb goes off. The Wogs are out for blood!"

As Sergeant Nelson talks his right eye blinks in the smoke of his cigarette. Pensively pursing his lips, he takes his left eye out, polishes it against the bosom of his battle-blouse, and puts it back again. "Is it in straight, Dusty?"

Sergeant Smith says, "A bit bolo."

Sergeant Nelson blinks hard. The glass eye stares rather angrily through the smoke. "You've got to close the left, or disengaged eye, when you fire," he says. "What's an eye?"

We wait, very quiet. We want to hear about the Wogs, the Arabs. Evening is coming. The moon is already out—a pale, thin little moon, no bigger than an eyebrow.

"Ah," says Sergeant Smith. "We used to see a bit of fighting in peacetime."

"Definitely, Dusty," says Sergeant Nelson, and his story goes on:

The Wogs was around us. The desert was alive with Wogs. You couldn't see 'em. You couldn't hear 'em. But you knew they was there. They can hide, those Wogs can, behind a grain o' sand. Ain't that a fact, Dusty? They wears robes the same colour as the desert. They digs themselves little bits of cover. Puzzle, find 'em. You *know* they're there, but they're invisible. And the Wog can wait. He can wait hours. . . . Then *bomp!*—and *wheeee!*—he's letting loose atcha. He ain't a bad shot at three hundred yards.

I

What was I saying? The Wogs was around us, quiet as mice, but all you could see was lousy sand. We come to a road block. We takes it down and marches on. Now mind you there's nothing stirring—nothing in sight, only the lousy great sun and the lousy old desert. I say we marches on. Quarter of a mile on, round a bend, we comes to another barricade. Walk on, and walk into a jolly old deathtrap. We about-turns and goes back. We definitely does.

Now mind you, nobody's seen anything. We rounds the bend and Sergeant Tuck says "Blimey." There lies both scouts with knife holes in their backs and their rifles and ammo gone. And the block we just took down, so help me Gord, it's up agen. Definitely up.

The officer says: "Well, it looks as if we've got to fight it out here." He talked like his mouth was full o' hot potatoes, but he wasn't a bad sort—I've heard that fellow swear something terrible, blinding and bloodying like a bargee, just like you and me. Didn't 'e, Dusty?

Then all of a sudden, poppity-pop! Old Charlie, my pore old china, pore old Charlie, he says *Gug!*—just like that, didn't he, Dusty?—*Gug!* and goes down plonkety-plonk on the road. Definitely plonkety-plonk.

And we see sort of . . . kind of bits of desert getting up and charging us. So help me Gord they seemed to be right atop of us. And somebody yells: "The Wogs! The Wogs!"—and we're firing for our lousy old lives, biff!—bosh!—bang!—with the Wogs going down like coconuts. Where one fell, ten seemed to spring up. Didn't they Dusty? Yelling. It sounded like "Lulu! Lulu!" Remember that, Dusty? That's their God—Lulu. . . . Allah? All right, Allah: but it sounded like Lulu to me, Dusty; definitely Lulu. Definitely.

Well. You rooks can grouse and grumble about discipline, but in a time like that you want it. You horrible little men. You over there— you funny creature, you—stop picking your horrible little nose and pay attention to me when I'm talking to you. Whaddaya mean, you *are?* In my day, if I'd answered back to a sergeant I'd of been run into the moosh so fast me feet wouldn't have touched the ground. Why, you miserable twillip!

Discipline. We was outnumbered about twenty-five to one. I was shivering in my shoes. I was dead scairt. Wasn't I, Dusty? We didn't stand the chance of an ice-cream cornet in hell. Definitely not the chance of a penny cornet. But we had to hold out to the last man, if only as a matter of principle. Our mob never say die. Definitely never. Do it, Dusty?

That was just about twelve, noon, when the fun started. Quarter past, was it? I would of sworn it was just on the hour. Well. The Wogs tried to rush us. But in a time like that, without stopping to think, mind you, you remember the stuff we knock into your soft little heads when we train you here. Don't you, Dusty?

We fired like on a range. The good old Lewis was going thumpity-thump, and the Wogs was going down. At last they got back under cover to snipe. And snipe they did—they snipe all right. And we gave it 'em back. But they had the advantage of cover. Poor old Muddy—you knew Muddy Waters, Dusty? The bloke what threatened the Sarnt-Major? Yeh, back in '28—poor old Muddy gets one, bip, right in the forehead. The joke of it was, it didn't kill him: didn't touch the brain; he never had no brains: he's in Palestine, now, still keeping the Wogs in order.

The day wore on. Didn't it, Dusty? Definitely it wore on. And about a third of our fellows was out. But we held 'em. Discipline. Morale. *Es pritty corpse,* to put it in Froggie lingo. And at last, towards sunset, we could see that the lousy old Wog was going to make one big, determined rush and scoff us that way. And the devil of it was, we was pretty near out of ammo. We was, wasn't we, Dusty? Are you listening to me, you, Dopey, over there? Give him a poke in the eye, somebody —he's going to sleep.

Near out of ammo. Okay doke. So now it's going to come down to good old cold steel. We see the Wogs gathering. They fluffed our ammo was out. They gathered in the open, luluing like mad—hundreds of 'em. We was absolutely certain we'd never get away alive. Remember, I shook 'ands with you, Dusty? Funny, wonnit? Then the Wogs charged.

We stood firm. We was going to die in proper order, by crummit we was. You don't get yourself took prisoner by no Wog, not if you use your loaf you don't. The Wog's a torturer. Well, over they comes, and we gets ready to snuff it.

And then, all of a sudden, what do we hear? That lovely old scalded cat of a lousy old bagpipe! *Mee-yow . . . mee-yow . . . mee-yow . . . !* And I says: "By God Almighty—the Jocks!" And the Jocks it was, screaming like madmen. Firing? Nothing! The pigstickers was out. It was knives, me boys, bayonets! They came pouring over the ridge, they did, and they tore into them Wogs from the rear like lions—and we comes out, we does, yelling red, white, and blue murder—*Yaaaah! Yaaaah!*—and what we leave of them Wogs is scarcely worth the trouble of picking up. Eh, Dusty? It was a whatsiname, definitely a whatsiname. A triumph. A triumph for training and discipline. Without it we'd of been wiped out in the first half hour.

And training and discipline is what you're going to get here. See? And if you don't like it you can definitely lump it. Because you're going to beat the pith out of old Herr von Fritz. You're going to batter the tar out of Old Adolf. You're going to kick old pigface Gooring from hell to breakfast. Ain't they, Dusty? Definitely from hell to breakfast. Don't let me hear no lousy old alarm and despondency about tanks. I'll spit in the eye of the next man who mentions tanks. England's an island, see? And while we hold this lousy old island, old Hitler's blocked. See? And we can make all the tanks we're going to need, given time. And if we hold out, we've *got* time. Get it? And with trained men we hold out. Men are more important than tanks. You can bust a tank. You can't bust a proper man. And I'm going to make proper men of you—you horrible creatures, you. You'll give old Hitler a coating in Africa, and Greece, and hell and all. You will! Won't they, Dusty?

Who said "What about Musso?" Musso? I don't count Musso! I could take on Musso and the whole Wop army singlehanded, five at a time, couldn't I, Dusty? . . . All right then, three at a time.

Remember the time I laid out three Wogs with a spare Bren barrel? Swords, they had—swords and knives. They was the mob that mutilated poor old Charlie. Ah, it was fun being in the army in peacetime. Definitely, Dusty.

Now, you mummy's darlings, get a rift on them boots. Definitely shine 'em, my little curly-headed lambs, for in our mob, war or no war, you die with clean boots on.

I

The Raw Materials

It was a big, dim, grim, high, wide, unhandsome room, smelling unpleasantly of too much cleanliness. Discipline has an odour of its own —a smell of scrubbing soap and floor polish mixed with just a little too much fresh air. You sniff it in prisons, workhouses, and other places where men abandon hope: the smell of organised scouring; the smell to end smells.

Men were talking; not loud. A beardless boy with a pink face and a queer mop of hair like a copper-wire pot scourer had been smoking a cigarette. He was holding the butt of it between finger and thumb, looking anxiously from side to side. A crisis was approaching: soon, he wouldn't be able to hold it; but how could he dare to throw it down and put his foot on it? A large plump man with a deep, round voice said: "Chuck it out t' winder, lad." The wire-haired boy said: "Ah, but say there's a rule agin it . . ." He pinched out the glow, rolled the remaining crumbs of tobacco into a little pill which he poised in his hand like some undisposable, incriminating mass. At last he put it into the huge cold stove, slammed the door, and walked hastily to the other side of the room.

"Scared, lad?" asked the plump man, and the wire-haired boy replied: "What, *scared?* Who, *me?* Me *scared?* Not me."

"Homesick, like?"

The wire-haired boy scowled. "No."

Two men were trying to play billiards with a sawn-down cue and three odd balls on a table not much bigger than a tea tray. The boy watched them. One of the players, a long, saturnine man, addressed the spot ball with elaborate care, and miscued. I heard the woody scrape, and saw the ball roll slowly away. The saturnine man swore briefly and bitterly, handing the cue to the other player, who took it, held it, stared blankly at it, and then said: "Ah dinna wanna play na more."

"No more do I. Let's turn it up."

"Play draughts?"

"No."

Somebody else asked the company in general what was going to happen to them now.

A glum blond man who had been turning over the pages of a bound volume of *Punch,* 1893–1894, said: "We get another medical examination. First of all we get our hair cut off. Then, if we're okay, we get injected."

"Injected what with?" asked the wire-haired boy.

"Germs."

"Oh, blimey."

"Germs," said the glum man. "Your arm swells up like a thigh. You throb like a damn great aeroplane. Your head aches fit to bust. A scab comes. Then it drops off. Then there's a scar."

"What's that done for?"

"Because it's healthy."

"And what happens then?"

"A trained sweat is put in charge of you. You go and draw your kit."

"Do we get rifles right away?"

"Yes. Then you're put in a hut."

"What kind of a hut?"

"A *hut.* Then you're squadded. Then . . ."

"Ah?"

"God help you," said the glum man.

"What d'you mean, God help you?"

"What I say. God help you. You're here. You're in the Guards. It's like being in jail, only there's one difference."

"What's that?"

"In jail you sometimes get a bit of time to yourself."

"Oh, blimey. Do they give you hell?"

"Hell," said the glum man, "hell. If they gave you hell, it wouldn't be so bad. Hell is Paradise to what they give you here."

"Can you go out?"

"After a few weeks they let you out maybe once, for an evening, every eight or ten days."

"And where can you go?"

"Nowhere."

"What's the food like?"

"Horrible."

"What are the officers like?"

"Terrible."

"What beds do you get?"

"Planks."

"What are the sergeants like?" asked the wire-haired boy.

"Son," said the glum man, "did you ever see a picture called *Beau Geste?*"

"Um."

"Remember the sergeant that put them dead men on the wall, and sent them blokes that was dying of thirst out into the desert without a drink o' water?"

"Oh, ah!"

"He chased 'em in the sun till they fell down dead, didn't 'e?"

"Ah!"

"Would you say he was tough, just a bit?"

"Not half he wasn't tough!"

"Well," said the glum man. "He was a Godfrey Winn compared to the sergeants here."

"Oh, blimey," said the wire-haired boy.

There is a silence; then a little outbreak of uneasy laughter.

"Join the Army to see the world," says the glum man. "Join the Guards and scrub it."

We look about us.

Each of us sees twenty or thirty other recruits, raw and inconsolable as new-born babies. The man with the volume of *Punch* is riffling the leaves, blackened at the edges by the fidgeting of countless uneasy thumbs.

This is one of those awful gaps of silence. You know such moments. Talk limps to the edge of a chasm and falls in. Ten thousand pounds couldn't buy a spontaneous word. Men become suddenly engrossed in silly trivialities. A big Nottingham man sits scrutinising a razor-blade wrapper with the intentness of a merchant poring over a rare vase.

The purr of the pages is the only sound we can hear . . . *prrrut* . . . *prrrut* . . . *prrrut.* . . .

The weather has got into us, also. The day has blown hot and cold, wet and dry, light and dark; and now, settling into a uniform dirty whiteness, threatens rain. The sky sags like a wet sheet.

From the asphalt below comes a *ka-rup, ka-rup* of disciplined iron heels, and a great, strained voice shouts: "Get a hold of the step! Get a hold of it! *Eff*—ite! *Eff*—ite! Eff. . . . Eff. . . . Eff. . . . EFF. . . . *EFF!*" It is a squad of Grenadiers being marched to their baths. In this place no man walks. A recruit represents two feet on a brown caterpillar: his paces are measured; his movements are predestined; his day is divided into equal squares. "Eff. . . . Eff!" The voice and the footsteps fade . . . walking *en masse;* a community-singing of boots. . . .

From an unknown distance, a flat, sore-sounding bugle blows a melancholy call of unknown significance. From different distances other bugles pick it up. The notes blend. They combine in a strange, sad discord . . . a rich weeping of vibrant brass. Then, right under the window, a little grim boy puts a bugle to his lips, puffs his cheeks, and blows. The red, yellow, and blue tassels on his coppery bugle hardly stir. A gathered flush empties out of his neck and face, into the mouth-piece, round the coil, and out in a great trembling note. He sounds the call again. Two scared swallows flutter from the roof. Simultaneously, a flat loud-mouthed bell in the clock tower clangs an hour; and sliding down a slanting wind comes a rattling volley of raindrops.

Somebody sighs. The man with *Punch* throws down the volume and yawns.

The bugle is our masters' voice . . . and the swallows will go where the sun goes, and we shall be here under the treacherous English rain, kicking the soil into mud for our feet to slip in.

But all England is here.

We men in this Reception Station are unreserved, inessential.

Individually, we are necessary only to the tiny nooks and crannies of England into which life, like a wind carrying seed, has dropped us. We have our roots, of course, like all men. Pluck us up, and an empty space is left. But not for long. Without us things do not change. Only the appearance of things changes. Life moves differently, but still goes steadily on.

We lived our peacetime lives; worked, enjoyed things a little, suffered a little; built what we could, struggling, more often than not, for just enough bread and rest to give us strength to struggle with; made homes and supported them, turning sweat into milk for the babies. We were part of the mass of the British.

We are here. The things we lived for are behind us. All the personal importance of our own lives has been washed down in the gulf of the national emergency. Other hands were there to take up the tools we laid down. The machines still drone. The fires still roar. The potatoes still grow, and will be plucked when their time is ripe. Our work is behind us, still being done.

And we wait here, to be made into soldiers.

There is scarcely a man among us who did not volunteer.

How does this happen?

We come out of the period between 1904 and 1922—that wild waste of years, strewn with the rubble of smashed régimes. The oldest of us is thirty-six, Shorrocks of Rockbottom. The youngest is Bray, eighteen, of London. Those of us who are not old enough to remember the war-weariness of the century in its 'teens, are children of the reaction of the nineteen-twenties—when "No More War" was the war cry; and the League of Nations seemed more solid than the pipe-of-peace-dream that it was; and the younger generation—our own generation—was sworn to eternal non-belligerence in the face of the futility of war. We haven't forgotten that. If only our own propagandists took a little of the blood and thunder that the peace propagandists so effectively used to move us!

From page after laid-out page, the horrors of war gibbered at us . . . stripped men, dead in attitudes of horrible abandon . . . people (were they men or women?) spoiled like fruit, indescribably torn up . . . shattered walls that had enclosed homes, homes like ours, homes of men, men like us . . . cathedrals shattered; the loving work of generations of craftsmen demolished like condemned slum tenements . . . children starving; nothing left of them but bloated bellies and staring eyes . . . trenches full of dead heroes rotting to high heaven . . . long files of men with bandaged eyes, hand-on-shoulder like convicts, blind with gas . . . civilians cursing God and dying in the muck-heaps of blasted towns. . . .

Oh yes. We saw all the pictures and heard all the gruesome stories, which we know were true. We were the rich culture-grounds of the peace propaganda that said: *If war was like this then, what will it be like next time, with all the sharpened wits of the death-chemists working on new poison gas and explosives, and the greatest engineers of all time devoting themselves to aeroplanes that can come down screaming like bats out of hell?*

When we heard that first siren on the Sunday of the Declaration of War, things like damp spiders ran up and down our backs. We expected the worst.

And then came a flow of something hot and strong. We went out and begged to be allowed to fight Jerry. We insisted on our right to do so, and to hell with the age groups. Men of sixty, who had seen the things at the pictures of which we had lost our breakfasts, and who had spent twenty post-war and pre-war years saying: "Never again," declared on oath that they were forty and beseeched the authorities to give them rifles. There was a rush and a heave. Because it wouldn't take us all at once, we cursed the War Office from hell to breakfast.

Men like Shorrocks, who had argued the futility of all war in his grocery shop in Rockbottom (cotton and coal; pop., 21,369; near Blackburn; finest town on earth), did a *volte-face* like the pirouette of a balletdancer. (I say nothing of his mulish insistence that Britain, being an island, had no concern in the affairs of Europe; nor of the imbecile satisfaction he seemed to suck out of the statement that there had always been an England and always would be. That Shorrocks, in his fossilivory tower!) He left the business to his wife, clapped on his durable bowler hat, and, arguing about nothing for fifteen minutes with an old sweat in the Recruiting Station, passed A1 and got his fifteen stone of maddening self-assertion into the Coldstream Guards.

It is what they call "Being there when the bugle blows." He sits by the window on a little collapsible iron bed, filling a pipe with Sidebotham's Unscented Cut Plug which, in the tone of a man who stands by some ultimate and glorious truth, he declares to be the finest tobacco on earth. Let his neighbour, Whitaker of the West Riding, swear that Sidebotham's is manure and there is nothing in the universe to touch Cooper's Fragrant Twist at one-and-five an ounce. Shorrocks stands firm. Jut Sidebotham's label on old bootlaces, and Shorrocks will smoke them and die in defence of them.

He is a big man. Assume that three of his fifteen stone are so much fat, food for worms. They will get that off him here, it is grimly hinted.

Meanwhile it fills his waistcoat, the good waistcoat of his everyday suit, which still has a year of wear in it. (The best suit—five pounds; no guineas; worth fifteen; made by Joe Hindle of Rockbottom, greatest tailor in Great Britain, one-time cutter to Jim Leach, finest tailor in the world, also of Rockbottom—hangs full of moth balls, ready for his homecoming. He will be back in one year. Germany will capitulate next spring. Who says so? He says so. Why? Because.)

All right. He will admit he has a few ounces of weight to lose. The Shorrockses eat well. You could not get Jack Shorrocks' Agatha's potato pie for ten shillings a portion at the Savoy Hotel, London—no, nor even at the Rockbottom Commercial Hotel. And he will say that, though careful with the brass, he begrudges nothing when it comes to food.

He knows what it is to go without. He doesn't mind admitting that he worked in the Mill. He saw Boom and Slump; knew Cotton as King and as Beggar. A man must not be ashamed of anything in the way of honest work. When circumstances demanded it, he got a job labouring, and happy to get it. The whole point is, the children ate, had shoes, and never had a day's illness. That's little enough to brag about, but at the same time it's something, he reckons. Well, gentlemen, he got together a pound here and a pound there, by going without everything except potatoes and sleep. He likes his grub but can go without it. He took a little shop, starting with a few packets of stuff on tick. Now he owes no man a farthing. It is a good business. It took him five years to make it what it is. He had a vast scheme for a mail-order business, a fair and square one on new lines, which, in another five years, might make Shorrocks as big as Sainsbury. He hasn't the slightest doubt that Agatha, though the finest lass in the world, will ruin everything. Well . . . happen she will, happen she won't. He'll still have his own two hands—

—that is to say, given reasonable luck. He reckons that very few men lose *both* hands. . . .

He sits, pink and stubborn, like a skinned bulldog. His expression does not change. He has got his left-hand dog-teeth into the hole they have bitten through the stem of his pipe; pincers could not wrest it from his mouth before he chose to lay it down. Somebody asks him why he volunteered so soon. A year or two might pass before the thirty-sixes are called; and in that time a lot might happen. . . .

"If we've to fight," says Shorrocks, "let's get it over and done wi'. Let's get on wi' it. I look at it lak this: it takes months to train a man.

Ah. A year, eh? Ah. I reckon that year between now and t' call-up o' t' thirty-sixes as eighteen months. Ah. Any'ow I don't like foreigners gettin' cheeky. So let's get on wi' it, and quick, too."

His little blue eyes glitter as he talks, and he spits rather than puffs the smoke of his pipe. You agree with Shorrocks or you quarrel with him. He is a man of unyielding spirit. He loves England for one smoky dent in her wind-blasted northern moors—the unlovely valley of Rockbottom which reeks to the rainy sky.

The wars of all the world never moved a hair of his scanty eyebrows. He never gave a damn for all the Japs in China. He wanted only to be left alone.

In this he gets his way, in the end.

There were other Shorrockses, just like this one. They were the dawn-men of Britain. There is little doubt that they looked much the same; had the same stubborn, rosy, primeval English face; the same stalwart carriage; and talked something like the same language. If Shorrocks on the bed wants to "talk broad," or lapse into Lancashire dialect, up pops the old Angle. He never yielded a thing—not even a phrase—to foreign influence!

The ancient Shorrocks went about his business in the same way and the same place when there was a bit of a Roman villa standing where the Jubilee Memorial Tower stands today. The Romans had come and gone. Shorrocks ploughed his land, and rose at dawn, and lay down at dark, and owed no man a farthing; kept a cautious eye on what came in and what went out, and cared not a rap for the heaving world. Yorkshire was a foreign land. Leicester was a traveller's story. London was a legend. Soldiers were a pain; they ate and drank but grew no barley for bread and beer. Shorrocks was unimpressible. He wanted nothing. He had Rockbottom. He had a world.

And when they said that the wild men were coming from the north —giants with winged helmets, swordsmen in long boats—Shorrocks snorted and sniffed and called the panting newsmonger a Silly Fewel, and told him to be damned.

But when he smelt the smoke of something burning, and heard that the long boats were up the Ribble, Shorrocks put down his scythe and put on a steel cap—not unlike his best black bowler—and got down a buckler and honed up an axe, and told Gurth to look after the swine, and kissed his wife, and went out to do battle with the raiders. He fought like the pig-headed yeoman that he was, and is. In due course he came back; or didn't come back. But he got what he gave himself for.

Rockbottom remained with the Shorrockses.

Snatch the cubs from under the she-wolf. Filch the kittens from the wildcat. Then try to take something that Shorrocks lay claim to—his wife, his child, his living, his prejudices; or England.

What is this strange stuff that runs in English veins? God knows, who shakes the cocktail of human blood. The English mixture is smooth and dangerous, always well iced, yet full of an insidious fire. Many elements go to make it. The English lay no claim to racial purity.

Racial purity! If blood were pure, man would still have no chin and walk on all fours. Even if there were unadulterated primeval blood, who would boast of it? A liquor might as well boast of being crude from the still. Rotgut might as reasonably vaunt its mad harshness over the gentle strength of a tempered liqueur.

The predominant English flavour is potent but bland, like good old blended whisky. You blend a whisky by balancing proportions of many different crude whiskies of various ages and qualities, until you happen upon something individual and of its kind perfect. In a blend, you mix the rough with the smooth, and so achieve a happy medium; power and sweetness.

Blood is like that, especially English blood, which of all the blood in the world is the most widely and subtly mixed.

Sometimes some ingredient predominates. Thurstan, for instance, although he has the national flavour, is a little too fiery. He is knockout drops, taken in immoderate quantities; best left alone. Shorrocks has the heavy, strong, fundamental stuff predominant in him—the Blend would be lost without it, but on its own it can become a shade monotonous.

Dale is one representative sample of the balanced whole—the decent Dale, who sits next to Shorrocks on the bed.

Dale is the Man In The Street if ever I saw one.

Abiding by all written and unwritten laws, right or wrong; adhering to all established beliefs, wise or foolish; patient as an ox, unopinionated as a spring lamb; moderate of appetite, diffident of manner—he looks at you with the clear, anxiously trusting eye of a child who has once or twice been unjustly punished. He is: he has: he is the English Man In The Street.

Dale is a Londoner. He was born in the black heart of that monstrous jungle of soot-eroded brick round Battle Bridge. Now, he has a home in Ilford, which, to him, is deep countryside; practically agricultural. He is a good, steady boy, married to his female counterpart who loves him and whom he loves. Their home is their own. They were saving up for a baby as for a piano when the War broke out. When they had so much put away, then they were going to have a family—for Dale loves to pay his way, and feels easy in his mind only as long as no man calls him debtor. He was happy on his wedding day; but even happier, in a deep and strange kind of way, when he posted the last instalment on the furniture.

Once he was an office boy. Now he is a fairly highly-placed clerk in the offices of a firm that has sold wine since 1755. Dale is proud of this date. If you take him to a pub, he will ask for a small glass of Sheraton Port, which is the produce of his employer. Not that he likes port very much: he is simply loyal in all matters, and feels that in supporting the Company he is also doing right by himself. If he worked for a brewer, then he would drink beer; though never more than a little of it, since any expenditure beyond his budget would take milk out of the bottle of his unborn son—or, as his wife insists, daughter. He knows his job and does exactly what is required of him. He can tell you that a hogshead of Claret holds forty-six gallons, while a hogshead of Hock holds thirty, and one of Brandy fifty-seven. Don't ask him why: it doesn't concern him. Dale will accept all the discrepancies of life without a murmur.

His face seems familiar to you. You feel you've seen it before. So you have. Where? Everywhere. Agencies pick that face for the type of Mister Everyman. The streets are full of it. At Cup Finals myriads of it make a great pink bank in the rain. It has straight, ordinary features; eyes neither grey nor blue; complexion neither fresh nor pale; hair neither light nor dark . . . everything about him is *ish*—greyish, bluish, brownish; in size tallish; in dress darkish—the whole noticeably unconspicuous and unmistakably English.

The coming night will be the first he will ever have spent away from his wife. He has started to write a letter, already, but having written the words: *Dear Mavis, I have arrived safely,* chews his pencil disconsolately, not knowing what more to say; or rather, having so many things he knows he wants to say, that he does not know where or how to begin. He won't sleep a wink. At home he couldn't shut an eye unless he was lying on the outside of the bed and could hear his watch ticking. Dale is a man of habit. His habits are chains which he has forged about himself in the thirty years of his peaceful and uneventful life.

Then why is he here, now, when others of his age group still await the call-up?

Ask Time. Ask History. A lamb to lead, a ram to oppose: such is Dale. He heard the trumpet and smelt the smoke. Somewhere in Dale's veins something craned up crowing like a fighting cock. He screwed the cap on his fountain pen and asked what they would kindly let him volunteer for. Vacancies in the Guards. Guards? Since Dunkirk, good God yes, alas! Dale is here for examination by the Guards M.O. (You need two A1's to get in here . . . but these townsmen, under their serge and shirtings, have good strong hearts and straight bones.)

He is thinking: *Tomorrow's Saturday. Mavis will spend her first week end without me, in six years.* He is depressed to the verge of tears.

There was another occasion, when another Dale spoiled his good wife's week end. Sunday was his only day off, too. He was a George Dale, exactly like this one. He ruined the family Sunday on June 18th, 1815, when he put in a bit of overtime from ten in the morning to five in the afternoon. He, also, worked in a counting house. But that Sabbath he put paid to the account of a Dictator called Napoleon, and the day of reckoning goes down in history as Waterloo.

Greyish-white as the paper on which Dale is trying to write; threatening as the sky; sullen as a thundercloud, Thurstan sits behind him, rolling a cigarette and staring at the floor.

He has the habit of staring at a thing as if he hated it. His eyes are holes full of shadows, in which dim, menacing things wait, slightly stirring. There is a rumour that he has been in jail. Who knows? Or perhaps his pallor is natural to him; some men are born pale. It may be that Thurstan has done time: lots of people have. If he did, it was for some outburst of violence, rather than petty larceny or sneak-thievery, for there is a savage recklessness in every line and curve of the man.

His lean hand with its bitten nails holds the tobacco against the paper. Blue veins like whipcord writhe over and around tendons that jump and snap taut like wires in a musical instrument. That would be a bad hand to have on your windpipe. The knuckles are dented and scarred. From one angle the hand looks like pincers: from another it resembles an old mallet. Thurstan is not a big man: he just touches the minimum five-foot-nine-and-a-half. And he is fleshless. His cheeks are sunken: he has had bad times. He can't possibly weigh more than nine stone. Yet there is about him an air of appalling force; a nervous power that could drive him through an iron plate. Was he a boxer? He won't talk. His nose is smashed to the four points of the compass . . . but boxers don't have such knuckles. You do not often see scars such as Thurstan has on his face. It is not that they are very terrible scars: simply that they are queer. High up on his right cheekbones there is a rough oval of white indentations. Tooth marks! Where he comes from, men fight with fangs and claws and hoofs. His forehead is marked with two depressions, circular in outline, equal in depth and size. You may make scars like that by hitting soft wood with a carpenter's hammer—and that is what somebody did to Thurstan, only there is nothing soft about his ferocious little skull. You would hate to receive such blows. You would hate, still more, to be the man who dealt them, if Thurstan lay under your hammer.

Life has beaten him like iron on an anvil.

He comes from the region of Durham City. That is, he lived there before he came here. His origins lie a little farther north. His is the wild blood of the Border. He was a collier, once. He knows what it is to lie in the hot darkness pecking tons of hard coal out of the seam. He doesn't have to tell you this: he wears the miner's trade-mark—blue freckles of buried coal in his face. He talks a dialect difficult to comprehend. Since the moment of his arrival, three hours ago, he has spoken only three words. A harmless old man, a Scripture Reader, called, and asked the recruits to gather in a far corner of the room. Thurstan said: "Ah no gang," meaning, "I will not go." He is a dangerous man, a rebel, inflammable as firedamp, touchy as a half-broken pit pony and equally willing to kick or bite—obstinate, morose, savage as a caracal, quick as a lynx, courageous as a wild pig and twice as hard to stop. He has a wife, somewhere in the stormy north, whom he has forgotten like a parcel in a bus. There will be trouble with Thurstan. We can smell it, like something smouldering.

There always was trouble with Thurstan. Hadrian built a wall to keep him out, but he came right in and thumbed his busted nose at the iron might of Rome. He was always something of a rebel and a raider. A Thurstan drew a wicked bow alongside Robin Hood in the black age of the Robber Barons. He is unblended firewater; a patch of unmixed hot stuff, here because he wants a fight. He comes to war as his grandfathers went to feud. He can't live without the thrill of the pounding heart and the slamming fist. He itches for the mad moment of the bayonet charge. When this moment comes, "controlled charge" will not include Thurstan. He will swell. He will yell. He will rush forward in front of everybody else, a live projectile, a horror, a bloodthirsty nightmare; the kind of fight-mad killer that panics an army. Whichever way he turns out, he'll be dangerous. Thurstan would butt against a bull, gore against a boar, trade bites with a leopard, impervious to pain or fear.

Disciplined, that force of his will be overwhelming. Discipline to him will be the brass shell round the packed explosive. But to discipline Thurstan, you must make him like you. God help the sergeant that has to break in Thurstan. But God pity the Nazi that comes up against Thurstan let loose. He is the old, old wildfire of ancient Britain.

In this room also sits John Hodge, a giant, reading a small black book which, under his huge thumb, looks no bigger than a playing card. His left arm hangs over the bedrail. It has hung like that for fifteen minutes, during which time he has pored, motionless, over the same page. His great square-blocked head droops, pressing his massive chin into folds against his chest. Hodge sits astride the bed, dwarfing everything; still as a man carved out of one mighty chunk of ruddy brown rock. You look twice at his back before you notice the rise and fall which indicates that he breathes.

Suddenly he moves. He closes the book. A grave suspicion has been whispered, that this book is a Bible: this is not the kind of accusation one shouts round the place, for fear of slander; but it has been whispered. It has black, shiny covers. Perhaps he promised his mother that he would read a page or two every day; in which case, of course, one may say that there are extenuating circumstances. Hodge raises his arms and yawns. Chest rises, belly flattens, things like ropes run taut under the bronzed skin of his throat. The Cockney called Barker says: "Blimey, it'd take a hell of a drop to 'ang that geezer." John Hodge is muscled like a Percheron stallion: his hands are hard and shiny like hoofs. A horse of a man; a work horse; patient, powerful, docile, and simple.

This is the story of John Hodge:

He was born to a farm labourer in Gloucestershire twenty-seven years ago. Fourteen years later he went to work on a farm. Week in, week out, for six hundred and seventy-six weeks, he worked stolidly. Then War came. John Hodge told the first lie of his life. He said he was a casual labourer, fearing that farming men might be reserved. The gentlemen gave him a railway warrant and four-and-six. He gave the four-and-six to his mother, who said nothing much, but privately wept. And he came here in a train.

Complete history of the main events of twenty-seven years in the life of a giant.

His father did the same in 1914. Back and back, generation upon generation, the seventeen-stone Hodge men, mild and unshakeable as the hills, went to the wars. There is something in their blood that makes them do it. You can slap a Hodge in the face without necessarily stirring him to fight; and in the event of an inescapable private quarrel he will go into action apologetically, uncomfortably. Ordinary insults arouse in him only a sad surprise. What does anybody want with him, Hodge who wants to hurt nobody? You could harness him to a plough, like a gelding; or to a millstone like Samson in Gaza. He asks only a little food and a bed, first for his mother and then for himself. He belongs to the earth; can tell you, intuitively, the productive potentiality of a field by the feel of a handful of its dirt; knows stock, and all the permutations and combinations of time and rain.

He wants nothing. He has got it. He is happy.

Yet he is here, a little worried about the subterfuge. Do you see?— he *wasn't* a casual labourer, so now he's a liar. He reckons that it was not a very bad lie . . . not like lying to avoid something, or to get something. Still, a lie *is* a lie. . . .

Once upon a time another of the Hodge men, also tearing himself up by the roots on a point of conscience, similarly told a lie. He was walking with a limp. Somebody asked him why, and he said he had a bad leg. Well, he didn't have a bad leg: far from it; he had a very good leg. But he couldn't very well say he had a sword hidden in his

breeches because he was going to join a band of good Protestants
farther west in a species of uprising under a certain Duke of Monmouth. God approved: the Law didn't. God, thought the ancient
Hodge, would overlook the lie.

The Monmouth affair turned out badly. Monmouth ran; that pretty,
gutless gentleman. It was a nasty business. The good peasants went
down like wheat under hail, calling upon Heaven for gunpowder.
Powder, for Christ's sake, powder! It must have been one of the most
piteous cries ever heard on a battlefield. The King's troops poured over,
and the good Hodge, laying about him like a stag at bay, died singing
a Puritan hymn, leaving an orphan son.

It was bad, for Hodge to leave an orphan son; but it would have
been worse if he hadn't—for here is John Hodge! May I be with him
at the last ditch!

In one of our fitful bursts of talk we had discussed the retreat from
Dunkirk.

The Cockney, Bob Barker said: "But it was a bit o' luck the sea was
smooth, anyway."

Hodge, opening astonished blue eyes, said: "Why, don't 'ee see? The
Lord God stretched out his hand over that water. He said: 'Now you
hold still, and let my children come away.'"

To that, Bob Barker said nothing. He knows when to laugh and
when not to laugh. He is sardonic as a general rule, and believes in
nothing much. If he laughs at Hodge, it will be in his sleeve. In his
odd way he draws his own kind of power from his faculty for laughter.
D'Annunzio told a story about a man like Barker in the last war.

I forget his actual words. The poet was looking over a little soggy
black hell of shot-harrowed mud between front-line trenches. A handful of British soldiers held a trench. They were wounded, and tired
almost to death. You must imagine the scene . . . the unutterable
melancholy of autumnal Flanders, and the rain, and the cold, and the
hopelessness, and the heartsickness, and the ache of throbbing wounds

and empty bellies, and the helplessness of exhausted ammunition. . . . Suddenly one of the soldiers shouted: "Are we downhearted?"

A pause.

Then, from a pit of mud out in No Man's Land, animated by its very last flicker of life a thing like a scarecrow out of a slaughterhouse leapt up, and screamed:

"*Nao!*" And died.

That could have been Barker.

He is a long, gaunt man of twenty-eight or so, with the kind of face one associates with adenoids. He hasn't got adenoids, but looks as if he ought to have. His eyes are prominent, under thick, arched eyebrows as mobile as caterpillars which almost meet at the beginning of his beaky nose. His upper lip is long and outstanding. His mouth is always half open, so that his chin, which at its firmest is far from prominent, seems to slip away down to his big, wobbling Adam's-apple. He has a bass voice. When he swallows his throat expands and contracts in the tight compass of the white rayon scarf he wears knotted round it. The ends of this scarf are tucked into a flash waistcoat. Barker dresses for show. It is for Barker that unknown heroines in mass-production tailors' shops sew on fantastic superabundancies of buttons, and fix incredible pleats in extraordinary coats. If anything new appears in the way of purple suitings or velvet collars, Barker will be the first to wear them. He knows, and carefully specifies, the circumference of his trouser legs—no less than twenty-four inches, though the heavens fall. He crams his big feet into torpedo-shaped shoes . . . unless the salesman tells him that America is wearing square toes, in which case Barker will wear square toes too.

For work, he wears his flash suits gone to seed. Barker shoves a barrow: fruit. He is the one permanent type of the Londoner—the indomitable, the virile, the astute, the nervy, the brave and cocky Cockney of the markets, who speaks a language, and has a background of colour and misery. His phraseology is debased. He uses slang. To Barker, a row is a Bull-an'-a-Cow; a suit is a Whistle, or Whistle-an'-

Flute; a kid is a Gord-Forbid; a car is a Jam, or Jam-Jar; talk is Rabbit, or Rabbit-an'-Pork; beer is Pig's Ear . . . and so on, up and down the language. He has a secret code; for sometimes Barker and his brothers have to hold their own against organised, English-speaking society: they can exchange conversation in slang and hint, spoken fast, and incomprehensible as Hungarian to the man or woman of polite pretensions. Barker has his own financial jargon. If the Stock Exchange can speak mysteriously of "Clo-to-clo" and "At the mark," Barker can refer to "Forty tosheroons" or "Six o' Clods."

He loves a rhyme, has as keen an ear for euphony as James Agate, and speaks in irony and satire. *"Who made that hole?"* asks the Rookie, at the shell hole; and the Old Sweat replies: *"Mice."* This is a Barker joke, pure and simple. If it is pouring with rain, he will say, not "Isn't it a terrible day?" but "Ain't it lovely?" As a free trader, he will starve rather than take a steady job. He has got to be his own master . . . even if he, as master, drives himself out at four in the morning and pushes himself round the streets with the barrow until midnight, when there is a chance of selling a bit of fruit at an advanced price to the girls and the drunks. He will short-change the prosperous without pity . . . or recklessly give stock away to the children of the poor. His father, a costermonger of the old school, was an Old Contemptible, who spent about a third of his Army life in the Glasshouse, but got a D.C.M. for some crazy impossibility with a bayonet against a machine gun. That same old man Barker, having, in his cups, bored ten thousand listeners with ten thousand bitter curses on the Army and all concerned with it for the last quarter of a century, now makes everybody's life a misery with his savage denunciations of the corrupt authorities who, just because he has only one arm, turned him down in 1939. He says he hopes Hitler wins. If he hears anybody else say that you have to admit that Jerry hasn't done too badly, he has to be held down while he brandishes his solitary fist and yells that Jerry doesn't stand a chance and asks everybody to wait till he gets hold of Goering.

Bob Barker is much the same, only he is young and humorous. If he goes out under heavy fire and saves somebody's life, he will say he did it because the man had some cigarettes. When he is decorated, he will curl his lip at his medal and call it a bit of tin . . . and secretly polish it for hours.

He says he volunteered out of spite, because of the shortage of bananas.

He admires above all things the quality of toughness. I don't mean toughness in the current sense of the term—not the toughness one associates with naughty little hats, tight lips, scowls, criminality, and offensive manners. I mean the quality of resistance: the quality that makes man survive. Galileo would have been a Tough Guy to Barker because he couldn't find it in himself to deny that the earth revolved round the sun. He would regard as tough the gangster who never squealed: also, Scott at the Antarctic or Sir Richard Grenville sailing into the guns of the armada of fifty-three, or Tom Sayres fighting with bare knuckles against Heenan, or Van Tromp hoisting at his masthead the broom with which he was going to sweep England off the seas, or Blake battering Van Tromp; or Ney fighting Wellington, or Wellington fighting Ney. Barker loves cold courage—in effect, the triumph of the soul over the nerves.

Thus, it is safe to prophesy a friendship between Bob Barker the Cockney and Harry Bullock of Bedfordshire.

Barker flips Bullock a Woodbine. Bullock gives Barker a light. He is a dark man, with a dour expression, a knotted forehead, a sombre glow in his eyes, and a swollen upper lip. Bullock is a bruiser. He is one of those boxers of whom nobody ever heard. His greatest fight was against one Nippy Oliver. Nobody ever heard of Nippy Oliver, either. Neither of those two fighters will ever get more than a five-pound note for an evening's mauling. Yet Bullock thinks he could beat Farr. Maybe he could. If he couldn't, Bullock would never know it. He has no idea of the meaning of defeat. If he lost his hands he would fight on with the stumps of his wrists, and feel that the advantage was somehow with him. He augmented what he earned in a boot factory by fighting in booths: shattering battles, murderous combats in which the ring ran red; for a few shillings a time. It began when the kid wanted a fairy-cycle for her birthday. He has never been knocked out. Something in Bullock holds on to consciousness and makes him always fight. He is big enough and heavy enough to fight anything on legs; gloomy, good-natured, taking all things seriously.

One of his front teeth is missing. This imparts something oddly wicked to his smile . . . to say nothing of the formidable look of his swollen lip, bridgeless nose, and left ear which resembles half a walnut.

Barker says: "Scrapper?"

"Yum."

"Fourteen stone?"

"Thirteen-ten."

"Ever meet Pinky Stallybrass?"

"Nump."

" 'E couldn't 'arf go."

"Yum?"

"A sof'-paw boxer. But stone me, wot a left!"

"Um . . ."

" 'Oo you met?"

"Nippy Oliver."

"Zat so?"

A Trained Soldier, with a pale, patient face fixed in an expression of permanent disgust says:

"Well, my chickerdees, come and get yer hair cut."

There is a dreadful finality about this. Condemned men in American jails feel the same cold thrill that we feel, when their head is shaved to facilitate the passing of the shock that kills them.

"Haircut. Then medical inspection. Then good night," says the glum man, rising and flipping away his cigarette end.

We go out. The wire-haired boy is as pale as ashes.

The rain holds off. The wind has stopped. The world is holding its breath. There is an awful silence in the barracks. I have a dreadful feeling that the world has paused in its spinning. Looking up, I see something that makes me jump. Sixteen barrage balloons stand still in the air. They look like bombs which have been falling but have stopped dead with the wind, the world, and time. In a moment there will be a sickening jerk. . . . Everything will move again. . . . Bugles will bray, the bombs will fall, and as life moves, so it will cease to move in one last red whirl of disintegration.

There is a dreamlike quality about this place, at this time.

First day at the Depot! It is too new to be real. We look round at the bare plane of concrete, as a new-born baby, being smacked into life, looks down at the counterpane. We don't see it, but it gets into our minds. We'll never quite remember, and never quite forget, what it looks like.

"If they spoil my quiff," says Barker, fluffing up his forelock, "blimey if I don't run away to sea."

We straggle into the barber's shop.

Later we were to hear dark, emphatic tales of barrack barbers; old soldiers' stories, punctuated with fearful oaths and paragraphed with pregnant pauses, of atrocities committed with 4-0 Clippers on unsuspecting skulls. Ah, the good Old Soldier! He will make a history of oppression and a drama of unutterable crime out of every grain of sand in the midday cabbage.

Months later I was to hear Sergeant Tug's tale of early sufferings in the barber's chair.

Tug, with burning eyes, talking of that barber as an Armenian might talk of Turks; thrusting forward his flat-nosed, stubborn-jawed, dour, hard face, morosely smiling, and saying:

"You're issued with a comb. Get it? A comb. And a brush. D'you foller me? A brush. What are you issued with a brush and a comb for? Answer me that? What for, I ask? I'll tell you what for. To comb and brush your hair. Do you see that? To comb and brush your hair.

Now listen to me. Some blokes round this camp are vague, if you get what I mean, vague about haircutting regulations. Right. Some say your hair mustn't be more than two inches long on top. Be that as it may. I say, *you got to be left with sufficient hair to brush and comb.* King's Regulations, by God! And to crop a man's head is to defy the King. To defy the King and country! Do you foller me? It's like saying Pooey to King George the Sixth. It's like putting your thumb to your nose and wiggling all your fingers at Winston Churchill and the whole British Government, to go and take all the hair off of a man's head.

"So. I was proud of my headervair. Laugh. But I had a headervair any woman might have been proud of. Oh, *I* know it's a lot of bull. But I was a youngster. And I tell you, I was proud of that headervair. And I says to the barber: 'Leave it on top,' and he says to me: 'God blimey, where d'you think you are? In a bleeding orchestra? Fond of music, are you? A pansy, ha?' And I says to the barber: 'I'm not fond of music—cut out the insults.' And he says to me: 'Bend your 'ead forward and cut out the back answers.' And I says to him: 'Cut off that top bit that waves and so help me I won't stand for it,' and he says: 'Oh, then lie down to it, Paderooski.' And I waits. And I feels them clippers going up my neck, and so help me God Almighty in Heaven, I feels them clippers going right up to the top of my head. And I jumps out of that chair and I runs out of the barber's shop, and I goes on parade with me hair uncut, and a sort of bald strip running from me neck to the top of me skull. And the officer says: 'What the devil do you think that is?' And I says: 'Sir, permission to speak, sir. Am I here to be shaved like a convict, sir?' And the officer says 'No.' And I says: 'Sir, permission to speak, sir, the barber wanted to shave my head, sir.' And the officer says: 'Oh,' and as true as I sit here that barber got fourteen days. Ah. Fourteen steady days. They run him into the moosh, they did, and they took him on Orders, and they give him fourteen solid days C.B. Yeah, it was jankers for that lousy rotten barber, for flying in the face of the King's Regulations. My headervair.

I don't mind telling you, it just about broke my heart, what they done to my headervair.

"That's a fact. I was a good boy till then. But after that, I didn't care for nothing or nobody, I didn't! I been made up three times and busted three times, and when I was a Corporal they bust me for something I never done, ah, they did that! But Detention, Spud-Hole, Jankers, Reps, Royal Warrant, and everything else—nothing 'urt me so much as what they done to my lovely headervair.

"Murderers! Murderers! That's what them barbers are, murderers! Jerry kills your body. But the barber, he murders your soul! Look at me now. Bald. Me mother cried when she saw me last. She cried, I tell you, she broke down and she cried like a child, and I don't mind telling you that I broke down and cried with her, too. . . . I was ashamed of myself, but I couldn't help it. I sobbed as if my heart was breaking, I did. And my old dad, a lump came into his throat; he couldn't touch supper. I can show you a photo of myself with a headervair that'll make you look up a bit . . . just like a mop. Call me a liar if you like. I say a mop. Everybody used to talk about my headervair. Girls used to say: 'Tug, I envy you only one thing; your headervair.' I got a picture of myself took in Ramsgit in 1910, when I was seven. Curls down to me shoulders. The Army ruined all that. I forgave 'em everything, but I'll never forgive 'em that."

And Sergeant Tug, who led a bayonet charge on the road to Boulogne, or thereabout, and carried six men's equipment twenty-six miles, and looks upon the awful discipline of the peacetime Brigade of Guards as "cushy," and has seventeen years of service behind him, and is as impregnable as a tank, fingers his scalp, from which the hair just naturally receded, and sighs, and scowls at the memory of the barber.

Somebody says: "Sarnt Tug—you got shot in France, didn't you? What's it feel like?"

He replies: "What's that? Feel like? Oh . . . sort of hot and cold. Golden, it was . . . spun gold, my mum used to call it, and I'm not telling you a word of a lie. Spun gold. That's life for you."

"Where d'you get hit, Sarnt Tug?"

"Machine-gun bursts: thigh and backside: two in the face, teeth splintered to hell. Blimey, I was proud of that headervair . . ."

Recruits have been pouring in. The Corporal in the barber's shop is harassed. Recruits are dreary cattle to shear . . . terrified, dumb, stupid, paralysed with novelty.

The floor is sprinkled with clippings, red, yellow, black, brown, and, above all, plain English mouse. The grim soldier is playing barbers: there are two cut-glass bottles on the shelf in front of the chair.

We cram ourselves into the room. The Corporal says: "Well, siddown, siddown, siddown, siddown, siddown . . . don't block up the gangway."

The wire-haired boy is first to take the chair. There isn't a mirror: we can't see his face; but a look of terrified expectancy spreads, somehow, to his neck. No doubt a neck looks like that when Monsieur Paris has his hand on the string of the guillotine. There is a *tickety-tickety-tickety-tickety* of clippers. It is like husking a coconut. Out of a mass of fibre emerges something pale, oval, top-knotted, and seamed. "Next," says the Corporal. "What?" says the wire-haired boy. "Fancy a nice shampoo?" says the Corporal. The boy who used to have wire hair says: "I don't mind."

"Any particular kind of shampoo?"

"I don't know. I don't mind."

"Ashes of Roses?"

"If you like."

"Or would you rather have violets?"

"Well, I think I'd rather have violets."

"Oh. And a friction? Or a nice massage?"

"Never mind about that. Just a shampoo."

"Just a shampoo?"

"Yes, please."

"Well go and put your head under the bloody tap. *Next!*"

The boy rises unsteadily, feels his head with an incredulous hand, blinks, looks at his palm as if he expects to find blood upon it. "Where d'you come from?" the Corporal asks him.

"Widnes."

"Then," says the Corporal, "you ought to be ashamed of yourself. *Next.*" He cuts a man's hair in about forty-five seconds.

"It ain't 'umane," says Barker. "You ought to give us gas wiv 'air-cuts like these."

"*Next.*"

Hodge's naked head emerges, still massive. Thurstan, shorn of a dense dark growth, looks blacker and paler and even more dangerous.

"I've seen your face before," says the Corporal to the glum man. "What's your monicker?"

"Alison."

"You been here before, ain't that so?"

"That's right."

"And now you're back, eh?"

"Worse luck."

"You pore thing."

One by one we pass under the clippers. He shears us like sheep. One man lurks near the door, half in and half out of the shop, as if he contemplates flight. He is very young and slender, dark and sunburnt yet lacking the look of one who lives in the open air. *Town* is written on his forehead, so to speak; the streets are his destiny. You can't help feeling that he got his tan in a city park: like inordinate skill at billiards, it seems to indicate a misspent youth. This is John Johnson of Birmingham; of Brummagem, gentlemen, the breeding-ground of the fly boys from time immemorial.

He has talked too little and too much during his few hours in the Depot. He wants everything tough—in the silly sense of the term. When Bates, that garrulous and amiable brewer's drayman from Leicester, said: "Well, Oi 'ope they'll fill moi teeth," it was John Johnson who snapped, in his aggressive burr: "Oi want 'em to take all moine out. Oi can't be bothered with teeth." He has a lank, saturnine face; eyebrows which collide in a black plume in the middle of his low forehead; little green eyes, and a sloping chin. He keeps his mouth compressed; sports a green coat, green flannel trousers, green suède shoes, green fancy sports-shirt with pompons; a tricky cigarette case which won't open and a cunning lighter which won't light—to say nothing of a novel watch on a doggy leather lanyard, which like Johnson, looks smart but doesn't work. When simple Bates said he earned a good, steady three pound two-and-six a week, Johnson said: "Oi drew twelve." He carries a box of fat cigarettes, and a paper packet of little black cigarlets, which, he maintains, are too strong for ordinary men. . . . The tobacconist warns you that you smoke those cigarlets at your own risk: if you pass out cold in a sweat of nicotine poisoning, don't come and ask for your money back. Nothing is too powerful for John Johnson of Brummagem.

Barker, to whom fly boys, both of Brummagem and The Smoke, are an open book, smiled at this, and said: " 'E chews nails and spits rust. 'E shaves wiv a blow-lamp." Barker knows fly boys as Professor Huxley knows flies . . . what they eat and drink, where they breed, if and when they sleep, how many eyes they have, and where they go in the winter time. But Bates permitted himself to be impressed, and said: "Are they noice?"

Bates, displaying his blond head, with anxiety in his big, bony Anglo-Saxon face; wide-eyed, wide-mouthed, wide-cheeked and friendly, says: "Do Oi look funny? Do Oi?"

Johnson replies, with patronage: "All right. You're in the Army now, yer know," and comes away from the door. He has lank black hair, heavily creamed, extraordinarily long, carefully arranged with a parting one inch to the left of the centre. I believe he would sooner part with his right arm than lose that gallant mane. But he swaggers forward, now, and says:

"Cut it off, Corp-rerl. You can't cut it too short for me. Oi can't be bothered with it." *Tickety-tickety-tickety,* chatter the clippers.

"One o' the Brylcreem Boys, eh?" says the Corporal, with a little smile of enjoyment: he looks forward to heads of hair like this; they give a zest to his life; he talks of them in the Mess. *Tickety-tickety.* . . . Johnson is scalped. A raiding party of Iroquois couldn't have done a much completer job on him.

"That looks noice," says Bates.

"Honest?" asks Johnson.

"It makes yow look toof."

"Tough, eh?" says Johnson, and represses a smile of gratification. "Don't talk soppy. You wait a minute and I'll give you one o' my cigarlets."

Bates has said exactly the right thing, for the first—and perhaps the last—time in his life. He beams, that simple soul; his face cracks into a smile like a split pumpkin. He has given pleasure: he is delighted beyond words. He lights one of the little black cigarlets. It isn't anywhere near the stuff he rolls, for strength and irritant quality. Bates sucks in a cloud of smoke and blows it out.

"They're noice and moild," he says.

Johnson's lips tighten again.

Clipped to the bone we walk back and wait for the Medical Officer to send for us.

A dentist looks at our teeth. An old sergeant, who appears to be nailed to an invisible backboard, shuffles eye-testing cards. There are some unscrupulous recruits who, having bad eyes, try and learn the rows of letters by heart, and so slink into the Guards. They have several cards, which they change from test to test. A big Exeter man named Septimus Plimsoll, seventh son of a seventh son, but far from psychic, is cast out as astigmatic.

"But my hair! They've cut my hair! They can't turn me down now . . . they've cut my hair!" he says.

"Cutcha hair, son?" says the old Sergeant, looking at him.

"Yes."

"Well, I'll tell you what. You go straight to Corporal Philips at the barber's shop—tell him Sergeant Robson sentcha—don't forget to mention my name—and he'll give you your hair back agen. Next!"

We take off all our clothes except our trousers. Bodies emerge, pallid as maggots. You see, now, the herculean thews of Hodge; his biceps like grapefruit, his pectorals like breastplates; Thurstan, all tendon and gristle, with a back that writhes with muscle like a handful of worms; lanky Barker; the Widnes boy, still padded with puppy fat; the inconspicuous pale Dale; suety Shorrocks; Johnson, thin but fast-looking, with long flat muscles and not enough chest; Bullock, dark and knotty; Bates, starch-fed, starch-white, but built for power; Alison, the glum old soldier, with *Death Rather Than Dishonour* tattooed on his left arm and *I Love Millie* on his bosom . . . outdoor workers with brown forearms and necks which make their torsos look like cotton vests . . . sedentary men, run to skin and bone . . . miners, with great backs and arms . . . a timber-feller, with wrestler's shoulders grafted on to the body of a clerk . . . a steel-worker, like a mummified Carnera . . . men who push things and have loins like Samson . . . men who pull things, and have deltoids like half-moons and hams for forearms. . . .

Barker says: "Hallo, Tarzan: if I 'ad me barrer ahtside I'd go an' get yer a banana."

The man he calls Tarzan smiles a slow, white smile. He is a tall, strong Cornishman called Penrowe; Barker's nickname will stick to him, for he has a hairy chest. Barker, looking at him for the first time, said: "Look—a Five." A Five is a Five-to-Two, or Jew. Penrowe has something vaguely Semitic about him—a swarthy skin, white teeth, glittering eyes of a hard hot brown, and a big hooked nose. Yet he, and his father, and his father's father, lived in the West of England all their lives, and no Penrowe ever was anything but a good Englishman. A Penrowe was among the first of the Englishmen who looked through a warm dawn and saw the New World loom on the western horizon. Sir Francis—they called him Franky—Drake knew the Penrowes. A Penrowe went out with Grenville off Flores, in 1591. A Penrowe terrified his fellow villagers by smoking one of the first pipes of Elizabethan Cut Plug; and a Penrowe got a Spanish ball in his head when the Great Fleet Invincible, the hundred and twenty-nine ships of the Armada, sailed against the eighty ships of England. Eighty ships, and Admiral the Northwest Wind. "God blew and they were scattered." But Penrowe helped, the black Cornishman; moody, calculating, proud, quarrelsome, hard man of the sea.

The sea is in his blood, and has been since the beginning of history. The sea washes its sons inland sometimes: our Penrowe comes from some messy hole in the ground where they get china clay. He has two brothers in the Merchant Service, at present engaged in the stout old Cornish sport of harassing the modern equivalent of the Dons on the high seas.

But what dark stranger left that complexion and that profile in England? Who left the name of Marazion in the West? The very first of all the sea-rovers, the Phœnicians; dark, Hebraic-looking gentlemen, out to do business, as usual. They called at Britain to barter trade goods for tin, before the Romans came, before the Three Wise Men cut their first teeth. The remote, forgotten grandmother of Penrowe saw the coloured sails of their great galleys, and saw them land— very dark, very suave, very well dressed, and smelling of perfume, with dress-lengths of exclusive materials and all kinds of household goods. They had come out of the Great Sea, over as rough a piece of water as anybody could wish to struggle against, right over the rim of the world, just to trade . . . the eternal, wandering Semites with their eyes that itched for new prospects. They were the first mariners. They came and went in Britain, always on friendly terms. The time came when Ancient Briton women brought forth dark, curly-headed boys and girls in the far West of this country. And then, no doubt, there slunk into the blood a restlessness and a yearning . . . a craving for the unknown seas.

And here is Penrowe, English as Land's End but dark as high

Barbary, with his hairy torso and high square shoulders, holding up his trousers and waiting for the M.O. to listen to the strange strong blood pumping through his powerful heart. . . .

Penrowe, swarthy Phœnician; Hodge, Bates, straight clear Saxon, fair as corn; Thurstan, black Gael. These are three rough, stinging, formidable elements in the Blend of Blood. What a devil of an island this is—this mixing-bowl of all that is most fierce and enduring in man, stirred by war in its beginnings and matured in its iron-bound cask of tradition in the rat-infested cellar of the centuries! Ancient Briton. . . . Ancient Roman—look at Allan of Cumberland, an English yeoman from the Pennine Chain, the Backbone of England—with the high-bridged nose and fine-drawn face of one of the Roman gentlemen who lived here, and laid the Great Wall, and Watling Street, and Uxbridge Road so long ago. The Romans were in Britain for four hundred and sixty-six years: they left blood, too! The red-headed monsters of Arthurian legend, the Saxons, came after them; and then the Norsemen cracked through. Johansen and Holm have been Yorkshiremen for centuries; yet there are no two between Heligoland and Hammerfest whom you could more easily visualise in a longboat under a ragged sail on a grey sea. And the Normans came, with a dash of Baltic madness and a dash of Gallic finesse; and we hated their guts, but assimilated all they had. Angle, Jute, Pict, Scot—it all soaked in. And you see it here, blended into a type, yet distinguishable in its separate elements . . . fermenting into Thurstan, mellowing into Dale—blood of the stolid Shorrocks, blood of the light John Johnson—blood of the cold English, the mad English—rough as Usquebaugh, smooth as Mead—strong red liquor!

Most of us are stolid and reserved, shy of strangers and of the sound of our own voices.

But there is a dark fire under the crust, and a hard current under the ice of the poker-faced Englishman. The expressionless Englishman, mouse-whiskered and talking at the ends of his teeth and greeting his best-beloved friend with a curt "Hallo," demanding mutton chops and strong tea of the luxurious restaurateur of the *Hermitage*, yet drinking like a Russian, duelling like a Hungarian, gambling like a Chinaman, or swearing like a Croat if the occasion demanded it, was always a little mad and curiously colourful to the amazed peoples of the Continent when he went on tour.

Heavy and immobile, or high-strung and variable blond; enigmatic black; mercurial red; or primary blond, red, and black ground into the prevalent common nondescript brown—in these men there is a strange wayward will. Dash of ferocious Britain, spot of aromatic Asia, jigger of crazy Celt, splash of gentle and murderous Saxon, tinge of iron Roman, shot of haughty Norman, drip of fierce Norse—the elements, even when they are blended to neutrality, give birth to something queerly individual. You can imagine the baffled astonishment of Napoleon, when Wellington, in Spain, imported some hounds and rode after local foxes in the blue coat of the Salisbury Hunt . . . grown men, tough soldiers, but serious gentlemen, *mon vieux,* dozens of them, all riding belly-to-earth after a species of vermin, blowing shrill notes out of a little brass trumpet! And these same gents, with the dead-faced shopkeepers who followed them and took it all for granted, were the rock against which the Irresistible broke itself.

Foul! . . . Wahnsinnig! . . . Loco!—quite crazy, demented, nuts—mad Englishman! Methodical in his eccentricity; cool to man and openly affectionate only to dogs and horses; stirred to applause or cat-calls by nothing in the world but the struggles of twenty-two men with a ball; seemingly more engrossed in the defence of three stumps and a pair of bails against a five-and-a-half-ounce ball, than in the defence of an Empire against barbarism; prone to forget everything in his eagerness to ascertain that one horse can run faster than eight others; regulating all combat by rules as of sport; unassuming as a mole and arrogant as a lion; an islander of islanders, regarding his salty wet rock as a universe, and the universe as too foreign for serious consideration;

looking upon himself, in a strange land, as the one Briton in a world
of gibbering aliens; blindly despising and blindly tolerating all outlandish things; incredibly blundering into chaos and fantastically
blundering out of it; conspicuously inconspicuous; insanely cheerful;
bland as a fat man in an asylum who thinks he's the Buddha; and mad-
deningly calm . . . always bewilderingly calm.

Calm. What looks calmer than a flywheel at top speed? What is
calmer than the heart of a whirlwind?

Men like this sailed on the *Birkenhead*. It is a simple story. They had
a pride of birth far deeper than any sentiment born of false reasoning
or well-hammered propaganda. The *Birkenhead* struck a submerged
reef. Think of the thing as a scene in a film: the night, the stars, the
heaving, shining sea. Then the crash, long and grinding. Furniture
goes mad: immovable things fall and movables fly. Women scream.
You catch a glimpse of men's faces in the vague half-dark: black gaps
of shouting mouths, pale teeth. Then the list of the gutted ship and
the swinging out of the boats. There is barely enough space in the life-
boats for the women and children, and the *Birkenhead* is sinking
damnably fast.

There are some hundreds of English soldiers aboard.

These were soldiers like any other English soldiers. The same kind
of men went down at Hastings and at Passchendaele—inveterate
grousers, individuals who would sometimes skive if they got the opportunity, and frequently chanced their arms in the matter of boots and
buttons. They saw off the women and children. Clouds came over.
Night had put on the Black Cap.

These condemned men were formed up on deck. I do not doubt
that even then, and there, there was a bucko sergeant who yelled "Order
yer arms when you got yer dressing!"—or words to that effect—"Dress
forward number three in the centre rank! God damn it, any soldier'd be
ashamed to stand in a rank like a dog's leg! Stand still!"

They stood still. The sea rose. The ship sank. The soldiers stood to
attention on deck until the water closed over them—Tom, Dick and

Harry, saying forever good-bye to beer and skittles, tea and wads, the dawn they'd never see again, wives and children, love and life. They drowned by inches in the cold, empty ocean, because it was expected of them that, there being no chance of getting away, they die like Englishmen.

That's an old story, like the death of Nelson. We—it is typical of us—hide our admiration in our hearts, and giggle at "Kiss me, Hardy," and "England expects . . ."

But Nelson knew exactly what to say on his last memorable naval occasion. Emotional as a ballerina, but calm as the Angel of Death in crisis; sick as a dog at the heave of a ship, yet dragged out onto the ocean by the ancient sea-wolf that tugged inside him; Norfolk Puritan salted with old Scandinavian—there was plenty of the pale firewater in his mixture; and something sweet, too, for he could be gentle as a woman. He was a very gentle Englishman; a very English gentleman.

But you can imagine the French admiral making a song and dance about glory, honour, death, the France, liberty, the Emperor, Marengo, Austerlitz, the illustrious memory of Monsieur Chose, and so to the peroration. Nelson merely said, in effect: "Being Englishmen, fight to the death."

That was the duty England expected of them. And there is no doubt at all that in every ship in the English fleet, sailors, treated much worse than dogs and scarred as much by punitive flogging as by battle, growled that England expected a hell of a lot. . . . England expected a bloody sight too much . . . and England could go and do something impossible to itself . . . and they were browned off, and to hell with England. Whereupon they fought furiously and won the day.

The Englishman, that inveterate gambler, has loved the feel of long odds against him, since the dawn of his history. You can't breed out what is in the old blood. And here, there is plenty left of the blood that got splashed about when Caractacus threw his handful against Rome—the Caractacus who said to Cæsar, as we might say to Hitler: "You fight to make men your slaves: we fight to stay free men." There is plenty of the spirit that came out best in affairs like Agincourt, where 9,000 knights and bowmen engaged an army of 27,000, and killed a man apiece and sent the rest flying. History is veined like an inflamed eyeball with our Thin Red Lines!

Crazy Englishman! Incomprehensible Englishman, who would die rather than admit his satisfaction in finding himself outnumbered and out-equipped, perched on a rock with all the weight of a swollen Dark Age in front of him, and three thousand miles of terrible sea behind him . . . who sourly smokes the wayward butt of a Wild Woodbine and gathers his strength for the most terrific struggle in the red calendar of homicide which is the History of Mankind.

II

The Foundry

THE CALENDAR says early August, but the sky says late September. The world is stuffy, like an unventilated room, and the clouds crawl slowly like melting grease under the dim sun. The brick and asphalt Depot has strange acoustic properties. It rings and echoes like a sore head. We shamble across to the Receiving Station. At this point we are neither flesh, fowl, nor good red herring. Clipped heads protrude from civilian collars; a bristly residue of our first haircut still clings in the folds of our ears. Yet we are in the Army. We are in the Guards, rather, which represents a fate somewhat worse.

We have had our first Army bath, in sinks under showers in cubicles which to some of us seemed strangely familiar. It was Barker who said: "Where's the clurk to write out the tickets?" Those cubicles were very much like the ones they have in pawnshops.

We were a little shy. Thurstan, strangely enough, went to extraordinary lengths to prevent anyone watching him as he washed. Even Barker stood like the girl in "September Morn"; while Dale seemed to suffer with a primeval embarrassment, and the wire-haired boy from Widnes crouched under the shower like shamed Adam in the rain. He couldn't adjust the temperature of the water and struggled with the lever of the tap, while his body became red, white and blue. Hodge just turned cold water on himself, and stood with an expression of dumb suffering, soaping himself conscientiously from head to foot. Johnson of Birmingham dashed madly in, protesting too much that he was not afraid, and repeating again and again that he bathed almost every day and liked it. Bullock the bruiser, inured to nakedness in little athletic dressing-rooms, looked at us with sombre astonishment. Alison, the old soldier, went through the process of washing as one who carries out a fine but hackneyed ritual: he bathed as some men recite the Lord's Prayer—as if he felt that it was doing him some incalculable good, but was best got over quickly. . . . "Our Far chart nevn, Harold bethy Name"—he was bathed and dried in no time at all, and out, gloomily smoking, in the dim humid daylight.

So we went for inoculation. Bates asked: "What do they do to yow?"

"Stab you in the arm," said the Old Soldier.

"Is it noice?"

"Horrible."

"What 'appens?"

"Your arm swells up. Sometimes you get a temperature. Some men have to go sick with it."

"And what 'appens when yow go sick?"

"You soon wish you hadn't."

"And 'ow do yow go sick?"

"You get a form filled up."

"And say yow're sick and don't go sick?"

"You get into trouble."

Bates became sad and thoughtful. At last he said: "Do yow get shot for deserting?"

"Not unless it's in the face of the enemy."

"Are we in the face of the enemy now?"

"It's hard to say."

"If they don't shoot yow, what do they do to yow?"

"Send you to the Glass House."

"Is that noice?"

"I've done twenty-eight days there," says Alison, and pauses, struggling between two strong desires. Like all old soldiers, he wants to terrify the recruit. Like all men who have been In Detention, he wants to laugh it off. He says: "You heard of Devil's Island?"

"Where there's crocodoiles and sharks?"

"Well, Devil's Island is like the Y.M.C.A. compared to Aldershot."

"Whoy did yow go there?"

"For nothing."

"Oh bloimey!"

The time will come when, to us, an inoculation will be just another Jab—when we will even hope for a serious one, which will mean forty-eight hours off duty, "Attend C, Bed Down." But now, everything connected with the Army is strange and slightly terrible. We file past the M.O. As we wait, we hear the thud of a heavy fall. A big buck Jock who would laugh at a bayonet has fainted at the prick of the needle. He is revived, and left to his shame: the world will end before that moment of weakness is forgotten. In years to come, on remote bivouacs in the hearts of awful deserts, or in the mud of questionable positions under earth-shaking barrages, there will be somebody who will say: "Remember Jock?" And somebody else will reply: "Got the D.C.M. Captured a tank with a jackknife. Won the heavyweight title in such-and-such a year. Nearly got a V.C. for taking on seven Jerry tommy-gunners with a Bren-gun cleaning rod, and licking 'em. Carried an anti-tank rifle sixty miles. Toughest guy I ever knew. They once mounted a three-inch mortar on his back and fired seventy bombs off him while he held it." And then the first speaker will say: "Yet—funny thing—first time that feller got a Jab, he went out like a light. It only goes to show." "You're right, son: it only goes to show . . ."

We emerge from the Receiving Station. Bates, by the power of suggestion, has a paralysis of the arm. Johnson maintains that it doesn't hurt; that no Jab can hurt him.

At this point there rises the banshee howl of a siren. Something in the upper air goes poppity-pop. We stand and gaze at a flattish grey nothingness, until an old sergeant, medal-ribboned to the condition known as "fruit salad," roars "Genna shelter! Gorn, you silly great things, you, genna *Shelter!*" We take cover, and sit still, looking at one another. Can it be that the Excitement is starting? An old sweat, decorated with a round badge bearing the words "Trained Soldier," says:

"Another 'Red.' *There's a Jerry in the sky.* Bah. I'll tell you the honest truth: I'm losing patience with this 'Itler. This is on the up-and-up: I'm gettin' browned off with this 'Itler. I'll tell you straight: sometimes I begin to get sort of annoyed with this so-called 'Itler. Oo do 'e think 'e is, *any*way, this '*It*ler? Shall I give you my honest opinion? Right from the shoulder—politics aside—every man is entitled to 'is own opinion, and I'm entitled to mine, and I tell you, between you and me and the lamppost, it's my candid view that 'e's beginning to get a swollen 'ead, this 'ere 'Itler. *Adolf.* I'll *Adolf* 'im. 'Im and 'is 'Mine Camp.' Adolf! If I come acrost 'im I'll say 'And oo are you?' and if 'e says 'I'm Adolf 'Itler,' I shall say: 'Never 'eard of yer.' And then if 'e cuts up rough—*bif!—boff!*——"

The Trained Soldier shadow-boxes. Shorrocks says to him:

"Been here long, lad?"

"What did you say?"

"Been here long, lad?"

"Lad? *Lad?* LAD? Now look. You're a Recruit, and as such you're ignorant. I pity your ignorance, Rookie, and so I shan't be 'ard on you. You're as ignorant as gorblimey, otherwise you wouldn't dare to call me 'Lad,' any more than you'd call Lieutenant Colonel the Earl of Romney 'Old Cock.' Do you realise who I am? *I am a Trained Soldier!* It's all right: don't be frightened. You didn't know. Well, you'll know in future. You always, always, mind you, *always* address a Trained Soldier as 'Trained Soldier,' and stand smartly to attention when you talk to 'im. In the Brigade of Guards, you address me as Trained Soldier; a Lance or Full Corporal as 'Corporal,' a Lance-Sarnt or Full Sarnt as 'Sarnt,' and everybody else as 'Sir,' and you stand smartly to attention. Nor are you, strictly speaking, supposed to speak unless spoken to. A guardsman is a man. A recruit is not a man yet. A recruit is a child. Bear that in mind."

Somebody asks him, with full title, how long he has been in the Guards. He replies:

"Seven years, four months, eleven days. And let me tell you, you get it cushy 'ere now. You ought to of joined the peacetime Guards for real soldiering. Ah, those were the days, son. Those were the good old days. You couldn't call your soul your own. Why, when I come 'ere as a recruit, like you, they pretty near broke my 'eart. Three suits o' scarlet, S.D., and everything. White webbing, mind you, and it 'ad to be perfect. Perfect? More than perfect. If it was only perfect, you went in the book. We used to blanco our webbing day and night. Then, if there was so much as a sponge mark on it, our Trained Soldier would chuck it plonk into the coal box. As for brasses, well, all I can say is, gorblimey. The slightest speck, and you was run into the cooler faster than your legs could carry you. As for chasings on the square, we used to faint in 'eaps. I remember when I was on a Buck Guard . . ."

"Buck?"

"Buckingham Palace. Buck is the Palace, Jimmy is St. James. I lowered my butt less than a quarter of an inch. I got seven days. Blimey. Some of you will be in my squad, I suppose. I tell you 'ere and now: do as you're told, and you'll be all right. Nobody'll worrry you, just so long as you make your minds up to do just what you're told. You've got to get yourself into the Army way of doing things. You've got nothing to worry about. All the worrying is done for you. Get that. All you do is, obey. If you've got a loaf to use, you'll be given a chance to use it later on. Meanwhile, you got no responsibility, except in obeying an order exactly as it's given you. My name is Brand, Trained Soldier Brand. Bear that in mind. . . . Ah-ah, there goes 'All Clear.' Now get outside. You rooks are going to 'ave to draw your kit."

There is a general feeling that all we need to do is, get a gun and a uniform, and there we are. But when we get to the Quartermaster's Store, we find ourselves in a kind of forest of equipment. There are sacred groves of boots, avenues of battledress, hanging gardens of slippers, a foliage of vests, undergrowths of socks. We hear the Quarter-master blasting a wicked man.

"So. Your slippers are too small. What size do you take? Eight. And what size are those slippers? It *says* eight? Then they *are* eights. And they're too small. Then why the hell didn't you take nines? Obviously, you take nines. You tried them on before taking them, didn't you? What do you mean, you suppose so? Stand to attention! You did try them on. You know you did. And weren't they too small for you then? What d'you mean, you don't know? Did they *feel* small? Oh. *Oh*. A bit tight, eh? They felt a bit tight, did they? And so you took them away, and now you bring them back, do you? Could you do that in Civvy Street? Could you do that in a shop? After you've worn them for three days? Who's going to wear them after *you*? No consideration for yourself or anybody else. Where there's no sense there's no feeling. Just because you're in the Army, you think you can take all kinds of dirty rotten liberties. All right. I've got my eye on you. Stand still. Give him a pair of nines. . . . Now, do they fit? Are you sure they fit?"

"Yessir."

"Are you positive they fit?"

"Yessir."

"They fit, then?"

"Yessir."

"You won't come back and say they don't fit, the day after to-morrow?"

"No sir."

"Then go away."

"Please, sir . . ."

"What is it now?"

"They're too loose."

"Oh God, give me patience! Oh, Good God in Heaven Almighty, give me strength! Oh God blind O'Reilly suffering Christ in Heaven above so help me! You . . . you. . . . Take him away. Take him away

before I tear him to pieces! . . . What's all this? Recruits? *More*
recruits? The Guards used to be exclusive, and look at it now! If my
poor father were alive to see it he'd turn in his grave. Lead 'em in."

The men who work in the Store have an eye for size. They can look
at you and issue, without wasting a word, equipment that more or less
fits you. Each man gets a blue kitbag. Then comes a cataract of clothing.

Boots, ankle, pairs, two; a pair of braces; socks, knitted, pairs, three;
slippers, pairs, one; shorts, gym, pairs, one; vests, gym, two; caps, F.S.,
one, and a hard cap with a cheesecutter peak that covers the eyes and
makes you hold your head up; two pairs of underpants; one stocking
hat; holdalls, one; housewives containing needles, thread, thimble, and
spare buttons—one; knives, one; forks, one; spoons, one; shirts, three;
suit of canvas, consisting of blouses, denim, one, and trousers, denim,
pairs, one; battledress . . . blouses, serge, two, and trousers, serge, pairs,
two, or one suit of Best and another for Second Best; a greatcoat. The
kitbag bulges. Trained Soldier Brand sweats and strains like a man with
a thirty-mule team. Do we think we're done yet, he asks. Oho. Let us
not think so for a moment. If we want his candid opinion, we haven't begun yet. There is Web Equipment yet to be drawn. We draw it . . . a
large valise, a small pack, two ammunition pouches, bayonet frog, a
tangle of strange straps with brass D's and dim buckles, a thing to contain a water bottle, and a water bottle for it to contain. Is this all? Ha.
This, says Trained Soldier Brand, is far from all. This is by no means
all. There is still a ground sheet to come; and an anti-gas cape; and a
respirator, and a respirator case, and a strap to hang it on; and another
kind of anti-gas cape, rubberized and obsolete, but useful for training
purposes; and a badge; and mess tins; and a canvas bag to keep mess
tins in; and a steel helmet complete with chinstrap and lining; and a
clothesbrush, and a button-stick, and a button-brush, and a shaving-
brush, and two bootbrushes, and a toothbrush, and a nailbrush, and a
safety razor complete with blades, one, unusable except by downy creatures not more than six months on the wrong side of puberty. Then, of

course, every man must have a rifle, a Short Lee Enfield, together with a bayonet.

There is a stupendous clicking of pressed triggers, and an uproar of "You're dead," until the Trained Soldier says, very sourly:

"Say there was bullets up the spouts of them rifles. Say there was live rounds. There couldn't be, but just *say*. Well, you'd all be dead. It is strictly forbidden to point your rifle in the hut. I'm decent. I'm good-hearted. I'm one o' the best, I am. But I can be a lousy, rotten swine if I want to. And I'll put any of you inside that I ketch pointing rifles or assing about with bayonets—fencing, and throwing 'em, and chopping up wood or anything. So don't you go and do it. School kids. Who goes fencing about with dangerous bayonets in huts? Soppy little girls do that, not Guardsmen. Now look. You're in Lance-Sergeant Nelson's Squad, Z Company, Coldstream Guards, Guards' Depot, Caterham. Got it? And I'm your Trained Soldier, Trained Soldier Brand. Got it? Well, get it if you ain't got it. This is your hut . . ."

We look. A great, scoured box; two stoves; ninety planks on sixty trestles, making thirty little wooden beds; a coal tub, two galvanized iron buckets, three brooms, a long scrubber, a mop, two scrubbing brushes.

" . . . This is your hut. From now on, this is going to be your home. And it will be kept as such—so clean you could eat fried eggs off the floor, just like you do at home. God help the dirty man in the Brigade of Guards. God help the man who goes around in tripe! Personally," says Trained Soldier Brand, in a burst of friendly confidence, "I never used to use a nailbrush myself, for the simple reason that I used to bite my nails down to the quick. But then I lost all my teeth. And look at my nails now. Look how clean. I want to see every man's nails like them. I'm proud of my fingernails, now.

"Everybody pick himself a bed. Keep it. You're responsible for the tidiness of your bed area, and everything connected with it. There is only one right way of doing a thing, and that is the Army way. I am

here to show you what to do. Come round me in a circle, and I'll have
a chat with you. I want to get to know you."

He looks us over. He says: "It takes all sorts to make a world . . . and
then what have you got? What's your name?"

"Shorrocks, Trained Soldier."

"What was your job in Civvy Street?"

"I was a grocer. I've got my own business."

"What's your religion? Not that I care a damn."

"Congregationalist."

"Well, every man is entitled to his own whatsiname. I'm a bit of a
Mohammedan, myself. But I goes down as C. of E. There's services for
C. of E-ers and Roman Candles. Any other fancy religions—Baptists,
Jews, Congregationalists, Methodists, Seventh Day Adventists, Peculiar
Methodists (whatever they may be), Mormons, and what not, get along
as best they can. If anybody's got any religious arguments to make, he
can go and have it out with the Company Commander. I 'ad a Buddhist
in my squad, once. A white man, mind you, but a Buddhist. Gord bless
you, *we* didn't mind.

"While I'm talking, by the way, you can take off them civvy clothes,
and put on proper ones. You're expected to wear your underpants. In
the first place, they're issued for you to wear. In the second place, it's
un'ealthy not to. When cold weather comes you'll be issued with long
winter ones, and woolly vests, and gloves. Roll up your civvies. They're
to be sent 'ome; it's illegal to keep 'em now. You're in the Army. And
look. I've got 'ere a cap badge. It's the eight-pointed star, the Coldstreamers' star. Look at it. I've 'ad it seven years, and somebody 'ad it
seven years before me. See? It's been polished and polished until the
pattern's almost all wore off. Can you read what's on it? *Honi Soit Qui
Mal Y Pense.* Evil be to 'e that evil thinks. Our motter. Got it? Well,
a soldier prizes a cap star that's wore down like this one. Now I'll tell
you what I'll do. You're a decent-looking lot o' fellers. The man that
gets the best shine on one of his pairs o' boots by the end o' next week

gets this star. I tell you, you could offer a quid for a star like that and not be able to buy it, but I'll give it to the best-shone pair o' daisy-roots end o' next week.

"I'm warning you, they're 'ot on shining in this mob; and rightly so. We got a tradition to keep up. Anybody who remembers the last war'll tell you 'ow the Guards went into action like a parade. Not only 'ave we got to fight better, and 'ave better discipline: we got to *look* better. We're the 'Ouse'old Brigade, and the oldest foot regiment in the British Army. I tell you, Jerry thinks twice when 'e sees us coming: we been getting ourselves a good name for thousands and thousands of years, ever since 1650, when Colonel Monk formed the Coldstream Guards.

"Other mobs aren't so fussy about cleaning, and I'll admit that when you're tired it can be a bit of a business, getting all spick-and-span. But it's worth it. You can tell a Guardsman anywhere for his smartness, especially a Coldstreamer. It can be overdone, this spit-and-polish, in wartime. But the principle of the thing is good. Like an old woman who's always spring-cleaning . . . it's uncomfortable, but the idea is all right. . . . Now what's your name, son? Thurstan? And where did you come from? Durham, eh? You been a miner, ain't you?"

"So what?" says Thurstan.

Trained Soldier Brand looks at him and says: "So what? So this: lemme give you a word o' warning. I know your type. You're tough, you are, or you think you are. Well, don't get tough with the Army, because the Army's tougher. See? And you'll get hurt. See? You're a miner. Well, you wouldn't 'ave a kicking match with a pit pony, would you? Well, don't try and beat the Army. Better men than you have tried to do it, and failed. You can be as tough as you like with 'Itler: you'll toe the line 'ere, for the sake o' discipline.

"How shall I put it? You ain't expected to be angels, but Gord 'elp you if you're not, that kind o' thing. I'm warnin' you, Thurstan, if you got any idea of playing up in this Depot, don't do it. We're 'ot on discipline. Discipline makes the Army. The Guards 'old their line and don't break: it's discipline that does it, and discipline means when every man has got confidence in his N.C.O., his Officer, and his pal. If you know just what everybody else in your mob is going to do, things are easy for you. That's discipline, and take it from me, it's essential. I've seen some of it working out East, and so has your Squad Instructor, Sergeant Nelson.

"Sarnt Nelson. A word of warning about him. He's the decentest Sarnt you could wish to 'ave. He never goes about punishing fellers. He never chases you more than you can stand. He won't bully you and chivvy you till you don't know where you are. He's never too tired to explain something to you. He'll stand by you through thick and thin in the event of trouble. Nelson is 'uman and a good bloke. But Gord 'elp you if you take liberties with Sarnt Nelson! Just that: treat 'im decent and 'e's a pal. Take liberties and 'e's a terror. You'll find that out, Thurstan, if you want to start something.

"You? Hodge? You're a big feller, Hodge, and they like big fellers in the Guards. What do you weigh? You don't know? Well, all I can say is, Blimey. Somebody told me you'd been seen reading the Bible. You'd be surprised 'ow things get around 'ere. Remember that, all of you, and be careful what you say. Some'ow or other, news gets about in this Depot quicker than at a tea party. Well, there's nothing against reading the Bible. I've never read it myself, but far be it from me. That is what I say—far be it from me. Why, we've 'ad blokes here reading poitry before now, and one of 'em used to write it. I'm glad to see you, Hodge.

"And you. What's your name? Bullock? Scrapper? Good. You won't get a chance to box 'ere: you'll be too busy otherwise engaged. We've 'ad a few decent scrappers 'ere in peacetime. Danahar. Jack Doyle. We used to 'ave some lovely fights in peacetime, but I'm afraid there's none o' that at present. There's a war on. Religion? C. of E. I've got to put down a religion because of Church Parades. The Roman Candles go to Communion. The C. of E-ers go to a service.

"Now I'll tell you roughly what you do. You get up at five forty-five, when the second Reveille sounds. Then you wash and shave with great

care, because they're 'ot on washing and shaving 'ere. Then you make
your bed up. You make it up nice and neat—I'll show you 'ow—because
they're 'ot on making beds up neat in this place. Then on top of your
blankets you lay out your 'oldall, containing your knife, fork, spoon,
button-stick, razor, and shaving-brush, all polished till you can see your
face in 'em, and your mess tins, also polished, laid end to end, like this
... with the canvas bag neatly folded in the middle ... so.

"Got that?

"Now your lockers must be kept neat and tidy, because they're 'ot on
lockers 'ere. In the top shelf, your battledress, neatly folded—they're
'ot on neat folding—and your stiff cap neatly placed on top. You will
polish your chinstrap till it looks like patent leather, and get the buttons
up till they sparkle, because if there's one thing they're 'ot on in the
Guards, it's buttons. Got it? Good. On the lower shelf you place your
brushes, all properly numbered, sandpapered, and laid in proper order.
You mustn't keep any personal property in your locker, because they're
'ot on that, too. When you make your bed down at night, you'll lay your
battledress down to crease: I'll show you 'ow, because they're dead 'ot
on creases in this Depot. Your boots go up there on top. Got it? And
you'll 'ave to work on them boots. They're full o' grease: you've got to
work it out, with energy, spit, and polish. Spit is the best thing for boots.
A little polish: a lot of spit; that's the rule. And your greatcoat must be
hung on the left-'and peg, with the buttons polished till they blind you;
because they're 'ot on that, I can tell you. Kitbag on the right-'and side,
neatly tied up.

"You've got to salute an officer whenever you see one. You'll be taught
'ow by Sarnt Nelson. That's 'is job, poor feller. You'll be 'ere for eight
or nine weeks. It used to be four months, and will be again shortly, but
at present recruits are kept eight weeks or so before going on to the
Training Battalion. You'll 'ave Inspections, every so often, to see 'ow
you're shaping with things like drill. You won't be allowed out o' the
gates for at least three weeks, and thereafter, once a week if you're lucky.
That's so as you won't disgrace the Guards by lounging about the streets

with a packet o' wine gums in one 'and and a bag o' chips in the other. In three weeks or so you'll *begin,* you'll just about *begin* to appear to look like sort of soldiers. It'll take a long time before you get the un-mistakeable Guardsman's Walk—straight as a poker, but supple as rubber; quick, regular, and easy. You watch Sarnt Nelson: 'e's a typical Guardsman. See? You're civilians, and walk as such, which is incorrectly. We've got to break you of the 'abits of a lifetime. You'll be sore at first. That's all right: it's good for you.

"You'll get your first leave in about thirteen weeks' time, maybe. You can never be sure. Maybe thirteen weeks. For that time, consider yourself right away from Civvy Street. The funny thing is, you'll feel uncomfortable when you get back to your own beds . . . and all the girls 'll fall for you. Everybody falls for the Coldstream Guards. You know the poem?

"Why should England tremble when the Guards go 'ome on leave?
It's only for a short while, so why should England grieve?

"Very well, then. You'll get a lot of Physical Training 'ere. They're dead 'ot on P.T. in this Depot. You'll get a lot of drill, too, and weapon-training. The Guards always make a name for themselves with bayonets. You ask Jerry. When the Coldstream Guards take up a front-line position, Jerry knows that sooner or later it'll come to cold steel. And 'e's scared. It pokes the wind up 'im.

"Well, you ast for it. You volunteered. It'll be something to brag about afterwards, mind you. Not everybody's fit for the Guards, even in wartime.

"Reveille, 5:45. Lights Out, 9:30. You'll be on training till about four. Then, from four till seven, you're on Shining Parade—you get your kit worked up and in proper order, and sit on your ground sheets going hard at the jolly old spit-and-polish, until seven pip emma. Then you're free to go and buy yourselves a beer or a tea at the Naffy. Got it? Or you can read books or write letters, or talk to each other. During Shining Parade, no talking or smoking is allowed, nor no singing, 'umming, or whistling. Dinner is twelve-thirty. Tea is at five. Breakfast, seven. You can buy pies and stuff in the Naffy if you can eat 'em. You'll be hungry enough, mind you; but Naffy pies. . . .

"You mustn't form a trade union. You mustn't get girls into trouble. You mustn't go about with your hands in your pockets. You mustn't be immoral. You mustn't smoke out o' doors while an Alert is on. You mustn't smoke in shelters. You mustn't desert. You mustn't go absent. You mustn't be late for anything. You mustn't gamble. You mustn't get anybody else, for money or moneysworth, to do any jobs for you. You mustn't have financial dealings with Trained Soldiers or N.C.O.'s. You mustn't address me, or any other superior rank, with a fag in your mouth. You mustn't get drunk. You mustn't use foul language or tell filthy stories or possess filthy pictures. You mustn't associate with bad women. You mustn't steal, bear false witness against your neighbour. You mustn't do anything not in the Army Act. I've never read the Army Act, but, put it like this—to all intents and purposes it's safest not to do anything, much, unless you're specifically ordered to do it by a Trained Soldier, N.C.O., or Officer. You will always be clean, kind, courteous, and what not. If you see an old geezer getting on a bus, give him a shove to help him along. If you see an old girl standing up in a public convenience, you will give her your seat. Conveyance: I always get them two words mixed up.

"But I am 'ere to show you the ropes. It's not my duty to lecture you.

"Everybody will buy a tin of black boot polish, a tin of dark tan, a duster, a slab of Blanco Khaki Renovator, a tin of Bluebell Metal Polish, and a twopenny-halfpenny brush. With the possession of these 'ere articles, your troubles begin, and so do mine; for your webbing must be spotless, your brasses must damn well flash like a gigolo's eyes. . . . Is there an educated man 'ere?"

A dark, quiet individual whom we call Old Silence, says: "I've been to school."

"Well, tell me. Is it *Gigolo*, or *Jigolo*?"

"Pronounced *Ji*golo."

"I thought as much. I was having an argument. Someone said *Gigolo*. Then someone else said *Jigolo*, and I agreed. Where are you from?"

"London, Trained Soldier."

"What business?"

"Unemployed."

"Do you mean you've got money of your own, or that you just couldn't get a job?"

"Both, Trained Soldier."

" 'Ow old are you?"

"Thirty-four, Trained Soldier."

"Well, son, we'll soon find you plenty jobs round 'ere. . . . And your name?"

"John Johnson," says the Brummagem Fly Boy suddenly.

"Not so much of the 'John Johnson,' you. Address me as Trained Soldier! Don't tell me where you come from: I know. You're a Brummy Boy. I can tell by your accent. Well, don't get fly here, son. It won't pay you. And you?"

"Bates, Trained Soldier. Oi come from Leicester. Oi was a brewer's drayman. Oi'm Church of Englernd, Trained Soldier."

"Married?"

"One proper woife, Trained Soldier, but she left me. She took all the furniture. Oi got an unmarried woife, now, and she's noice, Trained Soldier. Yow loike to see a pic-tcher, Trained Soldier?"

"In a minute. And what's your name?"

"Abbs, Trained Soldier. I got a brother in the Coldstream Guards. Did you ever meet him, Trained Soldier? Abbs, from Walsall. Jimmy Abbs. I'm Alfred Abbs. Thirty-five. I got six kids, all girls. My wife's uncle just died of a growth in 'is throat—big as a babby's head. I——"

"—Every morning," says Trained Soldier Brand, "the hut will be swept and tidied, and everything will be put in its right place. Every Saturday, it will be scrubbed from top to bottom, and your bed-boards and trestles will also be scrubbed till they are as white as snow, because I don't mind telling you, they're 'ot on that. Also, you better take care to scrub your 'oldalls till they're like *driven* snow. They're 'ot on 'oldalls, too. Got it? One other thing: don't keep things under your mattresses in the daytime. More men get put in the book for that than anything else. And for God's sake see your rifles are clean. A dirty rifle is a serious offence. Oh well . . ." He yawns. "Muck in," he says, with conviction, "that's the great rule of 'appiness. Muck in. Muck in. That's what the Bible says: muck in. Do unto others as you would 'ave others do unto you. In other words, *muck in*. Got it? What 'ave you got to do, Bates?"

"Not leave nothing under your mattress, Trained Soldier!"

"Oh Gord lumme, I want my mummy and the puddens she used to make!" cries Trained Soldier Brand. "Why should England tremble, eh? Did you hear me say 'Muck in'?"

"I thought——"

"You thought. Wot with did you think? You ain't 'ere to think. You're not in Civvy Street now. Why, if everybody went around think- ing, we wouldn't 'ave no army. Muck in. What did I say?"

Bates thinks deeply, and says: "Mook in, Trained Soldier."

"There now. You got it right that time, didn't you? You can do it if you try, can't you? That's the style. Go on like that and you'll be a Brigadier before you know where you are."

"Will oi really, Trained Soldier?"

There comes into the hut a man in shirt sleeves and a soft S.D. cap. You can tell, by his walk, that he is no ordinary man. He swings his legs out from the hip, and his iron heels cut little arcs in the floorboards. He is long and lean, sun-dried, wind-cured, boucanned, smoked, and sand-blasted. His face is brown as a kipper, and as expressionless. One of his eyes is fixed in a dreadful stare: it is of glass. The other blinks. There is nothing left of him but bone and sinew and vitals: years of service have sweated away all that was superfluous or decorative. He has an air of demoniac energy: a wild swagger, a steady, genial ferocity. Out of his neatly rolled sleeves hang arms as dark and gnarled as old Salami sausages. He has fists like mallets of black stinkwood; an aluminium ring; and a silly little blue bird tattooed on his left wrist. Quite effortlessly, he shouts, in a voice that makes us jump:

"I am Sergeant Nelson! (Ain't I, Trained Soldier Brand?) I am Sergeant Nelson! I've got one eye, but both me arms! I died at Trafalgar but they dug me up again, and when I'm mad I'm a one-man wave o' destruction! I'm poison! I'm terrible! I kill seven rookies before breakfast! I can spit fifty yards through the eye of a needle! D'you see that dead tree over there? They'll tell you it was struck by lightnin'. Don't believe 'em. I killed it! I slapped it down! You're my new squad! I'm your Squad Instructor! Silence! Nobody say a word! You do as I say or you suffer. You suffer 'orrible tortures! Now, when I say *Hi-de-Hi Squad!* you shout *Ho-de-Ho!*—and shout it loud! Now: *Hi-de-Hi Squad!*"

We roar: *"Ho-de-Ho!"*

"Right. Whenever I shout Hi-de-Hi, let me hear you reply pretty damn quick, or I'll chase you all round and round that square till the huts look like henhouses. *Hi-de-Hi!*"

"Ho-de-Ho!"

"Good. Now we're introduced. I'm here to make Guardsmen out o' you. Are you going to help me? Well, answer, you unsociable lot of squirts!"

"Yes, Sergeant!"

"Good. You'd better. Soldiers get buried in a blanket. I'll make Guardsmen out of you if you have to pass out of here in blankets. If you turn out flops, as soldiers, I'm responsible. *I'm* the one that drops something on account of you. And I'd murder me best friend if he got me into trouble. I'd murder me great-grandmother. I'd cut her heart out and throw it on the floor and jump on it—wouldn't I, Brand? Now on Monday you'll be Squadded, and you start with me on the Square. I've got to drill you. I've got to hammer four months of drill into you in eight weeks. It's impossible. But I shall do it. You'll see. But you've got to play ball with me. You've got to give me all you've got, with a good heart." Sergeant Nelson becomes quieter, and very serious.

"Ask anybody in this Depot about me. They'll tell you: I hardly ever punish anybody. I never, never bully my men. But you've got to work with me. There seems to be a war on. Isn't there, Brand? So you've got to take things seriously. If there's anything you want to know, don't be afraid to ask me. If there's anything you don't grasp the first time, ask me again, ask me a hundred times: I'll tell you. If there's anything you want demonstrated, I'll demonstrate it. I'm the best demonstrator on earth, aren't I' Brand? Definitely, I am. If you're in trouble over anything except money, come to me, and if necessary I'll march you into the Company Commander, or the Commandant himself. I'll stand by you. But don't try any funny stuff. If anybody tries to treat me rough. . . . By God! Call me Pig, and I'm Pig all through. Definitely Pig all through. Okay. Which is it going to be? Are you going to work with me?"

A chorus: "Yes, Sergeant."

He roars again. "Okay-dokey, my little fluffy-'eaded chicks! *Hi-de-Hi!*"

"*Ho-de-Ho!*"

"Good. Now look. Recruits are babies. In one second, Cookhouse is going to blow. By rights I ought to march you about everywhere, definitely everywhere. But I'm going to let you go on your own, just to show you I trust you. You won't get lost? Or make mugs of yourselves in any way?"

"No, Sergeant."

Come to the cookhouse door, boys, cries the bugle.

"Knives, forks, and spoons, and scram, then!"

We rush to the door.

"Halt!"

We stop, paralysed by that shattering voice.

"*Hi-de-Hi,* Squad!"

"*Ho-de-Ho,* Sergeant!"

We go to Dinner.

That afternoon we get our first Fatigue. There isn't much for us to

do until we are squadded. Hanging around, putting twice-ordered bits
of kit again in order, looking around, exchanging speculative horrors,
we wait, killing time by inches. One or two of us—Hodge, Dale, and
Thurstan foremost, as it happens—start on our boots. The surface of
these Ammunition Boots is what the shopkeepers call "Scotch Grain":
that is to say, it is all bumpy. This has to be smoothed out by the chemical
action of spit and the mechanical action of polish. We have been warned
that, at first, the more we polish the less there will be to show for our
efforts. "Think of the Foorer," says Trained Soldier Brand, "think of
Gobbles, think of Gooring . . . and spit." But the Ammos, or boots,
would absorb the digestive juices of a shark. John Johnson watches us.
Soon, he says: "You got no oidea, that's what it is, no oidea." And he
picks up a boot and a tin of polish, and, baring his sunburnt arms, begins to polish away with a mad enthusiasm. All the misdirected energy
of a little, misspent life, is being concentrated on a toe cap. He polishes
as if some strange fate has condemned him to it . . . which, indeed, it has.
"Oi'll get that cap badge," he says, "oi betcher a million pounds." A
Bedfordshire lad who used to work in a Nottinghamshire boot factory
talks of buffing leather. He takes out of a battered fibre case a toothbrush;
compares it with the Army issue, and finally strokes his boots with it.
Everybody else follows suit. As any gentleman's gentleman will tell you,
it helps if you beat the surface of a leather boot flat with a bone . . . but
you've got to put your weight behind it. Alison, the glum old soldier,
says that if you smear the surface of the boots thickly with polish and
then set light to it, you get the grease out quicker. Trained Soldier
Brand, hearing this, says: "That is a serious offence," and adds:

"Say you burn your boots. What happens? Boots are made of what?
Well . . . what, Bates?"

"Oi don't know, Trained Soldier."

"Leather and stitches. Burn the leather, and you burn the stitches.
Burn the stitches, and what happens? Well, Bates?"

"It's a serious offence, Trained Soldier."

"They bust. And if the stitches of your boots bust, what happens, Bates?"

"Oi don't know, Trained Soldier."

"One day your boots come apart. And remember—a soldier marches on his feet. On his . . . what, Bates?"

"On his feet, Trained Soldier."

"Good. You'll be a lieutenant colonel inside of a fortnight."

"Will Oi——"

"So. Don't burn your boots. If you're without boots, you're what, Bates?"

"Uh?"

"Say you've got no boots, what happens?"

"Oi don't know, Trained Soldier."

"You're barefoot."

"Oi know that, but——"

"Then why didn't you say so? You can't march, and the war is as good as lost. So no burning. Leather," says Brand, "comes from abroad. It takes sailors. Sailors die so that you wear boots. Get it? Them boots are covered in the blood of sailors."

Bates says: "Trained Soldier, Oi thought that was grease."

"God give me strength," says Brand.

We polish away. Later, a sergeant with a book under his arm comes into the hut and shouts: "Stand to your beds and listen! Is there anybody here who's good at painting and decorating?"

Two men stand up.

"Anybody play football . . . I don't mean just kicking a ball around: I mean, anybody who can play it well."

One man rises and says: "I played for Underwood Wednesday."

"And are there any market gardeners, or other men who know all about turfing and whatnot?"

Two more men rise.

"Excellent. Excellent. Lastly, is there anybody here of education up to matriculation standard?"

Old Silence stands up.

"That's fine." The sergeant with the book licks a pencil and says: "Names. . . . You will all report to the Green Lanes Cookhouse for spud-peeling."

("And let that be a lesson for you," says Brand, grinning: "In the Army, you never volunteer for anything except certain death.")

Those of us who have risen go out. A cookhouse sergeant says: "Do you mind eating spuds a little bit wizened?"

"No."

"Then bloodywell peel them."

The men left behind congratulate themselves, until a serious-looking Corporal, asking for men who know jig and tool making, the use of the typewriter, the elements of the banjulele and singing, salesmanship, care of livestock, bandaging, fire-fighting, bartending, building, hair-cutting, carpentering, ladies' hairdressing, platen-minding, typesetting, fancy lettering, high jumping, and box making, drags in most of the others for floor washing, and, tiring of the joke, asks, all humour apart, for one intelligent man. Johnson leaps up. "You read books, I bet," says the Corporal. "Ah," says Johnson. "Then go and swab out the library," says the Corporal In Waiting, and goes out, while Johnson swears that in this life there is no justice.

That Sunday is quiet. Recruits in the Naffy tell dark tales of discipline. Men three weeks squadded, already assuming the portentous air of old sweats, ask themselves rhetorically why they did not join something else. The Glorious Fusiliers, says one, do no drill; the Dagenham Foresters, says another, have dulled brasses for active service, and rightly so. Old Silence, pursuing the vexed question of spit-and-polish in the Brigade of Guards, asks the Trained Soldier about it.

Brand laughs. "You'll work your boots and brasses up," he says, "whether you like it or not. So you may as well do it with a good 'eart. When you get round to fighting, I dessay you'll be told to let your brasses go dull and grease your second-best boots. Meanwhile, you'll shine.

Why, you might ask. Because the Guards have got a tradition of smart turnout, that's why. I admit you work harder in the Guards than else-where. Well, that's the price you pay for the privilege of being in the 'Ouse'old Brigade. Don't worry—you'll learn as much of tactics and field-training and fighting as anybody in the Army; only you'll be made to get the 'abit of smartness in your appearance. Why? Because we're the Guards. We're the Lilywhites, the Coalies, the Coldstreamers. It's got to be kept up. At Dunkirk, our mob were still pick-outable on ac-count of some of them still shining up their daisy-roots and working in a quick shave, even on the retreat. It's crazy, I know. But personally, I like it. And so do you. Or if you won't you will. And if you don't, you'd better. Gorblimey, we've 'ad fellers 'ere like Wild Men o' Borneo, and turned 'em out neat as a new pin in a few weeks. Carriage! Smart-ness! That's the *real* uniform of the Guards. Because all battledress looks alike. And yet you could pick a Coldstreamer out of a thousand others. It may be a bit tough. Well, blimey, you've got to suffer to be beautiful ... Ain't you, you de-licious little peach-blossom?" he says, to Thurstan.

Before Thurstan can unload the insults which rise and fill his mouth, a bugle sounds, a siren moans, and Brand says:

"Jerry in the sky. Get in the trench."

The Guards' Depot exploits air-raids, and makes prompt action a part of Guards' training. We run to cover, and it is then that Sergeant Nelson, who, for eight weeks, will never let us out of his sight, tells us about the Wogs, "light of ear, bloody of hand," the Arabs; and tells tall stories in short sentences, of discipline and training in the Guards. "And if I make your blood run cold—don't worry, because I'll warm it for you when I get you on the Square tomorrow. Definitely."

The Square is vast and flat; black-grey asphalt tickled by mysterious eddies of pale-brown dust. We have to pass a half-finished building to get to it. Bricklayers pause and look at us with some pity. One old man, splitting a speckled pink brick with one flick of a trowel, says: "Now you're for it, my boys." He is a little old man, incongruously got up in soiled blue serge, with a stiff collar and a bright strip of medal-ribbons. "Ah well, I was at Mons." To this, Barker, who is hiding his nervousness under a great froth of funny talk, says: "No wonder they retreated. Are you sure you don't mean Water-bloody-loo?"

"Laugh, my cock-oh," says the old man, "you'll never see what I saw!"

Sergeant Nelson is there, waiting for us. "Sheep!" he says, in such a voice that the distant echoes answer *Eep*. "Sheep for the slaughter. *Hi-de-Hi!*"

"*Ho-de-Ho!*"

"Now listen to me. I'm going to teach you some elementary drill movements. You don't have to be a Bachelor of Science to do 'em. Millions have done 'em before. Millions will do 'em again. You don't need a matriculation certificate to do it. Just be confident. Don't be nervous. Keep calm, and do exactly as I tell you. *And work!* By God! Work with me and I'm as mild as your mummy's milk. But work against me and I'll kill ya! Look at me. I'm poison! I'm a rattlesnake! I kill more men than Diphtheria! Now for the time you're here, you'll shout the time of your movements out as you move.

"For example. Look at me. I'm standing properly at attention. See? Heels together, feet at an angle of forty-five degrees, fingers curled up, head perfectly still, eyes straight to the front, chin in, back like a ruler, and thumbs in line with the seams of the trousers. (That's what the seams of your trousers are for.) Now. I'm standing to attention. I get the order Left Turn. *Le-heft . . . Tyeeern!* The heel of my left foot becomes a pivot. I push with the toe of my right foot, and turn left. That's *One.* I count a pause—*Two, Three*—then raise my right knee smartly and bring my right foot down in the correct position at an angle of forty-five degrees with a smash that cracks the asphalt—*One! One . . . two . . . three. . . . One!* Get it? You'll only shout out the time while you're here. By that time, the correct pause will become instinctive. Now, you. What's 'Instinctive'? What's it mean?"

He has picked on Bates. Bates grins. Then he says: "Loike a dog, Sergeant."

"What d'you mean, like a dog?"

"Well, a dog's instinctive, Sergeant."

"Oh, so a dog's instinctive, is it? I'll dog you, you stuffed dummy, you. I'll instinctive you, you sloppy great Dane, you! You horrible thing! The correct movement—for the benefit of any brainless lout that doesn't know the meaning of the English language—will come to you without your having to think about it, and so will the correct time. Anybody here done any navvying? . . . Several of you. Well, do you have to think how to get hold of a pick or a shovel? No. That's instinctive. Definitely. Well, your arms will come to you like that. So will the proper use of your feet. Now listen," says Sergeant Nelson, dropping his voice to an ordinary, conversational tone. "Some of you guys may be sensitive. I dunno. Well, don't *worry* if I shout at you a bit and call you names. It's essential. It's impossible to get along without it. I've got to get you fairly proficient in eight or nine weeks. Always be sure that I won't dish you out more than you can take, and I won't punish any man unless he asks for it. Take everything in good part, and you'll be all right." He bellows: "Now, then! Come here. Lemme arrange you, like flowers in a garden . . . oh, you pretty-pretty bunch o' soppy-stalked shy pansy-wansies. God definitely blimey, blimey with thunderbolts, blimey with lightning! You, you rasher of wind!" He drags Old Silence into place. "Atcha, you great roasted ox." He pushes Hodge into position. "C'mon, you parrot-faced son of a son, Barker, or whatever your name is. . . . You, you gorbellier Geordie . . . yes, you, Shorrocks. There's enough of you there to start a sausage factory. . . . And you, Dopey . . . where are you from? Widnes? Get in there. . . . Gor damme and lumme! Why should England tremble, eh? *You*'ve been in the Army before, eh? I can see you have. Well, you come up here. Now look. You're in your positions. You'll always keep in those positions while you're here. Get it? When told to fall in, you will fall in in those same positions, one arm's length apart. Have you got it? Are you sure?"

To our left, thirty men, followed by a shrieking Sergeant brandishing a pace-stick, execute a left wheel which, to us, represents the ultimate perfection of military footwork.

"Gord milk the coconuts and stone me over the hurdles," groans Sergeant Nelson, "look at 'em. Three weeks squadded, and when it comes to a left wheel some of 'em right wheel, some of 'em about turn, some of 'em turn handsprings, some of 'em pick their noses, and some stand still. Definitely horrible. Now you're going to show 'em what you can do. To me, you look not too bad a squad. You might shape. Now look. Over there is a squad that came last week. I want you to do me a personal favour. I want you to beat them Things hollow. Your credit is my credit. I won't let you down. Will you let me down?"

"No, Sergeant!"

"I'm sure you won't. I like the look of you, you terrible-looking objects as you are. Now. You'll be on this side of the Square punctual to time. That is to say, ten minutes too early, always. You will be clean and tidy, smart and attentive. Now, I want you to try and stand to attention like this. . . . No, no, head straight, eyes straight to your front, arms straight to your sides, backs straight. . . . Now, when I say *Stand at Ease,* raise your left knee, so, and bring your left foot down with a *stamp,* your heels twelve inches apart; and simultaneously, shoot your hands to your rear . . . like this . . . your thumbs crossed, fingers straight, right hand over the left. Now don't worry if you can't do it properly first time. I don't expect you to. We've all got to learn. Now. . . . *Stand* at Hoo*oease!"* He looks at us. "Keep still. In the Army, right or wrong —keep still!" He walks round us, pushing up a chin here, tapping down a head there, straightening fingers, adjusting heels.

With the possible exception of a man in love, no man in the world is so desperately eager to please as the new recruit in the Army. He has his back to the yardstick of regimental tradition. For the duration of his time, his value will depend upon nothing but his proficiency as a soldier. The muscles of a rookie doing his first Stand at Ease are as taut as those of a man clinging for his life to a breaking branch.

"It'll come easy in time. *Squah*aad . . . Shun!" roars Sergeant Nelson.

"Speed. Speed is the word. Smooth speed. Definitely smooth speed. And let me see one of you not keeping his head up. I'll make him wish he'd died ten years before he was born. I'll have him running round this square like Mister Nurmi the Flying Finn. I'll hare him up and chase him down so that his plates of meat don't touch the ground once in five hundred yards. Stone me definitely blind! *Stand* at Hooo*ease!* Now, when I says *Stand Easy,* stay where you are but let all your muscles relax. Stand . . . easy! And when I say *Squad,* tense up again, stand properly at ease. *Squad.* As you were! *Squad!* Just tense yourselves back to the At Ease. All right, stand easy and rest for a minute."

"Please, Sergeant, a dog *is* instinctive," says Bates.

"Shullup! Are you out of your mind? Whaddaya mean, a dog? Who asked anything about dogs? Insubordination, eh? Insolence, eh? Shullup! . . ." Sergeant Nelson looks to Heaven and says: "All these years have I lived, and it seems like a thousand years; and never, definitely never, have I heard such a load of Sweet Fanny Adams as this horrible man comes out with. Gord forgive him. He's mental. . . . Now, about saluting. They're pretty hot on saluting in the Brigade of Guards. I don't care what they do in the Boy Scouts or the Church Lads' Brigade or the W.A.A.C.S. or the A.T.S., or the Salvation Army. Here, saluting being a matter of discipline and proper courtesy and respect, they are hot on it, and rightly so. Thus, whenever you see an officer approaching you, you will salute . . . head up, chin in, shoulders back, hand in line with the forearm, thumb pressed close against the edge of the hand, fingers all close together; the whole to come up like a steel spring, so that the right forefinger rests one inch above the right eyebrow.

"Now . . ."

A bugle sounds. "I'm going to dismiss you for now," says Sergeant Nelson. "Just for fun, see if you can do me a right turn, like I showed you. On the command Dismiss, you turn smartly to your right, count three and then scram. Try it. Dis-*miss!*"

He doesn't call us back, or give us an "As you were." It is, after all,

our first hour on the Square. We walk back to the hut to change for
P.T. The novelty of the thing has made this first Drill Parade quite
pleasant.

Bates catches up with the flying Sergeant Nelson, and says: "Please,
Sergeant."

"What is it, son?"

"When you whistle to a dog, 'e pricks 'is ears opp."

"Are you here again with your dogs?"

"No, Sergeant. Yes, Sergeant. Oi mean, a dog is koind o' instinctive."

"There's a lunatic asylum next door to here," says Sergeant Nelson.
"Either you'll go there pretty soon, or so help me, I will."

"Well, a cat, then," says Bates, earnestly. "If you go *pt-pt-pt*"—he
calls an imaginary cat—"it cooms running up to yow, because it knows
what yow mean. But a cat's got no sense. It's instinctive. It don't *know*
what it does, or *why* it does it, but it *does* it, don't it?"

"Oh, definitely," says Sergeant Nelson.

He reaches the hut before we do. As we enter he cries: *"Hi-de-Hi!"*
"Ho-de-Ho!"

"Slippers, shorts, gym vests and sweaters, and a rolled towel under
your arm. The muscle factory, you weeds! The muscle factory, you
spineless gobs of calves' feet jelly, you. It made me what I am today,
and I'm a one-man wave o' destruction! *Hi-de-Hi!*"

"Ho-de-Ho!"

"Trained Soldier Brand," says Sergeant Nelson.

"Sarnt?" says the Trained Soldier, leaping up.

"*I* don't want you," says the Sergeant. "I just said 'Trained Soldier
Brand.' Just like that. 'Trained Soldier Brand.' Just as you might say:
'Blind O'Reilly.' . . . Come on, *come* on, come ON! Ja wants valets! Ja
want ladies' maids? Ja want me to powder your little bottoms with
talcum and put your little shorts on for you? Get out of it! Form up
like I showed you just now, for P.T."

We march as best we can out to the hard green fields, where a Staff
Sergeant waits for us—an Army Heavyweight Champion of practically

everything, with the body of a boxer turned wrestler, the eye of a kind man embittered, and the face of an executioner who is kind to his children when off duty.

He bites off jagged spikes of verbiage and spits them out like fishbones.

"Come close. Listen to me. First of all I want to have. A few words. With you. Pay attention."

His grim grey eyes look us over; rest approvingly upon the huge thews of Hodge and the long, quick boxing muscles of Bullock; appraise the wiriness of Johnson, the sedentary slenderness of Old Silence, the stolid suet of Sherrocks, the ranginess of the wire-haired boy from Widnes, the neglected average torso of Dale. He rests a great dark hand for an instant on Thurstan's shoulder. Thurstan bobs up and back like a hammer in a piano, tense and defensive. The Staff Sergeant glances at him and yawns. Then he says:

"None of you are. Any good. Civilians. City-bred, some of you. Doughy. Sloppy. Unfit. Most of you'd be puffed after running. A mile. Hn. We'll alter all that." He clears his throat, and then goes on, in the voice of a lecturer, but with an undertone of weariness. (After all, he has been saying the same thing over and over again, day in and day out, for so very long.) He says:

"It is my duty to make you fit and strong in order that you may serve your country to the full extent of your capacity. Some of you went in for sports and physical culture in peacetime. All the better for them that did. You all ought to have done so. A man who neglects the body God gave him is worse than a beast. And if you've neglected yourselves and let yourselves get short-winded and soft, well, you'll suffer for that in the first week or two: it'll come hard, very hard. You get a lot of P.T. here. You've got to be hammered into shape. I can't show you any mercy, even if I wanted to . . . and I don't.

"I hope you enjoy the P.T. you get here. If you don't, it makes no odds. So you'd better for your own sakes. It isn't all arm-and-leg exercises.

Now, we play a lot of games and do a lot of nice running. Above all, we teach a new kind of thing which we call Unarmed Combat.

"What is Unarmed Combat? Well, it's nothing more or less than dirty, roughhouse fighting . . . self-defence other than Queensberry method. Call it All-In Wrestling . . . a bit of Catch-As-Catch-Can, Ju-Jitsu, Judo, anything you like. The idea is this: you're up against Jerry. Jerry is ruthless. Jerry won't lead with his left in hand-to-hand fighting: he'll more likely bite you in the face and kick. The principle is, that a break-hold, or a gouge, or a properly placed kick or twist, well applied, might save your life in an emergency. I teach you ruthless, unscrupulous, roughhouse tactics, to be used if and when occasion demands. And furthermore, Unarmed Combat gives you confidence in yourselves, and helps you to a proper co-ordination of eye and hand and foot. For instance . . ."

The Staff Sergeant reaches out, casually, as one might reach for a cigarette; and almost as effortlessly picks up a great Sergeant Instructor in a blue-and-red striped sweater and a Sandow moustache.

"This kind of thing," says the Staff Sergeant, hurling the striped one to the earth and hauling his right hand back between his shoulder-blades, "is useful sometimes. But you have to be *quick*, not necessarily strong, but *quick* to do it, and speed is always useful, in every walk of life."

The striped Sergeant is black in the face and moaning. The Staff Sergeant releases him. "Sergeant Paul," he says, "rush me."

"*Must* I, Staff? You've demonstrated on me twice already today."

"Yes, you must."

The striped one walks twenty feet away, and then makes a desperate rush upon the Staff Sergeant. He hopes to bear the grim one down by sheer weight and vigour. A second or so later he is spinning through the air. "Watch him fall," says Staff. "If he didn't know how to fall he'd break his neck. Or maybe an arm." The striped Sergeant rolls over and over, and finally rises, covered with dry grass and somewhat angry.

The Staff Sergeant turns back to us. He has the calm, languid air of a man who has just thrown away an empty cigarette packet. "You might go a bit easy on these demonstrations," says Sergeant Paul. "There was a stone where I fell."

"Well, the stone had no right to be there. All right. I just wanted to have a word with you. You can't be good soldiers unless you're fit. It's up to me to make you fit, and up to you to help me." And the Staff Sergeant repeats something we have heard before, and are destined to hear many times again:

"Work with me, and I'll be all right. Work against me, make things difficult, impede the progress of fitness and the war by any idleness, laziness, insubordination or funny business . . ." He grinds his teeth, leaving the rest unsaid but hideously implied.

Then he hands us over to the striped Sergeant, Paul, who lines us up and says:

"I'm the best fellow in the world if you treat me right. Work willingly and do your best, and I'm your pal. Play me up, and I don't mind telling you I'll make life a misery for you. I'll soon get that paleness off your faces and put some zing into those limbs. Now, let's see you run . . ."

An hour later we go back to the hut.

Sergeant Nelson grins at us.

"Well? Grown any hair on your horrible little chests? Get back into battledress. I, *I*, do you hear me, *I* am going to tell you about the Short Lee-Enfield Rifle. *Hi-de-Hi!*"

"*Ho-de-Ho!*"

Bates says: "Please Sergeant Oi think Oi've got a torn muscle."

"So what d'you want me to do? Darn it? Get going."

The little aches and pains of unaccustomed exercise affect different men in different ways. Some remember what their mothers told them about "overstraining" themselves, and fall into dismal panic. Others— heavy manual workers, and the like—consider them philosophically, without entirely ignoring them. Sedentary men, clerical fellows, black-coated workers like Dale, suffer considerably in the first weeks of

Guards training, but suffer like heroes, saying nothing at all except an occasional "Owch," like the parrot that laid square eggs.

Months afterwards, Sergeant Nelson, speaking to the N.C.O. known as Corporal Bearsbreath, said:

"Bearsbreath, I definitely admit that the wartime Guardsman is not the same as the peacetime Guardsman. In peacetime you can settle down to quiet training. You can chase your man into shape for months; and then again he's come into the Army because he wants to make it his job for a few years to come. Definitely. In wartime, you get all sorts and shapes and sizes of Guardsmen, within the height limits. But you have to hand it to one or two of them, the way they take it.

"There was a guy called Spencer, some sort of a salesman of some kind of biscuits or some such tack, that had spent his life sitting in a little motorcar driving from boozer to boozer hawking this here stuff. He come in at fourteen-stone-seven, puffy as pastry, carrying maybe three stone of superfluous fat, and dead out of condition. Oh definitely. Built to weigh eleven stone; carrying three stone extra: thinnish in the leg, softish about the thigh, not too good in the feet. Well, Bearsbreath, you know as well as I do that the chief trouble with Guardsmen is their feet. There's practically a disease: 'Guardsmen's Heels,' from excessive stamping. I thinks to myself: 'With all the good will in the world,' I thinks, 'this here Salesman wallah is going to turn out pretty poor . . . yes, I'm afraid he's going to be definitely steady.'

"And I watches him. Well, Bearsbreath, you know as well as I do that the first week or two cracks up quite a few rookies, for the time being . . . ammo boots on their poor little feet, and stamp, stamp, stamp on the Square; and the Staff Sergeant in the muscle factory; and the change of grub, and so on. This here Spencer drops weight like a Wop dumping his pack on the run. You can *see* stones and stones dripping off of him on the Square. Millions of stones that rook lost; billions. And sometimes, coming in at night to see if everything was hunky-doke, I'd see this here biscuit, or potato-crisp salesman, sitting on his bed with a pair of feet on him—I swear to God, Bearsbreath, they was like barrage balloons painted red, only bigger. 'Sore tootsies?' I says, and he always says: 'It's all right, Sarnt.' Conscientious? I never see such a conscientious rook. And I see him shape, and I say to myself: 'This rook is a dead cert for the tapes, and pretty damn soon at that.' What I mean to say is, I run into him the other day, and he's a lance-jack. I would have sworn he couldn't have stood the racket, and I wouldn't have held it against him if he hadn't, because there's some fellers that aren't cut out for it.

"What I mean, Bearsbreath, is; for sheer sand in the belly, grit, spine, nerve, and guts, some o' these soft-looking civvies take some beating. He went through hell, that rook did. He was over thirty, too. Definitely, Bearsbreath, the war brings out the what-d'you-call-it in some blokes. There's big buck navvies would have laid down and had kittens at half what this here Spencer went through. Now my point is this: the Army helped to make a man of that geezer. He wouldn't have known how good he was if it hadn't been for the Army. But that's neither here nor there. My point is this: the kid of eighteen has soft bones, and he's young—he don't feel the strain much because it's helping him to grow. The working mug that's shoved barrows, or handled a pick and shovel, *he* doesn't notice it so much, because he's been using his muscles all his life, more or less. But the clurk, Bearsbreath, the clurk, the shop-walker, the pen-pusher, the bloke that's never used his muscles in his life—he's the bloke I'm sorry for and take my hat off to at the same time. He sort of feels that he's got to stand up to it as well as anybody else. And he does. And he won't go sick unless he's absolutely *got* to go sick. He's ashamed to. Toughish; definitely toughish."

Bearsbreath said: "We was all Civvies once, Nelson."

"Were we?" said Sergeant Nelson. "To tell you the honest truth, I hardly remember."

That evening, as we come back from tea, Trained Soldier Brand says: "No talking, singing, or whistling. No smoking. No eating. Shining Parade. Remember, every morning the Officer comes round to inspect this hut. I noticed one or two greatcoats with buttons like old halfpennies this morning. I'm responsible for you. You land *me* in the muck if you don't watch out, and that is a serious offence. I want to see you fellers working till seven. Them gaiters have got to be blancoed every night. So's your belt, and et cetera. Remember, brush the surface of the webbing with water, first, then brush your blanco in thinly and evenly. Take your belts to bits and work on them brasses. A thin smear of polish, let it dry, and then rub, damn it, rub. Above all, work on them boots. I don't mind telling you, they're 'ot on boots 'ere. You'll be inspected soon. Say your boots is bad. What happens? The Company Commander hauls me in on Orders and says: 'Trained Soldier Brand, why is them men's daisy-roots in muck? Is this 'ere the way you maintain the high stand· ards of the Brigade of Guards? Are you a Coldstreamer? Or what the lousy hell are you? Why, you twillip,' he says. 'Take three drills just for a warning.' And if you think I'm going to rush round that Square with a pack just for you, you're wrong. So let me tell you something—any idle skiver I catch will find himself with such a load o' jankers he won't know where he is."

"What is jankers, Trained Soldiers?" asked Johnson.

"It's a sort of general kind of word meaning punishment. You'll get to know the call: Defaulters—*You can be a Defaulter as long as you like, As long as you answer your name*. It might be *Show Boots Clean*. It might be *Extra Drill*. It might be C.B."

"What is C.B., Trained Soldier?"

"Confined to Barracks."

"But we're confined to barracks now."

"Yes, but only while you're Recruits. After you're done here, you're Guardsmen, and have the right to go out every night, duty permitting. You get a Permanent Pass, allowing you out of barracks from After Duty to Midnight. But if you get C.B., you can't go out. Defaulters sounds five minutes after Reveille. You've got to hustle to the Square and answer your name double time. During the day, Defaulters blows about Dinner Time, and every hour after about five, till ten-thirty. You've got to answer your name every time. If you don't, you're for it.

Then there's extra drills, in Fighting Order—small pack, with ground-sheet and mess-tins, pouches, braces, belt, rifle, bayonet, full water-bottle. And you've got to be spick-and-span, or you might get another few days. The drills, usually, are pretty tough, too. The game ain't worth the candle. For instance, you're very likely to get seven days or so for a dirty rifle. Well, a dust over and a pull-through'll save you all that. Or being late for a parade: two minutes can land you seven days. Or over-staying your furlough, or being in possession of playing cards, or answering back, or not answering back (answering back is Insubordination: not answering back is Dumb Insolence), or not being properly dressed, or forgetting to salute an officer, or having a dirty cap star, or a dirty bayonet, or standing idle on parade, or being inattentive on parade, or speaking out of turn, or laughing, or crying, or using horrible —dirty words, or not walking properly, or not getting up at Reveille, or not putting out the lights at Lights Out, or skiving . . ."

"What is Skiving?"

"The same as Swinging It. Trying to get out of things; dodging a parade, wangling a fatigue, or otherwise chancing your arm. Slipping out for a tea 'n'a wad when on fatigue is, for instance, Skiving."

"What's a Wad?"

"Shiver-and-Shake. A Cake. (Get on with that shining!) There's no need to go round bobbing: just keep calm and do your dooty, and you'll keep out of trouble."

"What's Bobbing?"

"Oh . . . sort of bobbing; getting nerves, worrying. You, Dale, your boots are very steady."

"Thanks, Trained Soldier," says Dale, gratified; for to this good man "Steady" is the highest possible praise of a man or his job.

"Thanks? Thanks for what? In the Guards, son, 'Steady' means 'Absolutely lousy.' If you want to sort of spit in a man's eye, call him Steady. If, on the other hand, you want to give him a bit o' praise, then says he's Hot. 'Steady' means Awful, so get working. I know you're not used to it yet: don't get down'earted. Rub your polish well in, then spit nice clear spit, and rub it in with a circular motion. If you're using a bone, then bone your boots with a kind of smooth, stroking movement. . . . D'you hear that bugle-call? That's 'Yellow' . . . there's enemy planes about, so be on the alert. 'Red'—*There's a Jerry in the sky"*— he sings it—"means, go to the shelter with your tin hat and respirator. You also take your rifle and bayonet, to get you used to the feel of 'em. There's hundreds of calls: you've got to know them, from Reveille to Lights Out. There's little pomes to 'em. Frinstance: Picquet:

> *"Come an' do a Picquet, Boys,*
> *Come an' do a Guard,*
> *You think it's ruddy easy*
> *But you'll find it ruddy hard.*

"Or Officers' Mess:

> *"Officers' wives eat pudden and pies*
> *But soldiers' wives eat skilly.*

"Or Letters:

> *"Letters from Lousy Lou, Boys,*
> *Letters from Lousy Lou.*

"Or Commandant's Orders: After the Brigade Call:

> *"Justice will be done!*

"or

> *"Cri-ime does not Pay!*

"You'll learn, you'll learn in time. And what is Commandant's Orders, you ask? Well. If the Commandant wants to say something to you, he orders you to attend Orders, and you're marched in, first to Company Orders, and ordered to attend Commandant's Orders, and then you're marched into the Commandant's office, and get what's coming to you. Or say you've committed some crime, like being late, or absent. The Company Commander might not want to deal with the case himself. He might send you to the Adjutant for sentence, and the Adjutant might send you to the Commandant. So don't go and commit no crimes.

"Again, any man is entitled to interview the Company Commander, privately, about any matter. But he can't just walk in bolo and——"

"What's Bolo?"

"Cockeyed; anything not correct in the Coldstream Guards is Bolo. You don't just walk in and say 'Oi.' You see Sergeant in Waiting, and write out an Application for an Interview, and then, if the Captain is free to see you, which he always is, you're stood at ease outside the office, then, when your name's called you spring to attention and march in with your hands to your sides; mark time, halt; left turn, and, as your name's called again, take a smart pace forward and wait till you're spoken to. When the interview is over, you receive the order *Fall In,* and take a smart pace backward, left turn again, and out you go, fast, keeping your hands still. It's dead easy. A baby in arms could do it. If the officer says anything to you and you just want to say Yes, say 'Yes, sir'; not just 'sir.' The Billy Browns, or Grenadiers, say 'sir'; the Lily-whites say 'Yes, sir.'

"Another thing. Every week or two you'll have a Kit Inspection. That is to teach you to take proper care of the property entrusted to you. You have to show boots, battledress, both hats, one pair of socks clean, one shirt clean, sweater, gym vests, shorts, tin of black polish, tin of brown polish, tin of blanco, tin of metal polish, oil bottle, pullthrough, mess tins and cover, housewife complete with needles and et ceteras, knife, fork and spoon, steel helmet, respirator and respirator-haversack, slippers, button-stick, all your brushes sandpapered clean, and other odds and ends, all laid out in perfect order on a clean towel on your bed. Everything has to be marked with your number. They're 'ot on numbers, round 'ere. And when the officer comes to your bed you stand smartly to attention, and say this: 2663141 (or whatever your number is) *Recruit Smith. Two Weeks Squadded* (or however long it is.) *Kit Present, sir.* If anything is missing . . . it might be a pair of socks . . . you say *One Pair Socks Missing Otherwise Kit Present, sir.*

"I've got the numbering kit here, ink pad, stamps, and doodahs. You've got to get yourselves a pennorth of tape each; stamp your number on a lot o' bits o' tape and sew 'em on everything you can lay your hands on. 'Cause things have a way of disappearing.

"Failure to comply with all this 'ere is a very serious offence, and I don't mind telling you that they're 'ot on serious offences in this mob."

"Hot means Good, doesn't it?" asks Dale.

"Yes. But not necessary. Frinstance, if I say 'Your boots is Hot,' I mean, they're good. But if I say 'The Drill Pig is Hot,' that means 'e's pretty savage."

"And what's a Drill Pig?"

"A Drill Pig is a Drill Sergeant. A Drill Sergeant is a sort of super-sergeant-major, an assistant to the Regimental Sergeant Major."

"But why *Pig?*" asks a lad from the Elephant and Castle.

"You'll soon find out," says Trained Soldier Brand.

The same lad asks: "And wot's a Regimental Sergeant Major do?"

"Well, 'e's a kind of link between the officers and the other ranks. 'E's a sort of an Archbishop."

"And the Commandant?"

" 'E's sort of a Gawd."

The wire-haired boy from Widnes, having stared for nearly fifteen minutes at a photograph of a peacetime Coldstreamer on a Buckingham Palace Guard, says to the Trained Soldier:

"I wanna sign on for twenty-one years."

As seven strikes we rise from our beds like men in a fairy tale released from a spell. "If you're going anywhere at all, even to the Lat," says Brand, "you're supposed to take your respirators, tin hats, and gas-capes with you. This is to get you into the 'abit of carrying 'em wherever you go. And so you'd better. Say you're out one day on leave and the Gestapo sees you without your tin bowler and mask, you'll go in the moosh."

"Gestapo?"

"Another name for military police."

"Are they noice?" asks Bates.

Trained Soldier Brand says that while the Military Police are in-offensive to law-abiding soldiers, they can nevertheless be People Of Dubious Ancestry if they wish. "We got to 'ave 'em. I suppose," he says, "to keep law and order. If you pay rates and taxes you got to 'ave law and order. Personally, I don't pay no rates and taxes, and I don't want no law and order. But there it is. There's military policemen in every town. They got the right to arrest anybody in uniform. They're the Army's C.I.D., kind o' style. They're coppers. They ain't popular, therefore. Nobody really loves a Gestapo man. It's unreasonable, but there it is. There ain't a soldier living that's never broke a rule—with the possible exception of Freddie Archer, R.S.M. of Scots Guards—the most regimental man in the British Army. Once, being two minutes late off leave, he put himself in the report and marched himself in to be punished. When talking to an officer on the telephone he salutes and stands stiffly to attention. But what was I saying? Gestapo. Person-ally I dislike 'em. That's a matter of opinion. The beauty of this 'ere Democracy is, you can hate policemen and say so. But I ought to tell you that a Gestapo man is serving his country same as a sewer-man or a dustman. He's essential. And even if he wasn't, don't you go and get yourselves into no trouble, just for the sake of being properly dressed or anything.

"They sell beer in the Naffy. I, personally, have never met a man who could get drunk on it, though I have known many that tried. Wind pudden, that's what it is. All the same, it is alleged to be alcoholic, and if you bring any back with you you will have committed a terribly serious offence. They're 'ot on alcohol in barrack rooms in this mob, I don't mind telling you. Red-'ot. Boiling-'ot. This is a military depot of the Brigade of Guards, so you don't go round bathing chorus girls in champagne. A cup of chocolate, yes. A nice packet o' wine gums, yes. But beer? Beer is a serious offence."

We hurry to the Naffy.

In an immense room with an interminable counter, endless queues of

Guards recruits, Lilywhites, Grenadiers, Jocks, Micks, and Taffies, writhe and mutter while a few frantic girls in blue cotton overalls dash out cups of tea, great jammy wads of cake, tins of boot-polish, bootlaces, vaseline, fruit-salts, pies, biscuits, pencils, chocolate, dusters, writing pads, beans on toast, beer, cider, ink, cigarettes and sausages.

We wait in a queue. Everything is smoky and strange. A vociferous recruit with a brass leek on his cap is shouting: "That is unfair you are, look, to get a man in front to buy things for you, look! That is unjust it is!" And a dark recruit with a Cross of Saint Andrew worked into his Guards' Star says, in a fantastic combination of American and Glaswegian: "So hwhit?" A man on a remote platform singing a song about one Danny Boy is more unheard than a goldfish: he simply opens and closes his mouth. The uproar of the Naffy swallows his song, but he neither knows nor cares. There is some clapping. A sharp-starred Irish Guards' recruit near us says:

"There's a song that goes:

> *"You've lost an arm and you've lost a leg,*
> *You're an eyeless, noseless, spiritless egg,*
> *You'll have to be put in a bowl to beg—*
> *Johnny I hardly knew you.*

"I wish they'd sing that and cheer us up a bit."

But the singer, shoving his sharp tenor voice through a chink in the din, begins *Bless 'em all.*

> *Bless 'em all, Bless 'em all,*
> *The long and the short and the tall,*
> *There'll be no promotion, This side of the ocean,*
> *So cheer up me lads, Bless 'em all. . . .*

Spencer the salesman recognizes a jar of the product he sells, and is cheered and saddened at the same time. Johnson, the fly Brummagem boy, says with sudden vehemence: "Oi bet Oi'll be a sergeant insoide six months." A dozen of our squad have arrived to swell the slow-moving queue. Old Silence comes out of his taciturnity and says: "Will you all have a beer?" We all say we will, if we can get it; for there seem enough men before us to drink all that was ever brewed. "Why are these places so short-staffed?" somebody asks; and somebody else replies: "They're short-staffed because they haven't got enough people working for 'em." "Oh, is that it?" asks the interrogator.

A querulous voice says: "So I says to the Sarnt In Waiting, 'I wanna go sick.' So I goes sick. So I sees the M.O. So the M.O. says: 'Now what's your trouble?' I says: 'Me foot, sir.' He says: 'Your foot isn't trouble. Say what you mean. What's wrong with your foot?' I says: 'It's swole.' 'Let's see,' he says. 'Ah,' he says, 'merely a blister,' 'Blister?' I says. 'Blister,' he says, and he sticks a ruddy great needle in that ruddy great blister and he got enough water out of that ruddy great blister—may I never get out of this here Naffy alive—enough water to fill a reservoy. And he sends me back to duty. Cruelty!"

"I wonder how we'll like it here?"

"Somebody told me it's horrible."

"The Training Battalion is worse."

"The Holding Battalion is worse still."

"The First is supposed to be worst of all."

"The Second is hell, somebody told me."

"Whether we like it or not we've got to stay here, so the thing to do is, get used to it quickly."

Suddenly a dreadful silence falls. *Jerry in the Sky!* cries the bugle. We run out. Thurstan pauses to curse and stamp his foot. Understandably: for, having waited twenty minutes, he found himself right against the counter. And then Red blew. Barker looks as if he has suddenly been smitten with all the miseries of Job, and has not been left with even a bit of pot to scrape his boils with.

From the back of the night comes the melancholy note of a siren. It gathers volume; shrieks, fades, and shrieks again. The distance is now full of something like muffled drums. "Lousy with stars," says Barker, referring to the sky, which is clear and beautiful. We hop down into our trench. The guns mutter loud now. We hear the queer, pulsating drone of raiders. Antiaircraft guns bang. The night is full of steel.

Bates, in the middle of a story, will not be interrupted:

" . . . When Brummy Joe chucked this feller out o' that winder, 'e landed on 'is 'ead and split it open. 'E was proper frit o' Brummy after that, this feller was. Brummy could of showed yow some fight-ing. I see Brummy put 'is fist through a oak door. What? *'Urt* 'im? What, *Brummy?* A oak *door?* Don't be silly. Yow could a bashed Brummy wi' the door edgeways and not 'urt *'im,* not *Brummy!* Well, another noice feller from Ull as we called Tyke——"

The ground seems to heave like a wrestler's back. The raider is weaving among the shell splinters, dropping his bombs. The searchlights make strange patterns: shifting triangles, sprawling rhomboids, fabulous outlines that look like letters out of some half-formed alphabet. One great beam squirting up like a hose catches a silver speck and holds it. The batteries go mad. The sky twinkles with shell bursts like a spangled skirt in a spotlight. "By God we got him!" somebody says.

". . . So this feller asks Brummy for his two bob back. 'Yow want yow're two bob back?' says Brummy? 'Ah, Oi want moi two bob back.' 'Yow do, do yow?' 'Ah.' 'Oh?' 'Ah.' 'Roight yow are,' says Brummy, and picks up a eight-inch crowbar——"

The pulse of the raider has stopped. The searchlights wave uncannily. *"Look!"* There is something like a dust mote in a moonbeam. It is a man, falling with a parachute. There is something pitifully insignificant about this little thing, this bit of life drifting down out of the darkness suspended on threads from the edges of a bit of silk, caught in a net of light. He comes down slowly. The great beam circles, bumping against a little cluster of clouds. Through it, flashing electric lights, passes a Hurricane, roaring. Another siren sounds, miles away. Then our own siren, fifty feet from us, revolves and fills the world with a terrific whoop of triumph, so loud that you cannot hear it, but feel it in your bones.

We smile as we go back. It couldn't have worked out better if the

Commandant had arranged it. In that little half-hour, we have begun to feel like soldiers.

". . . Seventeen stitches over one of 'is eyes," Bates is saying. "Oi tell yaw, seventeen stitches."

"Sleep and refresh your pretty little selves," says Sergeant Nelson. "Because tomorrow I'm really going to start in on you. Definitely, I'm going to chase you tomorrow. I got a liver. And when I got a liver I'd tear my own grandmother's tripes out and trample them underfoot. I'd definitely do all that and much more. Woho, am I going to chase you tomorrow! Any idle man here can make his last lousy little will and testament. Any chancer can go to the Ablutions and cut his scraggy little throat from ear to ear into a washbasin. Sleep! It's an order! *Hi-de-Hi!*"

We roar at the top of our voices: "HO-DE-HO!"

We have suddenly become cheerful. We are getting the hang of things.

Quickly but smoothly, week after week, Sergeant Nelson drives his stuff into us; tireless, patient, with legs of steel and a throat of brass. Step by step he teaches us to march and drill. Slap by slap he instructs us in the handling of arms. Screw by screw he uncovers the mysteries of the Short Lee Enfield, Mark Three. Lunge by lunge he divulges the secrets of the bayonet, from High Port to Butt-Stroke and Kill. We pass our second-, fourth-, and sixth-week inspections. The Company Commander says that we are doing tolerably well. Sergeant Nelson informs us that, in a long and varied life spent mostly among half-wits and the offscourings of the lunatic asylums of the earth, he has seen worse squads than us: which pleases us more than anything else. Like all Guards recruits, we have been working at concert pitch.

We have lived in a state of tense activity. We have become accustomed to the food. We grumble, as always. Once, when they gave us biscuits instead of bread for tea, and the officer came round to ask if there were any complaints, we all made barking noises; and the officer laughed, and we laughed to see him laugh, and even the Company Quartermaster Sergeant bared a terrible tooth in a bit of a smile. We have been lectured on gas, on regimental tradition, military law pertaining to the crimes of desertion, drunkenness, and neglect of duty. The Padre has had a few words with us. The Medical Officer has told us what every young Guardsman ought to know. The Staff Sergeant has been at us. The days in the beginning seem inexpressibly remote. We speak of recruits four weeks squaddled as Rookies. Eight haircuts have come and gone since the day we put off civilian clothes and looked at each other in brand-new khaki. Tactics are not altogether a sealed book to us. Our shoulders have experienced the pleasant kick of our rifles loaded with 303 ammunition. We walk very straight: it was a psychological rather than a muscular operation which brought this about. After three weeks we were allowed out for an afternoon: it felt good to walk in a street on our own, slamming down our great boots and swinging our arms.

And now we prepare for our last Inspection; the Commandant's Inspection.

If the Commandant approves of us, we will "pass out" to the Training Battalion, for another period of training. It doesn't occur to us, yet, that we have acquired merely the groundwork of Guardsmanship. We have yet to get down to the hard stuff, that makes Guardsmen into soldiers. The time is coming when we will know the fatigue of a thirty-two-mile route march, or of a midnight stunt in damp darkness among the bracken of a blasted common . . . the feel of a Bren Gun, like the stupendous gulping of wine out of a bottle . . . the smallness of a six-foot target at five hundred yards . . . the misery of half-dug trenches in a thin drizzle three miles from camp and an hour and a half from dinner . . . when there will be a C.O.'s parade every week, and other drill parades besides; and cross-country runs, and hardening exercises, and the tossing of live grenades, and the chance of seven days' leave, and the responsibilities of the ordinary trained soldier.

We dress with care. Debutantes flutter less than we do, as we put on our best battledress, with its cut-throat creases; and our best boots, glistening with quarts of spit and tins of polish; and our gaiters blancoed to a perfect pallor, and our brasses blindingly burnished. We help each other to dress. We pull each other's trousers over the web gaiters, and produce the proper blouse effect in our coats. We touch things at their edges. One thumbprint may destroy everything. We pull down the great cheese-cutter peaks of our best hats. Trained Soldier Brand follows us to the Square, and, when we have formed up, inspects us, and runs about us flicking with a duster, like a harassed housewife expecting overwhelming company. Then the Sergeant, the terrific Nelson, inspects us. Then the Superintendent Sergeant looks us over, with an eye from which all hope has long departed. *He* comes, a sturdy figure with a resolute stride. "Sergeant Nelson's Squad, eight weeks squadded, and ready for your inspection, sir." We stand frozen, stiff as overwound clockwork. We don't see the Commandant. We are staring straight to our front. We feel him as he passes . . . a Presence, an Eye. Seven or eight years pass. His voice is heard saying that our turnout is, on the whole, quite good. Sergeant Nelson's lone eye seems to heave a little sigh all on its own. The buttons on his S.D. jacket rise several inches, and then sink luxuriously. Then comes his voice. We thought we had heard him shout. We never did. He is shouting now. He is using his best Parade voice—a voice of Stentor at a Stannoy Sound System. He roars like a lion at a water hole. "*Squa-ha-haaaaaaaaaaaaAAAD . . . !*"

We stamp and wheel, right form and left form, salute to the left, the right, the front, and as improperly dressed. We take up arms, and slope, and order, and trail, and present them. We feel that we are doing all right. The Commandant questions us. We have swotted up everything he is likely to ask us, and, in fact, everything a Guardsman can possibly know. He asks us all that and a lot more. The autumn goes, winter comes and goes, more summers come and fade. Years pass. Our beards are long and grizzled. Our eyes are rheumy with advanced old age. He will dismiss us, and then we may lie down and die.

We are dismissed. It took about an hour and a half.

We drag ourselves away. "How were we, Sergeant?" And Sergeant

Nelson says: "You were not like Guardsmen. You were like a lousy crowd of wild, undisciplined Soudanese bloody Fuzzy-Wuzzies trained by illegitimate Wog corporals in a stinking pothouse in Tel Aviv in 1890. You were awful. I can never look myself in the face again. But all the same, you have passed out."

We raise a wild cheer.

"I daresay you'll leave for the Training Battalion on Tuesday," he says.

Cookhouse sounds. We laugh, if only to relax our stomachs.

"He saith among the trumpets, Ha, ha; and he smelleth the battle afar off," says Hodge, the Bible-reader. "Job, 39, 25."

"Who do?" asks Bates.

"The horse."

"I never heard a horse say 'Ha, ha,'" says Bates. "'Ave yow?"

Kitbag, big valise, little valise: Change of Quarters Order. We form in the road. Rather sadly, Sergeant Nelson cries *"Hi-de-Hi!"* We sadly reply: *"Ho-de-Ho!"* We are ready.

"Kill some Jerries," says Sergeant Nelson. "And *Hi-de-Hi!* for the last time, mugs."

"HO-DE-HO, Sergeant Nelson!"

"As for me," he says, "I got another squad coming today."

The order comes. Our left feet hit the dust.

We are on the march.

III

The Tempering

SOMETHING STUTTERS over on the Ranges. Five bangs on one string: that is the Bren gun burst. A squad is firing at three hundred yards. There is always one man who fires before all the rest: *tu-tu-tu-tu-tut!* Then the rest open fire. The air rattles like a dice box for sixty seconds or so. Then, *tu-tut!*—there is always one man who has a couple of rounds unfired. Hidden hands in the butts pull the targets down. A silence comes. Soon, somebody, somewhere, will make something go off bang. It might be a Mills bomb, or a mortar bomb; or in the distance the Artillery may fire a gun; or an N.C.O. may shoot fifty fat forty-five bullets out of a Tommy gun; or a learner may squeeze six hoarse and hesitant explosions out of a revolver. Only night, or fog, quiets the Ranges. This, say some, is why it rains so often. A military policeman from Gloucester, who talks and talks in a voice like the monotonous scrape and squeak of a rusty pump, breathlessly assures all who will listen that the everlasting banging shakes the clouds. "D'you yurr it? Bang, bang, bang. It shakes all the water out o' them clouds, experts reckon."

For here, when it is not raining, it looks as if it is going to rain; except in the hottest part of the summer, when one fears that it will never rain again. There is a perversity about the climate. It will pour all day. But when a Night Stunt takes place, which rain might cancel, then the sky clears and a calm falls, the Dipper hangs empty in a lucid heaven, and a fat-faced moon sneers down at the men who wallow in the mire that the day's rain has left behind it. The feet of innumerable Guardsmen have kicked the ground to powder. The earth, when wet, is of the

86

consistency of clotted cream. When dry it flies about. It is Passchendaele in the winter, and Oklahoma in the summer. One makes fantastic detours as the Quarter blows for C.O.'s Parade, to avoid puddles of unknown depth. But when the sun comes out, the very dandelions seem to blink in the dust. So say the old soldiers. From October to July, they groan, the place is like the countryside beyond the Malamute Saloon in "Dangerous Dan M'Grew" . . . it takes an Amundsen to get from the Post Office to the Y.M.C.A. From July to October, well, you might as well be in the Foreign Legion. And the flies, they say, are unnatural. The military policeman from Gloucester says that the flies are caused by the dust. "Dust creates flies, the experts reckon," he says, "just as earth creates wurrrums or shirts create fleas if you're not careful. It's a proof that thur's a God, the experts reckon . . ."

It is true that there are too many flies here in the warm weather; flies of exceptional intelligence, that might have come out of a Silly Symphony . . . flies that tickle and flies that drone; flies that bite, and flies that simply look threatening; dragon-flies, hover-flies, greenflies, even butterflies. On every side there stretches the decent, amiable Surrey countryside, full of gracious gardens behind trimmed green slabs of hedge. But the Camp itself is a shanty-town of huts. The adjacent villages are made up of skimpy little Edwardian villas, and look like little bits of Lewisham or Shepherd's Bush. The local barber complains that they know what you do in the village before you know it yourself: the other day his nose began to bleed; he hurried home, but his wife met him halfway with a wet towel—the news had preceded him, but only God knew how.

Some of the inhabitants complain of the soldiers: they dig trenches on the Common. . . . "Can't they make believe to be at war without digging holes?" The villagers are familiar with the bugle calls, which sound from dawn to dark and are audible for miles around: they hear *Lights Out* and adjust their clocks. All day long, manœuvring squads march out and back: Coldstreamers, singing *You'll Be Far Better Off in the Moosh,* or Scots Guards preceded by skirling bagpipes. They go out on Stunts, sometimes in the dead of night behind dim and sinister lamps; sometimes in column of route through spitting rain; sometimes armed with picks and shovels in the wake of a lorry-load of revetting hurdles and barbed wire. There is a coming and going of dispatch-riders, travelling like projectiles. All roads lead to the Camp. You get to it over a bridge that is all ready for blowing up. You pass a languid canal, brilliantly scummed with green algæ.

To the right of the road, going into Camp, lie the huts and the squares. To the left, the Messes of the gods and demigods; officers and sergeants. The road runs on, past the Y.M.C.A., past the Camp Theatre and the bright new huts that the Scots Guards live in . . . into a woodland of silver birch trees, and away to the unknown distance. To the right of the Guardroom, in the middle of a trampled desolation of clayey dirt, away from the jungles of gorse and bracken and bramble, lies a flat patch of beautiful turf. Day in and day out, in war or peace, a very ancient warrior strokes and caresses this turf, watering and anointing it, rolling it and smoothing it, clipping it and fertilising it, indignantly uprooting superfluous daisies with the forceful gentleness of a beautician depilating a lady's lip. This is the Cricket Field. Football is played at the back of the B. Lines Naffy, on rougher grass scattered with bits of metal—base plugs, springs, and scraps of cast iron that have come yipping and whining over from the little No Man's Land where live grenades are thrown.

By night, the Camp is labyrinthine and mysterious, more baffling than Pimlico in the similarity of its buildings and company areas. He who steps aside from the road is lost in the maze of the Black Huts. The newcomer must develop something of the cat's sense of orientation: if he steps out of his hut after dark upon a harmless, hygienic mission, he is not unlikely to find himself wandering, groping in an enchanted midnight on the downtrodden grass at the back of the lavatories. Newcomers from the Depot sometimes fall into a state of despondency at the sight of the Black Huts. The huts at the Depot are brand new: the Black Huts have a sombre air of extreme age; the curses and grouses of innumerable Old Sweats have soaked into their wooden walls. Some of them are said to contain mice. On one occasion, at least, three huge Sergeants were seen, pursuing with drawn bayonets and slashing coal shovels a miserable rodent no bigger than your thumbnail. The mouse got away, incidentally, but returned to forage that night, and caused Sergeant Hitchens of Wigan to shriek in his sleep by falling off a shelf on to his face. There is a rumour that two mice, bride and groom, consummated their union and brought up three families of baby mice in a suitcase in which a Guardsman known as Old Meanie used to hoard fruitcake. Meanie (says the legend) was in the habit of waiting until his comrades were asleep before regaling himself on handfuls of cake and pie; but one night he put the father mouse into his furtive mouth, and thereafter was a changed man. The legend is particular about the sex of the mouse.

Here, where recruits become Guardsmen, one is permitted to exhibit over one's bed photographs of wives, relatives, fiancées, or close friends. Bed heads break out in patchworks of snapshots. Men seize new arrivals by the arms, and, pointing to the blurred outlines of some non-descript form, say: "Isn't she a beauty?" or "Ain't she a smasher?" The correct reply to such questions is a sound which may be transcribed thus: "Mmmmmmmmmm-mum!" One N.C.O., who keeps three cabinet photos of his pretty wife on his bit of wall, takes them down in the evening, for he considers it indecent that these pictures should look down on the spectacle of thirty men undressing. Regular Guardsmen always exhibit postcard snaps of themselves in scarlet tunics and bearskins. One man displays portraits of Loretta Young, Ann Sheridan, and Frances Day, on which he has written loving messages to himself in assumed hands. Another sometimes talks to a small snap of a big woman, saying: "If you're carrying on with anybody while I'm away . . ."

Soldiers, here, have responsibilities. They must "make themselves acquainted with the Detail." That is to say, nobody tells them what they are going to have to do. No Sergeant leads them from place to place.

The blowing of the Quarter alone warns them that the hour of a Parade is drawing near. Baths and haircuts become, once again, the personal responsibility of the individual soldier. A hairy neck means trouble. "Dirty Flesh" is a serious offence. Men have got away with murder, but never with a rusty rifle. Beyond such matters as cleanliness, subordination, and punctuality, which are taken for granted, the Detail Boards are the Tablets of the Law. In the frames which hang on the walls outside the Company office, the Sergeant-Major pins the mimeographed will of the C.O., whose every word is an ultimatum. There one may read how it has come to the notice of the powers that Gambling is taking place, and the statement that this practice must cease forthwith; the game of Loto, or Housie-Housie, being the only indoor game officially sanctioned in the huts. . . . And it was there that the N.C.O.'s and men of the Guards learned that, in future, when rushing the enemy with bayonets, they must shout not "Hurr*ay*," but "Hurr*ah*"; at which everybody danced round everybody else, making savage points with imaginary bayonets and mincing "Oh, HurrAH, Duckie, HurrAH, HurrAH!"

But the Detail is The Word. Your destiny is written, not on your forehead, but on the Detail. Man disposes: the Commanding Officer details him.

And in this place many things are learned.

The handling, cleaning, and use of rifles, Bren guns, Tommy guns, mortars, and hand grenades, together with the firing, or throwing of same; tactics; marching; invisibility; trench-digging and revetting; cooking, if necessary and desirable; signalling; the manipulation of Bren carriers; wiring; moving silently; moving at night; how to be a corporal; how to avoid gas; how to put out fires, together with the handling of fire engines; map reading; the Army Act; how to be a military policeman; speed; presence of mind; falling down; getting up; swimming; marching in formation; reading and writing if illiterate; foreign languages; how to be a C.Q.M.S.; the selection of position in action; observation as a fine art; the laying of aims; the giving of fire orders; how to lead a section; how to mount guard; the whole mystery and art of sentry; the inner meaning and philosophic significance of applied discipline; how to drive military transport vehicles; how to crawl over enemy territory; how to attack; how to defend; how to fight, and when, and when not to fight; the timing of an attack, as it might be a punch to the jaw; how to harden the feet; what to do with bayonets, and when, and where to stick them; how to endure thirty-five miles on foot in rain or heat, with full fighting order; how to fire at aircraft; what to do when anything on earth happens, in any imaginable circumstances, in the teeth of any conceivable opposition . . . all these things are taught in official syllabuses. Above all, discipline; eternally and inevitably, discipline. Discipline is the screw, the nail, the cement, the glue, the nut, the bolt, the rivet that holds everything tight. Discipline is the wire, the connecting rod, the chain, that co-ordinates. Discipline is the oil that makes the machine run fast, and the oil that makes the parts slide smooth, as well as the oil that makes the metal bright. They know things about discipline, here. They have seen the Prussians with it, and the Arabs without it. Somewhere between those poles lies the ideal. The principle of discipline here is divinely simple: you lay it on thick and fast, all the time; the Englishman takes it to heart and then adjusts it to the national character. The result is the type of Sergeant Nelson, disciplinarian of ferocity and patience and infinite humour, who, if he told you to go to Hell, would be perfectly willing to lead you there; who might run you into the spud hole on Tuesday, but who would not fail to buy you a drink, and be damned to the regulations, if he met you outside on Saturday. Law and Order make the world go round: the stars of infinite space couldn't move without the parade-ground discipline of the heavens; and without the severe regimentation of the organs, no heart would beat. But there's a time and a place for everything. So says Sergeant Nelson, type and pattern of the N.C.O. He, above all men, knows the inner mystery of discipline and the value of the unbroken line.

Nelson on Discipline:

"You seen an old lawn. Have you or have you not? Rolled flat, smooth as a billiard table. Well, once upon a time, so a Yank tourist says to a gardener: 'Say, Buddy'—you know how Yanks talk—'how the gawdam hell do you gawdamwell get these 'ere gawdam lawns so gawdam smashing?' And the gardener says: 'You waters 'em and you rolls 'em, and then you rolls 'em and you waters 'em, and you goes on rolling and watering 'em for two or three 'undred years, and there you are.'

"It's the same thing with an Army. You work on it for hundreds and hundreds of years till you get a sort of foundation. That's tradition. That's the stuff that's got to be sort of lived up to, kind of style. Discipline sort of comes out of that. Definitely, English discipline comes from English tradition. Have you got that? Before you make an English soldier, you got to make an English *man*. And then, when you lay the groundwork, you see how an English soldier will sort of discipline himself. That's *proper* discipline.

"You treat the rookie a bit severe at first. But as soon as he gets the hang of things, you don't have to chase him. He takes everything in good part, and still stays a *man*. He fits into the machinery. On parade, he obeys an order like clockwork. Off parade, he'll argue the toss. That's what I like to see. But discipline, first of all, has got to be *taught*. You learn the ABC of it at the Depot. You pick up the grammar at the Training Battalion. Get it?"

The idea is, that by the time you leave the Camp you will be capable of translating things on your own, if need be.

And where is this Camp?

A balloonist found himself in this place, early in the nineteenth century. An old lady, looking out of her bedroom window into a pale pink sunset, saw a great white bubble drifting down on to the Common. Hastily putting on her bonnet, she ran out. A hundred yards away a billowing mass of silk rippled among the gorse. As she watched, a man struggled out of a basket. He said:

"Where am I, my good woman?"

Falling on her knees and whispering in a voice compounded of joy and terror, the old lady replied:

"Pirbright, please you, God Almighty."

A century later, an Austrian refugee in Pirbright village, hearing a thunder of engines shaking the sky, ran into his landlady's sitting-room and cried: "Listen, please!"

Ancient and frail as rare porcelain, the landlady quavered:

"Why, don't you recognise them engines, sir? Don't upset yourself; they're only Hurricanes."

It is still the same old Pirbright. Only times have changed.

Here, N.C.O.s sleep in the same huts as the men. The beds are of iron: like Antæus, they are strong while they stand on their own feet; but lift them, and they disintegrate. The coir-fibre mattresses look exactly like what they are called, biscuits. There are three biscuits to a bed. At night, they are laid end-to-end upon the wire bedframe, which, like the true-blue British institution that it is, has never bent or broken, or given way an inch under pressure. Hut No. 40, Z Company, contains thirty such beds, with their full complement of ninety biscuits; two six-foot benches of scrubbed deal; a galvanised iron coalbox, a tub, four galvanised iron basins, buckets zinc and buckets fire, a bass broom, two hair brooms, two scrubbing brushes, one long scrubber, a slab of yellow soap as cold-looking and uninviting as imported Cheddar cheese, and a stove. No luxury here; none of your Depot pampering. When you rise in the morning, you grab yourself an iron basin and rush out to the washhouse with it. One man who keeps his own little enamel basin is greeted, every morning, with derisive yells: "Where's your water jug, Darling? Where's your soap dish and slop pail? Ain't you forgot somethink? Where's your wardrobe and Jerry?" Sergeant Crowne fills a basin before he goes to sleep, so that he may shave in nice cold water the moment he gets up. He shaves with scrubbing soap. "Cold water, good rough soap and a bluntish blade," he says, "and you *know* you've 'ad a shave." Sergeant Hands, however, goes in for brushless cream, and washes in a bucket, so that Crowne calls him Ramon Novarro.

Both Hands and Crowne wear the Palestine ribbon. We ask them if they ever met Nelson.

"One-Eye Nelson?" asks Sergeant Crowne, reflectively. "Once upon a time we used to call him Lipstick. Why Lipstick? Well, when he was a Guardsman, he used it, once. No, I don't mean on 'is mouf, silly. 'E got a stain on his best tunic—scarlet, you know—so 'e thought 'e'd cover it up with some lipstick. So 'e borrowed some lipstick from a nurse called Pinkie."

"No," says Sergeant Hands. "The nurse's name was Jenny. We used to call her The Vest-Pocket Drill Sergeant. Pinkie was engaged to Ding-Dong Bell."

"That's right. Jenny. 'E borrowed a lipstick from Jenny, and smeared it over the spot. That scarlet used to stain as easy as anything: rain 'd spot it. Well, Nelson smears this 'ere stuff over this spot, and it turns out to be tangerine colour. So we called 'im Lipstick. Was old Nelson your squad-instructor? One of the best. 'E threw a plate of stew in my face once, in Egypt. Remember that, Hands? Best pal *I* ever 'ad. 'E didn't like to be called Lipstick."

Hands says: "You asked for that stew, Crowne. You would keep on calling him Gloria Swanson."

"Clara Bow. So 'e lets fly with this plate o' stew. 'Now am I Clara Bow?' 'e says."

"And what did you say, Sergeant?" asks Bates.

"I said: 'Of course you're Clara Bow.' After that we were best of pals."

Bates, who listens to everything with open mouth, says: "Oi bet it was noice in Palestoin, Sergeant."

Sergeant Hands replies: "A snare and a delusion. We was doing a kind o' police job. Oranges was cheap. We got them every dinnertime."

The giant, Hodge, with bated breath, asks if they saw Bethlehem.

"Certainly," says Crowne.

"What is it like?" asks Hodge.

"Little," says Crowne.

"Hot," says Hands.

"And Jerusalem?" asks Hodge.

"Pretty much the same," says Crowne.

"And what's all the trouble about?" asks Barker.

"Trouble?" says Crowne. "Well. The Yids make orchards and blocks of flats. And the Wogs want to cut in. So now and again a Wog shoves a knife into a Yid. Then a Yid goes and shoves a knife into a Wog. Then the Wogs get 'old of some live rounds and shoot a couple o' Yids. Then the Yids get 'old of some live rounds and shoot a couple o' Wogs. Then we come in and tell 'em to turn it in."

"And do they turn it in?"

"Yes and no," says Crowne.

"Who wins?" asks Bates.

"Order is kept," Crowne replies. "Order is kept."

John Johnson grins, and says: "Oi bet you 'ave a noice old toime, with all them Arabian dancing girls."

"No," says Crowne, "I can't say I ever did, not actually. They're fat. It's part of their religion to be fat. They ain't sort o' particular about soap. Their best friends are just the same, so *they* won't tell 'em. They ain't 'ygienic. Zmatter o' fact, I never saw a Arabian dancing girl. Beer cost about a bob a boll. I don't believe Arabian girls *can* dance: I never caught one of 'em at it. I 'eard one sing, once. It sounded like somebody was twistin' 'er arm. I got a nice sun-tan, though. Yes, I did get that . . ."

"Ha!" says John Johnson.

"What d'you mean, Ha?" says Crowne. "You're from Brummagem. aren't you?"

"Yes, Sarnt."

"I thought as much. A fly boy. Okay, fly boy. Let me tell you one thing. Don't you get too fly with me. Got it?"

"Oi never said anythink, Sarnt!"

"You said Ha. It's the way you said it. I can smell a chancer at five 'undred yards . . ." Sergeant Crowne looks around and his keen glance falls on Thurstan. "What's your name?" he asks.

"Thurstan."

" 'Ow d'you like the Army, Thurstan?"

"I dunna lak it."

"Oh, you don't, eh?"

"Na."

"Why not?"

Thurstan struggles for words, finds none, and shrugs.

"Oh, it's like that, is it?" says Sergeant Crowne. "Look, Geordie. I'll tell you something for your own good. Don't get tough with the Army. People 'ave tried it. You can't do it, specially in wartime. I'm not saying you will, mind you. But fellers get browned off sometimes, and some of 'em try going absent. They always come back, most of 'em of their own accord. Make the best of it, Geordie. A man that goes absent is a mug: 'e can't get away with it. Besides, it's a sign of yellerness: a man that goes absent 'as no guts. Say you go absent. After three weeks you're posted as a deserter; and then the police of the 'ole country are on your trail. You can't get identity cards, you can't do a thing, except perhaps lie low in somebody's 'ouse. And if you do that you lay them open to prosecution for 'arbouring you. You live like a rat in a 'ole. In the end, you come back. Then you go to the Glass 'Ouse, and you wish you 'adn't done it. Glass 'Ouse is tougher than a Civvy jail, Geordie."

Thurstan finds a few words. You can see them struggling to get out. Each broken phrase comes away from his white face like a limping, bedraggled, dazed chick from an egg.

"Civvy jell . . . Glass Oose . . . Ah'm no fred o't. Ah . . . Army, too. Ah'm no fred of nowt; life a deeth . . ."

Then Thurstan does something shocking.

He rises out of his condemned-cell crouch, crosses the room in two or three springs, and strikes the iron stove a terrible backhand blow. His bare fingers make it ring like a cracked bell. We leap up. Thurstan strikes it again. Then he comes back and sits down on his bed. A trickle of blood crawls from under one of his bitten nails.

"Ah can't be hurt," says Thurstan. As Sergeant Crowne lays a restraining hand on his shoulder, he shakes it off and mutters: "Let me gang."

I hear Sergeant Hands murmur: "There's going to be trouble with that geezer."

We are all a little nervous. If the Depot filled us with the shyness of boys at a new school, the Training Battalion finds us exhilarated but diffident, like boys in their first job of work.

Saturday morning finds us trembling on the brink of our first C.O.'s Parade. It is Sergeant Crowne who reassures us:

"It's a bit of cush. It's a slice of pie. The purpose of a Commanding Officer's Parade is mainly to see that you keep yourselves up to scratch. They are raising a stink in some of the comic papers about 'ow silly it is to blanco your equipment. Well, we're still 'ot on cleanliness and tidiness 'ere, just the same. Say you blanco every bit of web you've got— big pack and straps, little pack, braces, pouches, belt, sling, and gaiters— 'ow long does it take you? I say half an hour. You do it once a week. Praps you go over your gaiters twice. And you're neat and tidy. That's better than going about like Franco's Militia, ain't it? You feel better if you're neat and clean. In Civvy Street, you wouldn't go about your business with a filthy face and a ten-day beard and fluff all over your coat, would do? No. Well, no more you do 'ere. All these grousers do is shout. 'There's a war on.' Well, so there is. Certainly there's a war on. But that's no excuse for going about with your backside hanging out of your trousers and mud on your daisy-roots. War on! They're telling me there's a war on!

"Listen. War or no war, any man with dirty boots or dirty web or dirty flesh goes in the report. Now then. Grumble as much as you like, but wash! Moan your 'eads orf, but clean your boots! Grouse, but brush in that blanco! It takes a extra 'alf-hour. Alright. Let it. God strike me dead this minute—if I 'ad to walk out this very second to be shot against the wall, I'd prefer to die with clean 'ands and boots. It's our way. It's our style. Like it or lump it, by crackey you'll foller it. Do you get me?

"Look at young Sergeant Butts. You've seen 'im. 'E looks like a kid."

We have seen him. He does. He is very tall and lean, like the man in the O. Henry story who, if he carries any money with him has to carry it in one note folded lengthways . . . a man of six feet two, and no other dimensions worth mentioning. His face is round and innocent. He is all elbows and knees. When he walks fast he seems to have as many legs as a spider. There is such vigour in his skinny arms that he can draw a pair of new boots at five o'clock, and have a six-months' polish on them by a quarter to seven. Though fully twenty years old, he has not yet started to shave. Though merely twenty years old, he is already a Sergeant. His nickname is "Greengage," nobody knows why. He is purer than a girl in a convent school—he hasn't even any theoretical naughtiness. Sergeant Butts doesn't smoke. He says he enjoys a glass of beer, but nobody ever saw him drink one. All women, to him, are sisters. If he was born in sin, it doesn't show; or, like an unsuccessful inoculation, it never took. On the first blast of *Lights Out* he is asleep. One second before Reveille he is awake, ready to levitate rather than arise. He glows with soap and inner health. Upon his round pink head, with its Demerara-sugar-coloured hair, the cocky little S.D. Cap looks too ferocious. You feel that he needs a Scout hat and a pole. If a passing A.T.S. girl happens to say "Morning, Sergeant Butts," he blushes like a neon sign and grins like the Negro on the Euthymol poster, and says "He-he!" He finds it difficult to frown at new recruits, for he has no eyebrows. He has one accomplishment of which he is proud—stroking an imaginary dog. Sometimes, for the amusement of tired soldiers in his hut, he pretends to be coaxing a dog across the floor; fighting with it, tugging at it—he can lean back at an angle of something like forty-five degrees without falling over—and finally falling, overwhelmed by the dog's caresses. Sergeant Butts is scrupulously neat in his dress. His S.D. tunic is tight as an umbrella cover; it makes him look eight feet tall.

Young as he is, he has already had his baptism of fire and blood. He was in France when things cracked. The corporal they call "Bearsbreath" told us the story—that sour, hard-cased, gloomy corporal who always sits, tough and self-contained as a Brazil nut.

Bearsbreath tells of the retreat. "Roads choked. Civvies running. Bundles. Furniture. Everybody scramming; women, kids, and all. Once in a while some dirty Fifth Columnist yells 'Gas!' and starts a stampede. Kids trampled. I wish I could have got hold of one of those Fifth Column boys. I'd of shot him in the belly and let him dig his own grave wriggling. You know that our mob was the last to go. Covering the withdrawal. Jerries dive-machine-gunning, women and all. I saw the body of a boy of about five shot through the face. His mother was still carrying him: couldn't put him down. That's the kind of people you're fighting. Nazis. They'd kill anything. Kill your kids, too, as soon as look at 'em. Well, Greengage was cut off; him and about six men.

"He had about twenty-thirty miles to go to the coast. So he started out. His boots was pretty well scruppered even then. He dumped 'em, and slogged it barefoot, still carrying his equipment, till he found another pair. He polished 'em up, even then, just out of habit, whenever they stopped to rest. Two of the blokes with him, taking him for an example, shaved, honest to God, with bits of broken mirror to look in. No soap. But they had the habit of living or dying clean. Got me?

"Going was rough. Jerry came down from time to time, machinegunning. Our blokes tried to get one or two of 'em with rifle fire. Got one. Slogged on. Jerry got four of Greengage's men. The other two, dogtired, had to dump their equipment. Feet conked out. Greengage hung on to his bundook and about fifty rounds. Every time a Jerry dived, Greengage had a go. Not a hope in hell. But he had a go. And every time it came to a rest, Greengage swabbed his boots and tried to clean up a bit. Another of his men copped it. Greengage went on with one bloke. Bloke's feet conked out. So did Greengage's. But he couldn't give up. He was a N.C.O.: it'd look bad. Besides, it wasn't in him to say 'die'. He helped the other bloke along. They come to a wounded feller from Birkenhead. Greengage and the Guardsman carry him. Birkenhead feller dies on the way, so they dump him. Slog on. Get to coast. Guardsman says to Greengage: 'Go on, Sarnt. I'm not coming. Can't swim.' 'I can,' says Greengage, and tows the feller out. Three miles. Gets him to boat. Climbs aboard. Salutes the officer and passes out. It wasn't the tiredness. He had two ounces of shrapnel in his back, and some more in his leg. So there you are. He's a good soldier, Greengage. All that way, under what they might call trying circumstances, he did his best to keep neat."

When Bearsbreath told us this, Dale asked whether Sergeant Butts got a medal.

"Medal? What for?"

"Heroism."

"Heroism? He did his duty. Jexpect him to stay and get caught? Jexpect him to leave his pal behind? Ja mean, heroism? Ja think they *chuck* medals away?"

"So there it is," says Sergeant Crowne. "Take it or leave it. The order for C.O.s Parade is, belt and pouches and side arms, and rifle. You want to see them rifles are clean. Them barrels must gleam like Blind O'Reilly, and every nook and cranny must be dug out spotless. Mind your magazine springs: one speck o' grit and Gord 'elp you. There's a rifle inspection right after C.O.s Parade; and today being Saturday, the rest of the day is yours to muck about in. Got me? Geordie, be a good lad and 'elp me on with this stuff."

Thurstan holds up Sergeant Crowne's webbing. The Sergeant could easily manage on his own, but he is trying to win Thurstan's confidence.

Watching, we experience something of the thrill of the circus . . . The Tamer, with supreme confidence, kneels . . . the lion opens the red cavern of his mouth. . . . The brilliantined head rests, for a second, between the hungry-looking white tearing-teeth. . . . Then the Tamer, rises, bowing, and pent-up admiration lets itself loose in applause.

"Thanks," says Sergeant Crowne, buttoning his epaulettes.

Thurstan, feeling every glance focussed upon him, shakes himself. That man is dangerous.

A bugle sounds. "Quarter. Get outside to the Square," says Sergeant Crowne. Still unaccustomed to individual movement, we go down in a tight group.

Afternoon. It blows up cold. Yes, in from the North rides a muddy-piebald squadron of clouds, the spearhead of the advancing winter. All of a sudden the air bites. Lance-Sergeant Dagwood, a languid-seeming slow-talking, meditative, inexhaustible old soldier out of Birkenhead, breaks up some odds and ends of timber, using only his fingers and feet. He tears to pieces a piece of two-inch plank with quiet deliberation, as if it were a Japanese wooden puzzle to which he knows the key. He is a bony man with a plain, knobbly face: the best shot in the battalion, imperturbable as a carved image, with hands like wrenches, arms that have the lifting power of cranes, and only one hot passion— the game and play of football. Placidly smoking an absurd little pipe, Dagwood shatters a twenty-pound lump of coal to bits with one calm and awful kick of his iron heel. "The times I've done this for my old woman," he says. A match rasps; the draught sighs, then bellows. The stove is going.

"Where's Bullock?" somebody asks.

Barker says: "Boxing. Officer says 'Do you box?' Ole Bullock says 'Yes.' 'Amatyer or Professional?' 'Pro,' says Ole Bullock. The long and the short of it is, 'e's gorn to the gym. Gord blimey, I'd 'ate to 'ave to take ole Bullock on. I can use me forks a bit, but nothing like ole Bullock."

"Can he go?" asks Dagwood.

"Go? One smack from that right 'and, and yer jaw's just the place where yer teef used to be. 'E's a pro, I tell yer. 'E met Nippy Oliver."

Dagwood asks: "Who's Nippy Oliver?"

"Nippy went ten rahnds wiv Young Kilham."

"And who's Young Kilham?"

"No kiddin', Sarnt? Don't yer know? Young Kilham drew with Hymie Gold. Hymie Gold went the distance with Fred M'Aharba. Ever 'eard of M'Aharba? It's a sort of an Irish name, but 'e's a sheeny: M'Aharba is Abraham spelt backwards. 'E could of been 'eavyweight champion. No jokes, ole Bullock can fight."

"Did he beat this Nippy Oliver?"

"Certainly 'e beat Nippy Oliver. On'y 'e was robbed o' the verdict The referee was crooked. Everybody says ole Bullock won that fight, 'E's a wildcat, Sarnt, honest to Gawd."

"Well, that's all right," says Dagwood, easily. "He *looks* like a fighter."

"See that nose, Sarnt? See them ears? Oh," says Barker, hastily, "I know that sort o' thing don't count. But . . . well, talk o' noses. I knoo a feller that kept a pub, and to look at this geezer you'd swear 'e'd fought bare fists with everybody from the Pedlar Palmer to Joe bloody Louis. If ever there was any trouble in 'is pub, 'e'd simply lean over the bar and say: 'Anybody askin' for anyfink 'ere?' and people 'd shut up as if somebody's shoved a sock down their froats. Well, one night 'e got a bit you-know, soppy, and 'e told me abaht 'is face. It 'appened when 'e was a younkster—'e fell aht of a pear tree, and the branches 'ad sort of bopped 'im as 'e come froo 'em. 'E'd never 'ad a scrap in 'is life. 'E couldn't 'it 'ard enough to shake a blamange. Didn't 'ave the nerve, any'ow.

"But ole Bullock. I can size a bloke up. I've 'ad a few scraps in my time. I——"

Bates snatches this opportunity of saying: "Did Oi ever tell yow about Brummy Joe?"

"Shut up, you an' your Brummy Joe. I've 'ad a few scraps, and I can tell who to scrap wiv and 'oo not. I wouldn't start anyfink wiv old Bullock."

"To me," says Dagwood, "he looks a bit slow."

"Maybe, maybe not," says Barker. "But 'e'd be a swine to try and stop."

"Ah . . . that, yes," says Dagwood. "I don't say no to that."

Bullock comes back. He has a black eye, and a general air of calm satisfaction.

"Well?" asks Barker. " 'Ow dit go?"

"All right," says Bullock.

"Who d'you work out with?" asks Dagwood.

"Chap called Ackerman," says Bullock.

"What, a Corporal? A big feller? Jack Ackerman, of Y Company?" asks Dagwood, with interest.

"That's it."

"Now Ackerman is good, son. How d'you do?"

"Oh, I did all right."

"He got you in the eye, I notice."

"Oh, that? That's nothing."

"Give him a pasting?"

"No, we didn't go on long enough. We just played about."

"Think you could give Ackerman a coating, son?"

"Oh yes, I could give Ackerman a coating, Sergeant," says the serious-minded Bullock. "I went a bit easy with him. He hit me a bit. I didn't hit him much. But if I had to meet Ackerman, why, I'd get him all right."

"You'll have to be pretty good to get Ackerman."

"I've never been knocked off my feet," says Bullock. "Except once. It was a foul punch. I think it was an accident. A Jamaica nigger called Rube did it, at the Pilfold Stadium. He swung and got me in the groin. I don't think it was the nigger's fault. His foot slipped, or something. Even then I was only down for five seconds. They wanted to give me the fight, but I went on with it."

"But you got that blackie!" says Barker.

"In the last round," says Bullock.

Between Barker and Bullock a firm friendship has come into being.

I see Barker's eyes gleam with triumph. "There now," he says. "Ole Bullock could smash 'em all. Couldn't yer, eh?"

Bullock says: "I can't think of anybody I couldn't beat." He is not bragging. He really cannot think of anybody he couldn't beat. He contemplates his knuckles; screws up his face, and spits a little blood from a cut on the inside of his lip, his permanently swollen upper lip. "I think I could get most of 'em. I've seen Joe Louis on the pictures. Given time, I could get him, even."

Sergeant Crowne says: "What d'you mean, given time? You mean, if you could wait sixty or seventy years till 'e's nice and old, and slosh 'im when 'e's too blind to see yer?"

"Oh no," says Bullock, very earnest, "I mean, given enough rounds. I'd wear him down and then I'd get him. Give me twenty rounds, and I'd get Louis."

We look at one another, not knowing what to say. The boy from Widnes says: "Don't——" and then pauses; but he sees no aggression in the dour, battered face of the indomitable Bullock, and so goes on: "Don't be such a silly Git, Bullock!"

"Why am I a silly Git?"

"Joe Louis'd knock you silly in one round."

"Oh no he wouldn't," says Bullock.

The boy from Widnes protests: "I saw the picture of that thur Louis fighting Max Bur. He hit that thur Bur whurever he liked. And so he would you, Bullock."

"That's all right," says Bullock, amiably.

"Come 'n get a tea 'n' a wad," says Barker.

"All right," says Bullock, and they go out.

When the door has closed behind them, a stranger, a guardsman with a sagging, humorous face, not unlike Walt Disney's Pluto, laughs a peculiar quacking laugh.

"Joke?" says Sergeant Dagwood. "What's the joke, Hacket?"

The guardsman called Hacket says: "I've seen Bullock fight twice.

I saw him fight that nigger, Rube, at the Pilfold Stadium. And I saw him fight a kid called Francis in Bedford."

"Well, what's funny?"

"Well, nothing. Only he's duff. He's terrible."

"In what way terrible? Did he win like he said?"

"Yes, he won all right, just like he said. That nigger Rube was pretty lousy too; he must of weighed seventeen stone, and he was as slow as a dray horse—but even then, he was about ten times quicker than Bullock. He hit Bullock with everything he had. It sounded like hammering nails into a packing case. Biffity-biffity-biffity-bif! But poor old Bullock kept on coming back for more. Bullock kept swinging. He might as well have sent the nigger a postcard to tell him a punch was on the way. It was as easy as dodging a steam roller, I tell you! And that foul punch: it made me sick to see it. I thought it would have killed old Bullock. But up he got, bent double, and insisted on carrying on with it. Game! Game as they make 'em. But my God, what a lousy boxer! In the end, the nigger got discouraged: there wasn't anything he could do about Bullock. He was tired of hitting him. Then Bullock sort of crowded him into a corner and let him have a sort of a right hook. It sounded like snooker balls. The nigger just went flat. The same sort of thing happened with this kid called Francis, in Bedford. The crowd used to like poor old Bullock: they always got a laugh out of him. To see him sort of diving about after this kid . . . sort of doing the breast stroke, and missing every punch. He's a swinger, old Bullock. He can't box any more than a windmill. He just kept rushing this kid Francis, and in the tenth round, again, he managed to get in just one swing. It was like a buck navvy with a sledge hammer—just about as slow, and just about as hard. Hit this kid Francis on the shoulder and pushed him over. The kid was too exhausted to get up. But the funny thing is, he thinks he's as good as Jack Dempsey. He'd fight anything. Poor old Bullock. He doesn't know what it means to be licked. He just can't see it. The expression on his face after he beat that nigger— you'd think he'd just won the Irish Sweep. Not that you could see much of his face. It's hard to understand why a man keeps on at a mug's game like that."

"A fighter, born and bred," says Dagwood, thoughtfully.

"Yes. But a man ought to have the sense to see he's no good at the game, when he pays more than he gets at it."

" 'E wins, don't 'e?" says Sergeant Crowne, stiffly.

"Yes, but——"

"There ain't no 'but' about it. A man 'as a fight. 'E wants to win. 'E wins. That's all there is to it."

"But he doesn't win in the end; not in the long run," says Hacket. "Bullock'll be punch-drunk in another two years."

"In the end, in the end!" snarls Sergeant Crowne. "In the long run! 'Oo cares about the Long Run? If you're 'aving a fight, go in and win, and to 'ell with the long run! Let Gawd worry about the Long Run! If it's boxing, shake 'ands and come aht fighting! 'It 'ard and often, and the end 'll take care of itself. In twenty million-billion years' time, the world 'll come to an end. But it ain't my business to worry over that."

"In how many years did you say?" asks Sergeant Hands.

"Twenty million-billion."

"What a fright you gave me," says Hands.

"How?"

"For the moment I thought you said only twenty thousand billion."

"I like a man that doesn't know when 'e's beaten," says Crowne.

"But it can be carried too far," says Hacket. "Moderation in all things, as Voltaire said."

"Who's Voltur?" asks the boy from Widnes.

"Oh, some clergyman," says Sergeant Crowne. "What was you in Civvy Street, Hacket?"

"A book salesman."

"You know a bit about printing and paper and all that?"

"A bit."

"Then your swabbing job will be tidying up the area round the hut. You'll find plenty of paper there."

The man we call The Schoolmaster rolls up the sock he has been darning, and says: "How do we know what happens in the long run? It's not for us to consider. Why, even if som very wise man manages to calculate where things will lead in just a little while, he's lucky and clever. Sergeant Crowne is right."

The Schoolmaster is a long, calm, fair man with receding hair, and a concentrated, studious expression which makes him look at least seven years older than thirty, which is his age. He wears glasses, and is a Bachelor of Arts; speaks in a slow, carefully modulated voice, and even on a cookhouse fatigue manages to keep his large, thin-fingered hands in a condition of elegance. He has come into the ranks in order to get out of them—after his training here he will go to an O.C.T.U., from which he will emerge as a subaltern. Suspect, at first, on account of his accent, he won our hearts by plain good nature and unconditional mucking-in. It was Barker who said, one day, when the boy from Widnes muttered that the Schoolmaster made him sick: " 'E can't 'elp the way 'e talks. It's the way they're brought up, son; they can't 'elp it. Frinstance, you say 'Fur ur' instead of 'Fair 'air.' The ole Schoolmaster says 'Faiah haiah.' 'E's not smackin' it on. A certain class o' people talks like that. I know a Covent Garden flar merchant that made a packet and sent 'is boy to be a doctor. Well, the ole man—we call 'im Gutsache, because 'e suffers wiv 'is inside when 'e goes on the wallop—'e talks the thickest cockney even I ever 'eard: ole-fashioned slang, real market stuff that nobody can make 'ead or tail of nowdays. Ole Gutsache'll send a boy for 'is tea like this: 'e'll say: "Gemme a you 'n' a strike,' meaning a Cup of You-and-Me and a Slice of Strike-Me-Dead, or bread 'n' butter. Well, some time ago I run into ole Gutsache in the *Salisbury,* and there was ole Gutsache, runnin' on sixteen to the dozen wivaht openin' 'is mouf, talkin' to a youngster dressed up like a toff. *Les jum' in the jam 'n' gerra pig's 't Ella's,* 'e was sayin'. In plain English: 'Let's jump in the jam-jar (car), and get a pig's-ear (beer) at Ella's club.' And the youngster says: "Whay, certainleh, Fathah.' They'd taught Gutsache's kid to speak Oxford. But the kid wasn't puttin' on no airs: 'e just talked that way. Same wiv the Schoolmaster. Give 'im a fair chancet: 'e can't 'elp it, talkin' like that, any more 'n' 'e could 'elp it if 'e stuttered."

The Schoolmaster goes on:

"We all hope to live through all this, don't we? Yet every one of us is prepared to die if necessary."

We say that we suppose so.

"Yet," says the Schoolmaster, "I don't suppose that many of us here care much whether there's an afterlife."

Hodge says: "There is an afterlife. I know it."

For fifteen minutes, twenty men talk all at the same time, at the top of their voice. Afterlife: there is one, there isn't one, there must be one, there can't be one, there might be one, there is no proof of one, there are a thousand proofs of one, it says so in the Bible. . . .

"No," says the Schoolmaster. "We don't know where anything will lead to. We are all, so to speak, under Sealed Orders. We all pretend to live merely for our own ends, but it doesn't quite work out that way. If it did, we'd run away from the first threat of danger. We should live and die like animals, like rabbits. Nobody would ever go away from the safety of his own little place. No new things would ever be discovered. No new ground would be broken. Men would still be living in caves. No, there is something in men that makes them go beyond themselves. That is what makes us men. Right back in the beginnings, men had a queer instinct to *leave* something, to make something that should stay when they were gone. Some time ago a cave was discovered in which men had lived tens of thousands of years ago. On the walls of this cave there were pictures, very carefully dawn, of animals. Now why do you think those dead-and-forgotten savages, struggling naked in the very dawn of things, wanted to leave pictures?"

"It is a fact," says Barker, "that if you give a feller a wall 'e'll *'ave* to draw something on it, or write something. Step across the way and you'll see for yourself. You don't 'ave to go back no ten thousand years."

When the laughter subsides, the Schoolmaster says: "Men are always struggling against something. But the end must remain unknown."

"Mug's game," says John Johnson.

"I daresay that is what the Guards said in Nieppe Forest," says the Schoolmaster. "But in their hearts I don't think they believed it."

"What 'appened in Nieppe Forest?" asks Barker.

"Oh . . . last war," says Sergeant Crowne.

"I heard the story," says the Schoolmaster, "from a Captain of Engineers. . . . It was one of the things that made me join the Guards, as a matter of fact. I could never tell the story half as well as he did, because he was there, and saw it happen, and felt awfully deeply about it. He was one of the first men to become an expert in chemical warfare, after the Germans started to go all out in 1918. He had been working at something for three days and three nights, and at last, he, a Corporal, and a runner paused to rest on the fringe of Nieppe Forest.

"It was a Summer night. The officer and the Corporal took their turn to sleep. The runner kept watch. The night passed . . ." The Schoolmaster becomes a little dreamy. . . . "I suppose it passed in a timeless flash. They lay there, between a deserted village and a dark forest. And so dawn broke.

"The Engineer says that he awoke, instinctively almost, just before dawn. So did the Corporal. They listened. There was silence. Birds began to sing—first of all one little bird perched on the wreckage of something a few yards away. They watched it. Then, they realised that the enormous German push was coming. They blinked themselves thoroughly awake. And then, in the distance, they heard a gentle *shup-shup, shup-shup, shup-shup*. Men marching. They looked at each other. The noise came nearer. The men were marching into the village. They heard a terrific voice shout: *March to Attention!* Only one sort of soldier will march to attention through a deserted village. The Corporal said, in a hushed whisper: 'The Guards!' And so it was. My friend watched them as they passed, dusty with a tremendous journey along those terrible roads; but marching as if it were a Saturday morning on the Square under the eye of the C.O. . . . left, right; left, right; left . . . left . . . left. . . . They marched into the forest, took up firing positions, and settled down, that mere handful of Guardsmen, to hold back the entire German advance.

"What they did in that forest has gone down in history. But much later my friend had occasion to pass that way again. He found them still lying there. There hadn't been time to bury them. They had been wiped out to the last man. Even in death they still held their positions. Even their dead bones remained obedient to their will to stay unbroken."

A silence.

"Grouse about regimental bull-and-baloney," says Sergeant Crowne. "Go on, grouse!"

"All those lovely fellers," says Barker. "It sort of seems a kind of waste . . ."

"No," says the Schoolmaster. "An example of that sort has got to be lived up to. Look at Captain Scott, dying horribly, all alone in an awful desolation. He didn't achieve what he set out to do. And he died. He said: 'Had we lived, I should have had a tale to tell of the hardihood, endurance, and courage of my companions which would have stirred the heart of every Englishman. These rough notes and our dead bodies must tell the tale . . .' They did. I don't suppose anything could have been more eloquent. No man's gallantry is wasted. In the last war, for instance, hundreds of letters came to Scott's widow, saying that they could never have borne what they had had to bear without the strength that had come to them through Scott. Other examples can be futile. An example of pure courage never is. A true hero gives new power to all mankind. And if he comes of your own blood, it becomes impossible for you to let him down. And if he has worn your badge. . . . No. The traditions of the British Army may sometimes have given it a narrow mind, but they have never failed to make its heart very great."

"Did Oi ever tell you about Brummy Joe?" says Bates.

"Brummy Joe. Them Guards would a been frit o' Brummy Joe. They wouldn't o' held no positions if Brummy Joe'd been advancing again 'em. Eighteen stun seven and six foot three in his stocking feet. Mind yow, Joe's got a belly as stuck out like a basin. They said: 'One punch in the belly and Joe's finished.' Ah. But get there! I defy yow! Get near enough Brummy Joe to 'it 'im there. Joe Louis couldn't with a telegraph pole. When Brummy was on the beer the coppers went about armed. Once, when they pinched old Brummy, they broke seven cruncheons on 'is pore head. One night when Brummy went into a 'am-an-beef shop for a samwidge, the man didn't give Brummy enough 'am. Well, so old Brummy Joe picks up the 'am knife and cuts a slice off the man behind the counter. As true as I am sitting on this form, a lovely thin slice. Once, Brummy laid out nineteen Leicester boys in Chilliam's Dance Palace with a guitar. Talk about Captain Scott!

"Do yow know Chilliam's Dance Palace? Oi lived ten minutes' walk away, in Parrot Close, when Oi was married the first toime, properly married. Oi 'ad a noice 'ouse there. Moi woife was noice. She didn't loike me-ee. She fell in loov wi' moi best friend. It was loike going to the pictures. Moi friend came to me and said: "Oi loov Teena.' Oi says: 'Yow do, do yow? And does Teena loov yow?' 'Yes,' 'e says. So Oi says: 'All roight, Jim. Yow are my best friend, and so Oi give 'er to yow.' And so Oi pommelled 'im till 'e was black and blue, and Oi tells Jim straight: 'Oi don't loike to beat yow, Jim, but Oi don't want the neighbours to talk.' And so moi woife run off wi' moi best friend, just like the pictures. Ah. She was a foine woman, but she didn't loike me. Oi loiked 'er, but Oi didn't loike 'er cooking, so Oi used to 'ave my meals at my mum's 'ouse. And moi woife didn't loike that.

"So then Oi fell in loov wi' a loovly girl, and she 'ad a 'usband as 'ad deserted 'er, and Oi 'ad a woife as 'ad deserted me, so we couldn't get married, so Oi became 'er Unmarried 'Usband. It's all roight. The Army recognised it, and she gets moi money. It's respectable and proper.

"Oi gave moi married woife all moi furniture. We got another place, a cottage. But whenever moi unmarried woife went out shopping, moi married woife, as is jealous of 'er, used to wait for 'er and call 'er names in the street. And moi unmarried woife called moi married woife names back.

"Then moi married woife's mother, as thinks the world of 'er, used to wait outsoide where Oi was working and follow me 'ome, and call me names. Then my own mum and dad used to come and troy and make peace, but moi mum never got along wi' moi married woife's mum, and they used to foight in the street outsoide moi 'ouse. And moi unmarried woife's stepmother, as 'ates the soight of 'er, started wroiting anonymous letters to everybody about me. And moi married woife set Jim on me, and Jim used to wait for me to leave the 'ouse in the morning and pick on me, and Oi 'ad to pommel 'im. And then moi unmarried woife's 'usband turned oop, and 'e started waiting for me too, and Oi 'ad to pommel *'im*, only 'e was a rough 'andful and it took me some toime. So Oi 'ad to leave 'alf an hour earlier in the morning to attend to moi foights.

"One day moi unmarried woife made 'erself a new dress, and moi married woife waited for 'er and tore it off 'er back.

"The neighbours complained to the police about the disturbance. All the kids in the street enjoyed themselves and played Ring-o'-Roses round me whenever Oi went out. Moi mates started giving me nick-names, like The Mormon, and Ole King Solomon. Moi unmarried woife's stepmother scratched moi face in the street, and moi married woife came along and 'ad a foight wi' 'er; and moi unmarried woife came out an' joined in, an' all the kids started singing and dancing. That was on a Saturday noight. Moi unmarried woife ast me if loov was worth whoile, and 'ad 'ysterics and soom women came in an' soothed 'er down. Oi didn't get a wink o' sleep. Oi made up moi moind to join the Foreign Legion. Then, on the Sunday, war was declared. Oi was on the doorstep o' the Recruiting Office two hours before it opened. Oi loike war. War is noice: it gives yow a chance to 'ave a little peace."

"And what's all this got to do with Brummy Joe?" asked Sergeant Hands.

"Give me a chance to get a *word* in," says Bates. "Oi 'aven't started yet."

But *Cookhouse* sounds. We snatch up our knives and forks and go to tea.

In the course of this meal—mug of tea, slice and a half of bread, two-thirds of an ounce of margarine, and a Cornish Pasty, which Barker describes as "all pasty and no Cornish"—Dale, of all men on God's earth, does something silly.

He is at the foot of the table. He wants to attract the attention of Hodge, who is pouring tea out of a three-gallon bucket. He shouts. Hodge doesn't hear, for a couple of hundred men are eating at the tops of their voices. There is an odd crust of bread lying ready to hand. Dale takes careful aim and throws it at Hodge. The crust misses our gigantic friend and—it is one of those things that luck alone can achieve; a thing beyond human skill, like the falling on its edge of a tossed coin—drops very neatly into the hand of the Company Quartermaster-Sergeant, who happens to be passing at the moment.

The Quartermaster swells. His chin comes up; his eyebrows go down. "Who done that?" he asks.

Dale, white as paper, gulps and says: "I did, sir."

"Oh, *you* did. Do you realise that you're a traitor to your country? Do you realise that you're nothing better than a Nazi agent? Do you realise that if you took and blew up a power station, that wouldn't be no worse than what you just now done? Do you realise that this is Bread? Do you realise that Bread is the Staff of Life? Do you realise that thousands and thousands of sailors and marines drown every second for this here piece of bread? Do you realise that this is sabotage? Do you realise that in wartime, there's a death penalty for sabotage? DO YOU REALISE THAT THERE IS A WAR ON, YOU HORRIBLE MAN, YOU?"

"No sir," says Dale, losing his head. "Yes sir."

"What d'you mean, No sir, Yes sir? Are you a Hitlerite?"

"No sir."

"Then what do you commit offences like this for?"

"I don't know, sir."

"Are you mad?"

"No sir."

"Then why do you do things and not know you're doing them, or why you're doing 'em? Do sane men do that?"

"No sir."

"Then you're crazy, aren't you?"

Dale twists his face into a sickly grin and shrugs his shoulders.

"Oh," says the C.Q.M.S. "Laughing. You think it's a joke, do you?"

"No sir."

"Then what are you laughing at?"

"Nothing sir."

"Laughing at nothing. Raving mad. You must be, or you wouldn't chuck lumps of nourishing food about in times like these. Don't let me catch you at it again. Carry on."

Dale moodily eats his Cornish pasty.

"You should have nudged him," says the Schoolmaster. "In a case like that, the shock weapon is to be preferred to the missile weapon."

"What's a shock weapon?" asks Dale.

As we walk back to the hut, the Schoolmaster explains. "A shock weapon is something with which you strike your enemy directly."

"Like a cosh," says Barker.

"Exactly. Or a bayonet. A missile weapon is something that throws things and strikes your enemy from a distance, like a rifle, or a crust of bread, or a bow-and-arrow. The development of armies depends upon the development of missile weapons. Now we are highly advanced. An aeroplane armed with bombs and machine guns may be described as a missile weapon. So may a tank. The missile weapon is reaching its maximum efficiency. The rifle is being supplanted."

"Rifles have their uses," says Corporal Bearsbreath. "They're easy to clean, easy to use, and easy to carry. And when all's said 'n' done, a 303 bullet in your tripes is just as good as anything else. I bet old Wellington would have been glad of a few short Lee-Enfield magazine-rifles, Mark Three."

"I bet he would," says the Schoolmaster. "After all, any man trained to use a Lee-Enfield can be pretty certain of hitting his enemy, at three, four, or five hundred yards. In Wellington's day, when we carried the old smooth-bore musket known as Brown Bess, the Guards' musketry would have made you laugh. We practised at a hundred yards, with six-foot targets shaped like French Grenadiers. In the best possible conditions, the old brown musket misfired four times out of ten. You had to ram a handful of gunpowder down the spout, and put in a wad, and a ball, and then pour powder on the place where the flint struck a spark, and then pull your trigger and hope for the best. Training was at a high pitch at the beginning of the nineteenth century, when a Guardsman could load and fire about eight times in a minute. A musket, then, was like a cheap cigarette lighter—a matter of flint and steel. The chief concern of the soldier, then, was to see that his musket misfired as seldom as possible. So the first shot, loaded into the musket at leisure, was the most valuable. You had to make the most of your first volley.

"Thus, at the battle of Fontenoy, the Coldstream Guards in the front line advanced for half a mile up a slope under a crossfire of artillery against the French who were in trenches at the top. They received the French musket-fire without replying. Then, when they were right on top of the enemy, and one Coldstreamer in three had fallen, we let fly and swept them off the earth in an absolute hailstorm of bullets. If they had fired at longer range with their first careful loads, and then hastily reloaded, about 50 per cent of the muskets would have misfired, and the attack would have lost half its effect.

"Now do you know what I think? Our Guards discipline, which is the best in the world, has its roots in the old-time need to conserve fire; to keep a line, stay unbroken, hold the trigger finger back until the word of command, and then let loose one shattering volley. You see, the Coldstream Guards are the only survivors of the first highly-trained British Army. We have background. We have a start."

John Johnson says: "Oi wouldn't moind foighting in the Battle o' Waterloo. It was ea-*sy*. They didn't 'ave no shells and no bombs."

"They did. Major Shrapnel had already invented his shell."

"Ah, but nothing loike now. Them old cannon balls just bounced."

"If you saw an eighteen-pound ball of iron ricocheting and flying over the ground towards you, what would you do?"

"Duck."

"Do you realise that discipline was such that the British infantry were forbidden to step out of line, even in the face of round shot: and didn't?"

The boy from Widnes says: "I wouldn't like a bang on the head with an eighteen-pound ball of iron. As far as I'm concerned, it'd be just the same as a tank."

Hacket, whose rifle sights, having a film of dust on them, were described as "being lousy with spiders and cobwebs and dirty filthy rust and verdigris," says: "For my part, you can keep the Short Lee-Enfield."

"You ought to have a matchlock," says the Schoolmaster. "The first Coldstreamers lugged a thing about four feet long, firing a bullet weighing an ounce and a quarter. He had to pour a charge of coarse powder down the muzzle, spit in a bullet which he carried in his mouth, pour some finer powder on the priming pan, and set it all off with a match."

"Did they 'ave matches?" asks Barker.

"A kind of smouldering rope about three feet long. He took one end of the match between the thumb and second finger of his right hand, and then—bang! A fire order wasn't just 'Fire!' It was something like this: 'Take up your musket and staff. Join your musket and staff. Blow your pan. Prime your pan. Shut your pan. Cast off your loose powder. Cast about your musket and staff. Charge your musket. Recover your musket in your right hand. Shoulder your musket and carry the staff with it. Take our your match. Blow your match. Cock your match. Try your match. Guard your pan. Present blow your match upon your pan and give fire.' All that to get a bullet out."

"And now," says the boy from Widnes, "a Bren gun, weighing, I bet, less than one o' them thur things, can fire a hundred and twenty bullets a minute. I bet it took them about five minutes to fire. In five minutes, you or I could kill six 'undred men with a Bren gun."

"Now that's what I call civilisation," says Hacket.

Alison, the glum blond man, suddenly says: "My old woman talks tripe. She says, why don't Hitler and Churchill 'ave a set-to all by themselves and settle the war that way?"

"That wouldn't be fur," says Widnes. " 'Itler's the younger man. Old Winnie's getting on in years."

"Oh, I dunno," says the lad from the Elephant and Castle. "Old Winnie's got plenty of go in 'im. It's the fighting spirit, see?"

"Winnie breathes 'eavy," says the glum blond man.

"Don't you believe it," says Widnes. " 'Itler breathes worse."

"You know what?" says Bates. "If it come to that we could make Brummy Joe Prime Minister just for the toime being. Brummy Joe's a terror——"

"Tommy Farr'd be better," says Alison.

" 'E could go over wiv 'is Foreign Minister," says the Lad. "We could make Len 'Arvey Foreign Minister."

"War Minister," says Widnes.

"Nah, it couldn't be done," says Alison.

"Why not?" asks Widnes.

"Who'd do politics?"

"They could make an arrangement," says Bates.

" 'Itler wouldn't fight," says the Lad.

" 'E'd 'ave to," says the boy from Widnes. "It'd be a diplomatic arrangement."

" 'Itler'd fight dirty," says the Lad.

"So would Brummy Joe," insists Bates. " 'E carries a foot o' lead pipe covered wi' rubber bands orf beer bottles. Brummy'd feel naked without it."

"Would they charge an entrance fee?" asks Widnes.

"Bob a 'ead," says the Lad. "Make a packet."

"Oi bet yow there wouldn't half be some excitement," says Bates. "Wi' us and the Jerries in the audience."

"Proper rough'ouse," says the Lad.

"We'd all 'ave to go," says Widnes.

"It'd be just like a war," says Alison.

"But we're 'aving a war now," says the Lad.

"Blimey, so we are," says Widnes.

"It wouldn't prove anything," says Sergeant Hands. "Besides, all that kind o' thing is out of date. It'd make you laugh, Crowney, the way they used to fight in the olden times. You'd meet your enemies, and you'd bow, and you'd scrape, and you'd say: 'You fire first,' and they'd say: 'No, after you,' and then you'd fire at each other a bit, and so on."

"Don't be silly," says Sergeant Crowne. "War always was war, and when it come down to brass tacks, it was the same as it is now. You try and kill the other feller, and the other feller tries to kill you."

"It's true," says the Schoolmaster. "What Sergeant Hands says is true. Look at what happened when the Coldstream Guards fought the French at Fontenoy. They came face to face with the French Guards. They halted fifty yards away. Lord Charles Hay of the 1st Guards took off his hat, and drank the enemy's health. The Coldstream officers did likewise. The French Guards returned the salute. Then Lord Hay said: 'I hope, gentlemen, that you are going to wait for us today, and not swim the Scheldt as you swam the Main at Dettingen.'

"So Lord Hay turned to his own men, and said: 'Men of the King's Company, these are the French Guards, and I hope you are going to beat them today. Gentlemen of the French Guards, fire!'

"The French Commander answered: 'We never fire first; fire yourselves.'

"The English Guards then cheered the French, and the French Guards cheered back. They were thirty yards away from each other. The French Guards raised their muskets. A Coldstreamer said: 'For what we are about to receive, Lord make us truly thankful.' Then the French Guards fired. About nineteen Guards' officers went down, and a large number of men. Then it was our turn. We opened fire. Our musketry was known and feared all over the world. The British officers were walking up and down, tapping down the musket barrels of the men to make sure that they aimed low. We kept up a running fire, wiped out the whole of the French front rank. And so we cut through to the French camp."

"Well," says Crowne, "I'd see myself damned before I'd invite any Jerry to fire at me first. ''It first. 'It 'ard. Keep on 'itting.' That's my motto."

"It depends, though," says Dale.

"Depends on what?"

"Who you're fighting, Sergeant."

"No it don't. If you fight, fight to win, and get it over. If you got to fight, fight for keeps. If I *like* somebody, I don't fight 'im, and so I don't take my 'at off to 'im or ask 'im to 'it me first. . . . It makes a nice story, Schoolmaster, and if it's in 'istory, then it must be true. But that sort o' thing is a thing o' the past. If I 'ad to pick ten men to lead in a bayonet charge, I'd pick men that 'ated Jerry's guts and wanted to see the colour of 'em. I daresay there's two sides to any argument, but for my part I don't care a twopenny damn. My side's the right side, or I wouldn't be fighting on it."

"I agree with you," says Hands, "but you can't get away from being English."

"Who says you can?"

"Nobody says you can. You can't get away from your breeding, that's what I say. I've seen you myself, Crowne, with my own two eyes, during that bit of a riot. You were using your hands. In the heat of that fight, when there was a Wog coming at you with a knife, you boxed, Crowney, you *boxed*. If there'd been a referee watching you you couldn't have kept more above that Wog's belt-line. It's an instinct. It would have been all right for you to have used your feet. I used mine, I know. But it just didn't occur to you not to fight Queensberry. My brother talked just like you. But once, when he found himself wounded, in the same shell hole with a wounded Jerry, last war, he shared his iodine and dressings with him. Though he would have killed him in a fight, any day, mind you. It's drummed into your head as a kid. You can't get away from it. But I don't mind admitting that what the Schoolmaster told us about letting the Frenchman fire first is a bit too much of a good thing. Why, it's a wonder they didn't just come over and shake hands and call the war off, after that. *I* would of."

"It's good publicity," says Hacket. "I bet those Frenchmen said to themselves: 'What decent fellows these Englishmen are.' And it helped to undermine 'em."

Hands says: "English soldiers behave decent, instinctively; put Englishmen down anywhere and they'll be decent. Just as Guardsmen automatically form a straight line and keep their heads up. It's *in* them to do so. Isn't that what we're supposed to be fighting for?"

The Schoolmaster says: "A war can be an affair of honour just as a duel can be."

"You don't fight no duels with murderers," says Crowne.

"Hear, hear," says Dale.

Hands looks at him. "What are *you* fighting for, Dale?"

"Well," says Dale. "The Nazis have got to be stopped or they'll be everywhere."

"You, Widnes?"

"Because there's a war on, Sarnt."

"Hodge?"

"Hitler is bad. If you give in to un, you give in to wickedness. If you don't fight wickedness, you encourage wickedness. It'd be wicked not to fight Hitler, don't ee see?"

"Alison?"

"I don't know and I don't care, Sarnt. If the whole bloody country's fighting, what d'you expect *me* to do? Read a book or somethink?"

"Shorrocks?"

"No Dictator tells *me* what to do."

"Crowney?"

"I like what I like. I'm not satisfied with England, not by a long chalk, but it's *my* country and I'm used to it. You can, at least, grouse round 'ere. Get me? I'd rather die grousing if I fancy grousing, than live bottled up. And there's something about those soppy goose-stepping mugs that I 'ate the sight of. I don't know what it is, but they set my teeth on edge. They get my goat. I wanna kill 'em."

"And you, Schoolmaster?—and you don't have to give us a song and dance about the Battle of Waterloo."

"I'm fighting for the same as everybody else . . . to preserve what there is that's decent and good in the world."

"Barker?"

"Sarnt, shell I tell yer the honest truth?" Barker imitates the portentous tone of a politician. "I am fightin' to make the sea free for the banana trade."

"Bearsbreath?"

"Turn it up," says Bearsbreath. "This sort of thing bores me."

"Me too," says Crowne. "Turn it up, Hands."

"I'm trying to find out our War Aims," says Hands.

"Let 'em keep their sights upright, 'old their bunbooks firm, and squeeze their triggers," says Crowne, "and they'll 'it whatever they're aimin' at."

"Yuh," says Dagwood, slicing his last, precious bit of twist with a jackknife. In this knife you may find clues to the character of the good Birkenhead sergeant: he has guarded it for a dozen years, using it constantly. The big blade is worn narrow towards the point. He never uses the small blade: that is for emergency; but both blades are honed to razor edges. If the need arose, he could mend his boots with that knife, or cut his way out of a place with it, or pick a lock, or perform a minor surgical operation, or carve a doll for a small girl or a boat for a boy, or cut a man's hair, or kill him. "Yuh. You've all got to learn to shoot. You do some revision on rifle and Bren. Then you fire your course, wearing fighting order. Like the Schoolmaster says, musketry is always useful."

John Johnson of Brummagem says: "Oi want to get moi 'ands on a Tommy gun." Quite unconsciously, he says this out of the corner of his mouth. One can see the filmic fantasy with which he is entertaining himself . . . gangsters . . . the roar of fast cars . . . *tupatupatup!* —and an enemy falls on his face.

"They're handy little things," says Dagwood, "at fifty yards or so, they're handy."

"Give me a Bren every time," says Hands.

"A Lewis, for rough work," says Crowne. "A Bren is too accurate, sometimes. You put too many rounds in the same place. You can't miss with a Bren. Any mug 'ere could score well with a Bren. But say you've got a mob rushing you, why, then it's just as well to spray 'em a bit, if you get what I mean."

"The prettiest thing I ever saw in my life," says Bearsbreath, "was a shot with an anti-tank rifle. In France. Did you ever come across Cocky Sinclair? He got a Jerry officer and seven Jerries with one shot. It was as pretty as a picture. And that was the only time I ever saw an anti-tank rifle fired from the shoulder. I didn't know it was possible. It ain't possible. But Cocky was as strong as a bullock. He's a stronger man that Ack-Ack Ackerman, even: stocky, a neck like a damned tree. He hoisted that anti-tank rifle up to his shoulder and let fly. And down went eight Jerries, plugged as clean as a whistle. The recoil knocked him down. While he was sitting on his backside, a Jerry plane came swooping down. He reloaded, just like he was handling a short Lee-Enfield, and laid back, supporting the anti-tank on his foot, and fired at the plane. And so help me God he brought it down. I didn't learn till afterwards that the first shot broke Cocky's collarbone. The whole point was, he was annoyed."

"What 'appened to Cocky?" asks Crowne. "I put 'im inside, once. for insubordination."

"Oh, Cocky was always in and out of the moosh," says Bearsbreath. "He went absent once. The inside story of that was this: Cocky had a sister. See? She was all the relations he had. Cocky was sort of attached to this sister. Well, one day she got into trouble. Some bloke. This bloke treated her rough. She was a soppy sort of piece, and couldn't take care of herself. This bloke gave her a black eye one night when she asked him to sort of marry her. Cocky got to hear. He couldn't very well ask for a long week end just to give a bloke a hiding. And Cocky never told a lie in his life. He couldn't. If he tried, he got tongue-tied and contradicted himself. So he just done a bunk, and went home. He borrowed the fare off of me. That's how I knew. He got hold of this feller, and gave him the biggest coating you ever saw in your life. Then he came back, reported himself, and paid off fourteen days C.B. That was in peacetime. If he'd explained it to the C.O., I don't know, but I daresay the C.O. would have let him off light. He didn't like to. Said it made his sister out to be not respectable. The funny part is, this bloke married Cocky's sister, and has never raised a hand to her since."

"Where's 'e now?" asks Crowne.

"Oh . . . around, somewhere. I hear he pulled some bloke out from under a burning car outside Dunkirk: lifted the car up by the front axle and kicked the bloke away. I shouldn't be a bit surprised. He was a wild man in the Depot, but he got to be a good soldier afterwards."

"Some *are* wild," says Dagwood. "But as I see it, a wild man's all right, so long as he takes to a bit of discipline in the end. You've got to direct that wildness. Ever take the charge out of a .22 cartridge? It's little grey grains of stuff, sort of crystals. Put a match to it and it goes *phut,* a little puff of flame that couldn't hurt a fly. Pack it in proper, and that same pinch of stuff will send your bullet just where you want it, and pretty fast, too. Personally, I like a wild man. It's a sign of spirit. There are very few proper soldiers that haven't been inside once or twice. The officers understand that. They may talk all wrist watch, but they're not mugs, most of 'em. You can be wild, but wild in the proper place."

Now in the hut there sleeps a Corporal who is an instructor of physical training. They call him Stranglehold: he is an expert in Unarmed Combat. But his real name is John Ball. He came into the Army—it is an open secret—under false pretences, calmly perjuring himself. Ball said he was thirty-one; he is thirty-seven, but of the type known as "Baby-Faced." He needs to shave only twice a week. There is a juvenile bloom upon his pink-and-white cheeks. An accidental-looking pinch of ash-blond down on his upper lip represents the accumulated moustache of twenty years. His eyes are like the eyes of a baby, they are so full of quiet wonder and clear innocence: his teeth might be milk teeth. The merest draught stirs his fine-drawn golden hair. He weighs thirteen stone, is constructed like a Greek hero, spent seven years in a Highland regiment, and at thirty-odd made a living as an all-in wrestler under the pseudonym of "The Child Wonder." His voice is high-pitched and peculiarly flat and metallic, with the carrying power of a cowbell. When annoyed he can trumpet like a bull elephant. He spends most of his spare time writing interminable letters to a girl in Middlesbrough: she is a Baptist, and he is a Freethinker; his communications are oddly compounded of ardent love and passionate reasoning. He hates sentimental music. When he gets up in the morning he does handsprings, and sings at the top of his voice. Nobody has ever told him that he is tone-deaf.

Ball says:

"You talk about discipline and what not. Well, take a look at this." And he throws down a photograph. "Do you recognise me?"

We do and we don't. He is standing in a group. Seven or eight little men, dark little men, are leaning upon rifles. Ball towers over them, with his fair, shining face. He is carrying a rifle, also; but as the camera clicked he instinctively drew himself into a military atttitude, and so stands, stiff as a poker, properly at ease. He is dressed in a kind of forage cap, a shirt, and trousers. A blanket is rolled and slung about him. Fantastically, through his rags, there has burst the white fire of the good old British Regular Army. Everybody is covered with dust.

"Where's this?" asks Crowne.

"Spain," says Ball. "When the Civil War was on, I had a sort of crazy fancy to get into it. So I slipped into Spain and joined the Government Militia."

"Well I never!" says Dagwood.

"Bit of adventure, you know," says Ball. "I didn't care who won, so long as it wasn't Hitler and Musso. So I joined the Militia. I'd had seven years in the —— Highlanders. I thought I might put it to some use, you know. And I had the chance of seeing good men with bad discipline. Nobody bellyached about regimental nonsense more than I did before. But since then I'm dead regimental, as anybody'll tell you.

"Those dagoes had enthusiasm. They had nerve. They could stand the pace. But what bust them, apart from lack of equipment, you know, was their discipline. They'd got several different kinds of politics, too, you know, and that's always a bad thing for soldiers. They were *fighters,* you might say. But what was the use of it? Without discipline, they were a mob. The lousy Fascists were very little better, but they had better equipment, and what with one thing and another, they won. But it struck me that if my mob had got proper discipline, the Fascists could have been smashed up in Spain, you know; and then we'd have another ally at this present moment, instead of a Hitlerite in power in Spain. I did what I could, you know. But we were a rabble. With one battalion of Coldstream Guards, we could have taken Franco's shirt off his back."

"I bet you saw some sights," says Dale.

"I saw some sights. The Fascists had brought the Moors in. The Moors are used to torturing. Fascists like that kind of thing. I saw some of the things the Franco boys did, you know. We came into a sort of dusty, greyish-brown village. . . . Well," says Ball, "the other day I happened to look at somebody's bright red belt thrown down on a brown blanket. I happened to look at it while I was thinking of something else. And I didn't sleep that night, and when I did drop off about four o'clock I had dreams. You'd never believe what a woman can have done to her, and still live."

"But you gave them a taste of their own medicine when you copped 'em, I bet," says Barker.

"No," says Ball, "we didn't. You don't stop that kind of thing by doing it yourself. We strictly did not do anything of the kind. That's just where the Fascists are mugs, you know. They go in for tortures. That makes everybody hate them. They cut their own throats. I've seen the remains of people, all charred; soaked in petrol, you know, and lit. One of those dead bodies is a better argument against the Fascists than all the speeches in the world. And you don't think we were mugs enough to give them similar arguments against us? Besides, if you're fighting against a fellow because you don't want what he stands for, damn it all, you don't go and do just the very thing you're fighting to put a stop to. Do you? Even if you want to, you don't."

"I dunno," says Barker. "People must be mugs to stand for Nazis."

"People are mugs to stand for anything they don't want to stand for," says Shorrocks.

"Don't be silly," says Old Silence. "Remember that Fascism and Nazism live by *compelling* people, in the first place. And so the Nazi becomes expert at making you do things you don't want to do, *making* you stand for things, *making* you betray people you love . . ."

"——" says Sergeant Crowne, using a rude term of disagreement. "I'd like to see anybody or anythink make me do what I thought was lousy!"

"Me, too," say several others.

Old Silence strokes his lank chin with a long, dark hand, and says: "Assume something hard to swallow, Sergeant Crowne. Imagine—

just for the sake of argument—that England was sold, and made a dishonourable peace with Hitler. *It can't happen,* but just *imagine* it."

"Well?" says Crowne.

"You're imagining that. Imagine that England did as Pétain did. All right. You're imagining that. The war is over. We are disarmed. We become a sort of vassal of Hitler. Are you imagining that? They still call us 'England,' but it's only a name, a label. The Nazis hold all Europe. The Army is disbanded. Time passes. Are you imagining it? Ten years pass. Ten years. And after ten years, you, Sergeant Crowne, meet Sergeant Hands in, let's say, Holborn. All right. If Hitler won this war, this is the kind of scene you'd find yourself in, Sergeant Crowne. You meet Sergeant Hands. And you talk. This is how it goes."

And Old Silence, making patterns in the air with his smoking cigarette, tells his impossible hypothetical story:

"Look," Hands might say, "how about a beer?"

And Crowne replies: "Whatever you say. I don't mind."

"Beer, then. Look, we're quite near the old 'Red Lion.' What about there?"

"Like old times," says Hands.

"Ah, those were the days, eh? Remember Bella?"

"Do *I* remember Bella? What about you? You always had a bit of a soft spot for Bella."

"Not me," says Crowne. "Well, maybe a bit. But she liked you best. She said you had nice eyes. Remember?"

"Ah, that was a long time ago," says Hands.

"Well, well, well. After all these years . . ." says Crowne.

"Yes. I've often thought about you. Time and time again I've said to my old woman: 'I wonder what's happened to old Crowne.' Ellen always liked you. She said you had personality. Over ten years, and you haven't changed a bit. Good old Crowney! I knew you as soon as you came round the corner. That walk. . . . God in Heaven, how it all comes back!"

"They used to call us the Heavenly Twins."

"Didn't they, though?" says Hands. "Bella used to call us the Heavenly Twins."

"I'd have been jealous if we hadn't been pals," says Crowne. "But how is good old Ellen?"

"Best wife I ever had. Hardly a grey hair."

"And the kids?"

"All right, I suppose."

"What," says Crowne, "you only suppose?"

"No, no," says Hands, "they're fine. Only . . ."

"Only what?"

"Nothing. Nothing at all. But you know how it is. You sort of . . ." Hands pauses, and then says: "As an old pal. As one old soldier to another, and as man to man . . . you get sort of fed up."

"True enough," says Crowne.

Hands says: "I can see it in your face, too. Oh, well. In the old days we had our worries, but my God, Crowney, my God Almighty, we were *men,* at least. Remember when they called you Grouser Crowne? Those were the days, eh? You had something to say, and you said it, straight from the shoulder, right out, bang, and done with it. Good old Crowney! Grouse now and see what it'll get you!"

Crowne wants to change the subject. He says: "It's a nice day." But Hands is full, you understand, and he talks a bit.

"Once upon a time we could talk, we could grumble. Things were different, then. You were a man. You still had your soul. Your thoughts were your own. As long as you've got a voice in things, as long as you can still say: 'I like this and I don't like that,' things aren't so bad! But now! Honest to God, Crowne, you can't trust anybody. They've got our kids. They've educated our kids to think their rotten way. But I'm talking too much . . ."

"I'm your pal," says Crowne.

"I know it," says Hands, "but things have got me down. Still . . . you'd never betray me. You never let me down. And sometimes I feel that if I don't talk, I'll burst. I'll go mad . . . and then . . ."

"Beer," says Crowne.

"It's such a price," says Hands. "Remember? We thought the beer back in 1941 was bad. Well, I'd give a lot for a pint of 1941 bitter and a packet of real tobacco fags. What *is* this stuff?"

"Chemicals."

"And the tobacco . . . ?"

"Muck."

"Do you remember, Crowney, when you used to be able to walk into a place and buy a steak? Underdone?"

"With proper chips," says Crowne.

"And peas? Why damn it, cheese! Remember Cheddar cheese?"

"They used to *give* it away! Well, practically. . . . A few pence a quarter of a pound."

"We live on German leavings," says Hands. "On rubbish. And we'll die on it."

"Us," says Crowne.

"Englishmen," says Hands.

"We should have died first," says Crowne.

Hands goes on: "After the steak we'd have a cup of tea, with real milk and sugar."

"Real tea," says Crowne.

"And change a ten-bob note and get some silver back."

"Look at me," says Crowne. "I got a rise last week. Know how much I get now? Seven hundred thousand pounds a month! Paper. My kids are getting thinner and thinner. Bread at two thousand five hundred pounds a small loaf . . ."

"And what bread? Acorns, sawdust, filth! By god, Crowney, sometimes I want to rush out into the street and shout—give 'em the old shout, the good old shout that made the rookies jump!—shout: 'Long live England! Long live Liberty! Long live Democracy! God blast the

Nazis! Live free, or die fighting!' . . . and get shot down like a man, Crowney, like a *man*."

"And me, Hands," says Crowne.

"Honestly? Truly?"

"I saw my mother die of hunger," says Crowne. "Under my eyes she died. And my wife too. What do I keep going for? For my kids. They hate my guts. I'm not a proper kind of Fascist, or Nazi, or whatever it is. But they're my kids and I can't help loving them, Hands."

"I'm glad to hear you talk like that," says Hands. "Where are you living now?"

"Goering Boulevard. It used to be Victoria Road. Number 76. Always home by six. And you?"

"7, Hitler Avenue. Well I've got to scram. You'll keep in touch?"

"You bet," says Crowne. "It's like a breath of fresh air seeing you again."

"Well . . . (look out, somebody's listening!) . . . Heil Hitler!"

"Heil Hitler!" says Crowne. And so they part.

Hands walks East. Soon he pauses: stands, biting his nails—just as he's biting them now—and then goes into a telephone booth. He dials a number and talks:

"Give me 55X," he says. "Here is CBH/888. Take this down. *Crowne.* Got it. 76, *Goering Boulevard.* Got it? Yes. Seditious talk. Subversive activities. Spreading discontent. Treasonable propaganda. An enemy of the Reich. Go get him. He will be home at six."

A pause. A horrified silence. "What?" says Hands. "What? Do you mean to tell me that I'd do that? Me? Me, Hands? Why, you. . . . What, me? Turn nark? Turn informer? Rat? Me? On my pal? On my pal Crowne? Or on any man, let alone Crowne? You . . ."

Old Silence replies: "Listen a moment, Sergeant Hands. We were imagining a case. Still imagine that the Nazis came to power here."

"Well?"

"You've got a daughter."

"Two."

"And a son?"

"Two."

"In ten years' time, your daughters will be young women, and your sons young men. You love them, Sergeant?"

"Better 'n anything."

"And if a Nazi official threatened to send your girls to a House, for the entertainment of German soldiers, or workers? And to do some terrible things to your sons? You'd do anything on earth to stop that, wouldn't you? You'd consider your daughters and sons more important than your old pal, wouldn't you?"

With a strange touch of tenderness, the savage Sergeant Crowne says: "Hands. I wouldn't bear you any grudge if you turned me in to save your kids. I'd see your point, and we'd still be pals."

"By Christ," says Hands, quietly, "I wouldn't be alive to see that day, Old Silence. Not while I had even a tooth left to fight with."

"That is how Dictatorships are kept going, though," says the School-master.

"Over my dead body," says Hands.

"And mine," says Crowne.

Sunday. We rise thirty minutes later. This being a day of rest, we only have to scrub the hut. The Catholics go out early, for Communion. There is a United Board service; a spiritual coalition of Baptists and Congregationalists, held in the place called the U.B., in which there is a tea-bar . . . a good tea-bar, at which there presides an old soldier with one finger missing, and an Alsatian dog with a non-conformist air. Almost everybody else is marched off to Church Parade. The Camp is silent. In our hut only four or five men remain—three Catholics, a Jew called Shaw, and Old Silence, who is down as an Agnostic.

Shaw is the four letters in the middle of *Warshawsky*. The name was sawn down to fit English tongues, when Guardsman Shaw's father came West from Czestochowa, where the Black Virgin is, in South-west Poland. There had been rumour of a pogrom. In Kishinev, un-born children of Jews had been delivered prematurely and posthu-mously with bayonets. Warshawsky got out. Guardsman Shaw was born on British soil; but only just. He is a tallish, slender, pensive man, to whom are attributed strange rites and outlandish ceremonies. Dur-ing eight days every year, he eats no bread, because the bread of the ancient Israelites, delivered from the Land of Egypt and the House of Bondage, had not time to rise before they packed it. There is a period of twenty-four hours in which no food and drink passes his lips, and he keeps the Great White Fast in a synagogue, to the accompaniment of ardent prayers and strange, nostalgic songs. Here, he eats what he gets; but at home nobody would dream of cooking meat which did not come from a beast that chewed the cud and also had cloven hoofs, and had not been killed according to a certain ritual. His father has never shaved, in obedience to Mosaic law, and would die sooner than eat a milk pudding after a dash of meat, and wouldn't eat at all if he couldn't wash his hands first. Shaw has never tasted pork, oysters, lobsters, eels, rabbits, or anything that creeps or crawls, or any fish that has not both fins and scales. He gives away his breakfast bacon, and will not smoke after sunset on Friday until after sunset Saturday, on account of the law which forbids the kindling of a flame on the Sabbath. There is money in his family: his father made a good deal out of gowns. Guardsman Shaw, in civilian life, is an accountant. He went to a good school. A studious and on the whole unworldly person, he abandoned his office and volunteered for the Guards because he felt that in this manner he stood a good chance of getting at some Nazis hand-to-hand. Beneath his bookish exterior, something simmers. He is the type of the fighting student that held the walls of Jerusalem against Titus, and argued over the split hairs of the Law as the catapults quivered and the javelins hissed past. He smokes interminably, never drinks, and possesses a kipper-coloured violin upon which he plays melancholy music. He needs to be watched: otherwise, he will switch the radio on to a quartette in Something Minor or a Concerto in D before you know where you are.

A young Catholic named Dooley says, rather severely:

"You know what, Shaw? I bet they wouldn't let you do things like this in Germany. Believing what you like, and all that."

Shaw, who tends to sententiousness in argument, says: "They couldn't stop me believing. They could stop my expressing my beliefs," and he picks a phrase of Bach's Toccata and Fugue in D, pizzicato, out of the violin on his knee.

"You ought to think yourself lucky," says Dooley.

"I do," says Shaw; and tries to get the viola parts of Beethoven's Quartet in C Molle, but fails. "I am lucky. This is the best place in the world to live in. My father came from Poland, when Poland was part of the Russian Empire. He was astonished when he found that the English police were polite to him, and that they didn't expect bribes. He couldn't believe that I, his son, would have equal rights with any other British-born man. Jews had no rights worth mentioning where he came from.

"He came here just before I was born, with my mother and a sister of mine, two years old. Well, it happened that he did fairly well after a good deal of hard work, and after a year or so was actually able to afford a holiday at the seaside for us all. I was a very little baby. My sister could walk: she was a beautiful child. One morning, my father took my sister and me for a walk along the front. He was pushing me in a pram, very slowly, while my sister toddled along by his side, holding on to him. I believe he was just about to cross the road, when a great big man—my father must have told me this story a hundred times—a great big man in a check suit, with a beard and a fine swaggering air, stopped and looked at me, and gently pinched my cheek; and looked at my little sister, and patted her on the head, and said: 'Fine children.' 'Thank God,' said my father. The gentleman in the check suit then asked him how old we were, and my father told him: 'The boy is eleven months old, and the girl is four, bless them, Mister.'

Then the gentleman put a hand in his waistcoat, and took out a golden sovereign, and gave it to my sister; said: 'Good morning to you,' and walked on. My father, looking after him, saw men who were passing raising their hats to him. He asked somebody who it was. It was King Edward the Seventh.

"My father was overwhelmed. There was a country for you! A King, an Emperor! And he walked along without a bodyguard, and stopped a poor Jewish tradesman, and was civil to him and kind to his children, in the open street! And my poor old father, who had some very bad times still fresh in his memory, burst into tears. My sister cried too. I, catching the infection, howled at the top of my voice. After that my father walked with his head held high. He felt he was part of a wonderful country, and he would have died for England after that. So would I. Sometimes I feel that even the English don't realise what they've got, in England. That wireless. . . . The other night somebody got Hamburg, and we listened to Lord Haw-Haw: listened, and laughed, and of our own accord cut him off. Does it occur to you how marvellous it is that we can do that? Fascists and Nazis are sent to prison for listening to English broadcasts. And in the library, there's a copy of *Mein Kampf,* though nobody bothers to read it. Think myself lucky? I am lucky. So are you."

"And you, Silence," says Dooley. "I bet you wouldn't be allowed not to believe in anything anywhere else."

"And you, Dooley," says Old Silence. "The Catholics have been persecuted in their time, too. But who says I believe in nothing?"

"You've got no religion," says Dooley.

"Well?"

"Then what can you believe in?"

The man called Old Silence sits still and looks out at the bright morning, while Shaw, caressing the strings of his violin with the white bow, produces a gentle melody.

"The other night," says Old Silence, almost to himself, "I couldn't sleep. I was thinking. I was thinking of gods, and men, and prayers; and there came into my mind something . . ."

"What?" asks Dooley, for Old Silence has paused.

" . . . something that might be a prayer."

"To *who*? To *what*?" asks Dooley.

"*For* what?" asks Shaw.

"It went something like this," says Old Silence. Half-closing his eyes, and looking at a beam of sunlight in which the tiny dust-motes dance, he gravely declaims:

"I can't believe in the God of my Fathers. If there is one Mind which understands all things, it will comprehend me in my unbelief.

"I don't know whose hand hung Hesperus in the sky, and fixed the Dog Star, and scattered the shining dust of Heaven, and fired the sun, and froze the darkness between the lonely worlds that spin in space.

"The world flies through the night towards the morning.

"Oh Universe, so far beyond human understanding! I know that a thousand worlds may grow cold and die between two of your unending heart-beats. I know that all the sciences and philosophies of man— all his findings and seekings—all his discoveries and inspirations—are like flashes of a mighty, misty panorama seen through a chink in a rushing train.

"I know that man, in his little space of time, may catch only a glimpse of Truth, like the last desperate glance at Heaven of a lost wayfarer falling into an abyss.

"I know that suns wane and earths perish. But I also know that I can see the light of dead and forgotten stars.

"I am lost in awe at your beauty, immeasurable Universe! Yet I am not afraid of you, and so I know that between the handful of grey slime in my head, with which I think and plan, and the threads of my nerves which miraculously tie my thoughts to my eyes and lips and fingers, there is something more. It is something that is Man's. It is a Soul.

"About this I cannot reason. I do not know. I believe that the soul of Man cannot die. I do not know what it is, or why it is, or how it comes, or where it may go. It made the beast-shaped dawn-man conquer his instinctive terror of the elements. It looks out of me with calm love for

the greatness of things, with joy in its power to praise noble things and wonder at eternal things, and with hope in its yearning to cleanse from life the squalor of unclean things.

"Oh Life! Light! Universe! Let me have strength to struggle always and keep unsoiled my pride in the presence of Fear! Give me the power to bear with a straight back all the burdens that Life can heap upon me! Give me the will to find new horizons and build new things! I am a poor creature; a shadow. But since I stand on a mountain of dead men and breathe the dust of a million years of man's broken endeavours, let me be no less than the first speechless man who with fine faith and blind courage crossed the first river! Give me strength to live and work, knowing that every movement of the finger of the clock beckons me towards a hole in the ground!

"I know that this life, and the death that goes with it, are only phases. Let me keep out of my heart the ancient, terrified ape that clutches, howling, at the breaking branch! Give valour to this dust and dignity to this clay! Give me kindness, patience, understanding and endurance, so that I, who love poor lonely Man, may help him to find some happiness on his way upwards to his unknown end!"

"Dust of a million years," says Barker, who has come in meanwhile. "Let's get this swabbing over 'n' done with."

Beds crash back. Buckets clank down. Brooms clatter. Corporal Bearsbreath begins to shout: "C'mon! Thirty of you! This hut ought to be dug out and finished in thirty minutes! Get a rift on! Get a jazz on those scrubbers! Johnson, don't let me catch you skiving!"

The lad from the Elephant, in mad enthusiasm, hurls down a bucket of water and runs amok with a long scrubber.

In forty-five minutes, the hut is damply clean. Later it will rain. To-morrow the hut will be dirty again. For the next seven days we will conduct a sort of Lucknow against the detritus of the earth which the rain will turn to mud, and the warmth of the hut will turn back to dust . . . against the dust and ashes which always lie in wait.

"In the East," says Sergeant Hands, "there's whole cities buried under yards and yards of muck. That's what comes of not getting the place properly dug out. So be warned! Dirt buries you alive if you let it.

Furthermore, as senior N.C.O. in this hut, I get the blame if the place is in tripe. And that," Sergeant Hands mutters, "is worst of all."

Barker says: "My mum's been digging aht our 'ouse for forty-two years and a quarter. It's still as dirty as it was when she started . . ."

"You'll find," says Crowne, "that even this little bit o' dampness will get into your rifle barrels. Watch out for your barrels. They're sensitive as a young girl's cheeks. And you're going to fire your course. So nurse them barrels."

And so the course is fired. Those of us who flinched a little at first (when, on the thirty-yard range at the Depot, the noise of a .303 rifle shot seemed to smash and reverberate like a cannon) find a strange exhilaration in the clear, crisp bang of rifles in the open air. A nice sound, accompanied by a pleasant nudge which hints of huge power, and a clean, keen antiseptic smell of burnt explosive. Those good, noisy, bleak-looking ranges, muttering with echoes! We fire gravely, and with concentration. We lie down with bucko sergeants and fire our Bren-gun course, and see the sand splashing brown on the butts, and the black or white discs hovering, oscillating and coming to rest where our bursts have punctured the targets.

We are becoming soldiers. The first strange excitement wears off; and so does the first uneasiness. The Depot seems very far away. We swore we'd never forget Sergeant Nelson, and yet we have already begun to forget him. He, at this moment, is hammering the crude stuff of brand new recruits . . . working, as on us, with frenzy and patience; pleading, roaring, urging, damning, dropping rare hints of praise; manu-facturing more of us. But we, seeing new squads coming into the Train-ing Battalion, stand, in our baggy canvas suits, and comment upon the manner of their marching. "Not bad," we say; and "Likely-looking rookies"; and "They're not getting too bad a mob of kids at Caterham these days."

A C.O.'s Parade has no terrors for us. In the ancient days, seven or eight weeks ago, we dressed for our last inspection with the tremulous, dewy-eyed anxiety of brides on the last dawn of virginity. Now, rushing back five minutes late from P.T., and having fifteen minutes in which to change before the Quarter blows, we curse hideously but are not in the least dismayed, and turn out smarter than we ever turned out at the Depot, to march with something resembling the proper swing, the subtle swagger . . . "As if you owned this ground you march on! And if you owned the ea-hearth!" the R.S.M. roars, in his voice which shakes a little from its decades of thunder.

We are acquiring experience in field training. We begin to get the diagnostic intuition of the soldier looking for cover. We can keep an Arrowhead Formation without looking. Night and the open heath have rustled to our crawling, when we started to pick up the secrets of prowling on patrol. Any one of us can clean a Mills grenade, and put the fuse in it, and screw it tight, and throw it so that it bursts in a mean spray of jagged iron at thirty or forty yards. They have given us Bren until we are slightly sick of Bren; but we can handle that invaluable light machine gun with the slightly bored accuracy of mechanics with familiar tools. Night, dark midnight, has seen us marching away to the shadow-lands behind the golf course, where, in black invisibility, we have dug weapon pits. And we know all about trenches, because we have dug them: buck navvies in uniform have sighed with a strange joy at the feel of picks and shovels; and sedentary men among us, puffing and grunting, have learned the technique of making holes and paid for their learning with little coin-shaped bits of skin.

Some of us, who would have shrunk like tickled oysters at a hint of punishment, have committed crimes and paid them off with carefree laughter. Yes, the serious Dale, the good clerk whom a rough word depressed, got three days C.B. for missing a parade. He said he didn't know: the Company Commander said he ought to have known, and so Dale had to answer Defaulters three days running, and did some drill that would have reduced him to a gibbering heap six months before. And he said: "What the hell, anyway"; to which Sergeant Dagwood said: "That's the spirit."

There is no getting away from the fact that we are changing. Shorrocks is down to eleven stone ten, and there is, so to speak, meat-juice in the dumpling of his face. What is more, he argues less frequently, and lays down less law. He is the same Shorrocks. But he has seen something of the world; of the wide and varied world that is England. He'd never spoken to a Devon man before, for example. To him, Rockbottom still represents all that is brightest and best in England, but his contempt for the rest of the world is tempered a little. He has had to listen to people telling him things, for the first time since he left Rockbottom Wesleyan School. He has mixed with new men. He despises the Cockney, but concedes to him certain virtues; which he didn't before the war. He has acquired patience. He has lost flesh and gained outlook; narrowed physically, and broadened mentally. "There is no Rockbottom but Rockbottom, and Shorrocks is its Prophet." This will hold good until the Pennine Chain is down to its last link; but the dogma has softened, admitting the moderation of inter-county tolerance. Shorrocks, meanwhile, having decided that he has a genius for driving, and being attracted by the sturdy little caterpillar-wheeled Bren Carrier (which somehow resembles himself) has gone into a Carrier Platoon.

Hodge, the giant, the man impregnable; Hodge, of huge thews and rock-founded faith, never changed. There was never anything in Hodge that needed to change. Hodge is an elemental force. If ever Hodge struck down an enemy, he would be striking not a man but a wickedness: not that the man, as representative of wickedness, could hope to be spared! He has gone into a Suicide Squad. A man in a Suicide Squad does not want to commit suicide: his career in it is a denial of the possibility of death. The Suicide Squad man is a man with a mission. He, personally, discounts death as a possibility while his mission is unfulfilled. In the canal, Hodge swam like a fish and dived like a seal. On land, he was indefatigable. He was immense, but proportionate; could run like a hare, perform unheard-of leaps, and hurl things to uncalculated distances. To Unarmed Combat he applied a certain grave, sober concentration. Imagine a statue of the Farnese Hercules endowed with a will. Even Corporal Ball was clay in his stupendous clutch. Yet Hodge is gentle. His fingers, large as a baby's arms, have a strange delicacy of touch. The lad from the Elephant and Castle will tell you how Hodge took a splinter out of his finger, which no tweezers could reach. Hodge yearned to come to handgrips with the Devil. It was natural that he should go into a training-place for parachute troops. By now, his training completed and his vast arm embellished with a pale blue winged parachute badge, he will have been called back to get in the harvest; and that being done with, he will return to fight the good fight with all his terrible might—the old, elemental Anglo-Saxon.

Dale, as I indicated, has toughened. He always had everything in him that a man needs, but it took the rough society of soldiers to peel from his essential self the pale sheath of the city. A certain primness has dropped from him like a cloak, and there has come into his face a look of confidence. His shoulders seem to have set, as a boy's shoulders do when he loses puppy fat. It happens—I tell you, it happens! Dale was a man (pardon the expression) seated on his bottom. He has learned to use his hands and feet—and behold, the riddle of Samson is reversed! Out of the meat comes forth the eater, and out of sweetness comes forth strength. The Schoolmaster has gone to his Officer Cadet Training Unit. But that gentle soul has got himself a certain physical resolution which nothing in his life before could ever have given him. Nothing could ever make that man less than a gentleman: but he has got something more than a theory of manual labour, and something deeper than a bookish sympathy with the thing he calls The People. He has come across the units that go to make up the strange, docile, cantankerous, trusting, suspicious, colourful English Masses. He will be a better officer for that, and a wiser man.

Certain people, of course, don't change, and never will. Barker is the same. So is Bullock, his bosom friend. They remain the same for different reasons. Barker, the eternal Cockney, is supple. He is bamboo.

He is many-jointed, but straight and tough. He will bend with every wind that blows, because that is how he is constructed for the stern business of survival. He has only one real shape and attitude, and springs back to it. The hurricane thinks it has levelled Barker to the ground; but the wind grows tired, and Barker stands upright. Bullock is unchangeable because nothing but death will ever move him. He stands stiff, and will break before he bends. Dour, solemn, narrow-minded, cautiously good-hearted, his great flame of indomitability always burns hot and strong. He is intransigent; a gnarled tree. He met that smashing fighter, Ack-Ack Ackerman, and they fought a draw. A poor boxer, but a dreadful man to fight: that is Bullock. If he changed, there would be the end of him. We ought to thank God that such men do not change.

Widnes, the boy who used to have wire hair, has taken to the Army. You have seen, perhaps, a new-hatched waterhen slipping into a pond and instantly swimming? Widnes, as soon as he felt his way among the back alleys of Army procedure, found himself in his element. He has put on weight, and will put on more. He took a Corporal's Class, and, having triumphantly come through the hell that the drill sergeants hand out to prospective N.C.O.s in the Coldstream Guards, went On Orders and was told that he had been awarded the rank of Acting Unpaid Lance-Corporal. He is making the Army his career. Soon, he will be a Corporal, then a Lance-Sergeant, then a Full Sergeant, then Company Quartermaster Sergeant, then Company Sergeant-Major, then Drill Sergeant, then Regimental Sergeant-Major; and then an aged man, erect as a telegraph pole, with a voice like a football fan's rattle and an impermeable respectability—a man like the great Charlie Yardley of the Training Battalion, or Britton, whose voice still paralyses men at eight hundred and fifty yards. Wars may come and go. Widnes will perform his duty, and take world calamity in his stride. It is feared, in certain quarters, that he may turn out to be heartless; but Sergeant Dagwood says that this kind of thing passes, like the gloom of adolescence; severity in a Young Corporal, he says, like wildness in a Recruit, is not necessarily a bad sign.

But John Johnson changed. He, fundamentally, is the Brummagem Fly Boy. But the Army has dealt with Fly Boys, since time immemorial. When dogs bring forth cats, then Fly Boys will get away with things in the Guards. There was one incident which, I think, undermined Johnson's confidence in the fly technique. There is a shambling, big-boned man from the wildest moors of Yorkshire, a sort of peasant who falls down rather than sits, and has to get words up out of himself with a conscious effort. This man is called Old Jeddup, because Sergeants are always saying to him: "Hold yer head up. C'mon! Old Jeddup!" He weighs sixteen stone. A young subaltern, on a night stunt, tried to teach him how to move silently. Old Jeddup melted into the heather like a weasel and came back with a buck rabbit: he used to be a poacher. We have thousands of such healthily law-breaking sons of the soil in this Army. Old Jeddup, bar by bar, bought five shillingsworth of chocolate to send to his little son. He packed it in a small box. He fumbled and tangled himself with the string in the presence of the Fly Boy, and ultimately got the box tied up and tucked away in his tin of personal effects. Then he took it out again, and looked at it. John Johnson winked at us all and asked him how much he wanted for it. Old Jeddup said: "What's it worth?" Johnson, being as fly as they come, said: "Quick! Half a dollar!" Old Jeddup said "Cash?" "Cash," said Johnson; and Jeddup said "Done." He handed over the box, and took the half-crown. But the box he handed over was empty; he had prepared a duplicate in advance. Then he told Johnson how this was the oldest of all confidence tricks, and gave him back one shilling. It undermined John Johnson, who, thinking thereafter before he demonstrated, automatically became more wise and less fly.

Johnson, with all his false ideals, makes a good soldier, if only out of vanity; for he would die a thousand deaths rather than look silly. Bates, that simple man, has the profoundest admiration for him. But Bates is basically the simpleton. He has nothing in his nature more complex than a punch in the mouth. He is beloved. Bates is affectionate. He has a childish ingenuity. If somebody sends him for a left-handed monkey wrench he assumes that such a thing must be procurable, and won't go away until he gets it. He believes what he is told, and the more firmly a thing is said, the deeper his belief in it. Then if a mob-orator shrieked Fascism at Bates, would he swallow that, too? He might repeat as gospel what he had heard, but he is the last man on earth who could live in the state of affairs that would come out of it, because he sets a vast value upon his personal liberties. A bit of a fool, Bates: but never, if you value your profile, never push him around; unless you happen to be his wife. And even then, not beyond a certain point. But what happened to Thurstan?

The Hut. Evening. Sergeant Crowne sits, setting up a new S.D. cap. In order to achieve the rigid rectilinear front beloved of the Guards, men evolve arrangements of adhesive plaster and bachelor buttons that might have been worked out, in fun, by Heath Robinson. So Sergeant Crowne struggles, muttering.

I shall not forget that night. It was the death-night of my beloved friend Old Silence. The occasion fixed itself in my memory. It is possible that I may forget my name. But that time, that place, and that atmosphere I can never forget. I did not learn about Old Silence until later. He had got seven days' leave, to be married. He had been a lonely man, like Larra in the legend, living like a shadow on a horizon beyond the ordinary cares of humanity. Just before he had been called into the Army, Old Silence had fallen in love with a woman, who fell in love with him. Life, thereafter, had a new and fine significance for him. He discovered new things, deep and high. And so he had left us for seven days, singing in the cracked, uncertain voice of a man unaccustomed to singing, after we had slapped his back, and yelled encouragement, and helped him to put on his webbing, which John Johnson, of all men, had helped him to blanco. Everybody loved Old Silence.

The lad from the Elephant stole a horseshoe and made ready to hang it over the vacant bed.

He was due back that night. He did not come. A week later, when conjecture had exhausted itself after every man had rejected the possibility of desertion, a letter came. Old Silence had been married. There was a breakfast. The letter stated it nakedly . . . a small breakfast for four guests. He was a man who loved everybody, and therefore loved nobody in particular. He had few friends, for he had a habit of silence, as his nickname implies. A raider dropped a bomb, and the remains of Old Silence were found with those of his bride. He had arched his back over her, trying to protect her. They were both dead in their first and last embrace. He died with his song unsung. There are few of us who would not have interposed ourselves between a bomb and him. Peace to Old Silence in the immensity! This is not the time to tell of the kindliness, the magnanimity, and the strength of that man. He was my friend. He died that night.

The radio was on. Because, at that moment, there was nothing available that was more to everybody's taste, we tolerated a record of Caruso singing some *Ave Maria*. The Sergeant In Waiting, who, that week, happened to be Sergeant Hands, pushed his head into the hut and said: "Well . . . Humphrey Bogart's gone absent."

Thurstan was called by the name of that distinguished actor of criminal roles, because of a certain hangdog trick of the head and his brusque manner of speech. Besides, Humphrey Bogart can look every inch a killer; and although there was no actual resemblance, Thurstan resembled him in his manner.

"Gone absent," said Crowne. "That settles it."

"Pore——" said Barker.

"Why pore——?" asked Sergeant Crowne.

" 'E's crazy," said Barker. " 'E's not right. There's something wrong with 'im. 'E ought not to be in the Army at all."

"Mug," said Hands. "Where'll it get him? But I've been expecting this all along. He was working up towards it. I could see it. He's been in trouble since he's been here. Remember when he socked Tucker for touching his boots? He's never been out of trouble from the first week. You could smell this coming. I despise a man that goes absent just like that. It's a proof he's got no guts. Even if he don't like it, he ought to stand the racket. *I* didn't like it. Nobody does, at first. No. Well . . ."

Sergeant Hands went away on his bicycle, about the complex and endless business of the Orderly Sergeant.

It was the Schoolmaster who said: "You ought to understand Thurstan. I could see this coming, too. I'm about the only person who ever talked with him.

"Thurstan is a wild animal. But I assure you that he's all right. He's had a rotten life. Don't condemn him too quickly. He's a decent fellow and a proper man. Don't laugh at me when I say that. You don't understand what the trouble is with Thurstan. Shall I tell you what? He can't talk."

"How d'you mean, can't talk?" said Crowne. " 'E's got a tongue."

"Sergeant Crowne! You've got a tongue. But tell me—can you explain exactly what you mean by the first pressure on a trigger?"

"Well, no, not if you want me to put it altogether in words. No, I can't."

"Can you explain what you mean by a corkscrew?"

"In actual words? No."

"Can you describe what you see when you see a puff of cigarette-smoke?"

"No."

"But you've got a tongue. And a tongue isn't always enough. It's like saying: 'You've got a pen. Write a book.' I'm about the only person who has talked to Thurstan, and I'm telling you that the thing that has made that man ferocious is, that he's never been able to say what he's wanted to say. That sounds crazy. But I've had his story from him.

"His father was an animal. He used to beat his mother. She was a silent woman. Thurstan never really learned to talk. Nobody talked to him. He came from a village in the wilds of the North. He hardly went to school at all. Do you remember how he'd always ask somebody to tell him what was on the detail: usually me? He couldn't read or write. He's ashamed of it. He was ill-treated by everybody except his mother, and she never talked to him, and he was unable to express his sympathy for her. As soon as he was old enough—and he was a strong kid—he went into a mine. I can't get a clear idea of what he did, because I don't know the circumstances. But he was in charge of pit ponies, or something of that sort. And it seems that he had reason to be scared of one of them."

A Northern collier says: "Ah. They can be orkard."

"It seems there was a black pit pony. It went mad and chased him. He saved himself by pushing a lamp into its mouth. But he hadn't the nerve to go back. He was ashamed of that, too. When he went home his father beat him. He couldn't explain himself. He got a terrible thrashing. He ran away from home. After that he lived as best he could. He never learned to say what it was necessary for him to say. You know how necessary it is for a man to talk a bit. Thurstan never did, never could. He married. His wife was afraid of him. She found somebody else. He couldn't do anything except fight it out, and went to gaol for three months. When he came out, he fell in with a mob of dock rats. He went in for robbery. He was let down by his associates, and caught. He didn't talk: he wouldn't, and anyway, he couldn't. He did another six months. He went to Liverpool, and fell in love with a girl there. But he couldn't get around to talking to her. He not only had nothing to say, but he couldn't even begin to say the things that he felt he *had* to say. He didn't have confidence. He'd start a word, and end by grunting. You've heard him.

"Now everybody knows what it is to feel that he'd like to have a chat, and yet have nobody to talk to. Imagine poor Thurstan, poor old Thurstan. He comes of a race that loves to talk and tell stories. He felt he had a lot to say. But it was choked back in him. So he became silent.

The most dangerous thing in the world is, for a man to become silent. That's what happened to Thurstan. There was only one way in which he could express himself; by using his hands. He knew only one argument: physical violence. He felt inferior to things, except when he could hit them. He has had terrible fights. He's a fighter. But he's always run away. To Thurstan, there has never been any use in explanation: there was nothing he could explain. It was all in his head, but he could never get it out. When things became too much for him, he simply left them. It wasn't cowardice: it was that he didn't know any other way of dealing with things. He ran away from the pit to somewhere else. From there, elsewhere. He's horribly alone. Life was too much for him, and he welcomed the war. He ran away from life, as he knew it, into the Army. And then—poor fellow—the Army was too much. He felt he didn't fit. And so he's run away. And I am willing to bet on something."

"What?" said Crowne.

"He'll be back in two days," said the Schoolmaster. "He's never spoken, but he's listened. He'll go away from here, right into the teeth of everything he ever wanted to get away from. Here, he has men fighting with him, instead of against him. Here, people are willing to teach him things for nothing, even to read and write. Thurstan is silent, but only because he *can't* talk. He's no fool. He'll think it out. I'll bet a hundred cigarettes to twenty that he'll be back in two days. Two days from tonight. A hundred cigarettes to twenty. Who takes me?"

Pause.

'Well?" said the Schoolmaster.

"Taken," said Hacket.

It happened quite dramatically. At that moment, Sergeant Hands came back. "He's in," he said. "Reported himself to Sarnt on Guard. Talking! Says: 'Take me back. Here I am. Shove me inside. I'll pay it off. I'm willing to be a soldier.' And then he says it's on account of Captain Scott. Nuts, I tell you, nuts, crazy, crackers!"

With a radiant face, the Schoolmaster said: "Give me that twenty cigarettes! I'm telling you that Thurstan is a good fellow."

"Or the value thereof," said Hacket, and laid down one shilling and one penny; the price of twenty Woodbines. "Fags are scarce."

Fourteen weeks have eaten themselves up. Our Company Sergeant-Major, the Iron Duke, wily old soldier, case-hardened roughneck veteran, has warned us. The Detail confirms it. We are for the Holding Battalion. This is a sieve through which all Guardsmen must pass; a clearing-house; a pack from which one is dealt. Companies go there, stay a while to mount guards in London, and so depart to rougher and dirtier work. This parting, now, fills us with no such sense of amputation as we experienced when we left the Depot. We have almost lost—though we never could quite lose—our tendency to thrust out roots wherever we rest. We have forgotten what it means to have any but portable property. All that we need to eat with, march with, sleep with, and defend ourselves with, is contained within the ninety pounds or so of our equipment. We have the habit of mobility. We have become soldiers.

As we hammer down the stuff in our big packs—(with what hopping anxiety did we assemble our first Change Of Quarters Order in the prehistoric period before we came here!)—Sergeant Dagwood looks at us and smiles. He has an ugly, lumpy face, every wrinkle and pore of which is a secondary masculine sexual characteristic, like hair on the chest; this powerful, gentle Sergeant. It breaks into a smile of remarkable charm. Years of command have hardened it: you cannot shout an order and look pleasant at the same time. But when he smiles, friendliness shines through his countenance like sunlight through a bomb-battered wall.

"You're off," he says.

"Yes," says Bates, "we are, yow know, Sergeant!"

"Yump," says Dagwood. "It's a long time since I was at the Holding Battalion. I'll never forget my first Buckingham Palace Guard. As soon as we were took off, I was run into the cooler. I'd lowered my butt an inch in turning. *I* didn't know. What was it I got? I forget. I think it was seven days. I can't remember. It's nice to be going to the Holding Battalion for the first time. It's nice to be young. Look: do your best on guard at Buck or Jimmy. It's not nice to let the mob down. So do the best you can.

"You can be good to look at, and a good soldier at the same time. No, honest to God: the better you are, the better you look. It's true. It's a fact. There's no argument. Do your best: be good pals and do your best, eh? All the old regulars, all the old sweats, tough guys, were particular about putting on a good show when they just had to be show-soldiers. Harry Wyatt of the Third Battalion—Number 5854—he did a good guard, and he got the V.C. That goes for the Lance-Jack, Bill Dobson, too. And Brooks, and Tom Whitman, and Norman Jackson: V.C.s too, all Last War. It's not all bull and boloney. *I* tell you it's not.

"Last War. People used to say: 'We can sleep tonight: the Guards are in front of us.' Well, keep that up. As a personal favour to me, keep that up. The Last War was only a war, a sort of ordinary war, compared to this one. It starts slow, but it doesn't finish, you know, till one or other of us goes down. There's going to be rough stuff. There's going to be hell. Well, that's all right. You know me. I'm a Sergeant. It's been my duty to tell you what to do. You know that if I've opened my mouth and bit your heads off on parade I was always one of you, and your pal, off parade. Man to man—keep it up, for Christ's sake keep it up. After all these hundreds of years . . . no, it'd look bad, *bad!*

"Anybody got a light . . . ?

"The proper fighting hasn't come yet. It's coming. Now, in Civvy Street, old geezers of eighty are heroes. You can't do less than them. You won't. It's not possible. This isn't a lecture. I'm not demonstrating something out of the book. Just talking to you. You're Guardsmen now. You know the whole story. Well, fight good! Keep it up! It might be that any one of you finds himself alone, right in a ditch. Still keep it up! And keep it up in proper order. Go to heaven or go to hell, but wherever you go, go clean!

"But what am I talking about? *You're* all right. Good luck to you. The best of luck. In this mob your best pal never writes to you. It doesn't matter. He's still your pal: you know him and he knows you. I'll never hear of any of you again, unless you get a V.C., or something. That's all right, quite all right. Only: keep it up! Do you get me? *Keep it up!"*

At this point there comes into the hut a razor-lipped man with immense shoulders and the icy eyes of a killer, no less a person than Ack-Ack Ackerman. He looks down his beaked nose at Bullock, and says:

"Fair is fair. Wanna tell you. The worst smack I ever had in my life was that right you landed on me. My head rung like a bell. I could never wish for a better fight."

"Nor me, neither," says Bullock. "And thank you very much."

"Thank *you*," says Ack-Ack Ackerman. "Well . . . good hunting. And watch that left. Adieu, but not good-bye. . . ."

And so we march away.

IV

The Finished Product

EVERY MIDDAY the Old Sweats foregather at the Naffy. There is a company clerk, a crumpled man, who has seen more years in service than he cares to remember. He is the leader of the little group of elderly soldiers. They meet at twelve and drink a species of watered bitter. He always buys the first round. He says one word, "four," and the barman puts out four pints of mild ale. Then, the crumpled company clerk hands out the beer. An ancient warrior, medal-ribboned in all the colours of the rainbow, the withered man who waters the cricket pitch, snatches the first pint. This man is called Geordie, because he comes from somewhere far north. He snatches his drink, says "uh" then sips it; puts it down, and then invariably explores his right ear with a matchstick. He is a very old soldier; a sombre man of twenty years' service; but he was old when he joined. There is another man, also from the far north: they call him Jimmy, and it is said that in thirty-five years of Army life he has never quite escaped trouble. Jimmy has an outrageous, an uproarious cheerfulness. No press in any civilised land could reprint his language. His imprecations are horrible. His blasphemies are unbelievable. He invokes impossible diseases, strange gods, and non-existent physical organs of unmentionable saints. Thirty years ago he was a corporal. Now, in the twilight of his life he is a Guardsman; a wicked, old Guardsman, still huge, still terrible and still riotous. It is odd to hear the somehow youthful flamboyance of his language tumbling out of that ancient, sunken mouth. And there he sits, invariably to the left of Geordie; both drinking acidulous weak beer. With them, always, sits a little tubby tailor. Rumour has it that this tailor owns thirty houses, and is a man of landed property. Everybody applies to this tailor on questions of real estate. Tradition has grown up about him. If he died with nothing in the bank, the Guards would feel that they had been cheated.

He has a greyhound.

He calls it a greyhound. It is a long dog. He calls it Bartholomew. Between Bartholomew and the enigmatic little man there is a dark understanding. The tailor, though a warrior, I mean an old soldier, is a man of peace: yet one kind of talk with him is fighting talk—talk against the dog Bartholomew. If you cast any aspersion upon the heredity of that dog you have Tubby, the tailor, to contend with. It is a greyhound, a greyhound of greyhounds, compared with which Mick the Miller is as stationary as a bedstead and a mere thing on four legs.

If you give him half a chance he will not fail to tell you the legend of the dog Bartholomew.

"Listen," he says, "look. Just look. Look at that back. Look at that chest. That dog is all lungs. So help me God, if he took a deep breath he'd raise up into the air, so help me God, like a balloon. So help me God. And this dog, this here mortal dog, Bartholomew, you may believe me or you may believe me not, was the fastest thing that ever walked. The fastest thing, so help me God. And he was owned by a toff. Are you listening? Do you hear me talk? By a gentleman, so help me God, a gentleman. But this gentleman—it can happen to any of us—so he was down on his luck. And you know how, good God, there can be all of a sudden a sort of a stroke of sort of luck? Well, this here gentleman, so it seems he has a sister who has a dog (excuse me) a bitch, a greyhound bitch. It's all right! A bitch, for a dog, isn't swearing. Well, this sister of this gentleman, so she goes so help me God, to Southdown and this here bitch sort of goes out and then she sort of comes back and then she sort of has pups. Five. Five pups. Well, this gentleman's sister is a judge of dogs.

"These five pups.

"Two, so help me God, she drowns. Three she gives away, but one she keeps.

"Did I say five? I said six.

"Now, this gentleman's sister, so the pup she keeps is this here pup. And no sooner can this here pup walk than—so help me God it runs. Listen, I am telling you something. I suppose you know that every living thing when the sun shines upon it casts a shadow. There is a law about it. Look. This here dog, this lovely dog Bartholomew, if he took off—and so help me God he did take off pretty frequent—you could see, just for a second, a sort of black patch on the ground. Not for more than a second, mind you, he left his bloody shadow behind him. But of course, only for a second.

"Well, the gentleman, this here gentleman, he was down on his luck. So he says to his sister: 'Irene, lend me a monkey.'

" 'Monkey,' she says, 'I ain't got no monkey. But I'll tell you what I'll do. I'll give you this here dog Bartholomew.'

" 'What do you mean you will give me this here dog Bartholomew,' this gentleman says. But they take him out on the Sussex Downs, and they say 'Run!' and so help me God this here dog runs so that this gentleman who is a judge of dogs swears that he has never seen anything like it in all his life.

"So this gentleman says 'Thank you very much,' and takes the dog to Brighton, and trains it up and down the Palace Pier. And so help me God it is a fact that nothing that ever ran was one millionth as fast as this here dog Bartholomew.

"And so, this here gentleman he goes here, and he goes there, and he borrows a fiver from this one, and from that one, and he raises two hundred and fifty nicker, and he enters this dog, this dog Bartholomew, for a race, and he shoves this here two hundred and fifty nicker on this here dog Bartholomew.

"O.K. O.K.? All right, O.K. Comes one day before the race. All this here gentleman has to do is to take this lovely dog to the White City for the race he has entered in. But this takes train fare. And this gentleman—mind you, a proper toff—has not got the price of the fare. He asks his sister. No go. He has sort of tapped his sister sort of heavyish in the past, and she will not stand for any more of it, no, not even for tosheroons. Well, so this gentleman finds some mug, and this mug has a motor-bike, and what does this gentleman do?

"No, no, that's all right, not a drop. Well, half a pint. All right, a pint.

"This gentleman borrows the motor-bike and a couple of leather straps. He straps this here dog Bartholomew on to the back of the motor-bike and, so help me God, he burns up the distance between Brighton and London, and then when he comes to unstrap this dog Bartholomew, the wha'd-you-call-it—dumpity-dump—vibration of this motor-bike has imparted itself, as they call it, to this dog Bartholomew. And he trembles, poor thing, like a leaf. He bobs like a recruit. I am telling you that this here dog Bartholomew has a nervous breakdown on account of the vibration of the motor-bike, and when he is let out of the trap at the beginning of the race, instead of running after the rabbit, he runs the wrong way. He bites three stewards, he does a sort of a death howl, but nevertheless he does something like half a mile in something like fifteen seconds. But, so help me God, in the wrong direction. And so, the gentleman sells him to me for a dollar to get his fare back to Brighton where he hopes to tap this here sister of his.

"And even to this day this here dog Bartholomew, whenever he hears a motor-bike, has hysterics. Otherwise this dog would make Mick the Miller look like something that crawls on a whatsiname. You may laugh."

And the dog Bartholomew crouches at his feet. It may be a greyhound, but a purist would call it simply a long dog, with too much chest and too much ears and too much tail and not enough legs. But the tailor's faith in that dog is something beautiful and profound, and nothing in the world could shake it.

To this group there also attaches himself a military policeman, a member of the dreaded Gestapo. He is the weather expert whom I have had the honour of mentioning once before: a man with a mild face and a West of England burr—a man whom, at one glance, anybody might recognise as the father of a family. He upholds the law, but with apologies. He joined the military police because he felt that this, somehow, would keep him closer to his wife and five sons. They call him Himmler. He resents this. He is a mine of misinformation upon every subject under the sun. If you wish to know the opposite of the truth about anything, ask Himmler. It is Himmler who knows that to have your ears pierced is good for the eyes. He knows that a cancer is either male or female, and, when removed by a surgeon, cries out of its own accord. If you want to know all that the moon can do, ask Himmler; for it is he who can tell you that the moon, and nothing but the moon, turns hair white, breeds fleas and is responsible for dust.

The group sits. Between the library and the main body of the restaurant, there is a kind of a closet containing a bar scarcely more than three feet long. This dog-end of space belongs to the group. The Old Sweats. They sit here from precisely noon until the stroke of two, after which they go about their unknown business.

The Old Sweats sit, full of small beer and big talk, puffing pungent Woodbine smoke. They are mostly Camp Staff. This was a Summer Camp before the War: they used practically to hibernate in that canteen throughout long winters, spinning endless tales of which nine-tenths were lies. Sometimes they are joined by a dried-out old Scots Guardsman and a fifty-year-old Grenadier nearly seven feet tall.

The Grenadier, whose origins are in Cumberland, has a gift of dramatic diction. He can make a story out of anything—nearly always a tragedy, an epic of martyrdom and injustice.

"Ah!" he says. "I knew Harry Nicholls."

"And who's Harry Nicholls?" asks Geordie, scornfully.

"What? You don't know Harry Nicholls? Why, he got the first V.C. in this war!"

"It's a dirty lie," says Geordie. "A dirty, filthy, rotten, stinking lie.

The very first V.C. in this war was won by one of our kids, a Coalie, d'ye hear?"

"I know this for a fact," says the Grenadier, with a tremendous gesture. "The first V.C. since 1935. Number 2614910, Lance-Jack Harry Nicholls. He boxed for the Battalion. Heavy Weight Imperial Service Champion. May 1940, he was wounded in the arm by shrapnel. But he led his section on. Over the ridge they go, the whole company. Do you hear this? And then, biffity-bif! The Jerries open up with heavy machine guns, at pea-shooter range. So what does old Harry do? He gets hold of a buckshee Bren, he does, and he rushes forward firing from the hip. From the hip he fires. He gives one machine gun a burst, and he wipes it out. Then he gives another one a burst, and silences it. They filled Harry full of lead. But he went up to a higher bit of ground so he could get a good look at practically the whole of the Nazi infantry. And he shoves in another magazine, and lets the Jerries have it. He killed about a hundred of 'em. But he didn't stop firing till he had no more rounds left. It is the truth, as sure as there's a God in heaven, kids—my old pal Harry Nicholls held back the whole German army single-handed, and got his company safe across the River Scheldt, though he was filled so full of bullets that there wasn't room in him for any more and he was walking in a great splashing pool of red blood. What happened to him then? He was dead. He must have been dead for half an hour. But the soul of that man was such that he couldn't stop firing until he hadn't a round left to fire with. So the company gets over the Scheldt, by crackey, and poor old Harry was left behind. Dead, says you. Dead, says they. Dead says all of us, and the King gives his widder a V.C. on his behalf. And then what news comes through? Why, Harry Nicholls wasn't dead at all. You can't kill a Grenadier. I'm telling you, you can't. Nicholls is alive, in a German hospital, getting over all them wounds. And God help Jerry when Harry Nicholls gets better again! He'll come smashing out, he will, he'll come crashing out of that heap like a fire engine out of a shed, and he'll be back. My old pal Harry."

"Your old pal nothing!" says Geordie. "You never met him."

"Say that again!" cries the Grenadier.

"You 'eard," says Geordie. "How *could* you of met him?"

"Never you mind how I could or could not have met my old pal Nicholls," says the Grenadier. "My old pal Harry was the first V.C. of this war, and that's all there is to be said about it."

Geordie says a naughty word, laughs heartily, and says: "A Coldstreamer was the first V.C. of all. A chap called Strong. Crimea. Shell comes over and drops in among a mob of our boys. All right, laugh. A shell, I tell you. A sort of holler iron ball, crammed with gunpowder, and fizzling with a fuse. Like a firework. Only dangerous. This thing comes plonk at their feet. It's due to go off in a split second. It's too big to run away from, and too heavy to lob back over the parapet. So Strong, a Coldstreamer, picks up this shell, and hugs it to him, and runs and runs and runs, gets to the parapet and tosses the shell over, just as it bursts."

"He wasn't the first V.C.," says the Scot, and the argument that follows may be heard a hundred yards away through all the noises of the Camp.

Then somebody says: "What d'you mean, 'first V.C. since 1935?' There wasn't a war on in 1935."

"Get out of it," says the long Grenadier. "There's always a war on There's always something, anyway. Up on the Indian frontier, there's raids, and there's all manner of skirmishes all the time. Nobody hears anything about 'em. But there are. And I tell you that medals get won every day, war or no war."

"You're a liar," says Geordie. "I don't believe a word you say. You and your Harry Nicholls. Don't make me laugh."

"I tell you it's true."

"Was you there?"

"No, I admit that I wasn't exactly there."

"Then how d'you know?"

"Why, you ignorant ——, you, it's history! Do you think they give V.C.'s away for nothing?"

"I don't know! Why, you lousy Billy Brown, I've earned the V.C. a thousand times."

Roars of laughter.

Geordie shouts: "I have! Thousands of times. And what did I ever get? Damn all is what I got. I don't believe anything about anything. If you ain't seen it with your own eyes, you don't know it's true."

"Dinnot talk rubbish," says the Scot, sourly; and says no more.

"Ever see a conjuring trick?" asks the Grenadier. "I once saw a man cutting a woman in half. All right. I saw it. So was it real? Was that man really sawing that woman in two?"

"Well, not properly, not thoroughly," says Geordie, evasively.

"Then how can you believe what you see?"

"I don't believe nothing!" cries Geordie.

"Look," says the Grenadier. "You can be mistaken. But if a thing *actually happens* to a lot of people at once, it's *true*."

Geordie replies: "A lot of people all at once see that man sawing a woman in half."

"That didn't actually happen. They was made to think it was happening."

"Same thing," says Geordie.

"Why, you obstinate swine, you swining obstinate pig! Don't you dare to fly in the face of History. You drunken slob! Didn't you once tell me with your own two lips, you dirty liar, that you'd seen a ghost outside the Y.M.C.A. one night?"

"And so I damn well did," says Geordie.

"You're a one to talk, then, about not believing in anything. That's what *you* are: I fluff you, all right. Truth, scientific fact like a V.C., honest scientific fact like my old pal Harry, you don't believe. But ghosts, oh yes! You fairy!"

"That was no joke," says Geordie. "It was sober truth as true as I sit in this chair. God strike me down dead this minute if I didn't see it.

Outside the Y.M.C.A., I tell you. And it wasn't nighttime, but broad staring damnation daylight. I was going along that road, and coming the other way there was a bloke covered wi' dust from head to foot, and walking as if he had sore feet. I takes a look at him, and I see he's got a funny sort of a uniform on. Red coat, knee breeches, and a long sort of cardboard hat. So I thought he was one of these so-called Czechs, but he comes up to me and says: 'Comrade, have you heard the news?' So I thinks he's one of these Communists, and I say: 'No, Comrade, I ain't. What news?' And he says: 'Napoleon is back,' he says, 'and I've got to rejoin my regiment.' And I says: 'Are you trying to take the mike out of me? Or are you just potty? Or what are you?' Then he looks at me, and shakes his head slowly, and with my own eyes I saw him sort of get thinner, thin-drawn-out, kind of smoky. And then he wasn't there any more."

"It could have been a dream," says the Barman. Geordie glares at him, and growls: "It was no more of a dream than you are, you squirt! Why ain't you in uniform, anyway, you . . ."

The Grenadier, who has been smiling on one side of his face, says:

"You and your dreams. To you, Geordie, dreams are real. Well, look. Look at this and tell me if I lie about Nicholls. Look." And from a deep pocket of his S.D. Jacket, the tall man takes a bit of newsprint, creased almost to nothingness, but religiously preserved between two bits of cardboard. It is a copy of the London *Gazette,* dated Tuesday, 30th July, 1940.

"Look," he says. "No. 2614910 Lance-Corporal Harry Nicholls, Grenadier Guards. And there's the story. Dead true."

"Then why didn't you pull out that bit o' paper in the first place?" asks Geordie.

"Because you ought to take my word for it."

"Anyway," says Geordie, "I knew it was true, because I see it in the papers at the time; and I believe I saw this kid Nicholls box, once."

"Well then, what did you say you didn't believe me for, then?" asks the Grenadier, angrily.

"Just for the sake of a argument," says Geordie. "What's a V.C., anyway?"

"A honour," says the tailor.

"Point is," says Geordie, "there comes a point where you got to go forrard or get kilt. You take a last chance, and fight mad. If it comes off, you're a hero. If it don't, you're a corpse."

"That depends," says the Grenadier. "I've seen plenty men surrender, Jerries, in the last bust-up. I've seen plenty of 'em raise their hands and shout for mercy. They're like that when cornered, though they're cocky enough when things are going their way. But I never saw one of our mob doing any surrendering. Did you, Geordie?"

"No, never."

"It's a matter of temperament," says the Grenadier. "Some people are made one way, others another way. Englishmen hate to look silly. So they go and die rather than make a laughingstock of themselves. Anything for the sake of proper order! I've seen a man crawl out over, good God, a bit of No Man's Land that was a death trap where a man stood no more chance than a fly in a gearbox—go out under machine-gun fire, and shrapnel, good God Almighty, with the Jerries limbering up a flammenwerfer, a flame-thrower. He crawled out when the odds must have been say two or three hundred to one against him getting back at all, and thousands to one against him getting back unhurt. He went to pick up a bloke with a busted hip lying out in the open. Now as things were just then, it was about a million to one against any of us getting out alive, because there was only nine or ten of us, and Jerry was advancing under a curtain of heavy stuff, and we was cut off and hopeless to look at. But this bloke goes out to get this wounded man, who wasn't even a china, not even a pal in particular. He couldn't help it. It was in him to do it. Once an Englishman, always an Englishman. Medals don't make any difference. You don't go and get a V.C. because you think it'd look nice pinned on your coat, or because there's some twopenny-halfpenny little pension attached to it. You aren't a hero on account of a medal."

"A medal encourages you," says Geordie.

"Don't you believe it," says the Grenadier. "A medal is a bit of tin. A *medal* don't encourage you. I've seen Italian colonels covered from head to foot with crosses, and stars, and bits, and pieces, and medals of every possible variety and shape and size. And they ran like rabbits. No. It's the *act* that is the encouragement. A bloke like my old pal Harry Nicholls, now, what's a bit of a bronze cross to him? Or to anybody? But when kids get to hear about him, when they read stories about old Nicholls, they say to themselves: 'It'd look silly if after all that we went and let Nicholls down.'

"And again, look at my old pal, Lance-Sergeant Rhodes. He had a Lewis gun section. Well, so Rhodes sees the Jerries leave a pill-box. Our own barrage was coming over thick and strong. It was the good old death trap again. But Rhodes, after picking off Jerry after Jerry with the Lewis and with his good old bundook, went out single-handed, with machine-gun fire right on him, and the shells bursting right in his face; and God only knows how he done it, but he took that pill-box, single-handed, he did, and brought back nine Jerry prisoners. All alone he did it. They give him a V.C. for that."

A dark and excitable old soldier with a brass leek in his cap says:

"And what about my friend, look, Bob Bye, a Glamorgan boy, look! Did he not do all that and more? With these eyes I saw him do it. He took two German blockhouses, *two,* that is! First of all, look, he rushes one blockhouse and kills the whole lot of the garrison, all alone. Then he takes the second one with his company. Then a party was detailed to clear up a line of blockhouses which had been passed, see. Bob Bye volunteers to take charge. He cleans them all up. He takes a third objective. That is a man, he was! A Glamorgan boy, from Penrhiwceiber. Like me."

The Scot says, with a grim air of acrimony:

"Did you hear of Freddie McNess, in 'sixteen? He was wounded so that his neck and jaw were pretty well blown away, while organising a counterattack. But he went through a bomb-barrage alone, to bring us fresh supplies of bombs; wounded and alone. He kept us going, shouting and swearing and cursing and laughing, throwing bomb after bomb like a mad machine. And then he fell down with hardly a drop of blood left within him. Hum. V.C."

"Tom Witham did pretty much the same," says Geordie. "A Burnley boy. Coldstream Guards, 1917. V.C."

"And Johnnie Moyney?" says a giant Mick, an Irish Guardsman with a stiff leg, and a shrapnel-pocked cheek. "Old Johnnie Moyney. Didn't he hold the post with us for ninety-six solid hours without water and with no food? And on the fifth day didn't he take us out and give Jerry hell with the Lewis and Mills bombs; and cut a way back for us; and cover our retirement, and bring every last damned one of us safely back? There was a V.C. for you, a real V.C.! I wonder what happened to Johnnie Moyney . . ."

"I daresay the same as what happened to Olly Brooks of the Third Battalion," says Geordie. "Blown to hell and back at Loos in 'fifteen; recaptured two hundred yards o' trench: feared nothing. I daresay he's one of two things. Alive, or else dead. V.C.s. Oh, *phut!* Some are noticed, others aren't. Some get V.C.s. Others get headaches. It's all the same in the end. Have another beer. Hi, you, you twit! Pour these out agen. To hell with the bits o' tin and brass! Medals! I saved an officer's life once, and ought to have got a V.C. for it. Near Loos. I lifted up a burning car that he was pinned under with these two mitts, I did. I was as strong as a bullock then, and still arm, too! I lifted up that car by the front axles, and it was blazing like a busted lamp, flaring like crackey. I turned that car over. Sandow couldn't have done it. I felt sort of strong, with all the shells bursting round me and the little bits o' red-hot shrapnel yipping and wheeing in my ears. Yes. I saved that officer's life. But he was dead. So nobody knew about it, and I didn't get no medal. Waste o' time."

"Did you know he was dead?" asks the Grenadier.

"How could I have known, you stupid? Would I have gone to all that trouble and burnt the skin off of myself for a corpse? I kind of suspected that he might be dead, mind you, but I thought I'd give him the benefit of the doubt. And much good it done him or me."

"Ah," says the Grenadier. "If I could have my time over again!"

"What'd you do?"

The Grenadier has not the faintest idea. He covers his confusion by picking on a young recruit who has edged into the alcove and is lighting a cigarette. "You," he says, "what do you mean by coming here and eavesdropping on our conversation?"

"I wasn't eavesdropping, I was just listening."

"Oh, you were. What's your name?"

"Dobbin."

"How old are you?"

"Nineteen."

"Where are you from?"

"Luton."

"What work you do in Luton?"

"Nothing."

"Do all right at it?"

"How d'you mean?"

"Didn't you have a trade?"

"No."

"Like the Army?"

"No."

"It's the greatest life in the world, son."

"Yes?" says Dobbin, with a grin. "It don't seem to have got *you* anywhere."

"Shall I scoff this little nit?" asks Geordie.

"Let him alone," says the Grenadier. "It's not for you to say, Dobbin, where anything has got us. It's not any man's place to say. Do you hear? We've been in the Guards all our lives, and we might grouse and grumble day and night, but we're proud of it. You see us now, son, getting on a bit in years. As the Dagoes put it, our roads are nearing the sea. But there's more to a thing than you see in one second, at one time. You

bear that in mind, Dobbin. You might see an empty brass cartridge case
lying on the ground, and you might kick it aside without a word. Yet
that cartridge case might be the one thing that won the War. Yes. You
might see an old rusty nail lying around, and throw it away. But there
was a time when that nail was bright and sharp, and for all you know
to the contrary, that nail might have been the thing that held the very
roof up over your head, in its time. If you saw us rolling about in Rolls
Royce cars, I daresay you'd think we really had got somewhere, wouldn't
you? When you've knocked around as long as we have, you'll know
that everybody goes the same way to the same place in the end. A
shilling blanket or an oak box with brass handles: there's only one way
for any man to go, Dobbin. What a man has got, doesn't matter. *What
a man has done, and what he's stood or fallen for, that's what matters.*
That's where he's got. There was a City man that made millions out
of swindling. On the Tuesday, you would have said he'd got to the top
of the world. But on the Wednesday he blew his head off and the whole
town knew him for an empty crook. Where had he got? Really and
truly? Nowhere. *Never* anywhere. Us, we've got nothing. We've got our
pay and our grub, and not too much of either. But we were keeping you
and your mum safe in your beds when you were too little to walk, and
keeping this country all clear for you to grow up and do nothing in.
Where have we got? Into the Guards, and into a bit of history. That's
something, if there was nothing else, Dobbin. We held our lines, by
Jesus, and we came out fighting and we managed to get through. We've
been hurt. Nothing can hurt us much any more. No, the rain can't wet
us, the cold can't freeze us, the wind can't shake us, and the sun can't
burn us. There's no man, or beast, or nightmare, or bluff that can throw
a scare into us. There's no force that can put us off a thing once we go
towards that thing. Not even a lump of iron through the head can
stop us, because we are the ones that hand on the stuff that makes us go.
Put us in a desert, and we can make ourselves at home. Put us in a hole
full of mud, and we'll still keep calm and play the man. We've got no
homes. A plank is comfort to us. A bit of meat is luxury. If we ever

had any folks, we just lost 'em. The hut is our house. Our feet feel funny out of ammunition boots. We've known what it feels like to come face to face with a day or a night that must be the last . . . only somehow we came through, and saw the dark, or the daylight, and laughed it off whatever we felt. We've had our share of troubles. We can take an injustice and swallow it. We grouse, but never whine. We yell before we're hurt; but never because we're hurt. We'd lie for a pal, but not for ourselves. We break all the laws except the important ones. We can lie doggo under destiny like Arabs, but we never give way to it or anything else. We don't believe in anything except that we've *got* to be on parade when the bugle blows, whatever the parade is, and wherever it is. And we like to keep ourselves clean, and don't do too many dirty tricks. Where has it got us? Son—didn't anybody ever tell you? Manhood! That is what it's got us. We may be a bit dilapidated, but we're men! Isn't that something?"

A heavy old voice says: "Well said, my boy."

It is Old Charlie.

Although he is neatly dressed in a blue tunic and trousers; although his boots have upon them a dye, or shine, such as only years can impart; and although he has an air of smartness, a dapper alertness, a prim elegance such as only Guardsmen acquire—turned out, though he is, with a calculated neatness, he somehow looks as ragged as a battle-tattered banner. There is that about him which suggests that he is death-less. He looks as if he might be some trophy over which nations have fought. Perhaps he is. He is one of the oldest of all the Coldstream Guards.

His forehead is something against which Time has sharpened its scythe: it is scored and creased and wrinkled beyond the aspect of flesh. Some strange fatality has saved him, throughout incalculable years, for some unknown destiny. He was born in 1860. Charles Dickens was a man-about-town when he was a boy. Once upon a time he was a child, and then he was devoted body and soul to an elder brother whose name —what a pig this Time is, that snuffles up everything!—he has almost forgotten. This brother, with the Foot Guards, went to a place called Russia on some fool's errand and came back with one leg and a thousand tales. Where is this brother? The worms know. But it was out of hero worship for him that this old man joined the Guards, the Coldstream Guards. There was, in his mind, some bluish picture of smoke—some strange blurred scene—a haze, in the midst of which men in red struggled hand-to-hand with men in grey: some adolescent fantasy of Inkerman, where the Guards fought tooth and nail and, turning their muskets round, banged down the soldiers of the Czar with the butt of Brown Bess. He should be dead. He belongs to another day and age. His father remembered Waterloo. He can tell awful stories. Geordie has seen him looking at a short Lee Enfield rifle and shaking his head—it seemed to him such a small thing, with such a small hole in it. How could so petty a weapon stop a man? In spite of everything, years or no years, he stands erect. Nothing but putrefaction will bend that back. He is rigid with the uprightness of sixty years of service. The last time a sergeant told him to hold his head up was in 1881. He was an old soldier before the Boer War. His age had reached two figures—about ten years—when his mother, with a look of vexation, said: "This Napoleon." She was referring to Napoleon the Third.

They call him Old Charlie. It is impossible for him to appear without some outbreak of badinage. Even Geordie says: "Where's your bow and arrow?" There is a legend that he was put In The Book for having a dirty powder horn at the Hougoumont Farmhouse. Apart from the fact of his long service, his antecedents are wrapped in darkness. He never had a home. If he ever had a wife or children, nobody ever heard about them. He is a legendary figure, like the old horse that still survives in the depot at Caterham—the slow, stately regimental horse, which represents nothing but a half-forgotten sentiment. He says little. The oldest have borne most. He knows it. He carries the weight of years and memory. None of us will ever live so long. Age has worn his cheeks into little pits and nodules: he is a monolith. Geordie is an old soldier, but Old Charlie might have had a son older than Geordie. "You may be young," he seems to say, "but you never saw 1860. Live as long as you like, you never will have seen 1860."

Sometimes he comes into the little bar; says nothing, drinks nothing, does nothing—simply looks about him with an expression curiously compounded of bewilderment and ineffable dignity. It is then that the nonsense starts; not that there's any man in the place who would not defend Old Charlie with his life.

There is only one person to whom he talks. This is a little girl whom men call Star. She is the daughter of some old sergeant who lives beyond the camp. They call her Star because her mother, drenched in regimental matters, has embroidered the eight-pointed star of the Brigade upon the grubby yellow jersey which she invariably wears. She is a naughty little girl, sullen and intractable. Her face is fixed in a forbidding scowl. She got that from her father, a savage old N.C.O. She is not like other little girls. She is not interested in childish things; nor has she any of that budding womanliness which is common and proper to little girls. I believe that her real name is Jess, or Tess—anyway, it ends in "ess." She likes soldiers, but in no flippant or flirtatious way. She likes to contemplate them. When the long brown lines go out in column of route, she may always be seen standing still as a graven image by the roadside; not cheering, giving no sign of recognition—merely gravely watching. Her lower lip protrudes; her upper lip is compressed. Her brow is corrugated; there is a ferocious look in her small dark eyes. This is a peculiar little girl. Nothing can melt her. If you offer her coins or sweets she takes them gloomily and thanklessly. She seems to be full of trouble. She plays only one game, and that seems to have no meaning. She walks up and down dragging after her a peeled branch of silver birch—saying nothing, and never smiling; simply dragging the branch. Her mother says that she is eight years old, and will grow out of it. It is alleged that she takes after her father—a man whom nobody loved, nobody understood, and nobody wanted to understand.

She has one boy-friend. This is Old Charlie.

They have assignations. They meet, by a kind of instinctive arrangement. At about a quarter past one every afternoon the little girl Tess, or Jess, walks gravely past the Guardroom and walks, as it were accidentally, up and down the road outside the Sergeants' Mess. She is self-possessed, preoccupied and rather sombre. She never ceases to frown —in fact the habit of this facial contortion has already cut two tiny lines between her eyes. She walks swinging her arms, her small fists clenched. At other times she might drag her branch; but never at one-fifteen. She walks up and down. In due course, out of the Officers' Mess where he is employed in some not to laborious capacity, Old Charlie comes striding, dressed all in blue. The mystery of it is, that in all those years—all those years—awful, monotonous years of military service —he has never managed to acquire even two stripes. Lance-Corporals of the Coldstream Guards always wear two stripes: (it looks, somehow, better) old as the hills, he is less than a Lance-Jack. Was he stupid? It seems hardly likely. Was he a bad man? A bad soldier? One would say not. The fact remains that he is ending as he began, having got nothing in the service but age, which any man can get anywhere if he lives long enough. He walks solemnly and pauses just by the Catholic Church —a cold old man with moustachios like icicles, disciplined and aged beyond ordinary humanity. The little girl walks to within four or five paces of him, and then she stops, boring the toe of her right shoe into the gravel. She has all the appearance of one upon whose shoulders rests the weight of the universe. She looks almost as old and almost as responsible as Old Charlie. She pretends not to have seen him. He pretends not to have seen her. His huge right hand, which resembles a bunch of red West Indian bananas, slowly opens: he always carries his pipe in his hand, for fear that the bulk of it may spoil the outline of his skin-tight blue mess suit. From a trousers pocket he produces a match; strikes it, lights the pipe, spits once and lets a big blue cloud crawl up to heaven while he contemplates, with God knows what strange sad thoughts, the bare and hideous Guardroom, the White Huts, and the hidden distance which ends in the trees beyond the cricket field.

This never varies. His forefinger, indestructible as asbestos, tamps down the glowing ash in his pipe. Holding this pipe in his right hand, while his left arm hangs straight down; slightly inclining his head in deep thought, he walks up to the Guardroom and stands still.

The little girl watches him out of the corners of her eyes. Then she follows him, walking exactly as he walks—in long, stiff strides. They pass each other three or four times. The ancient one pauses and his tangled white eyebrows come down in a savage and forbidding scowl. His poor old washed-out eyes, which might be blue or grey or green, fix themselves upon the little girl in a glare which is meant to be terrifying, but which, alas, is nearly vacant. She in her turn, glares back at him and in her glance there is something oddly lonely. They confront each other: the child, dark with the clouds of sorrows which nobody will ever understand; and the old man, inarticulate and encumbered with an awful weight of half-remembered things.

He clamps the teeth the Army gave him down upon the yellowish stem of his burned-out pipe and holds it unsteadily between his wavering jaws. Then he shoots out his right fist clenched tight, and slowly peels away from it one finger—the fourth. The little girl looks at it, frowning, and then grabs this extended finger in her left hand. No word is spoken. They walk off together. It is believed that neither of them has another friend in the world. Old Charlie has outlived everything and everybody; and Jess (?) or Tess (?) seems to feel that she is going to have much to live through.

A meeting of the currents of Life and Time. They walk away, past the Officers' Mess, past the Pioneers' Yard, to the Y.M.C.A., and then back.

And it happens that only I have heard what they say to each other.

Near the nice new huts of the Scots Guards, between the road and the canal, lies a strip of woodland, mostly silver birch. From here they cut twigs to make revetting hurdles. Men go in with slash hooks, and come out with great armfuls of slender and elegant budding branches; yet, the woodland remains dense and almost primæval. We come here sometimes in field training: there are dents and gashes in this strip of earth which present all the varying features of potential cover. From the road it looks like . . . merely trees, but if you go in among these trees, you lose sight of the road . . . the dark grey dreary road . . . and find yourself under a pattern of foliage which waves gently and mysteriously, and among slim, straight, speckled silver trees which stand between you and the world. Men come here sometimes on Sundays or on Saturday afternoons, when they want to be alone. There is a time when every man wants to be alone, for a little while, among trees.

It was Saturday afternoon. I was lying there and looking up. In the distance rubber tyres purred over tarmac; and some bird, some high-flying bird with a voice of ineffable sweetness sang a song in four notes. The branches moved. In that moment I forgot all the grandeur and misery of the war and the world, and almost fell asleep. I heard them coming, but the sound of their feet seemed to come from far away and hardly penetrated the gentle coma into which I had fallen. I saw them —the very old man and the very young child, both scowling, she clasping the little finger of his right hand in a determined left fist. This must have been a place to which they often came. They walked straight to it and sat down upon a patch of grass between two banks of bracken. I could not see the little girl: she was too small, and the fronds hid her. But the stiff blue back of that impenetrable old soldier stood up sturdily, conspicuous against its background of green. He took off his cap. I don't know why I was surprised to see that he had no hair.

He spoke:

"Woman. Look. Trees. Do you like trees, woman?"

No doubt the child nodded; she said nothing.

"Listen."

The birds still sang.

"Do you like birds?"

Silence. She must have nodded again, for he went on:

"I like birds too. Birds are nice things. Wherever you go you find birds. Anywhere you like, there is always birds. Go to Africa—right out into the desert, where there is nothing at all; and there are still birds. Out on the veldt: you look, and you see nothing. But fall down, just you fall down. And what will you see then? Why, woman, right up, right up in the sky, as it might be a speck, a tiny little speck, you'll see something coming down. What is it, what is it coming down out of that empty sky right down on to that empty land?"

The little girl said "God."

The old man said: "Vultures. A kind of a bird. They wait, hanging up in the sky so high that you can't see them, but all the time they're watching you, watching you all the time. And when they see you fall, or if they see you die, they drop. They don't fly down. They wrap themselves up in their wings and fall like stones, and then, two or three hundred yards off the ground they spread their wings out all of a sudden as it might be, great big flowers opening, and you hear them go slap! Yes, slap! And they slide down, and they stand round you, wrapped up in them wings of theirs, like cloaks, and they wait."

"What for?" she asked.

"They wait for you to die."

"Why?"

"So as to eat you."

"Not till you're dead?"

"No."

"Ah."

Silence again. Then the little girl said: "What are they for?"

The old man replied: "To clean up. You can't have things lying around all over the place. They clean things up. They are . . ." he paused and then said, "on fatigue. They get a wilderness dug out. If it wasn't for them horrible birds the desert would stink. Because everything is dying all the time. Yes, in them hot places it is easy to live. If you put your walking stick into the ground, roses would come out of it. And if it is easy for one thing to live, it is easy for another thing to live; and it is easy for you to get along, and also for your enemy likewise. Yes, woman, the easier it is to live, the easier it is to die. But woman, you look at me. I'm ten times older than you are, and I'm alive. I'm eighty."

"Eighty's not much," she said.

He went on rather dreamily: "I see every day fellas fretting—fretting like prisoners behind bars—at being in this Army. But woman, do I say to them: 'Young fella, I have been in this Army over sixty year'? No I don't. I don't say nothing. Woman, I don't talk to 'em. I ain't got nothing to say, woman. Why? Because talking makes no difference. Talking makes no difference. Talking never helped anybody nor never will. There is nothing to be said woman, nothing. Sometimes I think that in the Army the first thirty years is the worst but woman, when I think again I don't know. Everything is rotten while you're going through it, and everything is lovely when you look back on it. I don't know woman, and I don't care. I'm old. But I will see 'em damned before I die. I ain't going to die."

He said this almost to himself. Then he seemed to remember something, and his tone changed. He said: "You like me, don't you? And I like you. I think you're a nice little girl. You like holding on to my finger don't you?"

She made a noncommittal noise: "Mm."

"If I had anything to give you, I'd give it to you. But I ain't got anything. No, after all these years I got nothing to show. But does that matter? You take it from me woman, having something to show don't matter. Show yourself to yourself, at the end of everything, and if you can pat yourself on the back and shake hands with yourself and like yourself—like yourself like you might like a stranger—well, that's all right. I've seen rough times. I've had field punishment. I've seen wars. Yes, woman, I've drunk my medicine. When they lay me out, there'll be some marks for them to see. But that don't matter. I was saying, if I had anything to give, I'd give it to you, or to your mum to hold for you. I had a matter of a hundred and eighty-two pounds that I saved up. But I ain't got it any more. I give it away. Tell me, woman, am I crazy?"

Her voice said very firmly: "Yes."

"Yes, says you, yes says everybody. So I don't talk. A certain party comes to me and says: 'Charlie, I've got to find a five-pound note.' So I thinks. 'A five-pound note,' I says. 'All right,' I says, 'I will give you a five-pound note.' So I draws out a five-pound note to give him. And then I says: 'What do you want with the dirty money? What have you saved it for?' And I draws it all out, and I gives it away. I gives it to charity. Never mind what. It makes no difference, I give it away, woman, and I felt the better for being without it. I'm a soldier, see? And I travels light.

"There's a young fella they calls Bearsbreath. A sort of a lance-corporal. A kid, a little kid, a kid of no more than thirty-six or seven. And yet, woman, I see that kid Bearsbreath, with these two eyes I see him give away everything he ever had. And do you know what it was? A belt. Do you understand?"

" 'Course I understand."

" 'Course you understand. You're a woman of the world and I'm a man of the world, and I'm talking to yer, because you got savvy. Me, I joined the Army—do you know why? Because I idolised my brother. He was in this mob. He was at Inkerman. That was in the Crimean War. Why," said Old Charlie, with a kind of hushed amazement in his voice, "if he had lived Edward would be ninety-five. But he's dead. Everybody's dead. That was a battle, Inkerman, woman. The Coldstream Guards come over, and when their guns was empty they picked up stones off the field and beat the Russians' 'eads in with 'em. Yes, we took that position with sticks and stones, that's what we did. And we'd do it again, woman, we'd do it again, sticks, stones, boots, or just bare fists.

"But this kid Bearsbreath. What was I saying? Oh yes, his belt. Young Bearsbreath has been in this mob all his life, practically. He was a Barnado's Boy. Do you understand what that is, woman? He didn't 'ave nobody. He didn't 'ave no mum, he didn't 'ave nothing. I believe they found him in a basket outside a door. Soon as he was old enough

he went into the Army. Guards. Coalies. Got 'im nowhere. Regular
old sweat like me. Never had nothing and never will 'ave nothing.
Except what? Don't laugh, a belt. Dirty old leather belt. You understand, woman? 'Course you understand. An old soldier has a belt.
Wherever he goes and makes a friend he gets a badge. He swaps
badges, with whatever pal he might make in another regiment. And
he fixed this here badge on to his belt. Time comes when his belt is
covered with badges, and that is a very nice pretty thing. This here
young fool of a Bearsbreath, he had a belt.

"Hah! Well, so there was a kid in the drums. Ginger kid. I don't
know his name but they called him Ginger. One day, so there's a re-
hearsal for a pantomime or a concert, or something. Somebody or
other says: 'What's the dateth today?' and somebody else says: 'The
dateth today is the nineteenth.' This kid Ginger—you wouldn't cry,
would you, woman?—this kid Ginger busts out crying. Well, young
Bearsbreath says to young Ginger: 'What's the trouble?' and young
Ginger says: 'Nuffink.' This kid Ginger was a good drummer. It was
a pleasure to hear him blow Defaulters. This kid Ginger says: 'Nuffink'
and this kid Bearsbreath says to 'im: 'Somebody been bullying you,
Ginger?' and Ginger says: 'No.' Then Bearsbreath says: 'Why did you
bust out crying when they told you the dateth?' and this kid Ginger
says: 'I wasn't crying.' 'I should bloody well think not,' says Bearsbreath.
'A big boy like you. 'Ow old are you?' And this kid Ginger says:
'Sixteen.' 'Oh,' says Bearsbreath, 'you're a big boy for your size, and
when was yer sixteen?' This kid Ginger says: 'I'm sixteen today.'
'Why,' says Bearsbreath, 'what's that to cry about. You ought to be
laughing. You should be thankful you're alive, or something. Gord
blimey,' says Bearsbreath, 'whether you're thankful or sorry, God damn
and blast it all, you should be ashamed of yourself for crying. Are you
a man or are you a woman?' 'I'm a man,' says Ginger. 'No you're
not,' says Bearsbreath, 'you're not a man, crying like that! Why,' he
says, 'what's the matter with you? Did you want your mummy to come
and wish you many happy returns or something?' The kid Ginger

says: 'I ain't got no mum.' 'Oh,' says Bearsbreath, 'you ain't got no mum. And I suppose next thing you'll tell me is that you ain't got no dad.' 'Well, what if I ain't,' says Ginger. 'Ain't you?' says Bearsbreath, and Ginger says: 'Well, no, I ain't.' 'Brothers, sisters, uncles, aunts?' says Bearsbreath. 'No,' says Ginger. 'Oh,' says Bearsbreath. 'A sort of orphan.' Then Ginger says: 'Sort of.' 'Well,' says Bearsbreath, 'then you ought to be ashamed of yourself,' and he walks out. Well, about five minutes later he comes back into the hut with four tuppeny bars of chocolate, and he gives them to this kid Ginger and he says: 'Oh well, many 'appy returns,' and hands these bars of chocolate to young Ginger, and Ginger says: 'Thanks.' "

"Nut-milk chocolate?"

"Yuh—that's right, nut-milk chocolate. And then Bearsbreath sort of stands on his two legs wide apart, and he says: 'I'm surprised at you. You and your birthdays. Blimey,' he says, 'what's the younger genera-tion coming to. Personally,' he says: 'I never had a birthday in me life,' he says. 'Only sissies have birthdays. Only effiminate young women 'ave birthdays. Why,' he says, 'personally, I'd be ashamed to own to 'aving a birthday,' he said. 'So,' he says, 'you ain't got no mum and no dad and you ain't got nobody, and you go around 'aving birthdays, do you? All right, young fella,' he says, and this kid Bearsbreath shoves his hands under this here rubbish, this sloppy stuff they call battle-dress, and takes off his belt. Bearsbreath was proud of this belt. It was a good bit of cowhide with a big brass buckle, and this kid Bearsbreath had stuck on to it eleven or twelve regimental badges of all sorts, and in particular a silver stag's head of the Seaforth Highlanders, and a Scots Guards warrant officer's starred cross in some sort of silver metal. He was proud of that belt, because in a way, apart from a sort of a stiffness in the back and a sort of way of walking, this belt was all that young Bearsbreath had to show for about twenty years in the Guards, woman, twenty lousy years. Bearsbreath takes off this belt, and I thought for the moment that he was going to give Ginger a lamming with it. (In case you want to know, a belt of that sort is very handy if it comes

to a roughhouse.) Bearsbreath drops this belt into this kid Ginger's lap
and says: 'Here you are, you little crybaby. Here's a birthday present
for you,' and walks out. Young Ginger sat there sort of staring, and a
couple of other drummers who had been pulling his leg about him
piping his eye stood around and sort of went green with envy, and
somebody says: 'God blimey, I wonder what come over old Bearsbreath,' because, you understand, woman, that that belt was much more
than money to a man like Bearsbreath. Dammit, woman, that was his
Army life. That was bits and pieces. That was all he had to show.
That was all he'd ever have to show. A Lance-Jack, good for nothing
but the lousy Army . . . but that belt, well, that belt was something.

"Me, I only gave away a bit of money. That was nothing. Money's
nothing."

"Have you got a belt?"

"Yes, I've got a belt."

"Can I see it?"

"Yes, but you mustn't touch it."

"I won't touch it."

"Honour bright?"

"Honour bright."

I heard the snick of a buckle, and a little scream of admiration.

"Isn't it lovely."

"Yuh, isn't it? There's badges on that belt that you'll never see the
like of again. Do you see that one there? That dates back to 1855, and
that's pretty nigh a hundred years ago. There's twenty-two badges on
that belt, woman, and every one of them badges belonged to a good
comrade of mine, a good friend. And every one of them men is dead
and that's all there is to show, so what do you think of that, woman?"

A silence.

Beyond the frail branches of the silver birch trees, the bird still sang.
The ancient soldier had risen to his feet and was putting on his cap.
I could see the little girl now, for she had risen too. Her forehead was

smooth. Her eyes were clear and wide open and the frown was gone from over them. For a moment they looked at each other.

"Your belt," she said.

The old man said: "Keep it."

He stuck out his little finger and she clutched it, and then they walked away.

EPILOGUE

Nelson on Death

PIRBRIGHT VILLAGE: the pub called "Fat Fan's." Once upon a time the "White Hart" was owned by a plump lady. The wife of the present landlord is slender; but in the Army, tradition dies hard. Go to the Brigade Naffy in Pirbright Camp any day at noon, and you will see a little knot of old, old soldiers in the wet canteen, drinking a species of ale so weak that it falls flat as soon as it is poured out. The most ancient of these warriors is a Coldstreamer of about thirty-five years' service—a veteran of every military vicissitude, old as the hills and as indestructible; wise as Gideon, in battle, though not so wise out of it; huge, uproarious, heavy-jawed and voracious; a drain through which half the beer in England has passed; a graveyard of Naffy pies; a dictionary of strange language; a mine of information about the other ranks. He has been in Pirbright since time immemorial, but has never heard of the "White Hart." But "Fat Fan's"—oh, *he* knows "Fat Fan's." Let outsiders call the place the "White Hart." Coldstreamers and Scots Guards in every square of Mercator's Projection know the place as "Fat Fan's"; and "Fat Fan's" it will be for ever.

I say: Pirbright Village; the pub called "Fat Fan's."

The carriage trade gets there now. Captain Hobdey, who took the place, dug down through strata of wallpaper and found, like a gem in a Christmas cracker, an ancient inn. Bits of the "White Hart" thus discovered strike old soldiers as new-fangled. The seventeenth century is all very well, but it is nothing like the good old days. Nevertheless, they drink there, because it is "Fat Fan's." If a cataclysm washed the

178

place out, the naked site would still bear the name . . . Fan's, Good Old Fan's, Old Fat Fan's. There is nothing to be done about it.

Sergeant Nelson is down on a visit. He was entitled to seven days' leave. He had nine pounds in credit, and has drawn the money. Beyond the Army, that one-eyed hero would be lonely. It is true that he has a relation here and there; but nothing that you might describe as a family. To him, Sergeant Crowne's handclasp is the touch of a vanished hand, and the faded echoes of the Pirbright bugles the sound of a voice that is still. The Black Huts are home sweet home. The ranges are the lost horizons of sweet youth. "Fat Fan's" is a tender memory of the springtime of things. Time is a swine that snuffles up everything; but some things Time can never swallow.

You can imagine with what grimly-suppressed eagerness he made the roundabout journey. But he comes into "Fat Fan's" with perfect nonchalance. It might be his own mess. His heart bounds like a rabbit in a bag as he sees Crowne, Hands, and Dagwood, at the bar. But his face remains rigid. Only his eye celebrates. He says:

"Ah-ha, Crowney. Ah-ha, Hands. Yah, Dag. Drink?"

"Ole Lipstick," says Sergeant Crowne.

"Whattaya mean, Lipstick?" says Nelson. "Tcha gonna drink?"

"Mild," says Dagwood.

"Bitter," says Crowne.

"Brown," says Hands.

"Place changed hands? Lady! Two bitters, a mild and a brown. Big 'uns. Well?"

"Well?" says Crowne.

"Long time since we met," says Nelson.

"1937," says Hands.

"8," says Dagwood.

"7," says Hands.

"9," says Crowne.

"7," says Hands. "What d'you mean, 9, you Burke?"

"What year did war break out?" asks Crowne, patiently.

"I can tell you," says Hands. "It was the year Big Arthur threatened the Drill Sergeant with a bayonet."

"That was 8," says Dagwood.

"1938?" says Crowne. "You sure? Well, all right. 1938. Big Arthur threatened the Drill Pig in 8. The year the war broke out was the year I got a Severe for sort of 'itting a feller that 'it me first. I know, I got this Severe, and then the war broke out. Yeamp, I got it: the war must of broke out round about September, 1939. Ye-amp, it sort of broke out then."

"Definitely," says Nelson.

"So what's been happening since then?" asks Hands.

"Oh, nothing, nothing," says Nelson. "You?"

"Nothing," says Crowne. "Sort of squads you gettin'?"

"Oh, just squads," says Nelson. "I teach 'em: you skive with 'em."

"I unlearn 'em all you learn 'em, and then I learn 'em proper," says Crowne.

"*Phut!*" says Nelson.

Hands introduces a newcomer, a burly Sergeant with a blue scar on his nose: "Know Clark? Nobby, this is Nelson."

"Stameetcha," says Nelson.

"He was in the Foreign Legion," says Hands.

"Well, have a drink. Have a short one. So you were one of these Foreign Legionaries, were you? Was it like on the pictures?"

"The uniform was," says Sergeant Clark.

"There long?"

"Five years."

"How d'you come to join that mob?"

"I was a kid. I saw *Beau Geste* and got tight afterwards. When I come to, I'd joined the Foreign Legion."

"That's how I joined the Guards," says Nelson. "Well, was it all right?"

"All right."

"Tough?"

"I done tougher marches with our mob in Egypt."

"Well, well, so we meet again," says Sergeant Nelson.

"Um," says Crowne. "Well? Drink? Same again please miss. So what's goin' on, Nelson?"

"Browned off," says Nelson.

"'Angin' on to you," says Crowne. "Need instructors. Won't let you go. Yah?"

"Definitely hanging bloody on to me," says Nelson. "I'm browned off."

"Me too," says Hands.

"I'm thinking," says Dagwood, "of getting myself bust. Then I might get abroad."

"Me too," says Crowne.

"And me," says Nelson.

They have been talking like this for about seventeen years.

Nine-thirty.

Private lives have been discussed and disposed of in five minutes. Grievances have filled two hours. Reminiscence has scuttled in and out of everything; ubiquitous, irrepressible and unreliable as a pup. It all comes back to shop; soldiering. All roads lead to that.

"They'll do all right," says Nelson.

"Mmm-yeah, maybe," says Crowne. "Some of 'em are steady. But on the whole, they'll do. I 'ad some of your kids."

"What kids were they?" asks Nelson.

"They came in the autumn. Sort of October, round about."

"Oh yes. I remember. It was . . . no it wasn't. Was there a kid from a place called Brighton that worked his ticket on account of asthma?"

"No. There was a bloke called Thurstan that kept on getting into trouble."

"Glass House?" asks Nelson.

"No," says Crowne. "Went absent once. Came back. Went straight. Bit mental, but 'e come to 'is senses."

"Some people definitely do, and others definitely don't," says Nelson. "I remember the wallah you mean. I could see there was going to be trouble with that geezer. Definitely. So, he turned out all right, eh?"

"A nice kid," says Dagwood. "Well, anyway, not so bad."

"Wasn't there a po-tential officer they used to call The Schoolmaster?"

"Yes," says Dagwood. "A bookworm."

"Kay?"

"Yes," says Crowne. "Okay."

"When he left," says Dagwood, "he wrote a bit of poetry."

"What, made it up?" asks Nelson.

"Oh, I shouldn't be surprised." Dagwood rummages in a breast pocket and gets out a greasy little autograph album. "Look."

Looking over his shoulder, Nelson reads:

> *Here dead we lie because we did not choose*
> *To live and shame the land from which we sprung.*
> *Life, to be sure, is nothing much to lose,*
> *But young men think it is, and we were young.*

"Now there you are," says Nelson. "Dead we lie, and all that sort of bull and boloney. Life to be sure is nothing much to lose. Now where do they get that stuff? God blimey, where do they think that kind of tripe is going to get 'em? Education. There's a man of education, and look at what he makes up. Before they do anything, they've got to write something on their own gravestones. They've got to make a song and a dance about it. Definitely, they've got to make a fuss. We were young! He *is* young! What's the big idea, Dagwood? What's the big idea? Crying over their own dead bodies before they're killed! Here dead we lie. So what if here dead we lie? Eh, Crowney? A pack o' tripe. I'd like to see anybody sort of encouraging a squad of rooks with that sort of slop. Me, I give 'em the old Hi-de-Hi! And I make 'em give me the old Ho-de-Ho! Dead we lie. Why, we been dead dozens of times. Haven't we, Crowney? Or pretty near dead. As good as dead. But what did we say? We said: 'Let's give 'em rough stuff and bust through.' Didn't we, Handsey? We did, Dag, didn't we? Definitely we did. Where do they get that stuff? God blimey, I nearly did a Dead We Lie on the way along: I nearly went smacko on the line. I tripped over a sort of trunk on the platform. Why, Dagwood, old cock, we lie dead, more or less, every five minutes from the time the nurse smacks our backside, to the time they chuck dirt in our face. But do I write poetry about Dead We Lie? Did you ever catch me at it, Dagwood? Definitely not. Did he, Crowney? Well then. Tear that page out and—"

"Order your last drinks, please," says the landlord.

"Last drinks? *Last* drinks? What d'you mean, last drinks?" asks Sergeant Nelson, ordering one more round. "Well, mud in your eye, old skivers! This time next week payday on the Field! It'll be nice, ha? The dear old Active Service! Death? I spit in his eye! *Last* drinks. Not by a definitely very long chalk, my cocko! Here's looking at you!"

"Time, gentlemen, please," says the landlord.

"Yes, Time—that's all we need—Time!" says Nelson.

PART TWO

The Nine Lives of Bill Nelson

I

The Statement of Butcher the Butcher

BUTCHER THE BUTCHER, a cutter-up of Army meat who works in the cookhouse, came off a seven-days' leave twenty hours late, and was put under Open Arrest. Sergeant Crowne muttered: " 'E was pushed once before, back in 1931. 'E was due back at midnight. 'E didn't get in till midnight-forty. Forty minutes pushed. It was 'Case Explained,' though. Butcher'd got run over. There was what they call a Bright Young Thing: she sort o' fell for old Butcher. She ast Butch to a party and give 'im . . . what do they call them? Mahrattas?"

"Manhattans," said Sergeant Hands.

"Some Indian drink. So Joe Butcher walks into an Austin Seven. Actually, it'd take a Dennis truck to make a dent on Butcher. I b'lieve Butch smashed up the Austin Seven. Anyway, the police detained 'im, and 'e came back forty minutes pushed. I mean to say is, if Joe Butcher's pushed twenty hours, there's a good excuse. I lay five tanners to two Joe Butcher's got a good bar. A smart soldier, Butcher the Butcher. Could of got tapes: but no ambition. Got blood pressure. Blood pressure! Stick a pin in old Joe Butcher and it'd come out like a bust water-main. Bags o' pressure. I ought to know: I was first squadded with Joe Butcher."

Then Butcher came into the hut. He is a garrulous man, but this afternoon he was silent. His mouth was shut tight. His shiny black crescent moustache lay still, like a shard of broken gramophone record. He had left camp in his best suit, the suit of Service Dress which he had preserved for twelve years and which he filled as a hard red apple fills its skin—a burley, bloody-faced, full-bodied old soldier, instinctively meticulous in his dressing as only a Guardsman can be.

Now, no military policeman would have let him pass unchallenged. A triangle of cloth had been ripped from his left sleeve. The edges of his creases were blunted. His cheeks were yellowish: only his nose was red, with the sore redness of inflammation, where something had hit it hard. There were dark, stiff stains on his tunic to mark the trail of the blood. The jetty shine of God knows how many months had been kicked off the surface of his beautiful best boots. He had been burnishing his cap star for twenty years, until, of the *HONI SOIT QUI MAL Y PENSE* around the cross in the middle, nothing but *ON . . . IT . . . MA* remained. But the badge was gone. With my own ears I heard Butcher the Butcher refuse ten shillings for that badge—ten shillings in cash, and another badge thrown in. But he only laughed. Three of his tunic buttons were gone—regimental buttons polished away to blank domed surfaces. The cloth under his armpits was split: some terrible effort had burst it. He dragged his respirator on a broken sling. And where was his tin hat? The bayonet scabbard which Butcher had shone brown and bright as a house-proud woman's rosewood piano, was scratched beyond spit, polish, bone-friction, and elbow grease—"scratched up all to Hell." Butcher the Butcher was encrusted with stuff like ashes mixed with curry powder. He was bone-weary—a strong man drained and exhausted, a bled beetroot, a force used up, a chewed fibre, a weariness in mud-defiled webbing. There was a pouchiness about him.

The wireless was playing *Lord, You Made The Night Too Long* when he came in. Sergeant Hands was particularly fond of this song. But at the verse which says:

> *You made the mountains high,*
> *The earth and the sky,*
> *And who am I to say you're wrong . . . ?*

there was a *bip* as Hands himself knocked up the switch and said:
"Happened, Butch?"

Butcher the Butcher said: "Raid."

"Get hit?" asked Sergeant Crowne.

"Only by a house," said Butcher.

"You're pushed," said Sergeant Dagwood.

"Yeh, yeh, I'm twenty hours pushed. I'm under Open Arrest."

"Okay?"

"Yeh, yeh, *I'm* okay."

"Where was it?"

"Groombridge."

"Railway terminus?"

"Yeh, Groombridge. Helped dig out few civvies. Due back: so what? Drill Pig says, 'No excuse.' Well, sod the Drill Pig. See people buried, you dig people out. Hauled lumps o' house for eleven solid hours. Basement. No trains. Nobody gimme a lift. Slogged fifteen mile. I'm whacked. Forgot to get myself a chitty from the Rescue Bloke. Bleeding Drill Pig thinks I was in a fight. Oh, well, *I* sha worry. Lem gimme fourteen days! Lem gimme Royal Warrant! Lem semme to Devil's Island frall I care. *Ffphut!*" Butcher the Butcher tries to spit with a dry mouth.

"Lively, eh?" says Dagwood.

"Bit," says Joe Butcher. "Moo . . . moo . . . moo! Sireens. Like old cows; like lost cows, cows in pain. Ever hear a cow that lost a calf? Moo . . . moo . . . moo! Then these bombs go whizz, and bong! Ssssssssss —wheeeeeeee! Civvies in shelters and what not. I'm hanging on for a train. So I'm in a caff, getting a tea 'n' a wad. Caff shuts up when the raid starts. I scrams. All va sudden ole Jerry drops one on a house. I goes arsover tip: blast . . . Dust! Talk about egg-wiped: Egypt was cleaned bright and slightly oiled compared to that dust! 'Stonishing dusty thing, a house. Sticks to the roof a your mouth like Banbury cakes.

"Sort o' residential houses with shops underneath, kind o' style. Busted like a Christmas stocking. There was a lil sweet-stuff shop. I got hit in the face with a choclit marshmallow. Honest to Jesus, a choclit marshmallow. I scooped it orf me forrid and ate it. I got a tiny little bomb splinter in me leg, too; like a pinprick.

"There's another house gorn nex' door. Front wall down. I swallered a good bit o' that wall. Shook meself clear o' the debreece. Then some geezers comes up out a shelter; one old dear more 'n a million years old come Pancake Day yowping: 'Me Georgie! Me Georgie! Upstairs! Me Georgie's upstairs!'

"I says: 'Upstairs, Ma?' She says: 'Upstairs, son.' There's practically no stairs. But this old geezer's leading orf about 'er Georgie this, and 'er Georgie that, and 'er Georgie upstairs. It seems this Georgie's the old girl's old man. So I goes up. Looka my ankle where I shoved it through a busted plank! Old girl comes up after me. First floor back. I chucks down a ton o' rubble, busts a way through, kicks down a door. I asks: 'Who locked this door?' and the old girl says: 'I did.'

"Bedroom. Proper old-fashioned kip. Bloody brass bed like park railings . . . millions o' brass. Bags o' vorses and orlaments on the mannelshelf, millions o' chairs, and an aspradaspra on a stand all broke. On the bed there's an old kite with a white beard, lying quiet. I says: ' 'E looks okay to me, Ma: kind of asleep.' The old girl says: 'As long as 'e 'asn't fallen on the ground. 'Slong 's Georgie's still on the bed, everythink's all right. You see, young man, we're burying 'im tomorrow.'

"So I goes on back down. I carries the old girl. Then they say there's people in the basement. So there isn't much of a rescue squad, and they can sort of hear people kind o' yelling out, so I has a go at the stuff with my bare forks. Look at me fingers!

"We clears a way. We cuts a bicycle inner tube in two and pushes it down. 'Soup, Ma!' we yells. And an old girl buried down there calls back: 'Wish it was beer!' I mean to say is, you can't get some of these old girls down. Then she sort of screeks up the tube: 'You better look sharp, there's a young man 'oldin' up the ceiling!' So we digs like mad. Hours. Hours. They brung me tea, but I was sort of carried away. We gets down.

"There's a sort of a basement, a kind of a cellar. In this kind of cellar there's an old girl, dead. Heart, or somethink. One old girl dead. Another old girl, cheerful as a cricket, very much alive. A kid of seven or eight, scared stiff, but alive. A gel o' fifteen in high-sterics. A lil boy less 'n ten year old, smashed dead. And arched over 'em, like a sort of brick kind of arch . . . guess who?"

Silence.

"Well, who?" says Crowne.

"Guess," says Butcher the Butcher.

"I give it up."

"Remember Bill Nelson? Lance-Sergeant now. Squadded with us. Old Bill Nelson. Remember him?"

"Well?"

"Well, there was Bill Nelson. Been visiting friends. When the house come down, old Bill Nelson sort of kept the roof of the cellar up. He was thin, but he was wiry, old Bill Nelson. He sort of jammed himself up against the bricks and held 'em off the old geezer and the kids. Ribs busted, face busted, head busted. He was smashed up but he stood sore of in one piece. Gord knows how. He was busted everywhere, internal and out. There was a spike in the brickwork, a sort of blunt spike, drove right through him. But he held up. Some men can do it. I don't know. Some men can. It ain't strength. Just, somehow, some men sort of *can*. You knew old Bill Nelson. I knew old Bill Nelson. We fought the Wogs together. We was Guardsmen together. Once I borrowed a dollar off of him what I never give him back. Once he borrowed a dollar off of me what *he* never give *me* back. He was my pal."

"Was?" says Sergeant Crowne, very quietly.

"Smashed to hell," says Butcher the Butcher. "In the Groombridge Central Hospital. Can't live. So you can say goo'bye to Bill Nelson. *I* knew old Bill Nelson. We was chinas. Decent when he was a Guardsman; decent when he was a Lance-Jack; decent when he was a Lance-Sergeant; decent when he was a full Sergeant. Quarter-bloke, C.S.M., Drill Pig, R.S.M., or Officer—Bill Nelson would of stayed the same. Decent. One of us. He'd of give away his shirt. He'd of give away his eyesight and his right hand. He chased you; yes. But he'd go first, wherever he chased you. Good old Bill. So now he gives away himself in a cellar, for some old geezers and a couple o' kids. That's Bill, all through. Conscientious. He ought to of gone down in a fair fight in the open air, with a couple o' dozen Jerries spread about and a pound weight o' lead in his tripes. But no. On a seven-day leave, on a visit, down in a dirty ole cellar . . . that's where Bill Nelson gets his. Not that he cared. Old Bill Nelson wasn't scared o' anything. But it ain't proper. It ain't right. Groombridge. Bill. Groombridge!"

"Where is Groombridge?" asks Corporal Bearsbreath.

"Oh . . . let me rest," says Butcher the Butcher. "Be quiet and let a man get a bit of rest . . ."

"Nelson was born at Groombridge," says Crowne.

"So he died at Groombridge," says Butcher, and covers his face with a blanket.

I happened to know that at Groombridge Junction twelve tracks run precisely parallel out of the station and under the Iron Bridge. Beyond the bridge these tracks give off other tracks, which, in their turn, bristle like heads of barley with tributary tracks—and the tributaries branch, and the branches fork, and the forks reticulate, and the reticulations swerve, until, two hundred yards farther on, all the steel rails in the world seem to rush together, dreary and bewildering, twisting and converging, doubling and tangling, dully-shining like steel wool.

There is no peace. There is no quiet. Signals slam and thud perpetually. There is an everlasting smashing noise of shunting, a shouting of steam, a shrilling of little whistles and big whistles, a muttering of tortured iron. Sometimes, men between the tracks blow melancholy notes out of metal horns. When the fogs come down the Junction roars and hoots and bangs and wails, blindly worried in a hideous yellow dusk. Interminable goods trains stagger through. Twenty times a day some great express rushes past shrieking. For forty years, day in, day out, night after night, the Junction has known no complete hour of unbroken rest.

The smell of the railway—that ponderous, nostalgic smell of hot iron and sulphurous smoke—sticks to the surrounding suburb. Here, countless tons of coal go up in smoke and drift back to earth in a soft snow of soot. It falls, flake by flake, from year to year; gently irresistible, mildly corrosive, persistent and insinuating; quietly eating up brick and stone, suavely blotting out the sun, softly besmirching newly-washed clothes as they flap dankly in the lugubrious, stinking winds.

Here, dirt must prevail. It devours housewives inevitably as grave-yard soil. Sometimes they see, in a flash of awful perception, how they have spent their strength and beauty in the struggle against it; but they scrub on, soap-drunk, embittered and preoccupied, sore-eyed, raw-knuckled, enraged and engrossed, winnowed of hope. And still the smuts drift and the soot seeps in and coats everything, so that Groom-bridge is a black suburb, a chafed and miserable suburb, uncomfortable with dirt where it is not uneasy with scouring.

The dark, flat houses cling under the railway-bridges like ticks on the belly of a rhinoceros. The Railway owns them: railwaymen inhabit them. The mainstay of Groombridge Junction is the steady job-holder on the Railway—mechanic, porter, guard, or clerk. If you want slaves, offer men some kind of secure income, no matter how meagre—they will fight for the chance to fetter themselves head and heart, hand and foot, body and soul. Young men conspire to punch tickets in the Sta-tion. Expectant mothers, feeling the kick of unborn generations, think: *Please God, if it is a boy, his father will get him On The Railway, and so his future will be assured.*

The suburb and the people in it belong to the Railway, because its payday has the awful, the tremendous inevitability of an act of God. The well-behaved man on the Railway may look forward to a certain income, some promotion, and a little pension, with the calm assurance of a sectarian pietist contemplating a corrugated-iron-chapel paradise. He may buy things on the instalment plan, and firmly establish his mode of life. The railwaymen of Groombridge Junction are steady. Salesmen of endowment policies do well thereabout. Burial Societies flourish. Groombridge looks ahead: before the end of July it has already put down a deposit on its Christmas turkey; by the middle of September it has already laid the foundation of its next summer holiday. Here today, here tomorrow. Once you settle in Groombridge, you stay. You live in the shadow of the Railway until that great occasion when you ride in state up the High Street, and strangers raise their hats to you, and mournful smuts float down to fleck the wreathed lilies that are dying with you.

Good. You are buried in Groombridge Cemetery. The suburb, having swallowed you, then proceeds to digest you.

The Comprachicos sealed babies in jars. The baby grew: the jar stayed rigid. The child was curiously misshapen: its market value increased in proportion to its freakishness.

Groombridge, similarly, swelling to maturity within its narrow boundaries, has squeezed itself into queer shapes—and this is a sign of its enhanced value as real estate.

The Railway grew bloated. Warehouses rose . . . clearing-houses, new stations, wider lines, more stations, offices, more warehouses. Householders near the Junction were elbowed away. The Railway built them new villas. Old leases were bought in; old streets were demolished. Children cheered as walls tumbled down in swirling dust clouds, and old familiar wallpapers stared out. Rubble carts rolled away. The Railway sprawled over. The baby had outgrown the jar. Flesh and blood was squashed into odd holes and corners. Dumping grounds of empty tins, questionable paper parcels and dead cats—lifeless areas behind blackened hoardings or under thunderous arches—bits of bad land soaked in sour water and deader than salty Sodom—became housing estates constructed with the geometrical economy of honeycombs. The flimsy houses rushed up: the coaly air rushed down; in six months the most blatant biscuit-coloured brick was one with the dirty face of the

Junction. And still the Railway spread, swelling, muscling out, nudging people into unheard-of crevices.

Oh, stench! Oh, darkness! Oh, black and melancholy birthplace under a fog-hazed sun!

"Better a bloke like Bill should be born in a place like that, than not at all," snaps Crowne. "And what's the odds where you die, so long as you die game? It's dead cushy to die in a fight in the sunlight. But in a cellar, in the dark, with a 'ouse on top of you . . . no, if you die game like *that*, you're all right. And I lay any odds you like Bill died game."

"Cracking a joke," says Bearsbreath.

"He gave 'em the old *Hi-de-Hi*!" cries Hands.

"With 'is mouth full o' sand, I've heard Bill Nelson 'and out the old *Hi-de-Hi*," says Crowne.

"And the spirit of the bastard was such," says Bearsbreath, "that if you were dying in the desert with him, you'd shout back the old *Ho-de-Ho*!"

"But why should Bill die?" asks Butcher the Butcher.

Hands, who has a good, potent baritone voice, sings a verse of the song he likes so much. . . .

> *"You made the rivers that flow,*
> *The breezes that blow—*
> *You made the weak and the strong.*
> *But Lord, you made the night too long!"*

This plucks some string in the Butcher's heart. He turns his face to the blank wall and weeps.

II

Bearsbreath on the Nature of Man

CORPORAL BEARSBREATH, that tense, twanging man of iron frame and piano wire, plunges an arm into his kitbag and hauls up a chipped enamel mug. "One of you kids do me a favour," he says, in an undertone. "Go to the Y.M.C.A. and get this filled with tea. Here's twopence. Just put down the twopence and say 'Fill it'—you stand to get a buckshee penn'orth that way. And give it to Butcher. . . .

"Come on, Butch, out of it! Have a fag, Butcher. Was you the only man that was Bill's china? He was my pal, too. I'm browned off as much as you are, about it. So is Crowney. So's a lot of us. Me . . . I could spit blood. A feller like Nelson, he's entitled to live donkey's years. For ever! Never ought to die. You rookies, you don't know. You couldn't know what a feller like Bill Nelson *is*. Don't get me wrong. I'm not saying you're not all right. But . . . Christ, the years we've known Nelson! It takes *time* to make a feller like Nelson. They got to be brewed: they got to mature.

"Bill Nelson. *Argh*—Death! All these years I've seen good men go, and go! The best goes first. It's a fact. The better they are, the less they want to save themselves. And a yeller dog'll live when a white man goes down. Right. I'd rather be Bill Nelson dead than a lot of other men alive.

"Nelson was a man, a proper man. I was squadded with him. Don't I know? I only saw him act unreasonable once. It looked unreasonable. It was when he was a rookie, less than a week squadded. Somebody called him a bastard. Nelson went mad. He was thin, but wiry; a lanky kid. This was nearly twenty years ago. He went for this bloke and

196

knocked him cold. I said to him, afterwards: 'What made you sort of go crazy like that?' Bill said: 'He called me a bastard.' I said: 'What of it? It's a sort of name. Everybody calls everybody else a bastard.' Bill said: 'I know. But between ourselves, I *am* a bastard.' He kind of was one. Not legally illegitimate, but almost. I believe he was fond of his mum, and she'd had a sort of rough time on account of him. But he controlled it, after that. And soon he took things in the same spirit as people said them.

"We went around together a bit. Bill didn't have any home, and no more did I. We got miserable together, and we cheered each other up. Two people, both cheesed off, are better than one. You feel low, you don't want a clown to brighten you up. You want somebody to be jarred off with . . . you grouse it out of your system.

"We went up for the tapes together. We were Young Corporals together. We got into trouble together. We were lousy soldiers, according to the rules. I've been busted four times. After twenty years of it, Bill ended up as only a Lance-Sergeant, which is the same as a Full Corporal. After twenty years! Bill's conduct sheet looked black as pitch, on paper. He was even in the Glass House, twice. And do you know what? Each time Nelson got Detention, he was innocent. On my dying oath.

"That kind of thing happens. Talk about the Army making a man of you. It can do. But it ain't the exercise, the drill, and all that bull-and-boloney. No; it's what you learn to bear. That's what makes a proper man of a feller, if he's okay to start with. It spoils some, I don't say it doesn't. But they're softish to begin with—they'd spoil anywhere, anyway. You want to see what a feller's made of, give him what Bill Nelson got. Nobody got more injustice than Nelson, and he was the fairest man in the Army. You try staying just when they keep making you carry the can back.

"Bill Nelson was the honestest man on God's earth. He could lie like a newspaper . . . but only for a good cause. I've heard him swear black

was white, but never for his own sake. Bill was busted three days after
he got his tapes for the first time. You heard about that, Crowney.

"You other fellers: that is the kind of mug Nelson was:

"There was a kid that was always getting into trouble. Unlucky.
He'd got a sort of manner that got up the nose of the Sarnt-Major.
So everything he done was dead wrong. That can happen to you in
the Army, too. So this kid's life was a sort of misery. Once you start
getting into a kind of routine of being punished, God knows where
you can end. You're marked. You carry the can. You can't do anything right. Well, one day this kid comes out of Company Orders with
a three-days' C.B. for standing idle on parade . . . right or wrong, he'd
got it. Well, where we were . . . you know, the peacetime Guards'
turnout took big mirrors. We had a longish sort of mirror in the room.
This kid comes in and sort of lets off steam. He means no harm. There's
a scrubbing brush lying about: he takes a flying kick at it. This hand
scrubber flies up and goes bong through the mirror, and smashes it to
bits. The kid goes white as the ash on this cigarette. Here's another
offence for him to be dragged in on, and he looks sick.

"As luck will have it, the Sarnt-Major looks in just then. It was bad
luck: he'd heard the crash.

" 'Who done that?'

"And Bill Nelson ups, quick as lightning, and says: 'Sorry, sir, I did.'

" 'How?'

" 'I chucked that hand scrubber across the room, sir.'

" 'What for?'

" 'Just for a bit o' fun, sir.'

"Bill takes the rap for this mirror, out of pity for the kid. They took
away his tapes, that he'd only had three days. Less than that has poisoned
more fellers than one: broke their spirits. Not Bill. He never complained, and actually argued the other kid out of owning up . . . 'Give
'em a chance to forget you a bit . . . I'm glad to get rid of them tapes,
anyway.' That kid's an R.S.M. in a line mob now. But Bill? I nearly
said 'Poor old Bill,' but there never was anything Poor about Nelson!

"That was one thing. There were millions more like it. He was made up again in time. He got to be a Lance-Sarnt. Then one day a Guardsman comes to Bill with some Fanny about needing some cash, and Bill lent this Guardsman two quid. It's against the rules. No financial dealings between N.C.O.'s and men, ever. Still, it happens sometimes that men and N.C.O.'s can be pals, and between pals what's a quid? Bill lends this man two quid. Due course, this man gives Bill the two quid back. But like the mug that he is, he does it where the Drill Pig happens to be looking on.

"Bill goes inside. Taking money off a Guardsman. They can practically hang, draw, and quarter you for that. Bill knows it's no use talking. He's busted the rules by lending this geezer the two quid in the first place. He relies on the other man to speak up and tell the exact truth. A mug, Bill; but there you are. The other feller was a rat. He let himself out by blaming it on Bill: said Bill'd asked for the money and he didn't like to refuse. Bill went sort of white. In all his life I never knew that fool of a Nelson explain himself or make an excuse. If you're in the soup, you're in it: right or wrong, pay the punishment off and forget it; that was Bill. 'What's the use of talking?' he used to say. 'Who'll believe you? To go and lay the blame for this and that on Tom, Dick, and Harry,' he said, 'is not worth lowering yourself to do.' So he was not only busted again; he went to the Glass House for twenty-eight days.

"I would of murdered that Guardsman, only I didn't get to know about it till later. But Nelson simply shrugged his shoulders. He said: 'Justice?' he said, 'Justice is a thing that you deal out if you can. But only mugs cry if they don't get it. Justice is a sort of a kindness,' he said, 'a kind of a charity; a sort of a good turn. It's very nice to have it, but it's as well not to count on it. Like Christmas boxes.'

"Yet—God Almighty!—let any one of Bill Nelson's squad get so much as one drill that he hadn't ought to have got, and Bill was like a roaring lion. He'd thrash it out with the C.O. himself, and he'd get that man his proper rights. He never had a farthing. Every penny he ever drew his pals had for the asking. Ask any squad that ever passed through Nelson's hands if Bill ever punished a man. In twenty years he never put a man inside. And I've seen him with some of the lousiest showers of rooks you ever saw in your life. There was an idiot, actually a sort of idiot. Bill worked on that kid and made him a right bloke where everybody else'd given up. Because there's some fellers that are shy, or scared, or that have been pushed about too much all their lives; and these fellers sort of smack on a kind of mental look so as to protect 'emselves. It takes patience and it takes kindness. Bill could do all that. He had a brain. He could make a thing clear where I beat about the bush. He could put things into words. He had personality. He wasn't afraid of anything or anybody. His heart was too big for his body. He'd go up a tree for a cat, or down a well for a sparrer. He was as strong as a bull. He was as soft as a woman. He liked kids. He liked pretty nearly everybody. Right up to the last minute, he'd try and reason a thing out. Then when it come to the fight he was a wildcat. He could of been Prime Minister. He could of been a General. He could of been anything. Only he come out of a dump without a chance on God's earth. Okay. Better for him to be just Bill Nelson, maybe. I don't know. It's a funny thing he had to go back to Groombridge to die. What for, I wonder? God knows. I don't. I don't know anything. I don't believe there is a God, anyway. I don't believe anything. I can't believe Bill's dead. . . . It's all wrong. . . . Dead wrong, somewhere. The idea of Bill getting his in a cellar with old women is. . . . But like Crowne said: any mug can go over with a baynet and a ration of rum, with other mugs charging. It takes a proper man to wait for it in a broken-down old cellar and still give the good old *Hi-de-Hi*!

"Nelson was a proper man."

III

The Statement of the Budgerigar

THERE IS a man called John Sparrowhawk, whom men call The
Budgerigar. Once he was a Company Quartermaster-Sergeant. Now
he is only a sergeant. Vague outlines, like birthmarks, in the bend of
his stripes, indicate that little brass crowns used to be attached to his
sleeves. He was reduced. There was an incident. The Budgerigar was
in a café drinking a cup of tea. He says that he was quiet as a mouse.
The general opinion is that The Budgerigar could not have been quiet
if he was drinking tea. Anyway, he was interfering with nobody. He
tells his story with terrible emphasis:

"I was drinking my tea . . ."

"Then what happened?" asks Hands. "Somebody thought you was
drowning and dragged you out?"

"A civvie tries to pinch my respirator. He thinks I'm not looking
and walks out with it. So I taps him on the shoulder, and says: 'Excuse me.'"

"I know your taps on the shoulder," says Hands. "You probably
picked up a marble-topped table and tapped him with that. You probably drove him into the floor like a tack."

"I taps him on the shoulder and says: 'Excuse me, that's my respirator.' And this civvie tries to make a dash for it. So I caught him
by the collar."

"And his head came off," says Hands.

"His collar came off. Then a military policeman pinches me. A civvie
policeman pinches the civvie. He gets three months for trying to pinch
my respirator. I get busted for trying to stop him. Justice. Justice! All

201

right, so they busted me. But I'll be back. This isn't the first time I've been busted. I should worry. I been in this mob more than twenty years. I've lost all hope. I lost all hope more than twenty-five years ago, or I'd never have joined this mob. I never did have no luck. Say I play pokey-dice. I can throw five kings in one, but somebody's certain to throw five aces in one. Look at Hands. If Hands fell into the Thames he'd come out with a new suit of clothes on. With a pocket full of fishes he'd come out. But me, if I so much as spit it comes back and hits me in the eye. My luck is something unnatural."

Hands says: "You shouldn't smoke that pipe. That civvie probably needed that respirator."

"Stealing soldiers' respirators! Luck. Gah! The very first Buckingham Palace guard I ever did, just as the King comes in, I faints. It was my feelings. Could I help my feelings?"

"Lucky you did faint," says Hands. "If the King had seen you he'd probably have fainted instead. A face like yours."

Between Hands and The Budgerigar there exists a strange friendship. The Budgerigar, earnest and formidable, simple and singleminded, is a bull's-eye for Hands to hit. Hands pretends never to take The Budgerigar seriously: The Budgerigar pretends that he has never heard anything Hands has ever said. They talk at each other. This has been going on for nearly nine years.

On hearing of the death of Nelson, The Budgerigar is silent. He swallows that tremendous piece of news as a quicksand swallows the wreck of a great ship. But at last he says: "And I stole his girl."

"The blind girl?" asks Hands.

"I stole Bill Nelson's girl."

"No girl with eyes in her head could let you steal her."

"Poor old Bill Nelson was courting a girl for nearly eighteen months. So it took me to do the dirty on him. On old Bill Nelson. Me. Spit in my eye. I'm a dirty swine. I never have no luck. If I bite a penny bun, there's a stone in it. If I want to do a pal a good turn, I do him a lousy turn. I'm a dirty swine. Yet in a way, it could be argued, mind you, that I done Bill a sort of a good turn, in a kind of a style, it might be, perhaps. Who knows? I kid myself along I might have been doing Bill a good turn all these years. But on the other hand, I don't know . . ."

Hands says: "I know how it was. She was an old maid. What they call a spinster. She liked parrots. Parrots were expensive. She didn't like to steal one, so she let you steal her. How'd you like your birdseed cooked, Polly?"

"I never have luck. Unlucky at cards, unlucky at love, unlucky in the Army, and unlucky in everything."

Sergeant Crowne says: "Come to think of it, didn't you go and marry Nelson's young lady? What I mean . . . spliced, respectably married?"

Hands says: "Some people like horrible things. Look at the way kids like golliwogs. Look at Snow White and the Seven Dwarfs."

"It was the dirtiest trick I ever played in all my natural puff," says The Budgerigar.

"Well," says Crowne, "the funny thing is, Budgey, Bill Nelson was always sort of under the impression that he dropped you a——" and he names an essential appendage of the masculine anatomy . . . one of those troubles that never comes singly. To drop one of these, in the jargon of Guardsmen, is to make a serious blunder. To drop one for somebody else is to let him down.

"Nelson never dropped me nothing," says The Budgerigar. "He was courting a girl called Joan, a very pretty girl that used to be an attendant at the Kinema at Groombridge. Look—here's a pitcher of her in 1930."

The Budgerigar undoes a button, and pushes a hand into his tunic, and fishes out a wallet, and opens this wallet only a little way, squinting into it cautiously. Obviously, this wallet is full of secrets. He picks out a photograph. On the back of it somebody has written in a little peaky hand:

Dearest fondest love from Joan.

The photograph is of a young woman with an enormous quantity of light hair, one and a half times the normal area of eye and much more than her share of bosom. She must be a young woman who likes to make the most of what she has, whatever that may be. She has managed to get nearly twenty-two of her teeth into the picture. There is no doubt that she is holding her breath with a view to expanding her chest and pushing into the camera those organs that our grandfathers called Sacred Founts of Motherhood.

Sergeant Hands says: "She reminds me of Staff Sergeant Moggridge when he did an impersonation of Janet Gaynor at the concert in 1936. He got a bit of an old coconut mat for a wig, and put two pillows under his sweater. He done an apache dance with some sergeant dressed up like Rudolph Valentino——"

"Why, that was Piggy Hogg," says Crowne. "The third ugliest man in the Brigade of Guards."

"You're thinking of Porky Pye."

"I'm thinking of Piggy Hogg."

"You're not thinking of no Piggy Hogg, you're thinking of Porky Pye."

"I'm not thinking of no Porky Pye, I'm thinking of Piggy Hogg."

"Betcha."

"Wotcher betcha?"

"Betcha million pounds."

The Budgerigar says: "But have you ever seen a prettier-looking girl? She was sort of engaged to Bill Nelson. He used to send her all his spare money to save up for the wedding. It was Bill that introduced us. When he had to go away, I was stationed in the Smoke. He said to me: 'Budgey, sort of keep Joan company a bit when you got nothing better to do, Budgey. Because when I'm not there she pines. She frets, Budgey,' Bill says, 'so be a pal and cheer her up off and on, kind of style.' Right you are. I sees her off and on and takes her out for a walk, or for a drink. No use taking her to the pictures, because she works in them. She'd seen the *Love Parade* twenty-one times. Nothing like what you'd think went on between us. I didn't so much as hold her arm when we walked. So help me Jesus, I marched straight to attention at her side and I didn't open my North-and-South. I never said a dicky-bird, because I was there to cheer her up and nothing more.

"One Sunday—it was May—so she asked me to walk over Parliament Hill. So we sat down on top of the hill, and so we had an ice. A *sixpenny ice*. Then she started to talk about things. She asked me did I believe in love? Did I believe in love?"

The Budgerigar, by instinct, drops into the staccato monotone of an N.C.O. giving evidence at a court-martial:

"I said I did not believe in love. She said: 'Oh, but you must.' I said: 'What for?' She said: 'Lots of girls must fall in love with you.' I said: 'Not to the best of my knowledge and belief, Miss Joan.' She said: 'I know one who has, anyway.' I said: 'May I ast who?' She said: 'Oh, nobody,' and then she bust into tears. I said: 'Miss Joan, may I ast what is the matter?' She said: 'You are an experienced man. I want your advice. What would you do if you was a young girl, properly engaged to a man who had given you an amethyst ring, but who you had ceased to care for.' I said: 'Ho?' She said: 'Say you went and fell in love with another man?'

" 'If you was not properly engaged,' I said, 'I should go ahead. But then it would depend.' She said: 'Depend upon what?' I said: 'Depend on everything.' She said: 'What do you mean by everything?' I said: 'Nothing.'

"Then she said: 'What would you do if you were a young girl and the man you were engaged to had sent you money for furniture, and then you had gone and lost this here money?'

"Then all of a sudden I fluffed. I said: 'Do you mean to tell me you've gorn and lost my pal Bill Nelson's money?' She said: 'A matter of thirty-two pounds.' I said: 'Now exactly where did you lost it?' And she said: 'If I knew exactly where I lost it, I would know exactly where to find it, but I don't know, I just lost it.' I said: 'You should have put it in the Post Office.' She said: 'I don't trust Post Offices. Oh, what shall I do?'

" 'Well, I don't know what you can do,' I said, 'but,' I said, 'Bill Nelson is my chum,' I said, 'and you are his young lady. It'd be a pity for there to be trouble between my china and his young lady. So I'll lend you the money to put back,' I said. Because, you see, I had about forty-odd quid saved up. My old Mum left me a matter of seventy-five-odd quid not long before. I had lent a matter of twenty-odd quid to a certain party, and still had most of the rest, because I always was a careful man with my money. So I tells her that I'm prepared to let her have this little bit of dough.

" 'But then,' I said, 'do you mean to tell me that on top of losing my pal's money, you've gone and fancied some other geezer?' She said: 'I do. I have.' I said: 'Well, anyway, it is bad enough for you to go and break my pal's heart. But it is even worse to go and lose the money he has earned serving his country with the sweat of his brow, so I'll draw it out for you. And don't you go losing it again,' I said. 'You didn't go giving it to this other geezer, I hope? Because if you did, just point him out to me and with all due respects I will tie his legs in a hard knot round his neck and choke him.' She said: 'Oh no.' I said: 'S'matter fact, I think you better tell me who this kite is, so I can give him just a little bit of a hiding as a matter of form. Because you are Bill's girl, and I am entitled to protect you.'

" 'You can't do that,' she said.

" 'Why not?' I said.

" 'Because you can't give yourself a hiding,' she said, and at that she busts into tears again.

"I fluffed what she was getting at. 'What *me?*' I said. 'You,' she said. I said: 'Lemme pay for these ices and go.'

"She cried like a fire picquet. She cried like a hydrant. Since they caught me with tear gas that time when I had a faulty respirator and got the full blast of the stuff in that test chamber, I never see such spontaneous tears. She had prominent eyes, kind of style, and it was like squashing grapes. She said: 'Oh, you drag a confession out of me and then you run away . . . you and your Bill. I'll tell Bill all about you.'

" 'You'll tell Bill all about what?' I said.

" 'All about you,' she said. 'Making me love you.'

" 'Oo I never!' I said.

" 'Oo you did,' she said, 'and I shall tell Bill.'

" 'I never touched you,' I said.

" 'You never touched me on purpose,' she said.

" 'You're showing me up,' I said. 'People are looking.'

" 'My life is ruined,' she said, 'you beast, you beast, you beast.'

"I said: 'What do you want me to do, for God's sake?'

" 'You've got to marry me,' she said.

"I said: 'If I marry you will you promise to stop crying?'

"She said: 'Yes.'

"So I said: 'All right then. Stop crying.'

"I just can't stand seeing women crying. It gets me groggy. I can't bear it. I once promised to adopt a black woman's child because she was crying. That's why I joined the Army. A mulatto I wouldn't have minded, but this was as black as coal, and I'd never seen her before in my life. You promise a thing, and there you are. She said: 'Darling, all the time I knew you really cared for me.'

"I didn't have any money smaller than a ten-shilling note, except a lucky five-shilling piece that my Mum's aunt give me. I wanted to get away quick. I couldn't very well leave half a quid. I left the dollar. I couldn't hang about for change with millions of people laughing at me, and so there it was. I lost me lucky dollar. She said: 'When is it to be?' I said: 'Gord knows.' She said she'd arrange everything, and so she did. I begged and prayed to be sent East. They wouldn't let me go. I nearly run away to join the Foreign Legion, but I didn't know how to go about it. So we got spliced. We been married ten years. She's been ill with her nerves all the time. Sort of laughs and cries and tears her hair whatever goes wrong. If she is not well she's afraid she's going to die and she busts into tears. If she's *not* not well, she's afraid she's going to be ill and she goes off the deep end. And so that's how it is."

"Any kids?" asks Crowne.

"No," says The Budgerigar. "The first time I sort of tried . . . to kind of . . . have anything to do with her . . . she called the police. She said marriage was rude. So I never did. After losing that five-bob bit I never had no luck at all."

Crowne says: "And you think you did Bill Nelson a dirty trick."

"Well, I did steal his young lady," says The Budgerigar.

"A doctor did me a bad turn like that once," says Hands. "He stole a bit of grit out of my eye."

"Ah," says The Budgerigar. "But she said afterwards that the only man she ever loved was poor Bill. She said I was an adventurer. She said I was a Don Jewen. She said that she might have hit it off with Bill, but not with a beast in human guise. Meaning me."

"She sounds terrible," says Hands.

Sergeant Sparrowhawk, the broken quartermaster, the roaring lion of the parade ground, sticks out a jaw like the prow of a destroyer and thrusts forward a forehead like that of an ox. This forehead seems, somehow, directly linked with a neck like the stump of an elm tree. He hunches his shoulders and says: "You mind what you're saying when you talk about my good lady. Who knows? Maybe I ruined her life and Bill's . . . ?"

IV

The Man Who Saved Thurstan

THERE IS a man who appears to be a product of many different kinds of hunger, and his name is Thurstan. Everybody knows him. Nobody likes him. He is too tough. He has had to kick and bite his way through too many things. He has walked between great, grey overhanging circumstances, as between elephants: all his life he has had to look left and right at the same time . . . he has had to be prepared for a quick duck, a lightning dive, a tigerish spring and swerve. His life has depended too much upon the little efforts that he has been able to make. He was born in the badlands of the Border, and scraped a living out of the slag heads about the ironworks and the coal mines. He is scarred and silent. He has the obstinacy and the hitting power of a mule; a giant's strength, and something of a giant's tyranny. He squeezes whatever he picks up, and there is a certain venom in his friendliest nudge. He went absent twice. Once, he got seven days for hitting a man. The man borrowed Thurstan's best boots. There is a whole legend about it. The man had to appear on an Extra Parade. His boots were dirty. Thurstan's boots on the shelf next to his were brilliantly clean, and since Thurstan also wore a wide-fitting nine, he borrowed them for half an hour.

Thurstan came in five minutes after the man had left, and said: "Where's me boots?"

Somebody said: "Mac borrowed them for a minute for his Extra Parade."

Thurstan said: "Ah."

When the man came back Thurstan walked to within arm's length and hit him precisely, with terrific force, on the point of the jaw; knocked him out, and then, while Mac lay on the floor, methodically took his boots off and put them back on the shelf over his bed. There was a certain savagery about this. It horrified the other men in the hut. While Thurstan was in close arrest, they played football with his best boots, just to teach him a lesson. When Thurstan had finished his seven-days' C.B. (Mac got seven days, too, for borrowing the boots) he came in with a feral snarl and challenged twenty-eight men to single combat, one at a time, or all together. And such was the ruthless ferocity of this man that his challenge went unanswered.

Now, when The Budgerigar stops talking, and the men stop laughing, and there is little sound in the hut except the sibilant scrape of twopenny nailbrushes upon web equipment, a hard cracked voice speaks from a corner near the door. It is a voice that comes out in queer gulping periods. It resembles the noise made by a bottle of beer, too abruptly inverted. The mouth is reluctant to let the words go, but when they get beyond the palate the lips spit them out like cherry-stones. It is Thurstan talking. When he talks, men pause in their spitting and their polishing, and they listen in a kind of incredulous amazement. I was going to say that they listen as men listen to a well-trained parrot; this is not quite true. They listen without amusement . . . only with interest, interest born of distrust. Thurstan is not a talker. He has nothing to say, and nobody to say it to. Indeed, he is not talking to any man now. He is not even talking to the twenty-nine or thirty other men in the hut. He is talking to himself and the universe. He is hurling some expression of something into the teeth of the world which rolls in loneliness down space. He is just talking:

"Death.

"People die.

"Good job. They're not fit to live. When they're fit to die they live. When they're fit to live they die. Me father lived. He was fit to die. Me mother too.

"I wish death was a man. Then some would be alive that is dead and some would be dead that's alive. Nelson is dead.

"Everything good dies. Nelson's dead.

"I knew him. No one else knew him. I knew him. No one else knew me. He knew me. He knew me fine. No other man knocked me off my feet but he did. Ah, he did! The second time I went absent he caught me. No, he didn't. Nobody caught me. I gave myself up.

"The first time I went absent I gave myself up. It was because. . . .

"I don't know why it was. I did. I just came back. It was rotten in here. It was rotten out there. It was rotten everywhere. But there was a thing. I came back.

"I can't be in one place. Time comes I've got to go. Go away. Away. Anywhere away. So long as it's a long way. What do I care where? It came again. When it means fighting I'll not go away. I'll stay. I'll stay for the fighting. Hah. They know me. For the fighting I'll stay. But . . . maybe soon I'll go away again. If I must they can't hold me. I'll go, if I got to go.

"I went. I went quiet. Pass till midnight. I get a bus. I go. Midnight? Hah. Midnight in hell! Back? Me? Hah. No. I got to go away. I got to go a long way away. Where? Hah. Where . . . I got to go. Got to get out. I got. Where? Pound. I go home. There isn't a place. Old lass? God knows. Where? Hah. Get a civvie suit. Pinch one. Get out. Go away. Go away again. Anywhere away. They feed a lost dog. Or they kill a lost dog. Hah. Two weeks. Three weeks. Hah. You need grub. You want to eat. You can't work. You want papers. You're military age. They got you.

"You go down. You turn left. You turn right. You go deep. Deeper. Find a hole. Crawl in. Then rock. Nothing. Stay and die. Or crawl back. Absent. This regiment. That camp. No papers. Gimme a cup of tea. All right son. Cup of tea. Escort. Go back.

"He was my squad instructor. Nelson. No copper. No nark. A fool.

"Mad. Crazy. Him and another. He talks. . . . Still hungry, Thurstan? Ah. All me life. Fancy tea? Ah. There's caff. There's no food.

Tinned salmon sandwich. Fancy that? Ah. Another tea? Ah. Another
sandwich? Ah. Thurstan, you're hungry. You mug. You horrible man,
Thurstan, but you're hungry, brother. Ah. What did you go and run
away for, Thurstan? What did you go and do it for? You mug. Are
you yeller? Na. Na. Not yeller. I know you're not yeller, Thurstan.
I can see you're not yeller, Thurstan. I know what it is. Ah? Ah. Just
nuts. Want to get away. Run out. Get away from everything. Go up
in the air, and hide yourself, you horrible man, or go down right into
the guts of the earth and bury yourself there. Anything to get away,
isn't that it, you mug? Ah. Have another sandwich. We've got to be
getting back. It means a steady twenty-eight days for you, Thurstan.
The Glass House this time. You thought you had a tough break before,
but you never had anything like the Glass House. I'm sorry for you.

"Give him one of those cakes. With that sort of coconut stuff on
the top. And give the mug a lump of that stuff with dates in it. Eat
it while you can, you poor mug. Anything on your mind, Thurstan?
Na. You ain't got no mind. Na. I don't know what to do with you,
Thurstan.

"Nor me with myself.

"Why d'you give yourself up, Thurstan? Want to go back? Na.
Then why? To eat. You've ate, Thurstan. Ah. I've ate. Are you a
man or an animal, Thurstan? Whatever you like. Neither. Eating?
What's eating? Cats eat their kittens, Thurstan. Ain't you a man?
Na. Then be-Jesus I'll make you one. They done something to you.
Thurstan, you poor louse. You got something, but it's lost, lost in you
like a needle in a haystack. Okey doke—I'm a magnet, see, cock?

"Nelson. Crazy.

"It's a bit of waste ground and a dark lane and the station. Do you
want to bust loose, Thurstan? Bust loose and run?

"You go to the police. Deserter. I'm absent. Hear? Run and be
hunted down? I'll leave it to you. Go on. Run away if you want to.
Run away. You yeller dog.

"I smack him.

"He smacks me. He's light. But good. I'm stronger. But you can't hold him. We fight. I fight good. I fight mad. I can hit. Anybody want to see how I can hit? You know I can hit. Ask Mac. Ask anybody. I can smash a door. A wall. I can smash. But Nelson I can't. No. He's good. Come on, Thurstan. Or do you want to run away?

"There's something. I never run away from any man, in any fight. But the heart goes out of me and I run. I run in the dark. He doesn't follow. All over the tin cans and dirty dead cats and rubbish and muck on the waste ground and up the street and round the back doubles and over a court and the night as black as bloody pitch. Stop.

"Night. A bit of the coconut off that cake mixed up with some blood in me teeth.

"Hit the wall. Smash me hand. What for? For nothing. Think. Run away? Yes. Ah. But from a proper man? Run away from the Army, run away from the coppers. But Nelson? Drop him a——? I should be a mug. I should take meself back for him? A sergeant? Hah. I'm not a fool.

"And then I walk, I walk back, I walk right back. I walk right back to the station. Train. Not in. A bit of a light. A bit of a light on a bit of a brass star. Nelson and the other one. I say Got a fag? Not a word from that man. Not a word. He gives me a Woodbine. Hi-de-hi, Thurstan . . . made up yer mind to give me the honour of your company back to camp? Ah. Light? Light. Like I said, Thurstan, there can be a needle in a great big haystack . . . but there *is* a needle *in* the haystack, somewhere in that haystack. Wash. What we want is a good wash. Stick it out, Thurstan. Stick it out like a pal. Be a pal, Thurstan, and stick it out. It's lousy. It's dull. Monotonous. Unjust. Uncomfortable. Anything you like. But it ain't being done for you. Nor me. Nor the C.O. Not for anybody in particular. It's a thing. You got to stick. Because you're a man and not an animal. You got to stick it out on your own, day by day, night by night of your own free will. After the war's all over go to hell your own way. Till then, come to hell our way.

"Ah.

"Hi-de-hi, Thurstan!

"Ho-de-ho, Sergeant!

"By the Christ, he was a man.

"A man."

And a silence comes upon the hut.

V

Jack Cattle

THIS SILENCE lasts for about two seconds. Then Thurstan breaks it by throwing down his boots and going out of the hut. As the big, loose door rattles shut behind him Bearsbreath says:

"I think that feller is going properly mad. I don't feel safe sleeping next to him. One of these days he's going to run amok. Could you make head or tail of that rigmarole, Crowne?"

"Well," says Sergeant Crowne, "in a general sort of way I could, sort of. I think I fluff what that geezer is driving at. Bill Nelson kind of won his respect. Though I can't say that Geordie makes himself clear. Blimey, I've known Arabs and Jews that talked almost better English than that kid."

At this a Guardsman whose name is Jack Cattle says:

"Thurstan talks as you or I talk in our sleep. You've got to piece what he says together like a jigsaw puzzle. He doesn't hand you a line of talk, but clues, like a crossword puzzle. Of course Thurstan's nuts, and dangerous. But what he was trying to say was something like this. . . . You or I would say it like this. . . . *I've never known where to go. Civvie Street was hell, because I couldn't muck in there. The Army was hell because I couldn't muck in there either. All my life I haven't known whether I've been going or coming. All my life I've been short of grub and everything. I gave myself up because I needed to eat. I didn't come back of my own free will. It was hunger that dragged me back like a dog that's been on the loose. Nelson saw that. Nelson wanted me to be a man with a will of his own, and not some kind of a dog nosing round the dustbins. So he gave me a chance to break away, after he'd fed me some grub. Nelson took that chance.*

He gambled his tapes on a feeling he had about me. And then I really came back of my own free will and took whatever punishment was coming to me.

"Get it? That's what Thurstan would have said if he could have said it; only he can't say it . . . he fiddles about and fumbles trying to get it out; shy, not knowing what to do or say, not certain of himself, like a kid of sixteen trying to undo a girl's dress for the first time."

This man Cattle is one of the oddest characters in the Brigade of Guards. He is a regular Guardsman of more than twelve years' service. It is said that he comes of what they call a Good Family, and has been to good schools. Sergeant Hands says Oxford, and Cambridge, and Harrow, and Eton. When newcomers ask Cattle what on earth made him join the Army, he replies, quite truthfully, that he joined the Army because he liked it; that he doesn't want a commission or a stripe because he is really perfectly happy as an ordinary soldier. Cattle went into the Army as another man might have gone to a South Sea island. Here, he feels untrammelled. He has no responsibilities. To him, the routine is gentle, almost soporific. He enjoys cleaning his equipment as some men enjoy gardening: it gives him time to think, it leaves his mind in a state of pleasant detachment. He loves the simple rhythm of a route march, and finds relaxation in a drill parade. Musketry revision gives him infinite pleasure, because he knows it all already: it leaves him with nothing to do except think. To him, the assembling of a Bren gun is an enjoyable little fidget. . . . He puts together the groups pretty much as you or I would tinker with a familiar wire puzzle that leaves our souls free to contemplate the infinite. He likes to be left alone. It seems to him that the Army leaves a man alone. The general opinion is that Cattle is a little insane. He is imperturbable as a stone buddha. No man ever heard him raise his voice or saw him raise his eyebrows. He lives in a state of bliss, of sublime mediocrity. He is beyond good and evil; beyond hope and fear; beyond astonishment and anger. He is detached, unhooked, gently floating in a more than earthly serenity. His great limbs swing loosely on his powerful torso. His huge-boned face wears a sweet, rippling smile. Every month he receives one letter, registered and sealed with the seal of a bank, and this letter simply begs to inform Mr. Jack Cattle that he will find enclosed the sum of four pounds. This represents all that is left of some little income he used to have. When the money comes, he puts it in his pocket and seems to forget it until somebody wonders if he could oblige with a small loan. Then he pulls out his money like a little handful of crushed leaves, and says: "Help yourself." He makes notes in a twopenny book. It appears that once in a while he has a thought, which he writes down. Sometimes he attempts to draw somebody's profile on the back of an old envelope. He will talk about anything, always with academic calm. The nearest he got to intimacy with any man was when he discussed life and books with The Schoolmaster, who left to be an officer.

He talks on, now, in his strange lazy way, idly shovelling into his sentences whatever words happen to get on to his tongue:

"You know, people do talk an awful lot of nonsense about what men are, and what they might have been. I heard somebody say Sergeant Nelson might have been . . . I forget what, but something or other that was very learned and professional, because Nelson had a clear mind and a good brain, and a way of expressing himself that made everything clear and exact. He had a fine understanding of men. But I think that Nelson found his real vocation in the Army, as a sergeant. What would he have done with another kind of job? In any other capacity, well, he would have been something not very much out of the ordinary. But as a sergeant he was great.

"Do you remember Old Silence? Poor Old Silence that got blown to hell when he left on leave to get married? Oh yes, yes, yes, Old Silence was a nice fellow and I liked him very much indeed. And he was an intelligent man with plenty of imagination and plenty of guts, and I think the world is so much the poorer since Old Silence got killed. Well, one day Old Silence and The Schoolmaster and I were talking about one thing and another and we got around to people we knew and so we came to Sergeant Nelson. He was their first Squad Instructor, you know. I knew Nelson quite well. We were out East together, and I got to see a good deal of him. Well . . . The Schoolmaster and Old Silence were saying the most fantastic things you ever heard in your life about Nelson. Old Silence said that in a country like America, way back in the eighteen-fifties, a man like Nelson could have been President, like Abraham Lincoln. Don't you believe it. Nelson's genius was just rightly placed. He was cut out to be great, if you understand what I mean, only as a *man* and not as some professional with a career."

Sergeant Crowne asks: "And what did The Schoolmaster say Bill ought to have been?"

"It sounded funny when The Schoolmaster said it, Sergeant. I don't suppose you'd guess what he said in a thousand years. He said Bill Nelson ought to have been a poet."

"A poet?"

"I'll tell you how it came about. One evening, it seems that Nelson was talking to the fellows about active service, and fighting, and living and dying, and all that, and while he was talking it seems that The Schoolmaster, who was a literary kind of a mug . . . you know, he couldn't think of a sunset or anything like that except in terms of rosebuds, or poached eggs, or anything else that was red except the sun. . . . The Schoolmaster took down what Nelson was saying almost word for word on a lump of paper. Then, you see, when he came to read it over, it seemed to him that Bill Nelson (poor old Bill Nelson! I can imagine what he would have said if he could have heard about this), Bill Nelson was talking pure poetry. This is a lot of poppycock, of course. But The Schoolmaster gave me what he'd written down. And this is how it sounded."

Guardsman Cattle fishes out a tin box, and selects from a bundle of mixed documents a couple of sheets of Y.M.C.A. notepaper. He looks at these sheets, grins with indescribable languor and reads:

Me,

I

see
men
die!
When
men
snuff
out,
day
or night,
they
might
cut
up rough—
shout
about
lying
dying.

Some
come
out
wiv:
"I
can't
die,
Sarnt!
Sarnt!
Shan't
I live?"

And a few say "Ooo,
why should I die
by night?"
They pray:
"Lord Gawd let me see the day!"

When men falls,
one

way or another,
they're done.
Some calls "Mother."
Some,
for rum. . . . And then agen,
men passing out round about
dawn start arsing about
trying to stop dying
till night; and still fight
for breath to hold back death
till dark. Definitely.
Many stay dumb and die dumb.
Most 've lived that way; dumb.
Some lark.
Bright light, or deep night, or dirty dawn,
I say a guy'll die as he was born—
on his Derby-and-Joan.
So why moan?
Try to satisfy
some geezers! Jesus
couldn't please us all.
You bawl
for what
you ain't got.
If hell is hot, you yell
for ice.
If it's cold, you want a fire.
Fat lot o' good, that.
Touch wood, I'm alive.
Time and time agen
I've
seen men live and die.
And me! Blimey—here I am.
Theories
apart,
Gawd knows fear is
a worse curse than death.

Right inside
you, your heart hammers
and beats. You sweats. You burn,
you lie and try to hide. . . .
Oh well, and then
in your turn—
being proper men—
you learn to be what they say
is brave. You behave right
and stand tight, and put a bold
face on it, and hold fast to
the last with as good a grace
as possible.
And so you see fear go.
Yeah, the line stands
ready, and your hands
are steady as steel, and you feel
fine. All right. Say you die
there and then? Why,
you horrible men, if you
survive for ever, you'll never
have been so definitely clean
alive!

"When you come to think of it," says Hands, "that really was something like how Bill used to talk, though I can't say I ever noticed him making things rhyme. It only goes to show—you can talk bloody poetry all your life and not know it."

"We—ell," dragged out Jack Cattle, "any man who knows what he wants to say and says what he's got to say without wasting words talks better than poetry, you mark my words. But old Nelson was dead hot on what you might call philosophy. He knew how to live, that man."

"Feared nothing," says Crowne.

"No, he was a brave mug," says Bearsbreath.

A voice says: "Brave nothing! I knew Bill Nelson. He was a dirty, rotten coward."

VI

The Cowardice of Nelson

WHEN BEARSBREATH is polite, time, for an instant, stands still, and men clear a space. The courtesy of Bearsbreath is as the hiss of an adder. His voice becomes sibilant; his legs grow tense and his hands hang loose. It will turn out better for you if Bearsbreath calls you a stinking dog than if he solicitously enquires after the state of your health. Now, he rises in a tired way and whispers: "I beg your pardon, old man, I'm afraid I didn't quite get that."

"I said Bill Nelson was a coward to the bone."

And Oxley, also, rises.

He is a long, lean man with huge feet and hands; all bone, a giant skeleton bound to last for ever in a network of huge sinews. His face looks, somehow, transparent yet unbreakable, like rhinoceros born . . . it has the same greyish yellowness and dull shine. There is a white lock in his dry black hair. His nose looks as if God designed it for tearing things. It overshadows a strange jutting mouth with a thin upper lip and a thick lower lip, which protrudes beyond the sullen bony jaw. He has green eyes. He might have been a Quartermaster, by now, only somewhere in his soul there roams an unchained leopard. He never rose above the rank of Lance-Corporal. His patience could stretch up to a certain point; and then it would snap. And whenever Oxley's patience gives way his right hand comes up like the heel of a wild ass. Once he hit a recruit. On another occasion he hit a Sergeant-Major. So he fell like Lucifer and will not rise again. He knows Bearsbreath, and Bearsbreath's fighting whisper. As Bearsbreath strolls over to confront him, Oxley walks out to meet that terrifying corporal. Bearsbreath, also,

222

has a temper. You can smell trouble in the air like an escape of gas. One spark, and there will be a white light and a stunning explosion. But The Budgerigar, who weight eighteen stone, of which not more than seven pounds is superfluous; who, alone among the heavyweights of the Coldstream Guards, once knocked out the man they call Ack-Ack Ackerman—The Budgerigar puts himself between them and says: "Hold it." There is a certain rasp of authority in the voice of this big simple-minded man. Bearsbreath pauses and says:

"You're a Guardsman, Oxley, and I'm a corporal. But anybody can have my lousy tapes. I don't mind being bust for chastising any lousebag that runs down Nelson after he's dead. Coward? Why, if you are half the coward he was you'd be a hero."

"Right," says Oxley, between his teeth, pumping out his words in his violent way, "you say Nelson was a hero and I say he was yeller, get me? Yeller."

Jack Cattle's voice, thick and slow, drops like oil upon the menacing surface of the argument. "Everybody's entitled to speak of people as he finds them. If he happens to be wrong, or right, doesn't matter. But he's entitled to expressing opinion. Now why, exactly, do you think Bill Nelson was a coward, Oxley?"

Oxley says: "He was dead scared of me. He avoided me. He run away from me. Isn't that being yeller? If f'rinstance, you're having a scrap with a man, and just when you're beginning to get the better of it he picks up his hat and runs away, isn't that being a coward? If it isn't being a coward what is it being? I been wanting to run into Nelson for five years. Only I always missed him. I had a bone to pick with him. I had a fight to finish off. I wanted to finish giving him the coating I started giving him that time when he ran away like a dirty rotten coward.

"You make me sick, all of you, with your bull-and-boloney about poetry and tripe like that. Nelson was tripe. He might have kidded people he was this and that. But I knew him better and I'm telling you,

Nelson was dirty tripe. If you want me to tell you why, I'll tell you why."

Silence.

"I knew him ever since he first joined. I knew him at the Depot when he was a recruit. I didn't like him then and I never did like him. I can tell when there's something funny about a bloke. I could tell it about Nelson. He was too smarmy. He was too smooth. He talked too bloody much. Ah yes, Nelson was hot on talking, dead hot, but not so bloody hot when it came to doing. We never did hit it off. Mind you, he was always trying to suck up to me. But I wasn't having any of it. He didn't kid me, with all his fake good nature and all his smarmy, soppy bull.

"He was underhanded. He was an informer. It was him that got me bust, first time. He was always trying to make himself popular among the recruits. He used to brag about how he never punished anybody. He didn't have the guts to punish anybody, not straight to anybody's face. No, he'd go down on his bended knees to a squad of rookies, and say, 'Do me a favour boys ... be good boys ... let me tuck you in at night and wipe your little snotty noses for you ... oh please be good boys and do what I ask you.' Is that the way for a Squad Instructor to be? And yet it goes down, it goes down like cream, that sort of dirty rotten, yellow, crawling around. And now nobody can say a bad word about Bill Nelson. Well I can, d'you hear?

"Call me regimental. Right. I *am* regimental. If there's a recruit that's got to be put into shape, by Christ he's got to be put into shape. Say somebody give you a bit of iron to fit on to something, and said: 'Your orders are, to fit that bit of iron.' What would you do? You wouldn't go down on your bended knees to that bit of iron. You wouldn't stroke it. No. You'd show that bit of iron the shape it had to go to, and you'd knock it round.

"Right. Nobody could ever say I knocked any man about. I chased 'em. And rightly so. I chased 'em till they didn't know their heads from their heels. Why not? You don't make a soldier with coddling. You make a soldier, I can tell you, by letting him see he'll be miserable if he isn't a soldier, miserable. Right.

"Now. Bearsbreath here——"

"Address me as Corporal, you yellow-bellied son of a fat-faced dog!" says Bearsbreath.

"You? You, as Corporal? Why, I was a Corporal——"

"Okay, Regimental! I can be regimental if I want to be. You're a Guardsman now. Address me as Corporal, or so help me God I run you inside for insubordination!"

Oxley says: "Corporal Bearsbreath here . . ."

"That's better!"

". . . Corporal Bearsbreath here says . . ."

A pause. Oxley is looking for words. Somebody says: "Yes?"

"I forgot what I was going to say," says Oxley.

"Sure you did. I got regimental. I picked you up. I interrupted. I was hammering you round, Oxley," says Bearsbreath. "I made you call me Corporal. Well? Go on!"

Oxley bites words off and swallows them, and regurgitates them:

"You can't handle a rook proper and handle him with kid gloves. There was a bloody dirty-rotten raving idiot called Rivers. Anybody remember Recruit Rivers? He deliberately didn't do what you told him to do. It was dirty-rotten spite and dirty-filthy-rotten malice. He wanted to make you look small. I stood that bastard for three weeks. If I said *Left*, he went right. If I said *Halt*, he went on. He was trying to get me. He was laying it down for me. I fluffed his game and kept my temper; but I took it out of him in other ways.

"One day Nelson says to me: 'Leave that kid alone and he'll do the same as the others do,' he said. Now that is a lot of bull-and-boloney and dirty-filthy-rotten-lousy poppycock. Let him alone! I says to Nelson: 'Keep your nose out o' my squad.' I says, 'Arscrawl around your own dirty little squad, but leave mine alone.' He just laughed, to annoy me. He was always trying to annoy me. I said nothing. I can hold my temper.

"Then it comes the Fourth Week Inspection.

"Now there's Lieutenant in Number 25 Company called Lieutenant Leffnant. He was a Subaltern. This lousebag Rivers gets through his foot drill. Then the officer comes round asking questions . . . how many battalions are there, and when was the Regiment founded? and all that. And he comes to Rivers, and he asks Rivers: 'Who is the Colonel of the Regiment?'

"And what does this Rivers say? He says: 'Lieutenant Leffnant.' So help me God."

("Nerves," says Sergeant Hands.)

"My squad gets through this inspection, but it was boiling in me. This dirty little rotten dog Rivers! And later on I gets him aside and I says: 'What did you mean by saying Lieutenant Leffnant was Colonel of the Regiment? I'm your Squad Instructor. Were you trying to make a fool of me?' And he starts to laugh. 'Stop laughing,' I says, and shakes him a bit, but he laughs louder still. And then . . . well, I got self-control, everybody knows I got enough self-control . . . I says: 'What's the joke?' In my day I'd have been taken back of the latrines and beaten to death, pretty well. 'What's the joke?' I says, and this Rivers swine laughs all the more. So I smacks him in the face. I lets him have a smack in the face. Not a punch: a smack, with my flat hand. And he shuts up this giggling, and he starts to shake again. Then he has hysterics like a woman. He pretends to go into hysterics. So I shakes him again and says, 'Shut up!' Then he laughs all the louder, and I lose my temper a bit and bop him in the stomach, and he falls down. He lies there laughing and crying, and just then Nelson comes by.

"He looks at me, and he goes and picks this kite up, and he strokes him like a dirty-rotten cat, and says, 'There, there,' and gives him a fag. Then he says to this Rivers: 'You've got to report this, Rivers.' He didn't ask whether Rivers wanted to report it. He *ordered* him to report me for striking him. And Rivers did.

"Then Nelson said to me: 'What you want is a team o' mules, Oxley, not a squad o' kids.'

"I said: 'We'll talk about this later, you rotten-lousy-stinking officers' pet you.' He said: 'Okay.' And I was for Orders. Believe me when I tell

you? Nelson—so help me God Almighty—give evidence against me.
And I was bust. And I got fourteen days.

"I looked for Nelson for a long time after that. I wanted to get him
alone. I wanted to paralyse him. Who wouldn't? Answer me that. And
so it comes round to wintertime, November. I was at a point near
Caterham. I remember the date. It was two days before Armistice Day,
in 1937, November 9th. I was in Purley, on an evening off. I had a
drink in the 'Jolly Farmers,' and I went to see a picture. I came out of
this picture and went into the 'Railway,' and who should I see there
but Nelson.

"I said to Nelson: 'I want to talk to you.'

"He said: 'Go ahead.'

I said: 'Not here.'

" 'Private?' he said. I said it was private.

"And I said: 'Will you have it here, or will you step a little way
away?' I said, 'Cause I'm going to give you something I owe you.'

"He says: 'Oh-oh' . . . just like that. 'Oh-oh.' He's drinking a pint,
and he leaves it. He says: 'Look here,' he says. 'Get this over. I don't
want to fight you. Especially tonight, I don't. You done wrong, and it's
paid off. Forget it,' he says. 'But don't drag me into a fight tonight,'
he says.

"I tell him: 'There won't be no tomorrow. We're different places.
And so help me God in Heaven, if you don't come with me I'll start on
you now, and I don't care if it means fifty-six days. I don't care if it
means fifty-six years,' I says.

"He says: 'Lay off of me.'

"I says: 'I should think so. I been looking for you for ages. And we
settle this now.'

"He says: 'Settle what? What'll a smack in the teeth settle?'

" 'Yellow,' I says.

" 'No,' he says. 'But I can't start anything now.'

" 'You're a dirty coward,' I says, 'and if you don't walk over the common with me, I'll let you have it on this spot.'

" 'Right,' he says.

"We walk. We gets over the Common. I say: 'Ready?' He says: 'Be quick,' and we starts.

"We goes on for five minutes. I put him down three times. He puts me down twice. We clinch, and he starts fighting dirty. He used his head. He used his knees. But I had him going. He tripped me up, and when I went down he lets me have one with his elbow on the chin. But I was mad, I was going good. After about another five minutes, we slow down. I got him again, and he got me. Then I went all out, and put him down twice more. The second time, he asks me to postpone the fight. 'Make it another day, Oxley,' he says. I says: 'Now.'

"I stands back. I lets him get up, because I don't fight dirty like Nelson. He would of got me if he could, on or off the ground. Not me. Me, I stand back, and he gets up on one knee.

"Then, you'll never believe what he done. You think he's a hero. Oh yes, a hero. Oh sure, a bloody hero. Not half a hero! He reaches out a hand, and grabs his cap, and picks up his belt, and he's off. So help me God! He runs! He runs off in the dark, fast as his legs will carry him, in and out of the bushes, running like mad.

"Yes, he run.

"I followed him as well as I could. But he was quicker on his legs than me. He needed to be. He wanted to be a quicker runner than me! He got away.

"And he might be a hero here. Oh, yes, he might be a bloody V.C. round this place. But I know I fought him and he broke and run. I didn't catch up with him again. But I waited my time. Well, all right, so he's dead now. I wish nobody dead. But don't make him out a hero. Don't make out Nelson was a God or a Saint. No, because I know a thing or two about him. Run him down? I run him down when he was alive, didn't I? Then why should I start crying over him for a hero when he's dead?

"He run away from me. He run like a rabbit.

"Well?"

Butcher the Butcher turns away from the wall.

"You said Purley, Oxley?"

"You heard what I said. I said Purley."

"You said 1937?"

"1937."

"Two days before Armistice Day was what you said?"

"I did. Well?"

"That'd make it November 9th, 1937."

"Well?"

"What time at night?"

"About nine."

Butcher the Butcher sits up, and says: "November nine, 1937, nineish at night, eh? Oh. Then just you listen to me . . ."

VII

Nine-Eleven-Thirty-Seven

BUTCHER THE BUTCHER becomes fluent again. He can drop words as an egg-boiler lets out sand. Now, there being something in his heart, he grows eloquent. The voice of Butcher is commensurate with his bulk. It is a great, deep, meaty, bloodshot voice. You are surprised to hear it dance so fast from word to word. His talk is strong and heavy, yet quick. He is a wrestler in language.

He says:

"Nine, eleven, thirty-seven, eh? And the time . . ." He pauses, like a prosecuting counsel. "The time was about nine.

"You sour-faced liar! You slanderer and perjurer and taker-away of men's names! Bill Nelson could have smashed you and whopped you to tomato sauce, given time. You put him down. All right, you put Bill down. Okay! Okay! Dempsey's been put down! Yes, Luis Firpo, the Wild Bull of the Pampas, put Jack Dempsey down and right out of the ring—but Jack Dempsey came roaring back like a wild tiger, and he killed Firpo stone stark dead, he did. And so would Nelson have done you, you grousing mug! Oh, don't start giving me looks, Oxley! I know you're tough. But I'm none so stinking soft! You was getting the better of Bill. Yes, maybe. I don't deny it. Firpo was getting the better of Dempsey, but it took seventeen hundred doctors and fifty thousand priests to stick Firpo together agen when Dempsey had done with him. Do you think, you louse-bound twit, that you're getting the better of a man if you put that man down for a second! Shullup and lemme talk! Lemme getta word in edgeways. Why, Jesus Almighty, you could of put Bill Nelson down with a twenty-eight pound sledge. You could of put Bill down with a Numane Killer, with a dripping great pole-axe, you could of. But if it'd been a fight he wanted to win, he'd 've got up and wan it! I know. I saw Bill in the Milling Contest with Dusty Smith, Dagwood over there, and Sarnt Hands. I saw Bill Nelson fight many and many a time. You're bigger. Oxley. You weigh three stone more. But Bill had a spirit you never saw in your life. You got temper. Bill had spirit.

"And you of all people are telling me of all people on this dirty-filthy earth, that Bill Nelson ran away from you on the ninth of November, in the year of all bleeding years 1937.

"You! Me!

"I never knew he met you that night. I never knew until this very moment that Bill met you that night. Strike me down dead into the earth. I never knew. But I do know somebody else Bill met on that very same night, on or about that very same time. And I have documents in my very pocket to prove the words I say, and all men can step forward and bear witness!

"It's a thing I wouldn't have talked about, because it's a private thing, do you see? It's a thing that's nobody's business but mine, because it concerns me and my private life. On this very earth and no other, only Bill Nelson knew about it. He was my pal in the old days, and my pal always. I wish to God I'd died with Bill Nelson, but that wasn't the way it had to be.

"Listen to me. Everybody listen to me. Oxley here says Bill Nelson was yeller. It's a lie. It's a dirty lie and I'll say so to Oxley's face, or in the face of the C.O. himself now or before the throne of God.

"Listen. I was in the butchery business, and I had a very nice job. I was a manager. I was in a nice position, and knocked up a decent screw. I was going to get a business of my own. I knew Bill Nelson in those days, when he was just sort of drifting into the Army, and I was working my way up in business. Then, God forgimme, I used to jeer at Bill and say he ought to go steady and try and get into something proper.

"I had a nice few quid saved up, do you hear? A very nice few quid.

I was engaged to a young girl I was crazy about. I worshipped the ground she trod on, and I don't know how it was, but somehow or other I was jealous of her. She never looked at any other man, not once. But the less she sort of looked at anybody else, the more jealous I got. In the end I married her. Go on, talk about your Greta gorblimey Garbos and your Joan Crawfords and your blonds and your glamourettes. My wife was the most beautiful woman in the world, and I loved her like God Almighty. Yes, I did. Only I was jealous, I was crazy jealous.

"We'd been married about six months when one day I came home and found her with some geezer's arms round her. So I give this other geezer a dressing-down, and I give my poor little woman a smack in the face, may God forgimme, and I rushed out of the place, and I drew out of the bank the dough I was going to use for the business, and I went on the Cousin Sis, and after about six weeks I got through three hundred pounds, and I was flat on the ribs.

"I didn't think of going back and talking it over. I'm that sort of bloody fool. That's me, fool right through to the bones. I went and joined the Army. I remembered something I'd seen in a book, and I went to join this mob. That's how I come to join the Brigade of Guards.

"My wife sort of traced me. I never knew how. I know, now, that she traced me through poor old Bill Nelson. He had a heart too big for his poor body, my china Bill. She kept on writing to me, and writing, and I recognized her fist, and I never answered her letters. I never even opened 'em. It wasn't that I didn't want to hear from my little woman; only I was sort of mad, proud. I was afraid if I read anything she wrote, I'd go and reply by return, and make it up with her . . . and I thought she was making a mug of me, and I couldn't bear it. So I put her out of my head.

"Get me? That's how it was.

"Yes, you'd better listen carefully. You Oxley, listen to me. You can be as tough as God Almighty, but you won't chuck a scare into me. No.

"Comes round some time in November, and Bill Nelson, that was squad-instructing then, and a Corporal, says to me like this: 'Butcher. I want to talk to you about something very particular indeed.'

" 'What's that?'

" 'Never mind what's that,' he says. 'I want to talk to you. I want you to be in the "Farmers" at no later than eight-thirty pip-emma to-night. Get it? Eight-thirty, in the "Farmers." I know it's your night out,' he says, 'so don't fail me, because this is important.'

"I was his pal, and I'd meet him anywhere and at any time, and so I says okey-doke, I'll be there.

"There's nothing much to this. But listen, because I'm telling you.

"For the love of God listen to me, Oxley!

"I turn up at the 'Farmers,' and Bill isn't there. I knock back a pint, and then another pint, and still Bill doesn't turn up. I watch the clock, and I wonder what it can all be about. Eight-thirty. Eight-forty. No Bill, and this is a bit queer, because Bill turns up on time, usually. You can set your clock to Bill, as a rule. Ten to nine. Then all of a sudden a bloke comes in looking shocking and disgraceful, a disgraceful sight. It's Bill. He's got a black eye. He's got a swelled nose. He's got a puffed lip. He's got a lump on his jawbone. He's got an inflamed earhole. He's got a torn tunic and mud on his back.

"I don't want him to run the risk of running into the Gestapo in his condition, and so I leaves half my pint and goes to head him off. I meets him in the doorway and says, 'Come and get a wash, you Burke.'

"He says: 'Never mind washing. I want to tell you something. I never had a chance till now. I'd have been earlier, only I had a bit of an accident. Listen,' he says. 'That about your old woman was a big mistake. Your good lady is as respectable as your mother or mine,' he says, 'and I'll lay my life on it. She's off her head in love with you, Butch,' he says. 'She wasn't carrying on with nobody.' He says this breathless, gasping, as if he'd been running hard and fast. 'She never carried on with nobody. The bloke you see her with was drunk. He burst in. It came out after. She never see him before, Butch. There was other complaints. It was all cleared up. Butch, what you got to do is, make friends again. Don't be a fool, Butcher; don't be a silly horrible idiot. Come with me and have a cup of tea, and let me tell you . . .'

"We goes to a tea-and-wad-shop round the corner, and as we go in Bill Nelson grips my arm and holds me. I feel myself going round and round, because there at a table, with a cup of tea in front of her (she was never the woman to sit in a place without ordering anything), there she was, sitting with her heart in her mouth.

"She had come down on Nelson's responsibility, do you see? He'd paid her fare and found her a room. He knew that if I see her again I'd stay and apologize. He sort of *knew* it. More especially as she was about three months off having a kid, do you see? And he'd made a date with her for that night, that time, and swore he'd bring me. He knew I'd turn up for *him,* just as he knew that my rotten silly pride would stop me coming along to see *her.* Get me? He understood all that, and banked on it; banked on what he sort of had a feeling on in the matter.

"And when I saw her I just went like dried-up boot polish when you fan it with a lit match . . . I ran, I went liquid, I melted away, I got moist.

"I said: 'Hiya, duck.' She said: 'Hiya, Joe.'

"Bill had taken a room for us and paid the first week's rent in advance. I saw how right he was. But I'd signed on for twenty-one years. I didn't have the money to buy myself out.

"The kid was born nine weeks later.

"It died. It was a he. She died too. They both died. That last few weeks was all right, though. We got together and understood each other, like. She knew all about me, I mean . . . but I sort of understood her, and we kind of linked up, sort of style. She was the only one, always. Never mind all that bull-and-boloney, though. Do you think I'm going to forget nine, eleven, thirty-seven? The ninth of November, two days before Armistice Day, at nineish at night? If I live to be ten thousand million billion years old, do you think I'll ever forget?

"And you dare to tell me that Bill Nelson ran away from you, Oxley? You bloody dare to tell me that? As I reckon it, he felt pretty sure he could finish you off in time to get back and fix her and me up again.

And when time passed he just run. He run away, yes. But *from you,* Oxley? Never in your life. Not if you was an army of dirty lousy Oxleys with a Bren in each hand. A louse bag like you would of stayed and fought it out—which it was Bill's nature to do—and you would have let everything else go to pot. That's you. But Bill ran away. Not *from* you. *To* her, for her sake and my sake. . . . He only stood to lose. Bill always did stand to lose. But say he's yeller again. Say it now. Say it and I'll do yer, if it takes me ten years. If I swing fifty foot high. Now say it!"

Oxley shrugs his great bony shoulders.

"You don't scare me," he says. "But it don't matter one way or another. *I* shan't say it. I said it. If it was like that, all right, forget it."

"Take it back," says Butcher the Butcher.

"Well," says Oxley. "He might not have been yeller. But he didn't ought to have run off like that."

"You, what do you understand about anything?" asks Butcher.

"I'd rather he knifed me," says Oxley, "or kicked me in the guts. I don't like seeing a man running away. But taking it all in all, I'm prepared to overlook it."

VIII

A Kind of Pink Snake

OXLEY BROODS for a few seconds, and then says: "See what I mean? If it was a Jerry, or a Wog, or a Wop, well, if he run away it'd be no more than what I expected and so I wouldn't hold it against him. But a bloke in your own mob, no, he's not entitled to run away, not even from you. Where do you stand if blokes on your own side start running away all of a sudden? No disrespect to the dead, but say you found yourself in a trench next to a bloke that run away from you? Would that be good for your morale?"

His face softens. "I admit I never could stick him," he says, "but I will go so far as to say he marked me up a bit. Bill Nelson was a body-puncher. It didn't show much, but it felt. He sort of lifted up a kind of . . . I don't know quite what to call it, but a sort of punch as if he was lifting a sack of flour, and always at the body. It told. After a few of those, you felt sort of not quite so fresh. And I don't mind saying that if he'd put a few of those body-punches round about the head, well, I would have got up all right, but maybe I wouldn't have got up quite so soon. I couldn't stick Nelson at any price, but in a way he was like me in the matter of a punch—he put some sting into it."

"He was soft-hearted," says Bearsbreath. "He'd punch you in the guts but not in the teeth because he didn't like to do any damage that couldn't be repaired. He hated to leave a mark."

Hands says: "Mark! Hah! Did you ever hear about the time Bill Nelson and me got tattooed in Egypt?"

Hands rolls up a sleeve and uncovers something that is supposed to represent a terrifying reptile in faded red, tattooed on his forearm.

236

"What I really wanted to have done was one of those belly-dancers. The general idea is, they tattoo them over the muscle, and then when you wiggle your arm, they dance. Their little bellies kind of waggle, provided you got muscles enough to provide the background. That was my original intention when I got tattooed. But as it so happened, fate intervened."

Sergeant Crowne says: "It's a thing of the past, tattooing. Only kids and crooks get it done. Lots of old sweats have got a mark or two . . . a snake here, a crucifix there, or something like *I Love Amy,* or *Death Rather Than Dishonour,* but they only get that done when they're very young, and they're sorry afterwards. Skin is like wallpaper. If you got to live with it you might as well have it plain. Bill Nelson only had one tattoo mark that I know of, and that was . . ."

"Two clasped hands," says Dagwood.

"Nothing of the sort," says The Budgerigar. "It was a palm tree."

"As far as I remember," says Hands, "it was——"

"A skull and cross-bones," says Crowne, "and a motto, a motto which said: *My Mother Is My Only Sweetheart."*

"Now that I come to think of it," says The Budgerigar, "it could have been the Regimental Star done in blue and red."

"Listen," says Hands, "I happen to know that Bill Nelson had two tattoo marks. One was on his wrist, or thereabouts. It was a kind of a blue bird. And there was another one on the left-hand side of his chest which said: *I Love Daisy.* It was supposed to be over his heart, but the bloke that did it was some kind of a Syrian, and according to this here Syrian, Bill's heart was somewhere near his armpit. The coloured races are ignorant.

"It was the most ridiculous thing you ever heard of in your life. I don't suppose you ever heard of Sergeant-Major Twine? We used to call him Swine. He was a misery. He only made one joke in his life, and to this day nobody can be certain that he wasn't serious. First parade on board the ship going East, after he dismissed the parade, he said: 'All right. Dismiss. Nobody leave the ship.' He was unpopular, but actually I got on with him fairly well. He was regimental, but fair, and usually when he said a thing, he more or less meant it. I can't vouch for his loyalty, but he was once seen standing up for one of his sergeants during some argument or other. I forget what. He was a real old sweat. He had a wife and kid in Cairo, an Irish wife. Well, all of a sudden, this kid of his seemed to grow up like a mushroom, almost overnight. One day she was a skinny little girl with long legs, and the next afternoon she blossomed out into a raving beauty such as I've never before seen in my life. You know Ann Sheridan? You remember Marie Dressler? Well, compared with this kid Pat, Ann Sheridan was as plain as Marie Dressler. She was a blond, with black eyes, and very well developed for her age, or, for that matter, any other age. I dare say she must have been about seventeen, or probably less. She got about eleven proposals of marriage every twenty-four hours. As soon as you saw a feller putting scented brilliantine on his hair, you knew perfectly well that he was going to propose to Pat Twine.

"I was young and foolish then, and I don't mind admitting that in a way I fell for her myself. It was probably the climate. I hung around this kid like any lovesick mug. The funny thing is that I was quite serious then. So was nearly everybody else in Cairo. But she, I need scarcely say, was aiming no doubt at bigger game than mere mugs of N.C.O.s in the Brigade of Guards. After all, she had the example of her father before her to warn her what this mob can do to a man after seventy or eighty years of service. I don't think she wanted to be a soldier's wife at all, because she was a sharp kid and she could see what had happened to her Mum through being a soldier's wife. The old girl was pretty awful.

"All the same, although we all knew we were wasting our time, we hung around her. You know what kids are when it comes to love and all that kind of thing. Bolts and bars won't hold them. Well, one day, when I was off duty, I ran into her and began to chat with her a bit. You know how ridiculous these girls stand, twiddling their heels, and blinking their eyes, and swinging their arms about, and showing off their figures. She waggled herself about, and then got around to talking about some fellow called Finnan who, she said, wanted to marry her. Of course, I asked her whether she cared anything about this Finnan, and needless to say she hummed and hawed, and tried to make me jealous, and succeeded in doing so. And she said: 'Well, I don't know, Sergeant Hands, but I'm certain that Walter Finnan would make a very devoted husband. Do you know what he did, only the other week? He had my name tattooed over his heart, as a proof that, whether I would have him or not, he would never look at another woman as long as he lived.'

"And then I started to tell her that all that was nothing. I told her how real devotion to a young woman came from the heart, and was more than skin-deep. After all, tattooing was only skin-deep. She seemed to be offended at that and said that, after all, it was Finnan's business what he did with his devotion or his skin, and no business of mine.

"I had it bad. I could think of nothing and nobody but her, and I lay awake nearly all that night, unreasonably annoyed with this Finnan, who was a very harmless sort of mug, and somehow going into a rage about his having her name tattooed over his heart. And then I made my mind up to get tattooed with her name myself, the very next payday.

"Well, there was a little Syrian bloke whose name was Hassan, who did a good deal of Army tattooing off and on. There were better tattooers, but Hassan was cheap. I believe he used to either drink, or smoke opium, or take hashish. Or maybe he was just a bit of a lunatic, like everybody else connected with the Army. Be that as it may, he was pretty hot on *Death Rather Than Dishonour* and graveyard crosses with *In Memoriam* underneath them. Poor mugs of soldiers, their own silly skins are about all they can count on carrying about with them for certain in peacetime. And I'm not so sure about that either. . . . So I go to Hassan, and this little Hassan wallah is sitting down, rather like a pig in a trance. He asks me what I want and I tell him that I want *I Adore Pat* right over my heart, in blue letters of a reasonably-priced size.

"I've never had anything done to me that hurt me half so much. It hurts like hell, this tattooing gag. No more of it for me, I don't care who

I fall in love with. They ought to give you gas. It took him a long time, too, because he seemed to be somehow a little bit dopey. The more he hurried the more he hurt me, but at last he got through it and I paid him and scrammed. But as I'm going out, who should I meet in the doorway but Bill Nelson.

"'What you doing here, Bill?' I ask him.

"'Oh, nothing,' he says, 'nothing at all. I just come to make a couple of enquiries. I tell you what I'll do, Handsy—I'll meet you for a drink across the road in about half an hour's time.'

"All right. I go and get myself one lukewarm beer, which takes about half of all the money I have left, and I wait, and at last, after nearly an hour and a quarter, Bill Nelson turns up and sits down opposite me. He has the price of two beers, so he orders, and we sort of have a bit of a chat.

"Then he says: 'Handsy, what were you doing over there in Hassan's?' And I tell him that I've just gone and had one or two decorations put on me, and he asks what.

"Well, he's a pal, so I take him into my confidence and I tell him that it's practically impossible for me to go on living without this girl Pat, and so I've gone and had her name tattooed over my heart, since it seems that she likes that sort of thing. At this poor old Bill looks very down in the mouth and asks me: 'What did you say over your heart, Handsy?' So I tell him, and he says: 'Oh, Jesus.' I ask him what's up, and he says: 'Well, to tell you the honest truth, Handsy, I feel pretty much the same way about her myself. And to be perfectly frank with you, I've been and had my own heart sort of decorated with the same motto.' I ask him if it hurts, and he says it hurts like stink. Then I say to him: 'Bill, let's see what sort of a job that little dopey idol done on you.' He says: 'No, you let me see yours first.' So he undoes his tunic and waits, holding his great big hands over his bosom, like the naked girl in that picture of September Morn. I rips open my tunic and shows him my bit of lettering. I've got it here to this day. I dunno what to do with it. It has practically ruined my life, this bit of tattooing. Bill looks, and he kind of grins as if he's very proud of himself, and he says: 'I've got a dollar's worth of fancy scrollwork round mine.' I say: 'Let's look, Bill.'

"He lets me see, and I takes a good look and then I practically have to strangle myself to stop from busting out laughing. Because do you know what this nigger Hassan has been and done? Under the influence of whatever it was he took to liven himself up, he'd done a marvellous job of work, a smashing hot job. He'd put the lettering inside a sort of fancy heart, with twiddley bits all round it; but instead of the name Pat he'd gone and put Daisy. Don't ask me why. I dare say some other mug had got tattooed with the name of Daisy, and it had somehow sort of come to the front of his mind just as these things will when you're a bit tight.

"I said: 'That's smashing, Bill,' and he said: 'It'll be pretty hot in a week or so when the swelling goes down.'

"That night our tattooings swell up. Have you ever tried to do a slope with fresh tattooing on your chest? You want to try it some time. The agonies we suffered, nobody would believe. You couldn't read a thing; there was just blue and red blobs. Then, at last, the swelling goes down and the inscriptions stick out like a punch in the mouth, and Bill says 'Daisy? Daisy? I don't know no Daisy. There is something very funny about this.' I say: 'You better go and argue that out with Hassan,' and Bill, looking very much like business, goes to look up this here tattooer. I, in the meantime, go and look for this kid Pat, and I find her, and I tell her about this proof of my devotion and I undo my shirt and show her this bit of lettering. I'm not the man to do down a pal, but all is fair in love and war. I say to her: 'If I were you, Pat, I wouldn't take too much notice of Bill Nelson, who seems to be hanging around you. He has just got himself tattooed with a great big heart and the name of Daisy in it. Whereas, I love you alone.' She says: 'Oh Daisy, eh?' And leaves me standing.

"I saw Bill that night. It seemed that this tattooer, Hassan, had either died or otherwise disappeared. No satisfactory conclusion could be reached about this misprint on poor old Bill Nelson. And for days and days Bill went about with a face as long as a fiddle. But a funny thing happened. Young Pat started to run after old Bill. Wherever he went she was sure to be hanging about, and once or twice she collared him and asked him who was this woman Daisy who she had not heard anything at all about. This, of course, got poor old Bill embarrassed, and he gave her what you might call evasive answers. She, naturally, was not satisfied with what Bill said. And so the end of it all was, that instead of Bill running after Pat, Pat kept running after Bill, absolutely dying to get a look inside his shirt. This seems to be in the nature of the so-called sex. And so she developed a sort of infatuation for Bill, and the more she developed this infatuation, the more Bill wondered what he could have seen in her, until the end of it all was, he flatly told her not to keep hunting him down and making his life a misery. Yet there was not a man in the battalion who would not have given his right hand to be in Bill's position.

"It all comes out in the wash, pals, it all comes out in the wash.

"We shifted. We done a bit of the good old hand-to-hand with the good old Wogs, and that was that.

"As for the little blue bird, I believe that was done, so to speak, to relieve the boredom when we was out in the desert, by some Mick that had taken a correspondence course in tattooing. But we had some fun with the Wogs . . ."

IX

Dead Hot Shooting

"AND THERE you are," says Dagwood. "There's life all over."

"What's life all over? D'ya mean, life all over?" asks Crowne.

"Why," says the deliberate-voiced Sergeant, lounging on his bed, "what I mean is this. Here's dozens of us all talking about Nelson, who we knew well, and that was our pal, see; and here we are shouting the odds, and chewing the rag about Bill Nelson this, and Bill Nelson that ... and, well, I'm damned if we don't forget what he looked like. You can't even remember what like he was tattooed."

"Shut up," says Hands.

"Ah," says Dagwood, and there is a sad twist in his smile. "Who remembers what Bill Nelson looked like? What colour eyes?"

"Grey," says Hands.

"Blue," says Dagwood. "Light blue. What height was he, about?"

"Five foot nine," says Hands.

"About five-eleven," says Butcher.

"He was about six foot one or two," says Dagwood. "And he weighed no more than a pound or two under twelve stone. Hair?"

"Fair," says Crowne.

With some excitement, Hands cries: "Dead wrong! His hair was blackish."

"There you are," says Dagwood, "one says light, another says dark. One says blue, another says grey. He had hair the same colour as mine —mousey, or what they call Brown. Teeth? Any teeth?"

A pause. "Yeahmp, he had some teeth," says Crowne.

"Real or false?"

"He wasn't a horse, and I wasn't *buying* the man," says Crowne, annoyed. "Well? Real or false?"

"I never noticed myself," says Dagwood. "Distinguishing marks or characteristics?"

"He had a good walk," says Hands.

"A busted nose. Slightly busted," says Butcher.

"You're telling me," mutters Oxley.

"Scars?" asks Dagwood.

"Slight scars on forehead," says Bearsbreath, "from when his eye come out."

"And a deep scar on his jaw," says Dagwood. "I was around when that one happened. It was sort of an accident. I kind of shot him."

Dagwood opens his slim old knife and pares some frugal slices off a plug of tobacco. Between palms like little millstones he rubs the slices to shreds, and fills the untouchable-looking pipe Sergeant Brown gave him.

Every man has his little parsimony. Hands makes a tin of brass polish last two years: Crowne would lie circumstantially and bare-facedly to avoid giving away a metal fly button, of which he has accumulated a secret hoard of more than fifteen hundred. And Dagwood won't buy a pipe. It is fascinating to watch Dagwood trying to make somebody give him one. This knobbly-faced old soldier who never owed a penny and who maintains a sublime independence by disciplining his desires and needs will coquette for a foul old pipe like a glamour girl who yearns for furs.

He will say—picking up the carbonized remains of six-penn'orth of unseasoned briar—"Pretty far gone, Bill?"

"Think so, Dag?"

"All burnt 'n cracked."

"Bit of insulating tape 'd fix that up, Dag."

"I'll tape it up for you if you like, Bill. I got some tape."

"That's all right, Dag. Don't bother."

"That's all right, Bill; no bother."

". . . Leave that bloody pipe alone, Dag!"

"I was only looking, Bill. *You* don't want a pipe like this, Bill. Pipe like this is no use to you."

"No? I wouldn't part with that pipe for a million quid."

"*I* wouldn't mind smoking a rotten old pipe like that, Bill. I could do with a pipe."

"You'll get that pipe over my dead bloody body, Dag."

"Keep calm, Bill."

"I am calm, Dag."

"I could give you a lovely lighter for that pipe, Bill."

"What sort lighter?"

"I got it at home, Bill. I found it by a stroke o' luck when I was doing the drains. A lovely brass lighter, and all it wants is some petrol."

"Has it got a wick?"

"Well, not exactly a wick, no."

"Wheel?"

"Well, it might need a bit of a wheel."

"Flint?"

"To tell you the honest truth, I don't believe there is a flint. Not a *flint,* Bill, no. But all you need do is spend a bob on it for repairs and you've got a lighter that'd cost you quids."

"I wouldn't take a fifty-pun-note for a pipe like this, Dag; let alone a busted old lighter."

"I wouldn't take a man's pipe for nothing, Bill: I'd have give you a thirty-five-shilling lighter for it."

"For a pipe like this I wouldn't take fifty pound down and three pound a week for life, Dag, on my word of honour."

"Well, all right, Bill. I'll help you mend it if you like. A bit of tape . . ."

"Oh, go to hell, you scrounging, loafing bastard! Here you are, take the lousy pipe. I was going to chuck it away, anyway."

"Beg pardon, Bill? What's that? Pipe? For *me?* Why, that's very nice of you, Bill . . ."

The Budgerigar, also, has a weakness for very old and unspeakably foul pipes. Sometimes, he and Dagwood make an exchange." These two big, dapper N.C.O.s sit and haggle for hours over some blackened and stinking cherrywood, like tramps quarreling over the pickings of a dustbin.

". . . A deep scar on his jaw," says Dagwood. "I shot him."

"*You* shot Bill?" There is astonishment in the hut, for Dagwood is a born marksman, who aims a rifle as you or I point a finger. A man like Dagwood doesn't have accidents with firearms.

"Well, to be more exact, I missed him just there," says Dagwood. "It was sort of like this . . ."

We was together a lot (says Dagwood), from the time we were re- cruits together. There was a kind of friendly feed between us. A feed— when two fellers are out for each other's blood. Feud, is it? Right, feud. We could run just about the same, and jump and drill fairly equal, and box each other to a standstill so that it was always hard to come to a verdict when Bill and me was in the ring together. But the thing Bill was proudest of was shooting.

He was pretty fair. We were in the same Company. We fired that Empire Musketry thing together. Bill scored a possible, twenty bulls. So did I. It was hottish firing. The officer was dead pleased. He measured our grouping with a calliper, and so help me it was pretty well dead equal in each case. We both got a medal—one of those little silverish things about big enough to put in a Christmas pudden. Only there'd be danger of swallowing it. Soppy little medal, mannyfactured in Brum- magem by some Italian firm. But it's the honour of the thing that counts. I got my medal still. My old woman keeps it in a locked cupboard. I call it the Dagwood Plate. In the middle of the night she'll wake up and snatch a poker and say: "The burglars are after your medal." I should put its value at fourpence, but it's about all the silverware there is in the house.

Well, Bill and me go to the Training Battalion together and we fire

our course there. That time, I was a bit up on Bill's score. He said it was
because a fly got into his eye. It might have done, because Pirbright is
full of flies. I once asked a man what was the cause of all the flies at
Pirbright, and he said: "You know how flies and bluebottles and things
always get round a dead body? Well, Pirbright's mostly dead ground."
That was only a gag. But, anyway, I had a possible, and Bill was one
under. But next time we fired together, Bill was one up on my score.
Then, at a Company Shoot, we fired a possible each again, and the Company Commander gave us a hundred cigarettes each.

We used to call each other all the names going, but only in the friendliest kind of way, because we got along very well together on the whole.
He was easy enough to get on with. But we used to accuse each other
of cheating, foul play, and all the dirty tricks you could think of. But
whatever we did in competition with each other we came out even. Bill
and I, for instance, were in a lot of the Company sports. We always
jumped exactly the same height or length. It's funny. I don't know why.
On a cross-country run, for example, we both came in fifth, we dead-
heated for fifth place. However much I strained myself I couldn't throw
a grenade farther than Bill, and nor could he throw farther than me.
Although there was a certain amount of difference in our sizes, we must
have had exactly the same amount of strength or something. Later on,
when we got a bit beyond sports in general, it all boiled down to shooting. And for years on end we just about tied in our scores. I'm not sure
to this day which of us was better. I think, maybe, on the whole, Bill
was just a little bit better than me, but I was regarded as pretty hot.
People don't seem to shoot any more like we used to shoot when we
was young.

Well, what I was going to say was this. Bill and me went East in the
same draft. And I'm glad to say—because after all it was what you might
call a bit of an experience for us—yes, I'm glad to say that we got into
the riots together. Bill was the one to tell you about the Wogs. Old Bill
would talk about the moon, and the desert, and make a whole rigmarole out of it so that it was a pleasure to listen to him. And as a matter

of fact, I've heard Bill tell stories about places where he was with me and he describes things that I, personally, never saw happen. Some say he just made them up. I think that it was a better sense of observation. Be that as it may. I doesn't do to speak ill of the dead. I never could understand how Bill, at eight hundred yards, behind a hill, in the middle of the night, without a moon, could tell you not only the colour of a Wog's eyes, but also the expression on his face. . . .

Well, you sort of know how it was. In some villages we put down a few Wogs that wanted to get us with knives, treating them gently with pick handles and not firing a shot. We simply made 'em listen to reason and did little more than knock a few of them unconscious for longer or shorter periods. But then we had to go out right into the desert, and there's only a little tiny handful of us, and we had to get from one point to another point . . . sort of beetling around . . . and then all of a sudden there's a bit of an attack. I will say one thing for Wogs. They can hide themselves. They wear them long robes pretty much the same colour of that dirty white sand, and they can make themselves look like bits of desert, and I don't mind admitting that if you're of a timid disposition it *can* give you the willies when, in broad daylight, you hear a rifle go off at about two hundred yards, and a bullet cuts your coat, and there's absolutely no sign of where it came from—in wide open desert. But on the whole, once you get used to the idea of protective background you get along all right.

On this occasion, if you might call it an occasion, a fairly large number of Wogs cut us off and there is quite a lively little bit of sniping. They make a kind of a ring round us and it settles down to steady potting. Bill and me carried on with the good old competition. It was like a game of darts. We were almost chalking up our hits. I got a matter of six Wogs and so did Bill. And then, at about three hundred yards, some bloke with a beard like Santa Claus sticks up his silly great head and sort of goggles at us, and Bill says "Hi-de-hi" and fires quick and that makes him one up on me, because this Wog with the big beard goes up into the air like a sky-rocket and comes rolling down to quite near us. Well, all this was all very nice, but it was near midday, and we were short of water, and it was easy to see that we couldn't really hold out indefinitely, and the general point of view of the officer was that unless some poor mug got through this ring of Wogs and managed to get about ten miles to bring up another mob, we were in a pretty poor way.

I have only one thing against Bill Nelson, and that is that he liked to push himself forward. As soon as he gets to hear of this, before anybody else could get a word in edgeways, he said: "I got an idea I could manage it, sir." The officer says: "Have you, by God? Well, if you don't, I'm afraid I shan't be alive to mention the fact in despatches for the gratification of your next-of-kin." And Bill says: "I ain't got no next-of-kin," and off he goes.

Now Bill and me had done a good deal of individual movement, and Bill, who had one of those snaky figures, was rather better at it than most of us. He doesn't take a rifle. He does a bear crawl for twenty yards or so and he wriggles round a sand dune and disappears. And then I heard about fifty million shots going bang, bang, bang, and I knew the Wogs had spotted him. And I hoped he'd get through all right because our little shooting match wasn't what I would call over, not by any manner of means. We watched, me in particular, sort of anxiously, because a certain amount really does in a way depend on Bill getting through. For instance, our lives, and what not. But there is no sign of Bill at all. We are not chucking our ammo away, needless to say, and so we watch where we're shooting and do not use a round unless we're pretty sure where it's going to go. We wait, and there is a sort of silence from the Wogs, and the sun gets so hot we can hear our brains bubbling like pitch. Then I, looking through the heat waves, see a solitary Wog behaving in a very peculiar way. First, he crawls ten yards, and then he falls down flat and disappears. And then he wriggles and goes sideways like a crab and behaves in general as if he's gone a bit mad. Actually, what was mad about it was this: he was doing what looked like an Army crawl as taught to rookies in camp . . . only he was a Wog, all right, in Wog robes. He is maybe seven hundred and fifty yards away when I get a chance of a shot at him, and I fires. He goes down flat. And then he gets up again and goes crawling on. And I, shoving another round up the spout and cursing the heat waves that were spoiling my aim, saw another funny thing. This Wog I'd missed, crawling along, came face to face with another Wog, also crawling. It was funny. They stayed there for one tick, face to face, like two cats. Then the new Wog jumped on this one I'd missed and in that sunlight I saw a knife flashing like a signaller's mirror. And then, all of a sudden, I realized that the man I'd fired at and missed was none other than Bill Nelson. He had got hold of the clothes or at least the robe of a dead Wog (and my God, he didn't half have to be fumigated afterwards) and using those clothes as a sort of camouflage had managed to get just about that far without the Wogs suspecting anything.

And then he bumped into this other geezer. Bill was in a bad position. The Wog, on top of him, sort of thrusted with his knife, but he missed, and the hilt hit Bill on the forehead and dazed him a bit, and then Bill was on his back with the Wog on top of him kneeling on his belly. They were wrapped up together like bride and bridegroom. Only Bill was holding the Wog's knife-wrist and trying to kick him where it would do most good . . . and that sort of thing doesn't usually come until a little while after the honeymoon. Bill was sunk. There was nothing for it. I had to risk a shot. Mind you, this was at just over one thousand yards by now. I flick my sights right forward, and my back sight goes up like a fireman's ladder; and I wipe the sand out of my eye, and I take aim on those two and wait a second. Thank God there's no wind. But there's heat waves. That was the first time I'd said any prayers in about thirty-five years, as those two were rolling over. I said. *God Almighty, if I was you I'd clear this heat haze just for a tick! Honest to God, God, no kidding, God, for Christ's sake, God, bloody well clear this heat haze.*

And all of a sudden, just for one split second, the heat waves seemed to stand still, and I knew it in my bones that if I fired a shade to the right, a current of air would take that bullet right to the spot where that Wog's head was going to be. And I pressed the trigger, and the two of them lay still.

Then one of them got up, and it was the one without the beard. He rocked a bit on his knees, and then fell flat, and crawled out of sight.

About midnight the reinforcements come up. Bill Nelson wasn't with 'em. He was in dock. That shot of mine had passed so close to him—his face and the Wog's face were close together—that I'd cut a crease in his jaw. But that shot had got the Wog a quarter of an inch above his right eye . . . and that, believe me or not, was exactly where I knew it was going to hit him.

I told Bill about it, and he said, calling me all the names he could lay his tongue to, "So it was you that fired the first shot, was it?" And he showed me a mark on his backside, a wale, like a whiplash, where my first round had gone past.

I said to him: "Well, Bill, that makes our score even again, since I got the Wog at a thousand yards."

He said: "Strictly speaking, that was not a shot but an act of God, a miracle. But seeing it's you, Dagwood, I'll allow it. Now Dag, I'll tell you what I'll do to decide this once and for all. We'll go to the thirty-yards range and fix up a red-tipped match at thirty yards, and the first one to light the match with a .22 round, light it without breaking it, wins a dollar."

We both missed fifteen times clean. So the matter was never decided.

X

A Few Words About Deserts

"And," says Jack Cattle, "there you are again. The scar was a part of his face, and it went unnoticed. Well, well, well. Isn't it an odd thing? As far as the whole world is concerned, you, you *as* you, are what they see. And what do people see? They see something that looks like a silly little picture a kid might draw in chalk on a pavement . . . something with a couple of ears, and a couple of eyes, and a nose, and a hole that you put food into or take words out of. They see a body, and some kind of a limb at each corner of it. If you happen to have a hump or a horrible skin disease they notice that all right, the silly mugs. Their eyes! 'Radiant jellies, shooting stars!' And what good are their eyes to them? No good at all. As Sergeant Dagwood was saying, we have been mourning for Bill Nelson with all kinds of Goddamned maudlin sentiment, and we can't tell each other what the man looked like. There was a real Bill Nelson, a real and vital Bill Nelson, of which we only saw a little part. I suppose it's the same in all of us . . . though some men have more to be seen than other men.

"The best and the worst in a man is never seen.

"Sergeant Dagwood was talking about shooting, and musketry in general. Musketry was one of the things that interested Sergeant Nelson more than anything else. He liked the feel of a firearm. And he was right, he was damned right, because any bit of machinery that is made to do its work cleanly and well is a pleasant thing to handle. And among the most efficient jobs of work in general circulation is a common short Lee-Enfield rifle . . . the good old bundhook that gives any Tom, Dick or Harry the power to throw a crumb of lead with enough force and

accuracy to smash a man's skull a mile away. Bill Nelson was right. He
liked the feel of a rifle when it fires. I've watched his face. I could see
how he felt he had absolute control over a power. He liked that, and
so does nearly anybody. In a good kind of way, Bill Nelson liked power.
He liked to have the power to punish a man or push a man around,
just in order to refrain from punishing or pushing. I suppose it could
be argued that in point of actual fact all Bill Nelson got out of everything was a purely selfish pleasure . . . that if he gave away his week's
pay he did so to get the personal satisfaction of doing a good deed . . .
that doesn't really matter. It's a nice way of giving yourself pleasure.
There are plenty of sods in this battalion that get *their* pleasure by exer-
cising their two-penny-ha'penny authority. You will find lots of Guardsmen who have only one real ambition, and that is to be Trained Soldiers
at the Depot, where they are about as terrible as Gods to a squad of recruits for the first sixteen weeks. . . . If being a decent fellow gives a
fellow a selfish pleasure, well, damn well let it! Whether you like it or
not, you get something back for whatever you lay out in this life . . .
just as you have to pay for whatever you take.

"Poor old Bill Nelson went in for a sort of . . . I don't know what
you'd call it . . . a sort of philosophy. What I mean to say is, he tried
to build up little parables, and make one thing give a new meaning to
another thing.

"Sergeant Dagwood talks about musketry. Well, I told you how The
Schoolmaster, who, when all was said and done, was a bit of a bloody
fool, used to take down some of the things Nelson said and rearrange
the words to make a kind of rhyme. I remember once how Nelson was
talking about the elementary rules of shooting, and The Schoolmaster
managed to boil out of a few casual remarks a whole song and dance.

"Here's a copy of it . . .

> Foresight
> without
> backsight
> is nowt,

like Wednesday
without
Tuesday.
Result?
No score.
You're
ahead on pay,
but you
draw
for
the week that went before.
It's on your pass,
blast it,
that the Q
cuts you
in the future.
You get away
with S.F.A.
you can borrer
on to-morrer
like I did . . .
provided
there's a Yesterday.
I mean to say. . . .

Too much
foresight,
and the flight
of your shot
will not
be right
or true.
It'll fly
too high.

Too much backsight
makes it go
too low,

nowhere near
the mark.

Keep level,
and you
aim true
and shame
the devil
even in the dark.

It's funny.
Revally
is your past
by Cookhouse.
Time can fly
fast.
So mind your eye.

"That," says Cattle, "is the sort of a thing Nelson used to say and the way he used to think in general. To Bill Nelson, everything had to have a hidden reason and a secret moral. Everything was a story. Whatever he said to you, Sergeant Dagwood, I'm pretty sure that to him, that bullet which slid in between him and the Arab and saved his life was . . . well, the razor-edge of Fate, which can save you but might destroy you. It was always good to hear Bill Nelson talking about the desert.

"Some men like the desert because it makes them think of so many things. Really, what Bill Nelson said about that lousy, dry, murderous waste of sand, was worth hearing. People like me, and people like The Schoolmaster, and Old Silence, we think in terms of nonsense, in mere words. That is why we are always quoting other people's bits of rubbish just because they happen to have words in them that we like the sound of.

"Oh . . . all the nice dramatic poetic Sweet Fanny Adams one can say about the desert! How night comes down like a lid over an eye; and how, looking up, you see points of pure light that make you feel like a beetle imprisoned in a box in the lid of which somebody has pricked pinholes for you to breathe through . . . how this is the land, the rotting wilderness that God gave to Ishmael . . . and how there are rocks that the sun and the frost between them have cracked as a hyena cracks thighbones. . . . Bloody nonsense! Talk! Literature!

"One night Bill Nelson, talking to me about the desert, really said something.

"He said: 'Isn't it funny, Cattle, when you come to think that every grain of that sand was once a part of a great big stone? And bit by bit it rubbed away. And all the time, Cattle, those grains of sand are rubbing together and rubbing themselves away to dust. It only goes to show, Cattle, it only goes to show. Leave that dirty muck-heap alone and given time it'll rub itself out. So why worry?'"

Dagwood says: "Well, yes, Cattle. That's very nice; but what *I* liked about Bill was, that whatever he might have said, he was the sort of mug who'd go and try and clear up the desert with a bass broom if he felt it was right and proper to go and do so. *That's* what *I* liked about old Bill *Nelson*."

XI

Concerning Truth and Life

"It MIGHT be true," says Butcher the Butcher, "that there's all sorts of things a man keeps hid underneath. Maybe you never do get the truth, the whole truth, and nothing but the truth about a geezer even if he's your best friend and you know him from the cradle to the grave. Near where I used to live when I was a kid at home, there was a dear old girl that had a daughter of about forty. This here daughter of the old girl died one night of blood poisoning. The poor old woman couldn't make head nor tail of it, because that daughter had devoted all her life to her mum ever since she'd been eighteen years old—twenty-odd years she'd hardly set foot outside the house. And yet it turned out that every night for the last fifteen years there'd been a chap she used to let in, and he used to sleep with the daughter till daybreak. In the room next door to the old woman's. And the old woman never had any idea of it. I forget whether the daughter died of having a kid or not having a kid. One of the two, or both. But then and only then the thing came out—after fifteen solid years. What do you know about that?"

"Well, I admit we all do funny things from time to time," says Bearsbreath. "So what? Speak of Nelson as you found him."

"So I do," says the Butcher.

"So do I," says Oxley.

"There's different ways of looking at things," says Hands. "I remember once seeing a house on fire. It looked smashing, with all the smoke and what not coming out. I says to some feller standing next to me: 'Better than a firework display, chum.' And he says to me: 'I hope the poor people are insured.' I look at the fire and I think of fireworks. He looks at the same fire and he thinks of the furniture and what not. Well . . . as far as I'm concerned, a fire is a fire. And a man is as *I* know him. Do you know what you can do with the truth, the whole truth, and nothing but the truth? Do you know where you can shove it?"

Dagwood grunts: "I knew Bill Nelson well. I never knew what he thought about when I wasn't looking. I knew he was all right, and I didn't want to know any more. I'm no magistrate. Call me 'Pal' and I'm your pal. Call me 'Swine,' and I'm swine to the backbone. I'm a decent feller to most people. But I'm a rotten dog to a few. It depends what part of me you want to go and pick. But both parts are true . . ."

"The *whole truth,* though?" asks Butcher.

"Nark it," says Crowne. "Have you been in the Army twenty years, to start talking about the Whole Truth at your time of life? Tell the whole, plain, honest truth and you'll end up in one of two places: Colney Hatch or the Glass House. You just can't do it."

"That's true. You've got to lie," says Dagwood. "If only out of polite-ness. A man shows you a pitcher of some wall-eyed tart and says: 'Ain't she an angel in human form?' What do you say? You say: 'Sure she is, sure she is.' It's all right as long as you *know* what's right and what's wrong. And as long as you don't let anybody down. It's life. I've known Bill Nelson to lie many a time. Though I will say I never knew him try to wriggle out of anything . . . except in moderation."

"Bill?" says the Butcher. "Bill could swear that black was white, or green was sky-blue-pink; especially for somebody else. Lying's nothing; as long as a bloke don't kid himself along at the same time. Bill Nelson was a bit of a liar like anybody else. But he was the honestest man *I* ever knew."

"Lawyers are the biggest liars alive," says Crowne. "And they get to be Judges, and they sit down and sentence you to death, or let you off."

"Same as advertisements," says Hands. "Do you believe all they tell you in the advertisements, about pills, and draughts, and disinfectants, and all that muck? But the geezers that sell that stuff get to be Lords and Ladies."

"Politicians," says Crowne. "They promise you the earth. And they run the bloody country."

"Actually," says Bearsbreach, "if you're in a bit of a corner, and you kid the blokes along a bit. . . . 'We're nearly there. . . . Our reinforcements are due any minute. . . . One more mile . . .' you're lying."

"Newspapers," says Butcher the Butcher. "They don't *dare* to tell the truth."

"Doctors," says Bearsbreath. "Nor do they."

"Well then," says Dagwood. "Why begrudge a good pal like Bill Nelson a bit of a lie once in a while? The whole world is full of lies like a corpse is full of maggots. Once you get wise to that, you're grown-up. You've got to learn to sort it all out. You don't believe all you hear or all you read: you learn to judge for yourself as far as you can."

"All you read!" says Bearsbreath. "Go into any graveyard. Christ! You feel they ought to bury all the live bastards, and dig up all the dead."

"Ah," says Oxley. "Soon as a man dies, he's a saint."

Bearsbreath laughs.

" 'Sa joke, Bearsbreath?"

"All this Fanny Adams. You know bloody well what kind of a bloke Bill was. Dozens and dozens of geezers are supposed to've known Bill since he was first squadded. Everybody says something a tiny little bit different. But doesn't it all come back to *He was all right?*" says Bearsbreath. "Well, that's it. That's your truth. Bill was all right."

"I never started all this bull about Truth," says Dagwood.

"Truth! *Ppphut!* A feller tells lies like a cat eats fish: specially a soldier. If a man's okay, he's okay. Bill was okay," says Hands.

"But after all, Bill went through," says Butcher, "and after all the times he scraped out of getting killed, one way and another . . ." His voice bends and melts. . . . "To go and finish up in that lousy cellar . . ."

Cattle says: "For what it's worth, here's a story that I know to be absolutely true.

"Just at the beginning of the war, a man who was Managing Director of a big shoe-making concern decided to get out of London, away from any chance of getting bombed, you understand. He was a very wealthy kind of man, and liked to get about with a few nice squidgy blonds, and all that kind of thing. And he wanted to be safe, you see, because he liked to have a nice time.

"Well, he had a house in the country, well away from London, in as safe an area as you could wish to hide out in. And as if this wasn't enough, he built a shelter. This shelter he built was something pretty damned tremendous. Do you understand? He wasn't taking a single chance. He had it dug God only knows how many feet deep in the ground, and built in with absolutely tremendous thicknesses of reinforced concrete, yards and yards of it. It's an actual fact, Sergeant Dagwood, that he had it tested to be sure it would stand up to a direct hit from a thousand-pound bomb. See? He dug himself a hole that a thunderbolt couldn't have touched.

"And this shelter of his was made like a luxury flat. I'm not telling you a word of a lie: just like a luxury flat. There was one huge room, a kind of lounge, beautifully decorated, with concealed lighting made to look like windows overlooking the Mediterranean. It sounds crazy, but it's God's truth. Windows overlooking the Mediterranean! There was a bedroom, a kitchenette, a hoard of tinned and potted grub of every kind, a bathroom, a W.C., and an air-conditioning plant. That shelter was better than most West-End apartments, I can assure you, Sergeant Hands.

"It cost thousands. He didn't care, so long as he could feel dead certain of being safe and sound when the bombs began to drop. And when it was done, he threw a party. Yes, it's a fact, Sergeant Crowne, a party in a shelter, with champagne, and oysters, and a few selected boy friends and girl friends, and they made a very lively night of it.

"Well, look. This is how things work. I suppose the party must have eaten something like three or four hundred of the very best selected Whitstable oysters that night, and all those oysters were perfectly all right except just one. And that one had something wrong with it. And this man got that oyster. And in forty-eight hours he was as dead as Judas Iscariot.

"That is a fact. You don't escape from dying by going here or there, Butcher; and when the time comes, it seems, you just die."

A brand-new lance-corporal, who has been itching to say something, suddenly says:

"My grandfather fought in the Zulu War——"

"On which side?" asks Dagwood, and the lance-corporal is silent.

"I know a man," says Hands, "that knows a man who pretty well died about a hundred times. It's very peculiar. This geezer's name was something like Gomez, and it seems he's pretty well known in a place called Mexico City, in Mexico, as a man that nothing and nobody could ever kill.

"This dago used to be a bit of a rough handful in his younger days, it seems, and before he was twenty he got shot about a dozen times in one revolution after another—because they always have revolutions out there—and at last he was caught by some Government troops, and sentenced to death. They shove him up against a wall, and six men in a firing squad give him six rounds, and down he goes, and they leave him where he falls. See? Well, some farmer finds him, and he's still alive. All them bullets, at point-blank range, almost, had missed a vital spot; and he got better.

"Later on he joined the police. He was shot up three times more by some bandits. He was shot right through the forehead, but your brain goes in two halves like a walnut, and the bullet just went right through without touching his brain at all. Once, they thought he was dead and shoved his corpse in a sort of refrigerator that they have in the mortuaries over there. His wife comes to identify him, and then he opens his eyes. The cold had froze the blood in his wounds, and stopped him bleeding to death: he was alive all the time. He got better again. Since then he's been shot twice more, and knifed ever so many times. But he's still alive.

"And the joke of it is this: This dago, Gomez, is dead scared. It's on the up-and-up, dead scared. Do you know why he's scared? He says he thinks his life is being spared for something really bad to happen to him.

"Now what would you make of a geezer like that?

"The odds are, he'll get knocked down by a kid on a fairy-cycle, and snuff it that way."

"I knew a rent collector that fell down in a pub, and stabbed himself to the heart with his own pencil," says Dagwood.

Butcher the Butcher says: "Yet it's a fact that some geezers *do* get killed in battles in the proper way. Not all old soldiers die natural deaths like getting run over by fairy-cycles."

"Who wants to get killed in a battle?" says Bearsbreath. "I don't want to get killed in a battle."

The new lance-corporal speaks again:

"All the same, it's nice to see your friends die sudden. I mean——"

A dreadful doom is hanging over this young man.

Hands says: "Yes? You mean? Your grampa that fought in the Zulu War?"

"Oh yes," says Dagwood, "the Zulu War."

"Who was your grampa?" asks Butcher. "Prince Monolulu?"

"His grampa was a cannibal king," says Hands.

"Well?" says Bearsbreath. "Come on. What about your grampa that fought in the Zulu War? I thought you was a bit of a Kaffir."

"That ain't coloured blood," says Crowne, "that's dirt."

"My grandfather was as white as you or me," says the new lance-corporal.

"I bet he was white when he saw them Zulus coming," says Hands.

"There *is* such a thing as a white black man," says Dagwood. "I saw one, once, in a side show at Blackpool. They called him Walla-Baloo."

"That was his grampa," says Hands. "Hiya, Walla-Baloo."

"My grandfather was a Sergeant-Major in the Glorious Ninth," says the new lance-corporal, with heat.

"Maybe he was a sort of a Gurker," says Crowne.

"There *was* loyal Zulus," says Butcher.

"My grandfather——"

"All right, Walla-Baloo," says Hands, "we know all about your grampa."

"Walla-Baloo . . ." says Dagwood, with appreciation. "Walla-Baloo."

The Doom has fallen.

The new lance-corporal will become an old lance-corporal, and a full corporal, and a lance-sergeant, and a full sergeant, and a company quartermaster-sergeant, and a sergeant-major, and a drill-sergeant. He will achieve the dignity of a regimental sergeant-major. He may become Captain and Quartermaster.

But to his dying day and beyond, he will be known to all men as Walla-Baloo the Zulu.

"You shouldn't chime into the conversation of your seniors," says Dagwood, with pitying condescension.

The boy who will be called Walla-Baloo the Zulu—a nice, rosey-cheeked, serious boy, with straw-coloured hair and white eyelashes—gets up, fumbles in the pockets of his brain for verbal missiles, but finds nothing but adjectival fluff. He goes out, slamming the door.

"Young corporals," says Hands. "Why, in my time, if I'd shoved my oar into a conversation like he just did, I'd have been shot up into the air like a skyrocket."

"You've got to start somewhere," says Bearsbreath.

"And where do you end?" asks Crowne, sourly. "If you're not careful, you end up like them old skivers that mooch about the Naffy Library. The minute the place opens, in they dash. Blind O'Reilly, it's like a Gold Rush. They go for them four armchairs like pigs for swill. And there they sit, reading books all day long."

"And listening to the wireless," says Hands. "Not that that wireless ever works. It squeaks, it goes quack, it screams like a baby; but much they care. They sit and listen just the same."

"I believe Fatty Teedale's librarian now," says Dagwood.

"Fatty?" says Hands. "The only man in the Brigade of Guards that used to bite his toenails. Years ago he used to be in the next bed to mine, and it made my blood run cold to hear him. When he'd used up all his fingernails, he'd start on his toes. Then he got too fat to reach them. He was the worst nail-biter I ever saw in my life. You know what he used to do? He used to save up the little fingernail on his left hand for Sunday afternoon. He'd store up that nail like another man would store a cigar. And first thing after Church Parade, he'd sit down and have a long bite at it. It shook me."

"So he's librarian," says Butcher. "Him. What, can he read?"

"Read what?" asks Bearsbreath. "There's nothing in that library *to* read. One of the cupboards has got books in it, I don't know what's in the other. It's been kept locked since before my time."

"There was a rumour," says Dagwood, "that when Pig Guinness—the Drill Pig, not the other Pig—when Pig Guinness died, he left instructions in his will that he was to be locked in that cupboard. I don't believe it. Muddy Waters says that back in 1920, a librarian murdered a Guardsman and put his body in that cupboard. Then he threw the key away. Nobody ever had instructions to break the lock. There was only one key issued. So the cupboard stayed locked."

"There's everything in that library except books," says Cattle. "I remember, once, Geordie Minor took a fancy to read something, and went and asked the librarian for a reading-book. The librarian gave Geordie *Mother Goose's Nursery Rhymes*. Geordie read it from cover to cover. And when I asked him how he liked it he said: 'It's nobbut a pack o' lies.'"

"Geordie Minor," says Dagwood. "Wasn't it him that called the Adjutant——?"

"No, you're thinking of Geordie Binns," says Hands. "It was in private when he called the Adjutant a——. And the Adjutant (it was Pongo; old Pongo, a decent sort, but I once saw him go into Adjutant's Orders fifteen minutes late), Pongo says to Geordie Binns: 'Speak up, man. I didn't hear what you said just then.' Geordie had the presence of mind to say 'Nothing, sir.' And the Adjutant said: 'I'm glad to hear it, Binns; but don't say it again.' My God, but Geordie Binns could blind when he got annoyed!"

"Binns was nothing to Swearing Simmonds," says Dagwood.

"The worst swearer of them all was Atkin, the one we used to call Blinding Atkin," says Butcher.

"Yet," says Dagwood, "it's hard not to swear, and handle a squad at the same time. They can bust you for using language. But how can you train men with an 'Oh-Dear-Me,' or a few 'My Goodnesses'?"

"You have to invent new swearing," says Hands. "Look at old Spurgeon. He swears like a bargee, but he swears in a legitimate way. He swears in front of the C.O. himself, and gets away with it because he uses only clean language. He can let out a string of swearing, and nobody could object. 'Blind my grandmother's guts!' he says. 'Card stuff me gently! God's Buttercups and Daisies and Blazing Daffodils! Sweet Burning Splintering Flagpoles! Cord Spotted Cuckoo!' And he invents new names to call people. 'Twillip!' he says. 'Snurge! Twitter-bug! Bugscratcher! Spittoon!' and so on."

The Budgerigar comes out of a kind of coma to say: "The best thing is, to swear in a foreign language."

"Remember when Geordie Binns learnt French?" asks Crowne.

"That wasn't Geordie Binns. That was Geordie Twistle," says Dagwood. "He got hold of some Frenchman, one night, in a pub near Kensington, and he asks this Frenchman what . . . well, he . . ."

"He asked the Frenchman," says Cattle, "what *beer* was in French. The Frenchman said *bière*. Then he asked him what *cigarette* was, and the Frenchman said *cigarette*. 'Ah,' says Geordie, 'and what's *whisky?*' The Frenchman says: '*Whisky.*' 'And *football?*' '*Football,*' says the

Frenchman. And then Geordie says: 'Ha. There's nowt to 't. It's nowt different fra' King's English.' "

"I was talking to a Free Frenchman," says Dagwood. "He wasn't so bad. It's not their fault they were born that side of the Channel. Some of them seem nice fellers."

"You talk of Free Frenchmen," says Cattle, suddenly, "and that reminds me of a thing. Sort of connected with what we were saying before about death, and so on. I was talking to a Free Frenchman too, an officer. I know French pretty well. And like other people do, he got around to talking of dying, and retreating, and all that. I mentioned dying of old age, and I said something about most people saying they preferred to die before they got too old to care. . . . You know the kind of tripe; the kind of tripe we were talking just before that young corporal went out. . . .

"He was a queer little egg with one leg, and he looked as if he'd taken a bit of hammering, quite a bit of hard hammering. It was when I was on leave. I was in civvies. He could stand plenty of liquor. He was homesick for the taste of French wine. He talked a lot about wine. And so he got around to talking about France, and fighting, and Germany, and the war, and everything else. He was a good little fellow. I quite liked him. He had as much fight in him as a terrier. Men like that come back and fight some more if they're alive. I wouldn't mind fighting with —of course, I mean fighting by the side of—this little Captain Ix.

"He told me a wonderful story . . ."

XII

Ten Old Tigers

"You want to think of this," said Cattle, "whenever people get round to talking about the way people die, and what people die for—in general, when people begin to talk about things like Bill Nelson's death. Because there are times when there really does seem to be a Destiny that saves us like cards to be played at the end part of a game. We talked about France, about the fall of France, and the nice rough wines of this part of France, and the smooth wines of another part; and the way wine is made.

"Then Captain Ix said this":

"You may crush men like grapes in a wine press. You can trample all the sweetness out of them—stamp them down until they look like a flat, downtrodden mass of rubbish. Do that. But don't forget one thing: out of the smashed remains of the grape harvest, my friend, brandy is distilled. Not much of it, but potent. And one whiff of good brandy carries with it the character and quality of the whole ravaged vineyard. Do you understand that? So with men. Squeeze a nation! Smash it and flatten it and twist out of it the last drop of its blood. But listen: out of the trodden-out débris of the people there comes a strong and vital spirit. It is there, fermenting, growing strong. And out of the agony of the crushed grapes, remember, comes the glory of the wine. Out of the agony of the people comes the glory of the nation.

"You can squash out the external appcarance of a grape: but in doing this, you give it an ultimate magnificence. It is like that with a man. A man on his own is a soft thing that spoils easily—like a grape! The

267

press and the dark cellar bring out the undying spirit of the grape—as of a man!

"I am a Frenchman. I am one of the trampled grapes. But it is I who am telling you that even at this moment, in the dark, there is going on a stir, a ferment. And drip . . . drip . . . drip . . . drop by drop, there is gathering the rare, biting, imprisoned spirit of my people.

"Look here. I have been beaten like washing in a stream. I have been chewed up like grass. But it was I who went out to die with the Ten Old Tigers."

And Captain Victor Ix raised a glass of English bitter, and said, in a deep and resonant voice: "The Ten Old Tigers and the greater glory of France!" He gulped the beer; pulled a face. "Listen," he said:

I do not need to tell you much about our retreat. It was a débâcle and a crash. To my dying moment I shall carry in my nostrils the smell of that defeat—a smell, my friend, of doom: of high-explosive smoke mixed with petrol and burnt oil and dust and ashes. That was the smell of the Boche advance. They came on like driver ants in a jungle, over heaps of their own dead. The tanks roared like devils. It was like seeing a city on the move—tanks which looked greater than cathedrals, spitting shot and shell. And above them, aeroplanes as numerous and awful as the horde of Satan falling into hell—coming down howling, my friend; that is the only word. Their noise alone stunned us. But we held. My company did what was possible. I went mad. I raved. I swore like a maniac. But my little men went down; and my good old friend Xavier, the Lieutenant, he went down in a fine spray. The French Army was cut to slices like a ham—torn to bits like a pineapple. A bridge which should have been blown up was not blown up. The tanks came over in a black cloud. France was rolling over in her last convulsion. Germany was at her throat. The great thumbs of the tank and aeroplane offensive had a stranglehold, right behind the great artery. We could only gurgle and kick. And our kicks grew weaker. Our head swam. Delirium! Blackness! Of my company, seventeen men were left.

I took them away. Then I was ashamed and wanted to go back: but then they took me away, for I was slightly wounded and not quite myself.

Yes, the man you see before you now, Victor Ix, retreated with the washed-out remains of his company.

I thought that although we had been pressed back, the rest of our forces were holding out; that I could come back soon with a new company and beat the Boche back to Berlin, as before. I did not know that the way had been cleared for the Boches, and that France was sold. It did not enter my mind, because I thought such things were impossible.

To the downfall of all traitors I will drink even another glass of this execrable beer: and one more still to the Ten Old Tigers. . . . To the ten grey and magnificent Old Tigers of Tolly.

We reached a tiny town called Tolly. Now I knew Tolly, for I had lived there for a little while when I was young. It is a little town like other little towns. Nothing happens there. Nobody does anything beyond a certain dead-alive routine of living. Tolly had only one thing to distinguish it from a thousand other such towns: a kind of Soldiers' Home.

Many years ago, after the fall of Napoleon Bonaparte, a certain military-minded wine merchant endowed a small row of cottages. He gave them to ten old soldiers: veterans of the wars, who had permission to live there in their old age rent-free. The will of the merchant provided, also, some small weekly sum for the purchase of tobacco and wine. The town provided a few francs' worth of lighting and heating. Thus, with their pensions, the old soldiers who lived in those cottages and waited for death were able to rest in some little comfort.

These poor old men were pathetic.

They had spent their lives in camps and barracks. They knew nothing but soldiering. A clause in the will that provided for them insisted that only men without families could enjoy those poor little amenities. So the ten veterans of Tolly, who are now in Heaven, were men alone in the world: men who had devoted their entire lives to the Army of France.

When I was young and was at Tolly, I often saw them. They drew their pensions and spent the money on necessities. They were regimental, however, those poor old men. They received, every Saturday, a sum of three francs apiece for wine and tobacco; and so they went out to spend those few pence on wine and tobacco alone. And every Saturday morning, punctually at eleven forty-five, the ten old soldiers would march out to the Café Roche on the corner, and sit, each with his glass of red or white wine, smoking and talking. They amused people. It was funny to hear them discussing battles and skirmishes that everybody had forgotten, in places nobody had ever heard of.

Now and again, some person, slightly drunk and jolly, would say, "What about Indo-China?" And one of them, who had fought some shocking encounters out there, would square his thin old shoulders and begin to explain. . . . "We were here . . . they were there. . . . And then the Commandant said to me . . . and then I said to the Commandant . . ." Real old soldiers' talk. And then somebody would buy them drinks. Once in a while one of them would get rather drunk. The townspeople enjoyed this very much—the spectacle of a seventy-year-old soldier singing forgotten songs in the ghost of a voice and reeling, supported by a comrade of seventy-two, back to the alms-houses.

They were old and shabby. They had just enough to eat, but never quite enough to drink and smoke. They cadged a little. They sometimes attached themselves to total strangers and, talking of the weather, complained of thirst. Sometimes they were a bit of a nuisance. They tried to get small jobs of cleaning, or gardening, for the price of a litre of white wine and a packet of the worst tobacco. They used bad language when they forgot themselves . . . and as they grew older they forgot themselves quite often.

They talked mostly of battles; and when they talked, their skinny old hands lashed the air in savage gestures. One veteran of North

Africa, a Sergeant-Major of more than eighty, whose elder brother had fallen at Sedan, used to demonstrate, with a decanter, how he had killed an Arab with a rock, and so saved the life of his commanding officer. The breasts of all of them tinkled with medals. They all cultivated fierce moustaches. Most of them shaved every day, and walked upright.

The people of Tolly called them the Ten Old Tigers.

We got into Tolly, as I was telling you—used-up, finished, dead on our feet. The town was almost empty. The people had fled. There was an echoing silence. "What is this?" I wondered. We passed the Café Roche. There was a sound of merrymaking inside . . . a sort of crackle of senile laughter.

I staggered to the door. The café was empty. Only ten familiar figures occupied the centre of the place. They had bottles of the best wine before them. Eight of them were smoking cigars. Yes, they were the Ten Old Tigers. I was nearly dead of exhaustion. I heard myself saying: "What, Sergeant Bonenfant—is it you?"

And a very old man said: *"Vi l'capitaine,"* and sprang to his feet. He said: "It is fifteen years since I saw your face last. Let us see—only four of us have died since then. There are four new ones. For the rest, we are still here . . ." He was happy with wine. "Listen, *mon capitaine,* they have all run away. The café is ours. Drinks are on the house." This Sergeant Bonenfant was a wicked old man, who was disrespectful to officers and feared neither God nor man. He laughed, and said: "They think the Boches have beaten France!"

All the rest roared with laughter.

I said: "They are coming in tanks." Then I felt my legs giving way. I said to my men: "Find yourself to eat and drink." And I sat down. And then the place whirled round me like a wheel, and there was a redness, and a purple, and a darkness. . . . And I came to myself on the floor. One of the old men had propped my battered head on his bony knee. Another was pouring most of a bottle of brandy down my throat. A third was saying: "Bite his ears: that brings them to" . . .

and another was replying: "I have no teeth." A fifth was slapping me in the face: an old soldier's remedy for unconsciousness, it appears.

"My men?" I said.

There was a mutter of horrible oaths and curses. The old sergeant, Bonenfant, said:

"The ——s have run away. There is some fairy tale. There is some legend. The Boches are almost here, one says. Then why not go and stop them, I say. But no. The seventeen of them, your men, throw down their equipment and run off. They say, 'Against tanks, what use are rifles? Besides,' they say, 'we are betrayed and sold.' It is a question of morale. They run. As for me, I say: *Bah!*"

I sat up. "There is something here that I do not like," I said. "We were retreating, yes . . . but . . ."

There was a crash. There was a smash of glass. A very old man, the oldest of all the Tigers, none other than the old Sergeant-Major whose brother had perished at Sedan, had thrown a water carafe through the window into the street. It was not drunkenness. It was rage. Yes, rage. That old, old man was bristling like a grey wolf. He stood up. His time-worn throat jangled like a broken piano. He shouted:

"Silence!"

There was authority in that voice, my friend. We all listened, out of force of habit.

He let out a string of old Army endearments:

"Silence, you dirty maggots! Silence every one of you, you this-and-that offspring of so-and-so! You drunken, noisy dummy-headed blank spawn of little frogs! Shuttup! You in the rear—put down that pipe while I'm talking to you! Are you attending to me? Right. You'd better. You imbecile idiot scum of puddles! . . . Stop shuffling those feet!

"The Boches are coming. This is serious. Do you understand? They say that France is sold. I don't know. I know that there is something strange here. I know that in time the Boches would have come here only through a thin paste and that thin paste would have been me— and it would have been you, too, if I'd been your Sergeant-Major! I'd have blown myself to dust to get in their eyes! And so? What has happened? Everybody runs. Civilians, yes: they are only jokes. They ran. But when soldiers run, my comrades, there is something funny. Soldiers are paid to fight, not run. It is a career: to fight, not run.

"Then what? We are old men. But we are men. We are ancient soldiers. But we are soldiers. In Africa we stood alone against thousands, and we did not run. What have we fought for all our lives, if people run away now when we are nearly dead? What have we lived for, to see everything we made go away like tobacco ash in the wind?"

A growl of rage from the other nine Tigers. They were sober now, and they growled. And I felt myself growling with them. He went on:

"For myself, I have only about twenty years more to live. But—name of a name of a dog of a dog of a pig!—I have spat in the eye of death twenty thousand times ever since I was born, and got away with it! So have you all, you young pups! So have you all, you whippersnappers; for you're soldiers like me! Good. At Sidi-Faouzi the raw recruits broke like string. The veterans, the old ones, it was they who saved the day with pig stickers, with naked steel. Good. It is the veterans who will save France now. Look! They have thrown down their rifles and their pouches. Good! Here are rifles, ammunition, and bayonets. What more do you want? A regimental band? Bah! Get on that equipment! It is an order! To Arms! Long live France, and down with the Boches!"

And my friend, my friend, as if in a dream I saw those ten old soldiers, those aged, superannuated, worn-out, battered, broken-down veterans of all the wars of the Empire—I saw them stuff their pipes into their pockets (incidentally, like good old soldiers, helping themselves to packets of tobacco) and struggle into the belts and pouches my men had left. They put the stuff on wrong. It didn't matter. They had their bayonets on their shrunken left hips. They loaded their rifles. The youngest of them—a man of sixty-four whom they called Bobo, who had been in the cavalry in the last war—showed the old Sergeant-Major how to load his rifle. The present pattern was quite new to him: in his day he had handled the ancient *chassepot,* and the forgotten Lebel.

The Sergeant-Major addressed them again:

"Now, come on, you sons of dogs! Do you want to live for ever?" It was the greatest warcry I had ever heard. I tore a strip off the table-cloth nearest my hand. I tied it round my head where I was wounded. I rose. I stood as on parade. I bellowed at them:

"What the devil is this? Sergeant-Major, are you forgetting yourself? Why, confound and blast you, man, I'll break you for this if you don't watch out! Who's commanding this company? Did you ask permission to speak? Now then! Get into line, there! Why, you ratty mongrels— are you sons of men? Or are you rookies? As you were! 'Shun! As you were! Company . . . slooooope arms! By your le-eft . . . quick . . . *march!*"

It was a dream. It was a fantasy. At the head of ten men, the youngest of whom was over sixty—whose combined ages added up to something like seven hundred years—seven hundred years!—I marched out to hold back the shattering advance of the German tanks.

There went, up that ruined road littered with the debris of an army that had fled, seven hundred and forty-odd years of French glory.

I was the odd forty years.

The tanks had passed. The mass of infantry was following. I found a position in the face of the advance. It was a good position. There was natural cover. I hardly cared. To me, this was not a battle, so much as a gesture. It was my duty to die with France, I thought. And I was going out to die. Those wonderful old men had shamed me into it, and they were right.

We saw the Boches coming. We had only our rifles, and about forty rounds of ammunition for each man. I was lying next to Sergeant Bonenfant. He was crooning over the butt of his rifle, caressing it with his cheek, and crying heavy old tears of joy. His poor aged hands were clutching his weapon. I could see the blue veins like cords, and the dried old fingernails dead-white under the pressure of his grip. The Germans came in sight. "Hold it," I said. The word went along. At a hundred yards I said: "Ready." At seventy-five yards I said: "Fire!" I roared it, and picked off an officer. The ten other rifles went off in a ragged little volley, but nine more Germans went down.

They must have thought that there was some huge counter-attack brought up to surprise them. They stopped. They took cover. We fired at will, picking our men. Ah, my poor old Tigers of Tolly . . . their muscles could no longer work together with their eyes and their nerves and their memories! Only one bullet in five hit anything, although the Boche was horribly exposed. Oh, for a section armed with light machine guns! I could have inflicted astronomical casualties. But it was better as it happened. Yes, it was greater. They were great, those men dying of old age and feebleness, who had exhausted themselves in the quarrels of France.

We went on firing until our ammunition was exhausted.

Meanwhile, the Boches had let loose machine guns.

Bonenfant went down first. I saw one drop of blood, like a jewel, on his white moustache. No more. He died smiling. He thought he had hit the man he aimed at. But the man got up afterwards: he had simply ducked. I fired my last cartridge. "That for you, Bonenfant," I said. Then I got up. My head was beating like a heart. I yelled: "Charge!" In one hand I held a bayonet: in the other my revolver. "Charge!" I shouted . . . and even as I shouted, I felt a kind of hammer hit my knee. A ricocheting bullet had smashed it to pieces, and I went down like a skittle, sobbing with rage and disappointment. I wanted to die with my grandfathers-in-arms.

I lay, helpless. And I saw the last of my Old Tigers advancing with fixed bayonets upon the enemy. Four very old men, carrying their bayonets at the high port, ran as fast as their rheumatical legs would carry them—against twenty thousand German soldiers.

A machine gun went *at-at-at-at-at*. The old Sergeant-Major and one other tripped and rolled over. The last two kept advancing. I believe that even the Germans were touched. They held their fire. An officer stood up, and waved his hands, and shouted something. The last two

Old Tigers ran faster, with the little, jogging steps of exhaustion. The officer fired his pistol. One of them fell. With his last ounce of strength he tried to throw his rifle at the Germans. But his arm was too weak.

And so the last of them all came down on the great German army.

Ten yards away from the officer, he stopped. I could see his chest and shoulders heaving. He was exhausted. Not even his will could take him a step farther. I was mad with pain and misery, and the shame of having fallen. I screamed: *"Vive la France!"* The last Old Tiger found breath enough to cry back—such a poor, pitiful, quavering cry; and yet so stupendous and so noble that the earth seemed to stop in its orbit and the sky seemed to stand still . . . *"Vive la France!"* Then he simply fell dead, because his heart had stopped.

That was the end of the Ten Old Tigers of Tolly.

I lay there, nearly dead. I lay for three days. I was found, then. I lost my leg. I am glad I lost my leg. All of me could not be buried with those great old men: but at least a part of me is honoured by their presence in a grave.

A nation is great only as its finest sons are great. France is as great as the Ten Old Tigers. They are planted in the earth like seeds. Out of them there will grow something stronger and more beautiful than trees. Such men do not die. God send me such an end.

XIII

The Escape of Bill Nelson

"I wouldn't have give those old geezers no bursts," says Hands. "Would you, Crowne?"

"I'd give my own grandmother a burst if I was ordered," says Crowne, sourly.

"That's what you say. I bet you a million pounds you wouldn't have let loose the old Bren on those old geezers, if you was ordered or not."

"Only a Jerry'd give such an order," says Crowne.

"Only a Jerry'd take such an order. Only a Jerry'd obey it," says Bearsbreath. "They could shoot me for mutiny. I wouldn't. I'd rather die, the same as I'd rather die than have cancer."

"I can't see anybody giving you or me such an order," says The Budgerigar. "We'd most likely be told to go and bring those old gentlemen in and give 'em tea and wads."

"Bill would have give 'em the old Hi-de-Hi," says Hands.

"I never see anybody more polite to old age than Bill Nelson," says Butcher the Butcher. "He'd 'Sir' or 'Madam' the lousiest beggar in the street, if it happened to be old. If a horrible old bag sold him a box o' matches, he'd give her a salute and say, 'Much obliged to you, marm.'"

"That was on account of his mother," says Bearsbreath. "He used to idolize his old woman."

"Alive?" asks Crowne.

"Dead as a doornail," says Crowne. "I was around when he got the news. She dropped down dead of a stroke, it must be . . . when Bill 'd been in the Guards about eighteen months. The year Bunny-Rabbit

Bunney got busted for trying to nail Sarnt-Major Glint to the Company Office door with a baynet."

"I dare say she treated him all right," says The Budgerigar.

"She treated him like——," says Hands.

"If she was a mother, God strike me blind and deaf and dumb and paralysed," says Butcher the Butcher.

Cattle asks: "What happened?"

"She was a right cow," says Hands. "But I don't know the ins and outs of it."

"She never wanted him," says Bearsbreath. "She tried to get rid of him dozens of times. When he was born she didn't like him. He was born about a week, or something, after she got married to his dad. That's why he was touchy about being called a bastard. That much I know."

"I heard he nearly won a scholarship," says Hands.

"I don't know much about him before he joined this mob," says the Butcher, "but I do know he was glad to get away from whatever it was."

"Unemployment?" says Crowne.

"One thing and another," says Bearsbreath.

Now it happens that I know something about Bill Nelson in the old days, when he was a boy in Groombridge. I learned what I know from an old woman who used to live next door to his mother's house. I met her, by sheer accident, in "The Bricklayers Arms"—the new, big Tudor pub at the back of the Junction. She looked older than the world. Out of a big straw shopping basket she was pulling a mysterious bundle, which proved to be a stout bottle wrapped in a bit of some faded curtain. "A drop of stout," she said, "does me the world of good. But I wouldn't be seen carrying bottles through the streets like some of them round about 'ere. I name no names, but a Certain Party . . ."

And she was off. A Certain Party, not a hundred miles from there, had been seen carrying eleven quarts of pale ale in one day. A quart or two, she wouldn't mind. Far be it from her. She was neither a nun nor a saint to object to a quart or two of beer. But eleven quarts was carrying a good thing too far. . . . She went on to define the characters and private lives of several people in her street. Then, looking up at me, she said: "Why, you're a Coldstream."

"Yes, ma'am."

She fumbled in a handbag and took out a polished cap star. "That was give me by one of your boys."

"So?"

"William George Nelson, 'is name is. Billy Nelson. You don't know Billy Nelson, I dessay?"

"I know a sergeant of that name. Tall thin man with one eye."

"Oo no, not one eye, not *my* Billy."

I took out a photograph of my squad. Some local photographer took it when I was at the Depot, according to the invariable Caterham procedure. Guards recruits had to be photographed: there was no way out of it, when I was there. I hid in the latrine for fifteen minutes, but somebody got me out in the end, and lined me up. My face, unlovely at the best of times, scowls over Nelson's shoulder. Twenty-nine other recruits hurl their most martial expressions into the picture. They simply look stupid, as the finished print turned out. Bates looks exactly as if he had just had an Unfortunate Accident. I look as if I had just stabbed Johnson in the back, and so does Johnson. But Nelson, who is what they call "photogenic," comes out of it well. He looks good-humoured, tough, battered, fine-drawn, and ugly; indescribably dapper, although he is wearing his oldest suit. Nelson seems to sit among us like an old boiling fowl among fluffy chicks. Looking at that little photograph, you say: "God help those fellows, if that's the man who's handling them." Then, on more careful consideration, you say: "God help this sergeant if that's the squad he's got to lick into shape."

Of this photograph the Trained Soldier said: "You will keep that there pitcher. You will keep it, and in your old age you will look at it.

Follow? It'll bring back memories; if you want my personal opinion.
Keep it for your old age. It'll be something for you to look at."

So I was keeping it, meaning to look at it forty or fifty years later;
but not before. And, seeing that photograph and all those faces that had
managed to look so much more absurd than God had made them, I
experienced a kind of nostalgic twinge, a pleasurable pain.

"Good God," I said. "Good Blind O'Reilly!"

The old woman was silent for a moment, and then she said: "Why,
yes, that's my Billy!"

"Your son, ma'am?" I asked.

"No," she said, "no relation. But isn't my Billy aged? And slim?
What 've they done to poor Billy? My Billy used to 'ave a face like a
little apricot. My goodness gracious me, Billy's an old man there! Oh
dear, oh dear. . . . Time flies right away . . ."

"You know him well?" I asked. "Won't you have a drink?"

"Well, young man. I should hope so. I changed his napkins for 'im.
A little drop of port, if you can afford it. If not, a little drop of stout.
It does me the world of good. Dear me, dear me, poor Billy! So thin!
I'm not a drinker, sir; I get myself a drop of stout now and agen because
it does me good. I takes it like medicine, sonny; it don't appeal to me
as a drink. Doctor's orders, you see. Why, you've bin and got me a port
as well! Fancy you knowing Billy, now! Billy give me that badge. I'd
wear it, too, only I don't want the Milintry Police after me. I saw Billy
born, you know. O' course I saw Billy born! As pretty a baby as you
ever saw—just like a little doll, or a kitten. Eight pounds two ounces.
Why, I remember . . ."

Her name was Mrs. Fish. She was a good-hearted old lady, with a
certain birdlike charm and—concerning drinks—a delightful hypocrisy.

"I knew Billy's mother when she was a girl," she said. "I used to call
'er Etta. 'Enrietta was 'er real name, and 'er maiden name was Wright.
She got into trouble with a feller on the railways, Fred Nelson. 'E didn't
want to marry 'er, but 'e 'ad to, you see. Oh dear . . . oh lor. . . . Fred
was a good-looking boy, for 'is size. Only a little tiny feller, but all the

girls liked 'im, you know. It was a near thing with Etta: young Billy was born only about a month after the wedding. She 'ad a bad time with Billy. She couldn't feed 'im, you know. Oh no, she couldn't make milk, you see. She was narrer, no 'ips, no muscles. Me, I 'ad seven with less trouble than she 'ad that one. She couldn't 'ave any more after Billy; she wasn't cut out for it. These youngsters ain't breeders like we was, young man. I 'ad my first on the Thursday, and on the Saturday I was out shoppin'. I was, you know!

"Fred Nelson 'ad 'is own 'ouse. It was 'is dad's. Well, when they 'stended the Junction, they bought Fred's 'ouse and give Fred two thousand pounds for it. 'E 'eld out, you see, and they wanted the premises, so as to pull it down, you know. Well, as soon as Fred got 'old of that bit of money, 'e threw up 'is job and left Etta and run orf. 'E went to America, you see. Fred left Etta and poor little Billy without a penny. That was when they come to live next door to me. Etta thought 'erself a cut above me, you know. 'Er father 'd been in the groshery trade, with a shop of 'is own. But she was glad enough of my 'elp. She come next door just on a week before 'er time, you know. Billy was a job to get born. Poor Billy was knocked about as if 'e'd been in a fight. It's true. 'E was born with a black eye and a cut face.

"And 'e always seemed to 'ave a black eye and a cut face ever since. I never see a boy get into more trouble than my Billy. I call 'im my Billy, you know, because I was really more of a mummy to 'im than Etta. She couldn't stand the sight of 'im. I suppose it was on account of Fred; but she couldn't stick Billy at all. She never said anything to 'im except to call 'im names. And all she ever give Billy was smackings and 'idings. I saved Billy from many a beating, many a time. She was a cruel girl, that's what Etta was. I used to say: 'Why do you keep 'ammering into the boy for nothing at all?' 'E used to go about in terrible clothes, you know. She couldn't bring 'erself to put a stitch in anything for the child. I sewed up 'is jersey many and many a time. I never was a rich woman, but I used to go without my dinner to give Billy a bite, once in a while. 'E was welcome to it, poor thing.

"She didn't want 'im, and she told 'im so, and it used to make 'im cry bitter. 'E was afraid of 'er. She used to pinch 'im, and things. A smack round the 'ead does no kiddy any 'arm. But pinching is cruelty, spiteful, and I don't like to see it. I've see bruises on that child's arm bigger than plums.

"Then agen, you see, Etta was a terrible one for the men. She used to act like a cat when . . . *you* know . . . like a cat when it's got to go out and . . . you know. It was in 'er nature, you see. If she'd 'ad twenty 'usbands, she'd 'ave looked for twenty more. She was that sort of a girl, you see. And she used to go round and about to pubs with men. She used to come 'ere before they rebuilt this place. There was a lot of talk, I can tell you. Powder all over 'er face, and dressed up like a dog's dinner: and as time went on she got worse and worse. If you ask me, it was a bit unnatural. It was what they call Sex, young man. She drank more and more until she was never without a drop of gin inside 'er. Beer, yes. Wine, yes. But spirits? No, a woman didn't ought to take the food out of 'er kiddy's mouth to buy spirits. She used to go out to work, cleaning and things. But she didn't like to seem servantified, you know, and she give it up as soon as she stopped caring what people thought.

"They make Billy's life a misery, callin' 'im a *B*. Mothers wouldn't let their youngsters play with 'im, because 'e was considered to be almost a 'gitimate child. Other boys used to set about 'im. 'E was fighting every single day. But 'e 'ad a lovely nature. 'E wanted to be friendly, if they'd let 'im. The only wrong thing 'e ever done was to steal two shillings of mine. I saw 'im steal it orf my mantelpiece, but I never said anything. I was going to, mind you, but then I thought, *Poor thing, 'e don't get much*. And so I never said nothing at all. But one day 'e come to me with two shillings and give 'em to me. 'E'd earned it doing errands for Mr. Maxwell, you see, and 'e give me this two shillings and said: 'I pinched two bob off of you, Mrs. Fish. 'Ere's it back. I'm sorry.' I said: 'What did you go and pinch two bob off of me for, Billy? That wasn't a nice thing to go and do, was it now?' And 'e said: 'I dunno why I done it, Mrs. Fish. I just wanted to give it to Tommy Millbank.' I said: 'Do you mean to tell me you pinched two bob off of me to go and give to Mrs. Millbank's Tommy?' 'E said: 'Yes, Mrs. Fish.' I said: 'Are you orf your 'ead, Billy?' and 'e said: 'I dunno.' I said: 'Billy Nelson, I see you pinch that money,' I said. 'I thought you wanted it for yourself,' I said. 'And though it's wrong and wicked to steal, why, I wasn't going to say nothing about it. But to pinch my 'ard-earned money to go and give to Tommy Millbank is being foolish on top of everything else.' Then 'e burst out crying and said: 'I dunno why I done it, Mrs. Fish. I won't do it any more. I wanted to give Tommy Millbank something nice, and I didn't 'ave nothing to give 'im, so I pinched your money. But I won't do it again.' I said: 'But what made you want to give Tommy Millbank something nice, Billy?' And 'e said: 'Tommy Millbank said 'e liked me.'

"I thought to myself, *God spare you, you poor little creechur,* and I give Billy back the two shillings and said: 'Well, don't you dare do it agen. Now go and buy yourself somethin'. And when 'e was gone, I cried bitter at the thought of that poor child—'e was only eight—going and giving somebody something just for saying 'e liked 'im.

" 'E took the two shillings 'ome and give them to Etta. 'E said 'e did. There was a wale on 'is face. *I* think she didn't give 'im a chance to give 'er anything. She took things away from 'im.

"It's a strange thing, because she wasn't a bad-'earted girl. She just 'ated that kiddy, you see. *'Ated* 'im, worse 'n an enemy. And the more she 'ated 'im, and walloped 'im, and picked on 'im and worried 'im— the more she did all she could to 'urt 'im, the more 'e seemed to be affectionate to 'er. It was something pitiful. 'E was trying to make 'er like 'im. But the more 'e tried to make 'er like 'im, the more she walloped 'im.

" 'E went to school near 'ere, two turnings away.

"It 'ad a gravel playground. I was for everlasting picking gravel out of Billy's 'ead. 'E got the name for a ruffian. There was a lot of boys from our street and they kepp calling Billy a *B*. They called Billy's mother a *W*. You couldn't expeck a boy to take it lying down, now could you? 'E used to fight all playtime, and after school too. 'E was always getting caned for fighting. Poor little thing, 'e wasn't big, but 'e was quick as lightning and wiry, and in the end they didn't pick on 'im as much as they used to, because 'e could fight any of 'em.

" 'E won prizes, though, sometimes. I remember 'e won a box of paints for painting, and a medal for swimming, and a book—a medical book about some Doctor Johnson or other. 'E was educated there . . ."

You know the kind of thing.

There is a large school building, as red as if it has been skinned, in the middle of a playground. On one of the walls somebody has chalked a representation of a wicket, which stands out, pale and skeletal, against a background of dim bricks dotted with the marks of wet rubber balls.

Some hundreds of boys rush about, throwing things at one another and uttering appalling cries. In another segregated corral a large number of girls dash from place to place, squealing. Then a whistle blows, or a bell rings, and everybody goes into the big red building.

"Hands together! Eyes closed!" The children strike attitudes of supplication. Then they say:

> *I bleevn Gotherfather or might he,*
> *Maker revven nearth,*
> *Than in Jesus Crisis only sonour Lor*
> *Doo was concede by the Yoly Gose*
> *Bore nother Verge in Mary*
> *Sufferdunder punch us Pilate*
> *Twas crucified edden buried*
> *DEE*
> *Descended inter well*
> *THUR*
> *Dayeeroser gain fromer dead*
> *DEE*
> *Ascended interweven nan sithoner ritander*
> *Gorrafather or might he. . . .*

and so on, to *Zarection-a-body-a-lifer-lasting GAR-MEN*. Then, having swung through the Lord's Prayer:

> *Ow*
> *Farchar Tneven,*
> *Harold be thy name.*
> *Thy kinkum*
> *Thy wilberdun nearth thas tis never*
> *Gus day daily breadden fug giser trespsss sweef*
> *givvem a trespss gains Tus,*
> *Nleed snot into temptation*
> *Buddy liver us meevil*
> *Thine skindum pown glory evnever RAH-MEN,*

they have uttered their confession of faith and made their demands on Heaven. So they get to work. They learn Reading, Writing, Arithmetic. They "do" History, which is Kings and Battles. They take in Geography, which is rivers and mountains and imports and exports, and is contained in brown books. They learn passages out of the plays of William Shakespeare; and "have Art" which consists of pencil lines dragged round areas of paper shaped like jugs, cups, or bottles. In the middle of the morning they have a Playtime: they throw more things at one another, and utter more appalling cries, and tell one another the latest snippets of gynæcological misinformation. A whistle brings them in again. There are more lessons. At twelve they pray that the Lord may be present at their tables, and then rush away, howling, to eat. They return at two, thank God for their food and beg Him to give manna to their souls; and so go back to lessons. At four or four-thirty they pray that God will guard them against the perils and dangers of the coming night . . .

Thine skindum pown glory evnever RAH-MEN.

Thanking God in their hearts that the agonies of the day are over, they emerge, striking tremendous blows at every head within reach and hurling shocking epithets at their friends and enemies. Some go straight home. Others hang about looking for things to break. They have got over the arid wilderness of the afternoon. They have picked their way over the soggy morass of the things they have been given to learn. Somewhere between boredom and fear of punishment, they have picked up a few shreds of fact and nonsense . . . the technique of addition, subtraction, and multiplication . . . how to read and write a bit . . . Mark Anthony's speech out of *Julius Caesar,* which is already fading from their minds like a word drawn on a steamy window. Those who wouldn't do as they were told, or couldn't repeat what they had heard, were slapped about the head a little or beaten on the backside—which is not the place to hammer home the accumulated wisdom of the centuries.

They find it all a bore. It is a bore. They want to grow up quickly; get old, smoke in public, drink beer, muck about with girls, shave, spit, back horses, wear long trousers, and in their turn beat little boys with an iron adult hand.

I know just what kind of education they gave Bill Nelson.

He was a bright boy, Mrs. Fish said. He won a scholarship which entitled him to a free place in a secondary school. But his mother wouldn't let him go. He stayed at school until he was nearly fourteen. At that age he seems to have been morose and touchy, horribly sensitive about his wretched clothes, his lanky legs, his long wrists, and his uncut hair.

His mother had taken to bemoaning her lot. The boy Nelson was overwhelmed by pity for her. It makes a picture in my mind. I can see it clearly . . . a dark, depressing picture. On the one side, the mother, Henrietta, a tall woman carrying the wreckage of a certain hot-eyed beauty in an aura of recrudescent gin, cigarette smoke, Opopanax perfume and the perspiration of sexual hyperaesthesia . . . a big-boned, loose-mouthed woman got up in shoddy finery. On the other, the boy who had been born with a black eye, the villain who had nearly killed his mother in his desperate struggle to be born; the much-blamed, much-beaten child who had eaten and drunk at her expense; the offspring of

an absentee father; the walking liability, the living reproach, the breath-
ing encumbrance.

"She took up with a feller called Daly, a feller that worked for a
bookie, and this Daly used to be a boxer. Billy got a job with a man
that 'ad a paper shop, delivering things and 'elping in the shop. Every
farthing 'e earned 'e give Etta, but she was always crying to Billy about
all she'd done for 'im. Daly come to live with 'er, and there used to be
ructions when they rowed. 'E knocked 'er about a bit. Billy tried to stick
up for 'is mother. Once 'e knocked Daly down with a poker, and 'e was
only sixteen at the time, too. But Etta went for Billy bald-'eaded when
'e done that, and scratched all 'is face. Daly kep quieter after that,
though 'e sometimes went for Billy something wicked when 'e'd 'ad
a few drinks.

"Billy 'ad a lot of different jobs. Nobody ever troubled to 'ave 'im
taught a trade. Nobody cared about 'im. It's a wonder 'e didn't grow up
to be a burglar, or a waster, or something. 'E must 'ave good blood in
'im, a lovely nature. 'E was a bit rough with people sometimes, but
never with 'is mother. Whenever 'e talked about 'er it was like 'earing
er talk about 'erself, you know. All about the way she'd suffered and
what she'd been through. Then it all broke up.

"Billy was just over seventeen, and strong as a lion. I was in Etta's
kitchen at the time. Daly and 'er was 'aving words, and Daly called 'er a
W. Billy said nothing but walked over to 'im and 'it 'im straight in the
face. It was a punch that made my blood run cold. It sounded like a
mallet. Daly fell over and knocked 'is 'ead against the table leg. I thought
'e was done for then. But it was concussion. Then, when all the screaming and shouting was over, and Daly was bandaged up, Etta turns round
to Billy and tells 'im straight out that she wants 'im to clear out and
stay out. 'You only like making trouble for me,' she says; 'you've done
nothing but make trouble for me all your life. I 'ate the sight of you,'
she says. 'Go 'way, get out of this 'ouse. Get out and keep out. I mean it,'
she says. 'Go to 'ell. I can't stand you, and never could.'

"So Billy goes. 'E was crying. 'E didn't 'ave anything to pack, you see, so 'e went as 'e was. Crying. It broke my 'eart.

" 'E stayed on at 'is job, which was no good, much. And then 'e got fed up, you see. 'E said to me that 'e was tired of everything, and wanted to run away from it all. Then I didn't see 'im for a year or more, and then one day 'e comes to see me in a big grey overcoat and a brass kind of cap. 'E'd joined the Army. 'E sent every penny 'e 'ad, almost, to Etta. Then she was took bad and went to the 'ospital. She knew she was going to die, and she was afraid. Billy come to see 'er. She said: 'Forgive me, Willy' (she always called 'im Willy: it was a name 'e 'ated). She said: 'I've treated you like a dog.' And 'e said: 'You've always been a good mother to me.' Then she died, and she was buried, and Billy went away and I never saw 'im again ever."

So that is how it was.

Nelson went into the Army because at that time he wanted to get away from life. He took to the Army as another man might have taken to drink: he wanted to drown himself. He ran away into the Army as a wounded animal runs away into a solitude: he wanted to be alone with his wounds. The Army was a kind of wilderness, in which he could lose himself. So he lost himself; and found himself; and so he became Hi-de-Hi Bill the Bucko Sergeant, Nelson, the One-Man Wave of Destruction.

XIV

Corporal Bittern

But something prompted me to keep my mouth shut, and Bearsbreath went on:

"What does anybody join the Army for, anyway? Some join because they're no good for anything else. They've got no proper go in them of their own accord, and they've got to be forced by law and discipline. Some join the Army because they're browned off with the job they've got, or haven't got, in Civvy Street; and in the Army, at least, they can eat regular. I'm talking of peacetime. Some join because of women. Some join because they think they're going to see the world; or because it's easier for a Guardsman to get into the Police after he's served a few years; or because they fancy themselves in a Guard Order. Only one or two join because they're cut out to be soldiers."

"Some join because their fathers were in the mob," says Crowne.

"Some join because they're made to join," says the Butcher. "A kid's sent to the Duke o' York's School. He gets Army training from eight onwards. Then he becomes a drummer or a tradesman. I knew one that never grew up. He never grew beyond about four-foot-four. Tichy Seeds: remember Tichy? Forty years old, he looked like a kid, from the back: in the Sports he just made the weight for the little boys' tug-o'-war team. But from the front he had a moustache like a hand scrubber. And a voice! What a voice. A voice near as loud as Tibby Britton's. And he was a Full Sarnt. Drums, of course."

"Wasn't it Tich that got fourteen days for the bull about the Field-Marshal's Baton?" asks Hands. "He was a drummer at the time. Some officer's lecturing the drums about some regimental Fanny Adams, and this officer says something about 'In every soldier's knapsack there is a Field-Marshal's Baton.' And this kid says: 'Gorblimey, I thought it was me fife!' The officer heard, and thought he was being insubordinate. The kid thought he was whispering, only he had such a shocking voice he bawled it instead of whispering it."

"Trust a drummer," says Crowne. "Nobody gets into more trouble than drummers. Every Defaulters' Drill is lousy with drummers. You can't punish them kids—they've had it all before. The training they get, they can sing and dance a Defaulters' chasing. They're 'ard, them kids. I'd as soon 'ave a couple of fifteen-year-old drums with me in a scrap as plenty of 'airyarse Guardsmen I know."

"Once when I was in Pompey," says Butcher the Butcher, "I was going to the station with a drummer walking just behind me. I would of let this kid walk with me, only it doesn't do to chuck away your dignity too bloody much in a public place. A kid that looked as if there was napkins on under his greatcoat. A whey-faced runt about three-foot-two that ought to 've messed in a wet-nursery and carried a titty bottle instead of a water bottle. Well, so three Marines, a bit lit, come barging along and start some funny stuff, and it end up with a fight. This drum joins in. Him and me against three Marines, mind you. Well, we was still holding our own ten minutes later when the Gestapo broke us up. He could go, that kid. Maybe the bloke he picked on—a Marine about seven and a half foot long by about four across—was only playing at fighting 'im and didn't want to hurt. But you should 've seen that kid. He was little, but he was like a ghost with a hammer in his hand, like Jimmy Wilde."

"Little men can fight, very often," says Hands.

"I don't like 'em," says Crowne. "They sort you out. The littler they are and the bigger you are, the more they sort you out, and whatever 'appens you're in the crap. 'It 'em and you're a bully. Ignore 'em and you're yeller."

"Psychology," says Hands. He rolls this word on his tongue. "Psychology. Psychology means that a man's got to be handled with kid gloves in case he goes off the deep end. Recruits suffer with Psychology. So do little men. A recruit one week squadded 'll work himself skinny to show he's willing and ready to do his stuff. You'd die of strain if you kept on as you go on at the Depot. After you're trained, of course, you lose a good deal of your Psychology and start hanging round the Naffy like a good soldier. Well, with some little men it's the same. They want to show they're not afraid of anybody. They hit you back before you hit them first. It's exactly the same as a rookie moving before he's given an order. Some of 'em get so keyed up they have to go to the sick-bunk for Bromide. It's the best thing in the world for a touch of Psychology, a nice spot of Bromide."

"Nerves are ruination to a soldier," says Crowne.

"That's what training is for," says Hands. "To get rid of nerves. Look at me. I've got no nerves in all my body. Yet once I was a bundle of 'em. That's how I came to join this mob. You would have died laughing, Butch. I was standing looking at one of them posters. *Join the Army and See the World*. And as I'm looking there comes up a Recruiting Sarnt. They were on a nice racket in peacetime, them pigs. They got a commission, or something, on approved recruits. I'm talking of a few years back. I was so nervous—this is a fact, Crowney—I used to get bound up and have to take medicine: I was shy about making a noise. Honest to God. Well, this feller comes up to me, and says 'Hello.' I blushed like a pansy, from head to foot. I'd never seen such a man in my life. He was about the same build as Butcher, here, but he carried himself better and had a tash exactly like the horns on a sacred cow in India or somewhere. Chest like the Albert Hall. It went bloobety-boom like a drum whenever he talked.

"He said: 'Well, son? Thinking of joining the Army? See the world? Travel a bit? Put on a bit of bone and muscle and a punch like the kick of a grey-bellied mule in a thunderstorm?' He was using Psychology, there, you see, because I was as weedy as a clurk and doughy-faced. 'Be a man,' he says. 'Be a soldier. Come and have a drink and we'll talk about it.' I didn't like to, but I was too shy to say no. We had a mild ale.

He started reeling off the old bull-and-boloney about the Army. 'The Guards! Think of standing over there spick and span and trained to a hairbreadth guarding the body of your King and your Queen. Do you want to go East? Think of Egypt. I've been there many a time. Peaches and oranges growing on every street corner and plump little brides with eyes as black as charcoal ready to fall down and worship you like a god. China! Lovely sunshine, live like a Mandarin in silks and satins, cushy little drill parades for gentle exercise in the morning and romance! Talk about your picture palaces! Talk about your story-books! Little princesses with almond eyes and tiny little dolls' feet ready to cover you with silks and jewels. Palestine, the Holy Land! Are you serious-minded? Read your Bible? I'm a reading man myself, son. You get leisure and time to do whatever you like in the Guards, and get paid well for doing it; paid like a gentleman, and fed like a Prince, and treated like a Lord. You say you're a Bible-reading man?' (I'd never said any such thing.) 'Ah,' he says, 'many and many's the time I've read my Bible—Old Testament, New Testament, and all the other Testaments from cover to cover and back. Well, you'll be taken to see the Tomb of Jesus Christ Himself. You don't find a thing like that on every street corner, I don't mind telling you. . . . Or maybe you're an Atheist? So am I. An Atheist to the backbone. You're free to believe anything you like in the Guards. Are you a Roman Candle? I'm a bit of a Roman Candle myself. Or if you're a Jew, we'll send you to Synagogues: some of my best friends are Jews.

" 'But,' he says, 'don't think I'm trying to talk you into anything. It don't rest with me. I can show you the ropes. But you've got to be fit, because in the Guards, for instance, they take only the cream of the population and the salt of the earth. You look to me just the sort of man they're crying out for. And if you're not, you will be. Look at me. I go eighteen stone, all bone and muscle, and yet when I joined I was six-foot-five and weighed nine-stone-two. But now . . . I'm an old man now. But the other day some kids were trying to put the weight, and I just showed 'em how to do it. I didn't think I still could. I picked up that ball of iron and tossed it through the Orderly Room roof, two hundred yards away. Yet once . . . why, when I was issued my first pair of ammunition boots, I fell down when I tried to pick 'em up, and when I put 'em on I couldn't move my legs.

" 'Now look. What's your job? Nothing much, I'll be bound. Then why not just look in and have the doctor—a Harley Street Specialist: you'd pay him a hundred pounds' fee for the sort of examination we'll ask him to give you free—have him just look at you? It's my business to offer advice and help those that need help—not to try and talk you into anything or persuade you to do anything you didn't mean to do in the first place. Son, sonny boy, can't you see I'm trying to help you? Can't you see I'd give my right hand to do you a good turn, because I liked your face the minute I saw it? *Can't* you *see* that, kid? I'm only a weak old man, but I want to help the youngsters before I die . . . and I haven't got much longer to live. Humanity is my country. To do good is my religion. Come and serve your King and your Country. As the poet says:

> *What is your boasting worth*
> *If ye grudge one year of service to the*
> *lordliest life on earth?*

The poet that wrote the little red book of poetry said that, son, and it's true. The lordliest life on earth! Shall we just take a tiny little look in?'

"And before I knew what was happening," says Hands, "I'd joined the Coldstream Guards. As a matter of fact, I was on my way to have tea with my sister when I ran into that Recruiting Sergeant. But I was too shy to say I wouldn't join the Army after all he'd said. And then when I realized I was about an hour late for my tea, I was so frightened of what my sister would say that I'd probably have run away from home, anyway. I had some idea of signing on for about three years. Then some bloke says to me: 'Do you want to sign for twenty-one years?' I says: 'Yes, sir, no, sir.' 'What am I supposed to say to that?' he says. 'Yes, sir, no, sir. . . . Three bags full?' I says: 'Yes, sir.' 'Make your mind up,' he says, 'is it twenty-one?' To save further argument I says: 'Yes, sir.' And bang went the best years of my life. My feelings were such that I wetted myself."

"Any regrets?" asks Dagwood.

"What'd be the use of regrets?" asks Hands. "I look at it like this: Say I hadn't signed. What 'd have happened? I was a squirt, no good for anything much. I'd have gone stuttering and blushing on and on in some twopenny-half-penny job, without the nerve to ask for a five-bob rise or talk back to a kid of ten. But now? I'm under orders, yes. I'm not my own boss, no. But no more is Churchill, no more is the King, no more is the Pope, no more is anybody his own boss. Whole point is, I'm not afraid of any man or anything; with the possible exception of wasps."

"Funny thing—I'm afraid of caterpillars," says The Budgerigar.

"You're afraid they'll run after you and catch you and eat you, you big-booted lettuce-leaf," says Hands.

At this moment something happens. For the first and last time in recorded history, The Budgerigar has a flash of inspiration. He replies to Hands. He drops a pearl of repartee:

"And you? You scared a wasp might take your nose for a pot o' raspberry jam?"

But Butcher, picking on the word *jam,* stamps down The Budgerigar's one and only witticism by saying:

"Jam! Remember Blinding Oliver? I took him to a friend's for tea, once. He behaves himself all hunky-dory till he wants some jam. Then Olly shouts out, at the top of his voice: 'Pass the ——ing Pozzy!' So I pulled him up. 'Now then, Olly,' I said. And he said: 'Sorry, miss. I meant to say: "Pass the ——ing jam".'"

"Look who's here," says Dagwood.

"Joe Purcell," says Crowne.

Hands, of course, says: "She thought her little girl's nightie was white, till she met old Persil. Ha-ha-ha!"

Corporal Purcell comes in and says: "What's this about Bill Nelson?"

"Snuffed it," says Crowne. "Ask Butch."

Butcher the Butcher tells him.

"Pity," says Purcell.

Another corporal comes in. "Who said Bill Nelson was dead?" he asks.

This is Corporal Bittern, sometimes known as "Twice Shy." It would be a waste of time to ask him how he heard about Nelson. News spreads in camps. There is something telepathic about it: it is as strange and disquieting as signal-drums in a dark jungle. Who told who what? When? How? What little bird carried the whisper? Find the breeding-place of the herring—witness the mating rites of the eel—then try and trace the source of an Army news-flash or the place where a rumour gestates.

Butcher the Butcher explains again.

"Ha," says Bittern, and he draws a very deep breath. . . .

XV

The Retreat of Bill Nelson

THEN Bittern says: "It's a bit of a joke, when you come to think of it."

Bearsbreath shrugs. Crowne says: "Why, what's so screaming bloody funny?"

"I saved his life in France," says Bittern.

"It makes a bit of a change," says Hands. "Now somebody saved *Bill's* life. I suppose Nelson said: 'I'm dying for a smoke,' and you gave him a fag. That's how you saved his life."

"Oh," says Bittern, with unshakable calm, "I didn't earn any medals. I didn't mean to save Bill's life. It wasn't deliberate. It was partly an accident. Seen my shoulder?"

"All my life I been dying to see your lovely shoulder," says Hands. "Why don't you wear ev'ning dress? Gorgeous!"

"If my shoulder hadn't been in the way," says Bittern, "the bullet that hit Bill in the eye would have scored a direct hit and come out the back of his skull. That's all. I didn't mean to do it. Only that shoulder gave me trouble. I didn't begrudge it. Bill wasn't so bad, a pukka Guardsman, and we got on pretty fair. Taken all-in-all, now that I come to think of it, I liked Bill. Well, that's nothing; everybody liked Bill and Bill liked everybody. I wasn't sorry to have him with me that time. I've seen worse soldiers than Nelson. I've seen one or two worse than him in my time. So, Bill's dead. Well, we all got to die some time. The meanest louse bags hang on to their old age till it burns their fingers and goes out with a stink. Fairly decent chaps like Bill die first, always. What d'you expect?"

"Ah, I wish I'd been there," says Butcher the Butcher. "But I'm Employed. I'm supposed to have blood pressure."

"You should worry," says Bittern. "You didn't miss much. I could have got on all right without being there. Still, it gives you something to talk about. What else is a war for? You were there, Bearsbreath—*you* have a nice time?"

Bearsbreath shrugs again. He has nothing to say to Bittern. He dislikes that strange man, and his too-calm philosophic face. There is something about Bittern that reminds you of Cattle: only Cattle is at rest, and Bittern is not. You feel that Corporal Bittern's brain is like a mouse in a panel: behind his blank face it scratches and nibbles, disturbing his rest . . . alive, elusive, insistent, secretly procreative, hungry, watchful, always out of reach. You hear it; you smell it; it irritates you. But it won't let much of itself be seen. Cattle's calm comes from within. The calm of Bittern has been put on, fitted, and screwed down over something that is far from calm and nobody's business. Cattle accumulates experiences as an old maid collects string; ties up the odd ends and lets them accumulate without purpose, neatly arranged in a cupboard. But Bittern knots and unknots, ravels, unravels, splices, stretches, and restlessly tangles things into patterns. But he is calm and cool—that expression, under his raised eyebrows, is what reminds you of Cattle. He used to be some kind of clerk to some kind of merchant, in some small city somewhere. Then he joined the Guards, three years before the war. There is a bile-green tinge of misanthropy in his talk . . . a twang of sarcasm, a curl of the lip, a grittiness that gets men's tempers like the east wind.

The sound of Bittern's voice makes Bearsbreath savage. He gives Bittern a look that seems to bite like a splash of acid, and goes out.

Bittern grins. "I get that man down," he says. "I'm just like sand in his teeth. I wonder why?"

Lazily, Cattle says: "Nelson was everybody's pal round here, you see. And it's just a way you have of talking . . ."

Bittern says: "Don't get me wrong."

"Bitt talks bolo," says Purcell. "But Bitt ain't so bad. We met on that bloody road, didn't we, Bitt?" He lights the butt of a cigarette. "They was bleeding like pigs. *YeeeeeeaaaaaaaaaaaoooOOOOOO— bobobobobobobobobop!*—remember that noise, Bitt?"

"And—KARUP!" says Bittern, knocking over four clanging iron basins.

As these roll, reverberating, Purcell screams again: *"Mmmmm- eeeeeeeeeeeaaaaaaaoooooOOOO!"*

"KARUP!"

"Turn it in," says Sergeant Crowne, with menace.

Silence.

Then Bittern begins to talk.

It was rough, in a way. I can't remember being in many rougher places, in my time. As far as I could gather, it was a crack-up. We didn't know at that time what was happening. I never did believe much in anything or anybody. But Bill did, and Bill took it harder than me, in a way. I always expect the worst. But Bill was the sort of mug that couldn't see the worst ever happening. He wasn't made that way. The rumour got around that the French had broken. They said the Jerries were through, and coming in strength. Well, latrine rumours—you've heard them a million times and so have I. They'd been coming over. Then they started to come good and proper. To me it looked like one of those pictures you see of one of those whirlwinds that go round and round like corkscrews, picking up dust and stuff. They seemed to be coming out of the sky just like that. Purcell saw it too. So did plenty others. It looked like all the planes in the world peeling off and coming down, like twirling water out of a wet sock. Bombing and dive-machine-gunning is all right within limits. There comes a time when it annoys you. If it doesn't kill you it shakes you. Well, you don't want to let it shake you, because that's what it's for. When you hear a plane coming down on you, it sounds as if it's only a foot above your head. You duck down. Then they start dropping it on you.

Your eardrums aren't built to stand up to that sort of row. Nor are
your nerves made to stand up to that much shaking and blast. It seems
to get in your eyes and nose and guts. It's just then that you've got to
hold on to yourself, if you see what I mean. If you break, you're done.
When it began to get really bad we had to lie down and wait a bit. I
don't know about others. I'm talking about Nelson, me, and some others
out of our Company. I'll tell you a peculiar thing. One man, Gabb,
started to get out and run. The mug wanted to do something about it,
I suppose. I caught him by the wrist. Then I found myself holding
Gabb's hand, as if he'd been a girl next to me in the pictures. Just Gabb's
hand. No Gabb. They'll have a job to find that mug when they blow
the Last Trump, I think. . . .

In a bit of a lull, I said to Nelson: "What's happening, I wonder?"
He said: "Didn't anybody tell you there's a war on?"

Mulkin, Perch, Ted Dinning, and Clarkie went down before he got
the words out. We didn't have very good cover. Then somehow the
word came that we were retreating. I don't know how. But it got about
before we had any official word about it. Bill said: "It's a dirty, filthy
lie." I never saw anybody so mad with rage; only he kept fairly quiet.
"A dirty filthy lie! I'll nail the next bastard that repeats it to the next
bastard that listens to it! So help me God! Go on—somebody say it!"
Nobody did.

We stood that attack for about seventy-two hours longer. Imagine
you're in a concrete mixer. It was like that. Then we knew that the
French were done. We saw some of 'em. There was something crazy
about it. Fifth Column stuff. Somebody had opened the door. What
did we know about it, anyway? The foreigners seemed to be in a panic.
They felt they'd been sold out. They felt it was every man for himself.
We stuck on. There wasn't much of a chance for us to go and mix it
with the Germans, in any proper way. As far as we could judge afterwards, they were coming from the sides, as it were.

Then it seemed pretty certain that we were cut off. Nelson said to
me: "One thing's certain. If our mugs *are* getting back out of it for the

time being, this mob'll be the last to go. If there is going to be any kind of stepping back a bit"—the proper word stuck in his gizzard—"we'll have to cover 'em."

I said: "Why?"

He said: "Why? Why? I'll tell you why. In a hundred years' time they'll write books about it, and for the sake of regimental records and what not we can't very well *not* be the last out."

I said: "You're talking bullsh, Bill."

He said: "Shut up, Bittern."

Then the attack started again. God only knows what they were chucking at us. They were hammering us with everything they could find to throw. Most of all, there were planes. It was all very well for Bill to talk. It was as if we were out in a real blinding thunderstorm and a blizzard combined, in the middle of the moors on a pitch-dark night. It was like that. It was impossible to go and impossible to stay. It was madness either way.

Bill kept shouting and keeping everybody alive. "Coconuts!" he said. "Sing it, you horrible men! Sing it, you jelly-bellies! Hi-de-Hi!"

Back came the old "Ho-de-Ho!" And Bill started to sing *Coconuts*. He had a voice like a saw. A sort of cow-bell voice; hoarse, but it carried miles. I shouldn't be very much surprised if the Jerries heard us singing. I forget the exact words. . . .

Lots o' lovely coconuts!
Lots o' lovely balls!
Here comes me wife,
She's the idol of me life,
Singing roll 'em,
Bowl 'em,
Pitch 'em—
Penny a ball,
Gorblimey!
Roll 'em, bowl 'em, pitch 'em,
Penny a ball!

It was crazy as bloody hell. Everybody picked it up. Everybody started to sing, putting all his beef into it, while the bombs came down and the planes came over, and as true as I sit here the ground looked like a pavement in a thundershower with the bullets splashing up dust out of it. We all sang, and it broke the tension. You could see everybody's mouth moving, although you couldn't hear your own voice for the H.E. and the plane engines and the M.G.'s and everything else. Johnny Stallion died singing it, and so did a few more. . . .

> *Roll 'em!*
> *Bowl 'em!*
> *Pitch 'em—*
> *Penny a ball!*

I'll never forget it, not in all my life. When I was in dock afterwards, delirious, I was singing my guts out all the time: that same song.

Then, thank Christ, there was a Jerry infantry attack, after a style. A shower of them came over and we mowed 'em down and swept 'em back; and then they swept us back; and then we swept them back. And there seemed to be a bit of our artillery banging about somewhere. I said to Bill: "I wonder what the big idea is."

Bill said: "I somehow fancy either one of two things, Bittern. Either we're advancing or retreating. Either the Jerry tanks are right through and we're doing what we can to let the other kids slip out; or else we're waiting for reinforcements. I'm not quite certain which."

But then the officer passed the order, and we knew which it was all right. Back. Coast. We had to scram. We'd been left standing. It was true about France having been bought and sold, it seems. The officer said: "Don't worry. We'll be back."

Bill said: "Hi-de-Hi, sir!" But he didn't look like Hi-de-Hi just for that second or two. His face was twitching like a ferret in a bag. He'd had more strain than any of us. But he yelled like a mad lion: "Come on, you horrible men! What d'you think this is? A private hotel? Come on, you shower of women! Hi-de-Hi!"

They said "Ho-de-Ho!" We started to move, still trying to sing *Coco-nuts*. The men were dead beat. We'd had it for days and nights. Days and days, and nights and nights. We had plenty of rough ground to cover to what there was of the road. You go out fresh in the morning from here with a belly full of breakfast and clean socks and shirts on, for a little thirty-five-mile route-march, and you feel it's pretty hard. We were dead men before we started. We'd held out for (it seemed like) years; no grub worth mentioning; hardly any of us left, and those few so stinking tired we had to bite our lips to keep ourselves awake; bomb-blasted to jelly; thirsty; sick to bleeding death . . . the Jerry after us all the time, gunning for us, trying to stop us. We were rotten with tiredness. We were more exhausted than a man dying of fever. We had temperatures. Some of us were wounded. Some of us were scared. I would have lain down and died if it hadn't been for Bill. So would we all. The officer went down like a . . . coconut. Not too bad a kid. Shot in the head. Bill was in charge. I said I would have lain down and died. I wanted to. I really wanted to. I was too fagged out to live. But as a Lance-Jack I couldn't very well set the example. And Nelson was tireder than me, and he was going strong. He told us to dump our packs and stuff. He made us keep our respirators in case Jerry used gas. Rifles we dumped, and chucked the bolts in a pond so that they'd be no use to Jerry. We had no ammunition, only thirty rounds or so, which Bill took. He kept his rifle. He kept his pack. He was setting an example. I said: "What now?"

He said: "There's something like a matter of sixty-odd miles to go, as I work it out. Sixty to seventy. At the double. To the coast. That's why we're travelling light. Step it out for your lives, you bastards! *Hi-de-Hi!*"

It came back like a whisper: "Ho-de-Ho." Then one feller, dead tired, burst out crying. His nerves were all frayed out to string. Bill put his arm round him like a woman, and talked to him like a baby, and the feller hit the road. Yes . . . Bill got us on to the road. There wasn't one single hope in hell. Not one single hope in hell. If it hadn't been for Nelson we'd have stayed where we were.

But we started to walk. Don't ask me where we got the strength. Ask Purcell, he might know. I don't. If we'd been fresh that road would've been hell. And we weren't fresh. We were walking corpses. But we walked. You ask Purcell. . . .

XVI

Feet That Left Red Patches

"WELL," said Purcell, "if you ask me, we dreamt it all. We couldn't of done it. Walking corpses? We was dead six weeks and falling to bits. Dead? We looked like it, we felt like it, we smelt like it. . . . That road, eh, Bitt? That rotten road! You tell 'em, Bitt."

So Bittern proceeds:

I don't mind saying that I have felt fresher in my time. And as for the road . . . I've been along nicer roads.

We'd helped to cover the Stra-bloody-tegic Withdrawal, and now we were trying to get out ourselves. And I told you, and Purcell told you, we were whacked. I know I was walking along not feeling my legs any more. Then I felt myself running. Then I was flying. Then I was on the ground unconscious. I'd just dropped. Dropped like a poleaxed ox, and Bill was waking me up with the point of a bayonet. I got up and we slogged on, and on, and on. We'd hoped there might be some sort of a chance of a lift on a lorry. No. John Shanks' pony. Our boots were finished. We were walking on bare feet. Purcell's boots gave out first. He tied rags round his feet, and kept going. Then the rags gave out.

We weren't the only people on that road. There were others. There were some soldiers and a lot of civilians, all making for the coast; desperate. The civilians were the worst. They'd just run away in a blind panic. There was no holding 'em. The Jerries were coming. Bet your life the Jerries 'd spread the news beforehand, and started scares; poked the wind up the civilian population . . . got them to run, got them to choke up the roads and stop troop movement. It's a Jerry trick, that, a typical one.

There were millions of 'em, all mad with fright. They'd tried to get their furniture away, too. That was madness. I saw somebody with his old mum and a big clock on a little wheelbarrow. I dare say they were what he most wanted to save. His mother and a clock. He'd harnessed himself to the shafts of this barrow and was pulling for his life. And the old girl was screaming at him and shouting. All along the way there were bundles and bits of furniture scattered about. The mugs. They'd tried to get pianos and sideboards away. I saw one woman standing by a great big harp. A harp, with a gold frame. I was light-headed, and wanted to laugh, but I couldn't get it out. As we got along the people got thicker. Right in the middle of the road there was a busted two-wheel cart and a dead horse, and an old man tearing his own hair and beard out and hitting himself on the chest and face. He'd gone mad I don't blame him. I saw a woman squatting on her backside with a great bundle of crockery, nearly all smashed. She was sorting it out. But it was terrible to see some of the real old 'uns lying there by the roadside, dead beat, sort of waving to you as you passed, as if they wanted you to pick 'em up and carry 'em.

And the mob of refugees got thicker and thicker, and then, all of a sudden, while we were trying to get through, somebody yelled "Gas!" It was a Jerry trick, again: Fifth Column stuff. And you should have seen the stampede. People screamed and tried to run away. Men were trampling on women. Women were treading down children. And right in the midst of it all—Zing!—right down out of the clouds they came, Jerry dive-machine-gunners firing right into the middle of the crowd and cutting down dozens of them like nettles. God Almighty, you should have seen those Jerries come down on them evacuees! Some of us didn't dare to duck or fall down, because in the first place we'd have been too tired to get up again, and in the second place there was more danger of getting trampled to death than shot, because the people were mad with fright. It's argued that you're safer standing than lying when

they dive-machine-gun you, anyway. Bill tried to do something with
the few rounds he had left, but he couldn't do anything that I could see.
Then the bloody nightmare 'd start all over again. . . . "GAAAAAAS!"
And stampede. So we moved very slowly, and every step was agony.

I don't know how far we went before the thing I'm telling you happened. It was miles, millions of rotten miles. There was another bit of
Jerry-diving. Then somehow the mob thinned off a bit. A lot of them
got the idea of keeping off the road, I dare say. And then, under a tree,
we saw a woman. I forget whether fair or dark. She was sitting there
with a kid in her arms, and she was giving this kid the breast. There
was another kid standing next to her and sucking his thumb and looking down: a boy in a black beret, maybe four or five years old. Bill gives
her the "Hi-de-Hi," but only the kid standing up looks round. Then
Bill said: "So help me, she's copped it." It was just like he said. She'd
got under this tree to feed the poor little baby, and Jerry'd come down
and machine-gunned around the place. And the kid was killed while
he was sucking, and she was killed too. She must have had a dozen
rounds in her, chest and neck. She'd had some things with her, and they
were all scattered about . . . kid's clothes, mostly, and a little tiny baby's
pot no bigger than a teacup with a picture of Mickey Mouse on it, and
stuff like that. And there stood this poor feller sucking his thumb and
just staring. Not crying, mind you, but staring, staring and sucking his
thumb. *He* didn't know what it was all about. Maybe he thought it
was all a great big joke. It might have been fun to him, only I doubt it
very much; because he looked shocked and dead-white.

Bill says: "By God! Look, look at that!" His face was so white it
made the dirt on it look blacker, and he looked terrible. "By God! Look
at that!" And he says: "Halt!"—like a lion at feeding-time, and out of
sheer force of habit everybody sort of stopped on the right foot. "Look
at that!" says Bill, "look!" He couldn't think of anything more to say
for a second, and then he said: "Are you going to march, you bastards?
Are you going to get yourselves ready to come back? Or are you going

to stay here and die and let them get away with that down there? Look! Or do I have to rub your noses in it?"

One of the fellers fell down, asleep, exhausted. Bill picked him up, and dragged open his eyes with his fingers, and stuck his face close, and said: "Look!"

I was a bit scared of Bill then. I was scared he'd gone mad. He started to take off his big pack. He kicked it across the road. His feet were bleeding a bit and there were reddish patches where he put them down. He spat into the air. He was trying to hit the sky where the Jerries 'd come from. "You wait!" he said. "I'm coming back for *you!* But now I'll take this."

The kid was just staring at him. Bill's ammo was gone. He picked his rifle up by the nose-piece and slammed it down and broke off the butt. Then he picked up the kid, and said: "March or die."

Then a few minutes later, he said: "I'm sorry I lost my temper with you. *Hi-de-Hi!*"

Three of us managed to say "Ho-de-Ho," and the rest moved their lips.

And we slogged on, and we thought that road would never end, Nelson carrying the kid and talking to it in English, which the kid couldn't understand. The kid didn't cry. It sneezed once, and Bill wiped his nose for it with his cuff, having no handkerchief. Once we got to a bit of road that looked exactly like the place we'd come from first, and one of us had hysterics. But we were moving, Nelson talking to us and the kid about this and that, but I don't remember what he said very much, because my brain was beginning to go dead on me and I only heard things in bits, like you hear noise coming through the doors of a pub when somebody's just gone out and they're swinging backwards and forwards. One man died on the way.

There was another raid before long. The kid began to cry as soon as he heard the planes. It woke him up, you see: he'd been stunned with shock or something before. It was then that I got that bullet in the shoulder. We took cover, standing. Bill had his tin hat over the kid's head, and I was standing close by, swaying a bit. And then they started to spray us with bursts. I saw a woman about sixty years old jump into the air like a greyhound and come down sprawling. I sort of blinked, and said to Bill:

"Who're you pushing?"

Then I felt my arm wet, and knew it had been a bullet that pushed me, not Bill. It must have gone through a narrow part of the tree, straight through the soft part of my shoulder, and into Bill's eye. It was just about spent when it hit him, what with me and the tree being there first. He was holding one fist over his left eye. When he took it away, I saw the round about two-thirds buried in his eyeball. About another ten pounds of force behind that bullet and it would have been inside his head. I said: "For Christ's sake, Bill!" He said: "Pull it out, quick. It'll frighten the kid."

I remember reaching out two fingers and giving the bullet a hard pull. It came free at once. The next thing, I was on my knees, trying to get up and singing something to myself. It was *Coconuts*. I'd just passed out for a moment, and woke up again as soon as I'd hit the ground. I managed to get up, but I knew that if I went down once more, I'd lie there till I died or the Jerries found me. Bill had got hold of a bit of somebody's blue dress. He tied his eye up as he walked, and the feller we called Bullhorn—it was his real name—held the kid while he did it.

And he went on. That was a road. By Jesus that was a road. I don't know how long it took us. We had no feet left. I've got the scars on the soles of my feet still, and one toe gone where I cut the muscle of it on some glass.

The kid cried and cried, and then stopped crying. "He's asleep," said Bill, and managed to walk on without joggling it very much. But some miles later, he lifted up the kid's face with a finger under the chin, and said: "He's dead."

So he was. I don't know what he'd died of. It must have been shock.

His heart had just stopped beating when he stopped crying. Bill laid him down in a ditch, and said nothing at all, absolutely nothing.

We were on the bones of our feet, nearly.

And then we got to the beach.

It is Purcell who continues:

XVII

Journey from Hell to Breakfast

WHAT BITT says is dead right. Straight up, what Bitt says is a hundred per cent. We got there. When we got to the beach, Bitt keeled over and went spark out. So did nearly everybody else. I didn't. I was sort of stunned, but kind of awake. You know when you're just dropping down dead of needing sleep—and then all of a sudden you come spark awake for a second or two, or maybe an hour? The way I look at it, you've got a reserve of liveliness tucked away and you kind of rub down to it. Bitt was wounded, you see. It was only a flesh wound, but he was a bit tired, like the rest of us. I saw men lying down and crying like babies. It was all sorts of things. We'd got that far. But we could foot-slog on raw plates-of-meat . . . but not across the bloody Channel, not even we couldn't. I said to Sarnt Nelson: "Well?"

He said to me: "What d'you mean, well? Now we get an issue of divers' helmets and lead boots and bleeding well march to attention across to the other side."

I was light-headed, see? I said: "I don't get that, Bill. Divers' helmets?"

He said: "Listen."

I listened, but I couldn't hear nothing. "Listen to what?" I said.

And Sarnt Nelson said: "Deaf?"

I said no, I wasn't deaf, and he said I must be.

"Guns," he said. "Things what go off bang."

"Oh," I said, "them! I thought they'd been going on all the time."

Because guns was going from the sea. Only I'd had my head so full of 'em, I didn't notice. It's a fact.

"Well, Bill," I said, "I can't go much farther than this."

"Boats," he said. "Can't you see?"

I saw it all then. I blinked a bit and rubbed the gum out of my eyes, and it was like a fog lifting. The sea was like iron, dead flat. There was ships, bags of 'em, and bags of boats, all sorts of boats. They were coming ashore, you see, and taking bags of us off. And I'll tell you something. I don't listen to no bull-and-boloney about discipline being bad, not now I don't. I'm all for it. After that mob on the road, after all I'd seen, I could have cried my eyes out at the sight of them geezers lined up like a pay parade on that bloody beach, waiting for the boats.

Bill got our mugs on their feet and we joined the queue. I said: "Hadn't you better let me take over a bit, Bill? Your eye . . ."

He said: "That's right, Purcy, I did get something in my eye. But that's all right."

There was stuff coming out of it, and it looked horrible. I said: "It was a shame about that kid, Bill."

He said: "Never mind about the kid, Purcy. Keep these mugs on their feet, if you can." Then he gives 'em the old *"Hi-de-Hi!"* and back comes the old "Ho-de-Ho" with something like the good old spirit in it.

"Sing!" he bellows. "Sing! It's an order!"

And so we struck up *Coconuts,* and by the time we come to

> *Roll 'em!*
> *Bowl 'em!*
> *Pitch 'em!*
> *Penny a ball!*

that bloody silly song was running up the line like a heath fire. And we stood there singing our hearts out while we kept an eye on the sea for boats. No stampede here, my cockos! Go on, laugh at discipline! Slouch about bolo and do as you bleeding like, and feel free-and-easy!—The time'll come when you'll go down on your bended knees and thank your lucky stars for a bit of the good old Guards order, bags and bags of it, and the more the better!

They were lining up for them boats like people waiting for the eight-penny seats outside a picture palace. And you can believe me or believe me not, but some of our mob was putting themselves straight, as far as possible. Those that had any boots left was cleaning them up a bit. They were trying to look decent. It may be crazy, but there it is. And the sight of it cheered Bill up. He said to me: "Purcy, this is what I like to see. In a way it was worth while coming this far to see it. In a way it was. This was a mistake, Purcy. They dropped us a —— But you wait. I know we'll be back and wipe 'em up. I know it, Purcy, I know it! The whole of bloody England 'll be up and at it by five o'clock tomorrow morning, making stuff. Aeroplanes? Millions of 'em. Tanks? Bags o' tanks. Shells? I'll tell you something—shells so big it's going to take a day to walk round one of 'em . . ."

You see, he was a bit delirious after all he'd been through, what with that eye, which I could almost see the throbbing of; and the strain. Because he'd always kept in front, and carried more, and kept up a line of bull-and-boloney to keep everybody going.

He was delirious, you understand, and not in his right sort of mind just for a few minutes.

He said: "No profits, Purcy. No profiteers. Nothing of that kind! Every geezer with twopence 'll rush out and say: 'Buy a round of ammo for the Nazis.' Every geezer with one good hand left 'll rush out and say: 'Lemme do a spot of hard graft.' I got it now, Purcy. I got it. I grasp it. They will. They will, Purcy. I tell you they will. After that kid. . . . You saw the way that kid died, Purcy? Cried himself to death with a kind of misery? Everybody in England, from top to bottom, 'll come out in a mob to pay that off. I bet you everything I got. I bet you every-thing I ever had. I lay my head on it. Nobody 'll strike a light if it takes a drop o' petrol out of a plane to pay off that kid. Fat old women 'll sell their rings to pay off that kid. Did you see that kid's mother? And the little 'un, Purcy? Was it a girl or a boy? It was too young to have any sex, wasn't it? Why, they gave that woman a burst while the baby was sucking milk! D'you think anybody back home 'll take that lying down? I saw the milk still running down. Old millionaires 'll give everything they've got and go to work in factories shovelling coal, to pay that off. I know it, Purcy, I know it! Tomorrow morning, five o'clock, all England, Ireland, Scotland, and Wales 'll be up working to pay it off!"

And when Bill said that I *knew* he was delirious.

Then he let out a *"Hi-de-Hi"* like a wolf-howl; and hundreds of the kids heard it and gave him back the old *"Ho-de-Ho!"* It run up and down. And out at sea it was like shaking a sheet of tin . . . and the boats were coming up.

Bill went spark out then. I thought he was dead. I listened for his heart. It was going all right. I propped his head up, and he came to. I said: "I thought you'd snuffed it then, Bill."

And he said: "Oh no, Purcy, my little snowdrop, oh bloody no, Purcy my cocko. Some other time, perhaps."

And he got up on his feet and waited.

We were scared in case there wouldn't be enough boats and we might get left behind. But there was a boat. We got Bittern into it. Nelson wouldn't set foot on it till we was all in. Then me and Bullhorn dragged him in and we pushed off. There was others waiting. You could see by their faces they was scared of being left. It was a lousy few minutes for them. We had it ourselves when it was our turn and we waited on that beach. Some of 'em swum out. But the rest kept their proper order . . . as well as could be expected.

We got on a ship. We got back. We got some fags and chocolates and stuff. Bill's eye had to come out.

Later on we got some proper breakfast.

A titled woman give me an orange. It's not every day you can say a titled woman give you an orange.

"We'll never see the like of Bill again," says Hands. "You could go on talking about him all night and not get tired."

Epilogue

A Word from Dusty Smith

WELL, THE night falls deep, and everybody sleeps as only soldiers can sleep, and day dawns, as dawn it must. Sparrows twitter, a cock challenges the morning to come and be damned; the Drum Major's dog barks and the melancholy drummer blows a great screaming Reveille, and the Camp stirs. Defaulters is blown. The condemned men on C.B. rush madly out to answer their names, and the others go galloping to the washhouses to get the night's crop of manly beard hewn down and washed away.

Sergeant Crowne rises looking surly and confides to Dagwood his dread of the new shower of tripe the Depot is sending today. Dagwood says "Ah," and nods with an air of the profoundest conviction, and Hands breathes something that sounds like an ultimatum from Genghiz Khan; and Bearsbreath scowls at Butcher the Butcher. Out of the little radio a soprano at whose feet the Crowned Heads of Europe have thrown their kingdoms sings an aria from something or other, and an Instructor of Physical Training says to the loudspeaker: "Shut your jaw, you moaning cow!" Like the honking of wild geese breaks out the reiterated command: "Get these swabbing jobs done! Get this lousy hut dug out!" One of the men sweeping the floor finds a penny, which five others instantly claim. A blackout screen falls on Sergeant Crowne's head, and he gives it a look which almost makes it leap back again.

Breakfast is eaten and groused at. Crowne, in a state of unutterable melancholy, waits for the new squad, and, having seen something he didn't like in the day before yesterday's newspaper, wishes that he had the writer of it alone for five minutes . . . alone on a desert island, where there is no law but the law of the knife. Dagwood goes to get his platoon for a little musketry. Hands is due to conduct some live-grenade-throwing, and seems to contemplate some fearful act of sabotage. It looks as if everybody wants to assassinate everybody else. Only one Guardsman Clegg is cheerful, and keeps singing: "Oh, Believe Me If All Those Endearing Young Charms" on one note, making up for his ignorance of the rest of the words by crying: "Dee-dee-dee, dah-dah-dee, dwa-dwa-dahum!" Until he is told to shut up: a command which he obeys for one second before singing on.

The morning's work goes ahead. Dinner is eaten, and groused at. Everybody curses the coming afternoon. Life is going on much the same as it did the day before yesterday.

The new Rooks come in from Caterham in the early afternoon, marching with fierce precision and desperately anxious to make a good impression. Dusty Smith leads one group in, with the air of a man who has done this kind of thing just about once too often. In due course he goes to catch himself a pint of beer and a gallon of scandal, and a train back. He mets Dagwood, Hands, Bearsbreath and Crowne, and there is the inevitable conversational opening. . . .

"Ha, Dusty?"

"Browned off. Howya, Handsey?"

"Jarred off."

"Cheesed off."

"I'm more cheesed off than what you are."

"You can't be more jarred off than what I am."

"Nobody could be more browned off than me."

"Cha having?"

"Mild. This is my shout."

"Oh, turn it up, this is my shout."

"Ah, turn it in, I'm buying this."

Then they all buy one.

Hands says: "Lousy luck on old Bill."

"What old Bill?" asks Dusty.

"Nelson," says Crowne.

"What's the matter with Nelson?" asks Dusty.

"Haven't you heard?" says Dagwood. "He got killed in the blitz."

"When?"

"Couple of days ago," says Crowne. "We was going to whip round for a wreath."

"Crushed under a house over in Groombridge Junction," says Hands. "Butcher the Butcher was nearly killed too."

"What *is* this?" asks Dusty. "Bill Nelson killed? One-Eye Nelson? Old Bill Nelson, the One-Man Wave Of Destruction? Why, he's my best friend."

"Well, now you know," says Crowne.

"No, I don't know," says Dusty. "Bill turned up at the Depot this morning before I left."

"What d'you mean, Bill turned up at the Depot this morning before you left?" demands Crowne furiously.

"He come in before I left with my shower," says Dusty. "I don't believe in ghosts. Not ghosts of Bill Nelson. He was in tripe, and bandaged a bit, and about forty hours pushed. He had a good bar, though. It was on his pass. He'd been trying to get some geezer out of a shelter, or something, and got trapped. They dug him out a bit, and shoved him in hospital for a few hours, and then he come back. Bit of a bashing, it looks like. Bit of a hole where a nail, or a screw, or a beam, or something, stuck in him. I didn't have time to find out exactly. He did look about *half* dead, now you come to mention it. Bust his glass eye again. Can't keep an eye five minutes. Strained back. Dead? Shut up, Crowney! There's nothing left of Bill to kill except skin and bone and a couple of *Hi-de-Hi's* and *Ho-de-Ho's*. Why, I remember the time when Bill Nelson and me——"

"You can keep it," says Bearsbreath. "You can tell it to your squad.

But for now, do me a favour and put a sock in it. Nelson, Nelson, Nelson. All I hear is Nelson."

"Well, there it is," says Dusty. "He gave me the old *Hi-de-Hi,* and about a million rooks give him the old *Ho-de-Ho,* and he goes off to report to the sick-bunk. That's all."

"Butcher," says Hands. "I hope Butcher's bloody blood pressure bursts."

"I'll burst that Butcher," says Dagwood. "I'll splash him over seven hundred yards. Him and his Nelson!"

"Did I ever tell you," asks Dusty, "about when me and Bill——?"

"Who cares about Bill?" asks Dagwood.

"—Me and Bill was at——"

"Oh, for crying out loud!" says Bearsbreath.

GLOSSARY OF SOLDIERS' SLANG

BAR, *an excuse. An alibi.*

BOLO, *an elastic word meaning Disorderly, or Cockeyed, or in any way unconventional. Slightly queer: e.g., "You got your cap on bolo," or "Number 1252? That's a bolo number."*

BROWNED OFF, *fed up. Also, CHEESED OFF, JARRED OFF.*

CHINA, *a Pal, a Mate. Abbreviated rhyming slang, China Plate.*

CHASE, *to drill ferociously.*

DRILL PIG, *Drill Sergeant.*

DARBY-AND-JOAN, *alone; on your own; on your Darby-and-Joan. Rhyming slang like.*

DICKY BIRD, *which means Word.*

FORKS, *hands.*

GESTAPO, *Military Police.*

GLASS HOUSE, *The Military Prison, at Aldershot.*

NORTH-AND-SOUTH, *mouth. Rhyming slang again. Similarly PLATES OF MEAT means Feet.*

NAFFY, *The Navy, Army and Air Force Institution . . . a sort of co-operative canteen.*

PUFF, *means Life, but isn't used much now.*

POZZY, *jam—the stuff you smear on your bread.*

PUSHED, *late, or overdue.*

SMOKE, *The Smoke is London. London, you see, is smoky.*

WAD, *biscuit or cake.*

WOG, *Arab, or Moor.*

318